FIGHT OF THE FURY

THE HEAD, THE HEART, AND THE HEIR
BOOK SIX

ALICE HANOV

Gryphon
Press

FIGHT OF THE FURY

Gryphon Press

Published by Gryphon Press
Waterloo, Ontario

First Edition

Paperback: 978-1-998835-30-0
Hardcover: 978-1-998835-31-7
Special Hardcover: 978-1-998835-32-4
Ebook: 978-1-998835-29-4

Edited by Sam Pollock, S.E. Fleenor and Fantasy Slayer Editing. Cover design by The Book Designers.

BOOKS BY ALICE HANOV

Main Series

The Spare Who Became the Heir and Other Stories

The Head, the Heart, and the Heir

Broken Sons

The Heir Rises

The Last True Heirs

Revenge of the Forbidden Lands

Fight of the Fury

The Last Spell

Extended Omnibus Books

Volume 1

Volume 2

Volume 3

Other Books by Alice

Heart of the Siren

Dear Reader,

To all the readers who have been with me from the beginning, this book is the darkest of the series, and as such as a much larger list of cautions. Themes included but not limited to are violent bloody battles, amputation, murder, betrayal, self-harm, mutilation, appearance of fetal death (but not), and as usual the cliffhanger.

If any of these are problematic for you, then I suggest you read with caution. I'm happy to talk to you about how any of these are used before you venture in, just reach out, and ff you'd like a list of what exactly this book will touch on, (both warnings and tropes) please see my website, AliceHanov.com, or scan the code below with your phone.

Happy reading, and take care of yourself.
Alice

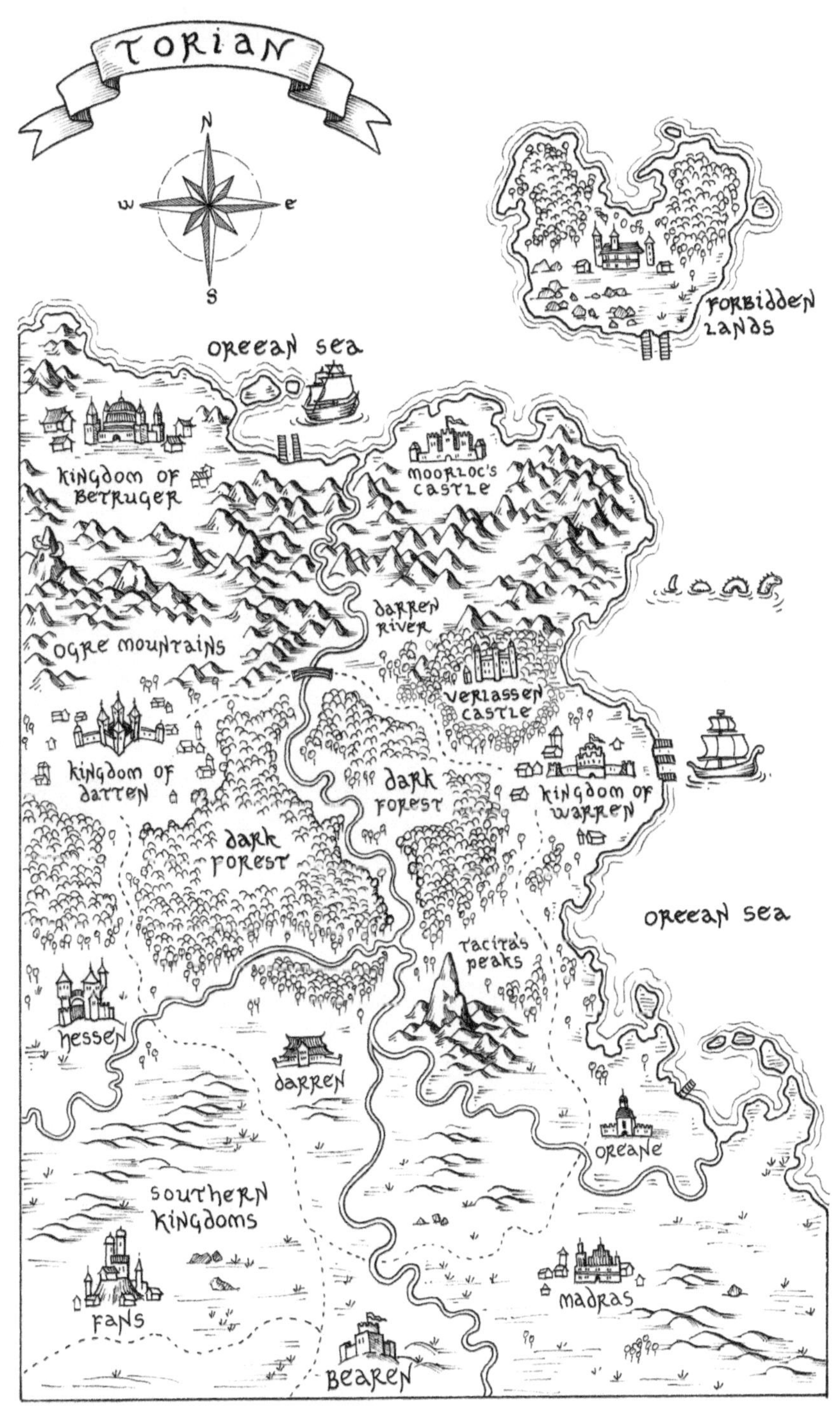

TORIAN
N
W E
S
FORBIDDEN LANDS
OREEAN SEA
KINGDOM OF BETRUGER
MOORLOC'S CASTLE
DARREN RIVER
OGRE MOUNTAINS
VERLASSEN CASTLE
KINGDOM OF DATTEN
DARK FOREST
DARK FOREST
KINGDOM OF WARREN
OREEAN SEA
TACITA'S PEAKS
HESSEN
DARREN
OREANE
SOUTHERN KINGDOMS
FANS
MADRAS
BEAREN

Forbidden Lands
Salem
Cassandra
Tiere
Merlin
Ares
Celtics
Mire
Hades
Mystics
Poseidon
N

PART ONE

GIVE ME BACK WHAT'S MINE

<h1 style="text-align:center">CHAPTER 1</h1>
<h1 style="text-align:center">AARON</h1>

Everywhere around him, Aaron could see a rainbow of leaves and flowers, most of which he'd never seen before. A sweet smell with a bit of spice and pine mixed in wafted around him. Trees taller than the castle spires in Datten towered over them, and underneath grew bushes and plants a brighter green than he'd ever seen back home. If he closed his eyes, it might have sounded like the Dark Forest, but nothing about this place resembled the familiar woods of his home.

Stefan reached out to touch a leaf, and his eyes widened in amazement when it came to life and flew away.

"Our butterflies are exceptional at camouflage," Birch said, rubbing her palms together. "Now let's go, you two. Finding this particular herb won't be easy."

Aaron and Stefan exchanged a look of annoyance, then hurried after her. "What herb?" Aaron asked.

"It'll disguise your lack of magic from those around us."

"Can sorcerers really tell if we *don't* have magic?" Stefan asked.

"Of course," Birch said. She waved her hand, and all the plants leaned to the side to make a clear path through the foliage. Birch motioned for them to follow her through. "Every sorcerer gives off a magical essence. I think you would call it a feeling. We can tell if someone is kind or not, powerful or not, drained or not. The herb we are looking for is notorious for exuding an essence so strong that sorcerers pursuing someone have often ended up in a giant patch of it."

"So, when we find it, we'll roll in it? Or are you going to make us all drink tea?" Stefan asked.

Birch chuckled. She held out two leather drawstring pouches. "We'll stuff these full, and you'll carry them with you. It helps that you're wearing Merlock's old robes. Some of his essence lingers on them, so we won't be starting from nothing."

The elder sorcerer had been a constant presence throughout Aaron's childhood, always in the background, ready to help get them from place to place or make a magical potion. Even after his death, Merlock was helping Aaron.

Birch and Stefan had slipped ahead while he was lost in thought. He picked up his pace.

"Aaron, you're too quiet. Out with it." Birch gave him a warm smile. "I've lived an unusual life, and with the risks we face today, I understand your curiosity."

"How could you leave Megesti behind for Gryphon?" Aaron asked.

Stefan coughed and shot Aaron a look of horror. Aaron pointed and mouthed, "She said I could."

"It's fine, Stefan. I left Megesti because I had to. Victoria predicted Gryphon's birth, and we knew if the future Head was left to his own family, he'd have become a monster. Some vile creatures are simply born that way; others are made by their upbringing and environment. Gryphon is the latter. If I hadn't stepped in, he'd have been a terror by now."

"But how could you leave your son for someone else's?" Aaron asked. Stefan smacked him, and he ignored it.

"I didn't want to leave him, Aaron. He was and still is my world. Should I have done nothing? Should I have let Gryphon be? He probably would have gone on to hurt, or even kill, Megesti. He would have laid waste to Warren, the kingdom that embraced us, and my best friend, and he would have done even *worse* things to her daughter. I made a tough decision, and not a day goes by that I don't think about it. You're a king. I'm sure you can understand that reasoning."

Aaron took time responding, considering the older sorceress' words. "I do. I wish we didn't have to make such challenging choices, but they are what they are."

"You'll understand better when you're a father. The love you have for your child will eclipse what you have for Alex. And while that seems unfathomable right now, it's a fact."

"That, I believe," Stefan said. "My father always said the only thing that kept him going after our family was killed was Jessica ... and you."

"Me?" Aaron said.

"His focus on training and raising you while your parents fell apart over your brother's death was the only thing that got him through his own grief."

"I never thought of that." Aaron had been so young and in so much of his own pain, he hadn't considered Jerome's.

"Don't worry about it," Stefan said. "It was hard on all of you." Stefan gave Aaron a nod of understanding, which he reciprocated.

Birch crossed her arms. "You can't deny that Alexandria did the same for you, Stefan."

Stefan shook his head and muttered, "Sorcerers."

"I heard that, young man," Birch said. She winked at Aaron, and they followed Stefan along the trail.

A tingle like a breeze blowing across his neck ran through him, and they found themselves in a large patch of deep purple flowers. The leaves and stems were dark green, the petals shaped like a horseshoe. Stefan leaned down toward one, and Aaron could swear it moved toward him.

"Oh good. They like you," Birch said.

Stefan jumped back. "Like me?"

"These are the ones we need. If you are a kind soul, they'll bloom for you, and their magic will be more potent. But if you're wicked, they will shrivel and die rather than let themselves be used to hide you."

"That's amazing," Aaron said. He bent down and used his index finger to gently pet a flower.

"I knew they would take to you," Birch said. "But I didn't expect them all to burst into bloom as they have. It would seem you are both more than worthy. You should each pick ten flowers and put them into these pouches."

Birch held out the small leather pouches, and the flowers faced Aaron and Stefan—

the way sunflowers turn toward the sun—as if they wanted to be picked.

"They won't bite," Birch reassured them.

Stefan picked a bunch and quickly stuffed them into this bag while Aaron took his time surveying the blossoms. Their purple shades varied, and he spotted a patch that reminded him of the way Megesti glowed when using his magic. *Merlin-colored flowers seem right.* Aaron stepped over the others to reach his chosen bunch. He picked them as close to the ground as he could and wrapped the stems in a circle, carefully placing them into his pouch. Finally, he secured the green twine that tightly sealed it shut.

"Time to see if they work," Birch said, and they left down the path toward the castle.

CHAPTER 2
ALEX

Alex and Michael squatted behind a bush with Kharon at their side. Sitting in the shrubbery, disguised as a boy by her pendant, reminded Alex of their time in the Dark Forest, when they were young. Anytime they got into trouble, they would hide in the bushes as long as possible to give Stefan time to calm down—he was always fairer doling out their punishment when they did. Back then, she would feel nervous excitement at hiding from her guard and pseudo-brother. Today, she felt only terror that they'd be caught before they even got inside.

Even from the bushes outside the hulking stone wall, Alex could feel power radiating from the sorcerer castle, though she wasn't sure if it was from the sorcerers inside or the building itself. She tried to calm herself with slow, focused breaths, but they weren't working. Michael squeezed her hand. He shared her fear, but his grip was reassuring.

Kharon hadn't moved a muscle since they took their position, but all at once their hand shot out in a warning gesture, and they all dropped lower in the bush. *Footsteps.* Alex held her breath. A sorcerer wearing forest-green robes walked past them, preoccupied with his own muttering. Once he left and Kharon finally motioned for them to stand, Alex let herself breathe again.

Kharon swiftly stood up from the bush and followed the way the sorcerer had come. Michael and Alex scrambled to catch up as they followed them to the gate they hadn't noticed from the bushes.

The stones were like nothing Alex had ever seen before. Flecks of rainbow colors sparkled from inside the gray surface. *They must be the ten-line colors.* Merlock had once told her that the Head's entire castle was enchanted with power from each of the lines, and that when a new head took over, the castle magically reshaped itself to the new leader. At the time Alex had lied when Merlock asked if she understood. She'd figured that facts about some far-off castle didn't matter. Now, walking alongside it, she was awestruck. *How do they get the magic of our lines into stones?* Alex opened her mouth to ask Kharon but then closed it. This wasn't the time to learn about sorcerer architecture, no matter how curious she was.

When Michael reached back to hurry her along, she realized she'd fallen behind. They rounded another spire and Alex gasped at the size of the steps. Each one would take two or three strides to cross. They were made of the same glimmering stone as the castle walls, and each immense step sparkled with the color of a single line, starting with the Hades gray, proceeding to Ares orange at the top. The magic was concentrated enough that each stone step almost glowed the color of the line.

Kharon paused at the bottom of the stairs. "We need to go slowly here. It's important that I place my foot on each step first, and raise the other foot last."

"Why?" Michael asked.

"The stairs can sense magic. If I touch a step, it will detect that I'm Hades, and as long as my foot is on it, it will still only detect Hades."

The oversized stairs loomed menacingly. "How did you figure that out?"

"Accidentally. Once, Lynx and I happened to arrive together. I was coming to tutor Gryphon, and she was to have a lesson with Imelda. We climbed the stairs together chatting, and when we arrived, Gryphon was waiting for me but Imelda didn't even know Lynx had arrived. It was then that I realized how they must work."

"Sounds simple enough," Michael said, and Alex bit back a giggle. He only used that tone when he didn't understand. She tapped his arm and held out her hand. He took it.

"We're ready," Alex said.

Kharon moved at a snail's pace. Every movement was exaggerated for their benefit, so Alex and Michael could hop onto each step as soon as Kharon's left foot touched the stone. What should have taken seconds to climb ended up taking almost ten minutes as they carefully controlled each footfall. Anyone inside would only know that someone from the Hades line approached.

Once they made it to the top, Kharon placed their hand on the large obsidian stone door and pulled. The area they'd touched glowed Hades gray. The hand mark vanished, replaced by the Hades tombstone. With a loud thunk, the door swung inward. Kharon motioned for Alex and Michael to follow and they scurried in behind them. The door slammed shut with enough force to throw Michael and Alex forward. Alex reflexively spun toward it, but no sound came.

Alex craned her neck to see how high the foyer went, her hood falling back, and she struggled to make out the ceiling. It reminded Alex of the cave in the Ogre mountains, the entrance to the labyrinth. When she'd come with Gryphon, they'd arrived in his bedroom, and she'd missed seeing the main areas of the castle.

Alex turned to Kharon, shocked. "Gryphon's room looks nothing like this."

Kharon nodded. "Gryphon's room is on the second floor, along with the others' bedrooms. The throne room is the tower in the middle of the castle and has entrance doors on every floor. Regardless of which door you take, you will arrive on the main floor of the room."

"Well, that's handy. I get lost easily enough in regular castles," Michael said. His hood remained up, but he clearly found the space as fascinating as Alex did. He kept rotating, trying to take in as much as he could.

"It isn't for simplicity, it's a show of power. Garrick can see anyone who enters from his throne."

Warren and Datten decorated their entrances with art, weapons, and symbols of wealth and history, but this foyer was bare. The extravagance lay in the stones themselves. Like the outside of the castle, these stones contained the colored flecks of the lines, but they were black rather than gray, and shiny enough to reflect Alex's face. Remembering her hood, she pulled it up to cover her entire head and face. Each stone had a name carved into it with line marks beside it, and the colored flecks matched the line marks etched onto them. Alex traced a Salem flame with her finger as she read the names on nearby stones. One had a mark through it.

"Names that are scratched out were killed by the Head," Kharon said.

"Killed, as in murdered?" Michael whispered.

Kharon nodded. "When a new Head takes power, they often will kill anyone who was loyal to the previous Head and deemed a risk for their rule."

"That seems unnecessarily violent," Alex said.

"No one ever said the Head was kind. Now let's go upstairs. We're supposed to start on the top floor and make our way down."

Alex and Michael followed Kharon across the foyer, but as soon as they entered the hallway, Alex's blood froze.

"What are you doing here, traitor?"

Ember!

CHAPTER 3

GRYPHON

"**I**s it time yet?" Megesti asked Gryphon, getting impatient.

"I never would have expected *you* to be so eager to rush into danger," Gryphon said.

"Danger isn't what I'm after. I just don't want to be useless. I spent enough of my life being left out of everything because my powers weren't strong enough to be helpful."

"That is no longer your situation," Harold said. "You have nothing to prove to us." He brushed some dust off his tunic. Everyone else had dressed for battle, but Harold would go before the sorcerers as King of Betruger to negotiate a peace between them. He had to look the part, so he wore his most formal attire, despite how the fur trim on his boots made his legs overheat. Megesti wore his Merlin Titan's robe. Gryphon had suggested it. The spectacle of a Usurper risking himself for the life of a mortal king ought to be enough to distract his father and hexa for a while.

As for himself, Gryphon simply wore his Ares robe, presenting the side of him Garrick hated the least.

"I think we've waited long enough," Gryphon said. "Deep breaths, everyone. We're about to head behind enemy lines, and will need to look thrilled to be there."

"Where exactly are we going to arrive in the castle?" Megesti asked.

"My bedroom. It's close to the throne room but will allow us to prepare in case we need to make a quick escape."

"Then take us," Harold said.

Gryphon nodded and cracked them to his bedroom. When Harold stumbled, he chided himself. He must be more anxious than he thought. *I can't even crack right.*

The trio stood there waiting for someone to barge in, making his room stink with fear. It had been a good idea to bring them here first. They needed to get their emotions under control to stand a chance against his father, or they'd be sunk before they had a chance to say a single word.

Megesti recovered first. "Where are your personal things?"

"That is exactly what Alex asked when she saw my room for the first time." Gryphon smiled a little and pointed to the books on the bookshelf that traveled around the highest part of the wall.

"You have a forceful personality," Harold said. "That you would have nothing in your room is odd."

"I have my books. But everything that meant anything to me was in my bedroom in Birch's cottage."

"The one that was burned down?" Megesti asked.

Gryphon avoided the question, selected a balm from his bookshelf, and rubbed it on his neck and face. As a safety precaution, he wore the bracelet Alex had crafted to keep him out of her mind. But with so much at stake, he'd do everything possible to keep his father out of his mind. He closed his eyes for a moment and found his father.

"He's in the throne room, exactly where we want him. Let's get our escape set up just in case."

The room was empty. "What escape?" Megesti asked.

"Birch and Lynx have been visiting me and influencing me for decades. Once my father discovered why I wasn't as insane as he wanted, he sniffed out what was causing my soft spots. So we had to create a way for us to see each other without him noticing." Gryphon used his foot to move his lion skin rug aside and waved his hand, revealing a trap door.

Harold stared at the floor. "Why does everyone have secret passages in their castles except me?"

Gryphon yanked on the large brass ring on the door, and a cloud of dust blew up at all of them, making him sneeze. *At least no one's found it and set a trap.* He let the door fall to the side and swung his legs over the now open pit. They all peered down into unending darkness.

Megesti braced him, but Gryphon laughed. "Don't worry, it's just enchanted." Gryphon launched himself into the pit and landed on a set of stone steps that appeared. "I wanted people to think there was nothing but storage in here."

"Clever," Harold said.

Gryphon hurried down a dozen steps into the darkness, stopped, and sniffed. "There is a faint scent of trees," he said, climbing back up. "This passage leads to the border between the Celtic and Tiere territories, so if I smell trees, the end isn't blocked."

"So how does this help us?" Megesti asked.

"Do I have to spell it out for you? If we get into trouble, you both know how to get out of here now. Lynx and Birch know it too, and I explained it to Alex and Aaron last night when I brought them the maps of the castle."

"Do we need magic to get out?" Harold asked.

"No. That's why it's so helpful. The pit is just an illusion, so anyone can walk through it. If you need to get out, not only can you use this tunnel, but it leads to the safest territory you could be in. The Celtic territory is peaceful and filled with a very thick forest, so it'll hide you."

"All right." Megesti nodded. "We have a safe way to get out. Now what?"

"Now you need to fix your robe, and we'll go see my father about a trade."

CHAPTER 4

AARON

Since the plants moved out of the way for Birch whenever she approached them, Aaron, Stefan, and Birch quickly reached the castle. She had them wait behind several thick rows of old-growth trees that bordered the Celtic territory. Aaron took stock of the sorcerer castle. The Datten castle was built for defense and durability, Warren's to be both aesthetically pleasing and welcoming. This one didn't seem to fit into either category. Although it was imposing with dark gray stones and lots of sharp angles and spikes on it, it didn't look strong. The stones sparkled when the sun caught them, but there wasn't anything special to the design that would be considered beautiful to Aaron. It was simply a dark and foreboding place. Stefan scoffed, and Aaron surmised he was just as unimpressed.

"It's not much to look at," Birch whispered. "But don't be fooled. Our castle shapes itself according to each Head. Garrick seems ruthless and single-minded on the outside. Once you are inside, you'll see the difference and understand the true chaos in him."

"Oh?" Stefan asked.

"The walls move," Birch said. "In the basement and the top floor. Most visitors will stay on the main floor, and that stays the same and looks imposing enough. But the basement is where he tortures those who disagree with him, and upstairs is his personal area, and his family's rooms. Neither floor is somewhere you want to get lost."

"We'll be sure to remember that," Aaron said.

"Aren't we going to the basement?" Stefan asked.

Birch nodded. "That's why I warned you. But the trees are telling me someone is on guard. We need to wait for them to go past and then we'll go inside."

They stayed behind the trees, waiting. Soon, Aaron heard footsteps. He and Stefan tucked themselves behind the largest tree in their vicinity and peeked out at the castle. A sorcerer walked the castle wall. Aaron recognized his green robe as being from the Tiere line. The sorcerer's features reminded him of Lynx, with the same sandy-colored skin and blond hair. *Could that be—?* Stefan's obvious rage confirmed his suspicions. The sorcerer guarding the entrance to the castle was Fenrir.

Aaron squeezed Stefan's shoulder firmly. Always calm under pressure and not one to lose his temper, Stefan could be trusted to be steadfast, but Aaron knew he seethed at the sight of Lynx's father. Seeing someone who hurt the woman he loved—someone who should also have loved her—and not being able to do anything was excruciating. Surprisingly, Stefan squeezed Aaron's hand back, much like Alex would. For a moment, the two shared an understanding unlike ever before.

Fenrir had reached the trees where they were hiding and stopped. Aaron and Stefan reached for their blades, ready to end the sorcerer rather than risk being caught, but Birch gestured for them to wait. Fenrir sniffed the air. The trio didn't even breathe for fear of being heard. Then Fenrir opened his mouth and howled. A flock of birds in the tree branches above them took flight and burst from the canopy in a loud and angry cloud. Fenrir muttered to himself about useless birds and resumed his patrol around the castle.

When he disappeared around a corner, they dashed across the path, slinking along the stone wall to avoid being seen from any other part of the castle. Finally, Birch found what she was looking for. She leaned into the wall and vanished. The stone wall seemed solid, normal, but Birch's head popped out of it with the rest of her still inside.

"This way," she said quickly, so Aaron and Stefan followed.

Alex had told Aaron of magical illusions that made walls appear to be there when they weren't. She had toyed with the idea of trying it when she came home from Moorloc's castle, but the spells proved to be more challenging than she expected, so she'd abandoned the idea. A chill ripped through Aaron as he crossed through the hidden wall and ended up inside the castle. The cold lingered in him as they stepped away from the door to face a dark tunnel.

"Do you think this is a good idea?" Stefan asked, his nervousness evidenced by his hesitation.

"We don't have any other options, Stefan." Birch waved her hand, and a torch in the path lit up.

"I didn't know you had fire magic," Aaron said.

"Lighting torches and cracking are things we can all do," Birch explained. "Control over fire is limited to the Salem line, but lighting something that was created to be lit is easy."

"I just assumed Merlock, Megesti and Alex could do it because of their Merlin line," Aaron said.

"What other magic do all sorcerers possess?" Stefan asked.

"Nothing you need worry about," Birch said. Mischief

entered her voice when she added, "You're both married to sorceresses. If I told you everything, I'd be spoiling the fun, wouldn't I?"

Aaron rolled his eyes. The frown on Stefan's face told him he was also unimpressed with Birch's reply.

"Come along. We should get to the basement and start searching the dungeons before it gets too dark to see down there. Garrick enjoys leaving his prisoners in the pitch black at night, so if he has Edward down there, we won't be able to use a torch to search without risking being seen."

Aaron picked up his pace and hurried after her. The path split into two. One curved up into a large spiral stone staircase, and the other sloped down.

"The stairs lead into Gryphon's bedroom," Birch explained. "When he was little, it's how I visited him with no one knowing. This path leads to the bowels of the castle. It's how Lynx, Kharon, and I snuck into the castle when we needed to save him."

"When did you save Gryphon?" Stefan asked

"He never told you?"

"I know his parents tried to get information about Alex out of him," Aaron said.

"They tortured him for months," Birch whispered. "Garrick's dungeons are designed to weaken our gifts. With how powerful Gryphon is, they kept him in a wet, cold cell made to keep his Salem and Ares powers weak, and they put two red steel bracelets on him to weaken all the others."

"Alex told us how bad it was in one," Stefan said. "How did he manage two?"

"He was in excruciating pain, but he didn't tell them a thing about Alexandria or any of you. He was so weak his father even burned him. As you can imagine, burning a Salem sorcerer is very difficult, and he still has a scar from it."

"How is one sorcerer so complicated?" Aaron groaned. "I learn from Ares that he was supposed to kill me as a baby, but he didn't because Victoria threatened him. But now I learn he withstood months of torture to avoid letting anything slip that would help his family come after us."

"That's the point, Aaron," Birch said. "Gryphon has his faults, but there is a part of him that is good. I like to think it's the part that Lynx and I nurtured."

Stefan scoffed. "He wants to do better, so he can be worthy of Alex." He patted Aaron's back roughly. "Like a certain prince did by ending a six-hundred-year-old war and attacking a mad sorcerer."

"I needed to prove myself in the eyes of the Datten people," Aaron said.

"Of course, you did." Stefan slipped past Aaron down the long tunnel.

They walked on in silence. The space reminded Aaron of the secret passages in Warren. The air wasn't as stale thanks to the open wall at the end, but the further down the sloping tunnel they went, the colder it got, and the mustier it smelled.

"We're here," Birch whispered. "We'll need to be very careful down here in case anyone was sent to patrol this area, but you two will have an advantage here."

"What do you mean?" Stefan asked.

In the dim light, Birch looked tired, almost slouching. "The dungeons interfere with our powers, rendering them useless, but since you don't have any powers, the area should have no effect on you."

"That explains why Gryphon insisted we take this area," Aaron said.

"He could have just told us," Stefan said.

Birch smiled as she pushed open a narrow door, and the three of them crept out into the hallway.

CHAPTER 5

GRYPHON

Gryphon briefly contemplated the look on his father's face when the three of them strolled into the throne room. An instant later, he cracked them into the space and left Garrick at the bottom of the steps that led up to the dais, which held the Head's throne. Gryphon put himself into his father's throne, with Megesti and Harold on either side of him, taking control of the seat of power.

The black obsidian stone walls and floors reflected back the firelight, and all around them hung portraits of previous Heads and the founders of the lines. Gryphon had spent countless hours over the years scrutinizing the paintings and looking for hidden meanings in them. For the most part he'd come up empty, but one or two had led to some very interesting research ideas.

"Hello, father," Gryphon said with a smirk as he lounged on the throne. He slouched, dropping his right leg over the armrest, and leaned back. It was large enough for two sorcerers, since it had been sculpted by the giant rock creature who had founded the Mire line, so he could spread out.

Garrick's eyes flashed blue, the same as Gryphon's. His expression was a compilation of rage sending the veins in his neck bulging.

Ignoring Harold and Megesti, who were busy gawking, Garrick instead trained his cold and calculating stare on Gryphon. He crossed his arms.

"What's wrong, father?" Gryphon taunted. "You don't look happy to see me!"

Garrick smoothed his robe and moved his hands behind his back. "Nonsense, Gryphon. I'm thrilled you finally saw reason and came home."

"Aren't you going to introduce us to your friends?" Eris appeared at the side of the dais. Her friend Orion stood beside her with his arms crossed.

"The little one looks like Merlock, with a hint of Birch. I think he brought us the Usurper," Orion said.

"This is Megesti." Gryphon motioned toward him. "As you correctly ascertained, he is the only son of Merlock and Birch, Titan of Merlin, and our current Usurper." Gryphon hoped their gambit would work, that his father's obsession with power—and the rare opportunity to have a sorcerer who could syphon another sorcerer's power—would keep him preoccupied.

"And the other?" Garrick asked. The other sorcerers in the room moved closer to them now. There weren't as many as usual, but it was clear his father had been entertaining some of his friends. They were all from the more powerful lines and ancient families.

Gryphon stood and rubbed his palms roughly together. "This is King Harold of the Betruger. After the incident with his castle, which I worked very hard to return, by the way, he requested to meet you. He's hoping to establish peace with you so you'll all leave his people out of this little tiff you have going on with Datten and Warren."

"Our 'tiff' you say?"

"Yes, a tiff. You want the Heart, and they are determined to keep their princess and queen, depending on which kingdom we're talking about. The Betruger want no part in this, and are hoping you'll be reasonable in agreeing to leave them out of it."

"Can the Betruger not speak for themselves?" Eris asked. She strutted toward Garrick with her arms crossed.

"Harold?" Gryphon kept his eyes locked on his hexa. She was not someone he could turn his back on.

Harold spoke. "As Gryphon said, your fight is with Alexandria and not us. We'd like to be left out of it. We will provide you with any assistance you'd like in retrieving your Heart, so long as our people and home remain unharmed."

Eris and Garrick considered his words.

"And what of the Usurper?" Orion asked from his place behind Eris. Always at her side, he was to Eris what Michael was to Alex—a friend, confidant, and protector, but with none of the mutual respect that Alex and Michael shared. No, Eris controlled people with fear, like Gryphon's father. Her power over people stemmed from her viciousness and her double Ares nature. On second thought, they were nothing like Michael and Alex.

"Megesti is here to make a trade," Gryphon said.

"What kind of trade?" Garrick asked.

He's curious. I was right! His father craved control, and the idea of having the future Head, Heart, and Usurper all under his thumb would be too tempting to ignore.

Gryphon smirked. He went over to Megesti and displayed him to his father. "My friend Megesti is here to take Edward's place."

Garrick walked up the steps to the top of the dais. "You …

the son of the most cowardly sorcerer I ever met, are going to trade yourself for the Heart's father?"

"I have two parents," Megesti snapped. "And my father was no coward."

"He fled our world because he didn't like me around his little sister," Garrick said, stepping right up to him.

Megesti didn't flinch. "He left everything he knew behind, so he could protect his sister from a deranged sorcerer. That's not cowardice. It's bravery. And just like him, I'm willing to give up my home and my friends to protect my family. So, if you return King Edward to Warren *unharmed* and leave the mortals alone, I will remain here. You might not get Alex and Gryphon right away, but you'll have the Usurper."

CHAPTER 6
ALEX

"I asked you a question, *traitor*. What are you doing here? Have you come to grovel for Garrick's mercy?"

Ember, the Titan of Salem, halted them in their tracks. Her fire red hair flowed around her pale face, making the gold in her eyes pop. Her maroon robe bore the line mark of Salem, a lick of flame glowed like a fire. Ember strutted toward Kharon, a vicious grin on her face.

Alex's heart beat so loudly she didn't know how the others around didn't hear it. Ember, she could deal with, but further down the hallway stood Lynx, frozen in place.

Kharon's stoic expression shifted to anger. "I don't need to grovel when I'm working for the Head."

Michael flinched behind him, and Alex felt her stomach drop. *Working for Garrick? It can't be real. He's making it up to distract her and let Lynx get away. Right?*

"You expect me to believe that?" Ember laughed.

But Kharon tightened their stance. "I don't care what you believe. The only reason you could ever become titan is because of Phobos' friendship with Garrick, and because you'll screw anything that moves."

"Don't be jealous that no one wants to share your bed."

"I don't want to share anyone's bed."

As the sorcerers bickered, Lynx crept along the hallway until she found what it was she was looking for. She gave a quick nod, and when she vanished from view, the tension drained from Alex's body.

"If you're working for Garrick, then why don't I know about it?" Ember demanded.

"Because, as I already said, you're simply a plaything to him. So go back to whatever pitiful little duty you were assigned and let the real titans get back to work."

Ember burst into flames and shoved him.

Kharon simply patted the fire on his shoulder out.

"Don't think just because you're descended from a god that you're better than me," Ember said. "Hades was the most useless founder, and you are even more useless."

"Garrick, it seems, believes otherwise." Kharon sounded like he could barely deign to address her and pushed passed her to continue down the hallway.

She stopped them when she noticed Michael and Alex. "You're bringing along your little apprentices to help. How important can this job be? You always have the ugliest apprentices too. It's as if you hate anything pretty." She wrenched Alex's hood back, examining her features for longer than Alex felt she could bear.

Panic flashed across Kharon's face, but they couldn't do anything without giving them all away. Alex allowed the terror she felt to show on her face, knowing the sorceress would see the boy version of her—she would see *his* terror.

The titan finally relented, shoving her back. Kharon had been right about not wearing the belt. "It figures. The one time you bring a decent-looking apprentice. This one even has red hair." Ember yanked Alex's hood back on her head so hard she fell forward, landing on her knees. The metallic taste of blood filled her mouth when she bit her tongue.

"Take your useless apprentices and report to Garrick," Ember snapped.

"You don't want to escort me?" Kharon asked.

Alex's heart stopped as she waited for Ember to reply.

"Of course not, you impotent excuse for a titan. I have actual work to do."

The maroon robe swished in front of her, and she stomped down the hallway. It wasn't until she left that Alex finally let out her breath. Michael and Kharon rushed to her side and helped her to her feet. She shook so hard she struggled to keep her balance. Michael steadied her until she calmed down.

"We need to go before anyone else comes by," Kharon said.

The trio walked down the long, empty hall until they reached the first set of stairs. It would be a long climb to the top. These steps were of an odd size, much shorter than the ones in Warren and Datten. Kharon didn't seem bothered by it, but Alex had to skip to make the steps line up. By the time they reached the top level of the castle, she felt winded and anxious. *I need to do more stair running. These are brutal.*

Kharon stuck their head out first to see if the coast was clear. Alex and Michael slunk into the hall after them. They made their way down the hall, walking on the balls of their feet so they wouldn't make any noise. Alex didn't know where they were going, but she trusted Kharon to take them to where her father was or to something that would help them find him.

They arrived at a large door inset with stones of a deep cobalt color that Alex had never seen before. As she moved her head from side to side, the stones almost seemed to bleed into the gray wall. There was no handle. They heard voices coming from down the hall.

"Kharon, how can we get in?"

Kharon slapped their palm against the door and swiped downward. The door vanished, leaving an opening. They pushed Alex and Michael through. The door reappeared behind them before a group of young sorcerers walked by.

They were inside an elaborately decorated room that reminded Alex of her father's and Harold's suites. Live trees formed the bedposts for the oversized bed, the bedding the same dark orange Gryphon usually wore. Alex couldn't tell what fabric or fur it was. The paintings on the wall were so realistic Alex had to go over and touch one to convince herself it wasn't a real person looking out at them. Embers on the ceiling glowed bright enough to light the room but no more. A sumptuous red fur rug covered the floor, and the wood furniture was a ruddy mahogany. Even her own room in Warren would look spartan in comparison.

"We shouldn't have come here," Kharon said.

Alex put the information together—*oh no*—they were in Eris' suite.

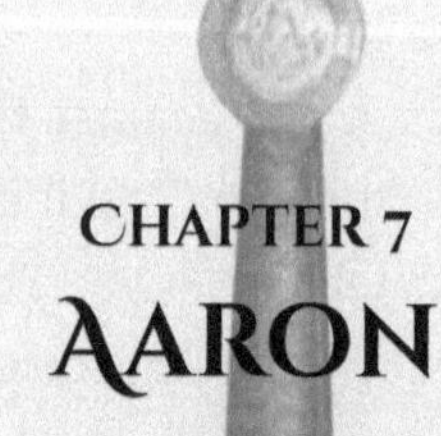

CHAPTER 7
AARON

Hard packed dirt floors led in opposite directions, and worn gray stones made up the wall. Aaron half expected to see flames on the ceiling but there were none. "Which way?"

Birch held up her hand and wiggled her outstretched fingers. "I'm trying to see if I can feel anything, but I can't. We're too close to the Celtic dungeons, and it's blocking my powers."

"Is there anything unusual about this area that we need to worry about?" Stefan craned his neck to examine the ceiling. "Other than the walls moving, of course."

"Oh yes," Birch said. "You should never go down a hallway with a dead end. The walls will trap you. They are an extension of the Head, and he hates you."

"If that's the case then we shouldn't split up," Aaron said.

"I would like to cover more ground, but I'm inclined to agree. Getting one of us caught in addition to Edward won't help Alex."

"We'll go this way." Birch motioned for them to follow her down a side hall.

The hall opened into a much larger hallway with solid wood doors on both sides. Though there was no sign of a dungeon, Birch rested her hand on one of the doors, making it light up in green. When the green reached the handle, the door clicked and opened slightly, revealing a storage room.

"The door was wood," Stefan said. "I thought the plants needed to be alive to do magic on them."

"As the Titan of Celtics, I can manipulate any plant matter. Lynx and Alex need them to be alive to influence them."

Birch stepped into the room first. Aaron followed, and before he could ask, Birch answered his question. "These storage rooms are enchanted. We're going to need to check each one."

The space should have been the size of Aaron and Alex's bed, but inside, it was as large as the Datten library. There were shelves filled to the brim with musty old books, various statues, and other knick-knacks, along with furniture that looked old but in decent shape. Aaron slid between the shelves in order to get to the back of the room.

"The rooms in the basement are the only ones that don't usually change when a new Head takes over," Birch explained. "The walls move to keep people from memorizing them too much, but these storage spaces, and the jail cells, have remained the same for a millennium. That's why there isn't a cell for Merlin sorcerers. The line didn't exist when they were made, and with how small the line is, no one has bothered to make a new one."

"Does that mean if Alex or Megesti were caught, they could escape?" Aaron asked.

"Maybe. They would have an easier time of it," Birch said.

"That makes me feel better." Stefan stood in front of the next door and waited for Birch to unlock it.

Many of the rooms were enchanted to be impossibly large on the inside, and searching them all was tedious. It felt as if each room had been set up in the least intuitive way, but Birch navigated the monstrous messes with ease. She could see something in the chaos that they couldn't fathom. After what felt like hours, they'd searched all the rooms in the small hallway and found themselves at a large junction leading into many directions.

"What's next?" Stefan asked.

"We'll start with the cells," Birch said. "Any preference which lines?"

"If they're trying to catch Alex, where would it be easiest for her?" Aaron asked.

Stefan stroked his chin. "Water is her best power, so I assume something that water defeats."

"We'll check where they held Gryphon. He was in the Ares and Salem area, so there would be lots of water and Celtic magic around to neutralize it. Alex would likely be drawn to it," Birch said.

"And which way is that?" Aaron asked.

CHAPTER 8

GRYPHON

Gryphon felt he might be sick. Garrick examined Megesti while the other sorcerers waited in silence. Gryphon forced himself to relax, putting his hands behind his back and tugging on the bracelet Alex had given him. The thin leather strap had been soaked in the spell she'd found to keep him out of her head. Now it kept his father out of his. It had a downside, though. He needed to work significantly harder if he wanted to look inside his father's mind. A faint pain still lingered from when he'd done it earlier. He was very tempted to try again to see if Garrick had actually been fooled. But even if it worked, he might vomit all over the obsidian floor.

Megesti stood tall as the Head, who walked around him for the second time. Gryphon had warned Megesti of his father's intimidation tactics. He attempted to make Megesti nervous, but the Merlin sorcerer was prepared. Gryphon could see the annoyance seeping through his father's face.

Gryphon laughed. "Would you like us to leave you two alone?"

Garrick spun on his son, snarling, but stopping short of saying anything.

Gryphon adopted an unimpressed expression. "I mean, he isn't going to grow or age in front of your eyes, no matter how long you stare at him. And his robe won't get any less violet. He *is* the Merlin Titan, after all, regardless of what his idiot cousin says."

Megesti raised his eyebrows. *Good. He knows I'm taunting my father.*

"Wait, where is the idiot cousin?" Gryphon asked.

"Lygari has his own duties to attend to today. We are trying to catch the Heart, and everyone knows Merlin and Cassandra can detect kin."

Harold laughed. "If you expect that boar to be of any use, you'll be disappointed. I've worked with all these young sorcerers, and Lygari is useless. He's by far the most arrogant, but with nothing to show for it. I suppose I understand why you like him."

"You come here to make peace, yet you insult our kind? Even the most useless sorcerer is more valuable than the best the mortals have to offer," Eris said.

Harold crossed his arms and glared at Garrick. Gryphon had warned him that Garrick would not respect him if he backed down, but pushing back too much would put him in danger. He walked a very fine line of being arrogant enough that Garrick would talk to him, but not so much that he found him cocky. When a mischievous grin spread across Garrick's face, reaching his eyes, Gryphon knew Harold had hit his mark.

"I do admire your bravery ... Harold was it?" Garrick said. "I will consider your peace request." He nodded to Eris, and she walked to the bottom of the stairs and whispered to Garrick, still staring at Gryphon. Garrick motioned for them to follow him.

"Come along, little Merlin," Eris said. "We want to see if you truly are the titan, as my daughter's son believes."

"Is that really necessary?" Gryphon asked, trying to sound lighthearted even as his heart pounded in his chest. It was undeniable that Megesti was the Usurper. Usurpers had a very specific magical essence that could not be confused with anyone else. Gryphon hadn't expected this.

"Unlike you, Gryphon, we take our duties seriously," Eris said. "And if you say he is the Merlin Titan, I want to be certain."

Gryphon hyperventilated as they headed down the stairs. Megesti would be fine, but while the ghosts of Heads past tested him, he would not have his powers. Megesti followed Garrick without batting an eye, but his terror was obvious to Gryphon.

Gryphon felt powerless. *What do I do? What do I do? We need Megesti's powers.*

Harold scoffed as he stepped off the stairs.

Garrick stopped. "Is something funny?"

"Of course not," Harold said, grinning, as he brushed non-existent dirt off his shoulder.

Garrick rubbed his palms together; a sign Gryphon knew all too well. His patience was nearly gone. He stepped up to Harold and scowled. "I insist."

"I merely found it funny that your most powerful sorcerer —you are their Head, right?"

Garrick nodded.

"Well, I just assumed a Head would be strong enough to know who a titan was, and if not, that he'd have better things to do than worry about which little boy is Titan of Merlin. I mean, if everyone knows he's this Usurper sorcerer, then how could Lygari possibly be titan?"

Garrick tilted his head to the side, revealing a flash of blue in his eyes. *You're cheating. You're looking into Megesti's head, or trying to see what the other sorcerers are thinking so you don't lose face. It's no wonder my hexa controls everything.*

Eris gasped and pulled up her sleeve, making Gryphon's thoughts quiet.

"What now?" Garrick barked.

Orion took her arm. "Someone's in her room."

Gryphon and Harold exchanged a terrified glance.

Garrick snapped. "Then you should make yourself useful for once, Orion, and go see which of my son's new little friends are snooping around my castle."

CHAPTER 9
ALEX

Alex hurried through the room, looking for anything that could help them find her father. She opened every drawer and rummaged through them for a key or a spell. Kharon attempted to summon one of the spirits he'd hoped would help them. Michael flipped through the books, but none had anything unusual between the pages. The final drawer stuck, so she ended up slamming it shut, and it shook the table.

"Try not to make so much noise," Michael whispered.

Alex's shoulders drooped. "Maybe she doesn't know where my father is."

"She knows," Kharon said. "But she may not have written it down."

Alex groaned and moved her hands to rub her eyes and face. "Then what do we do now?"

"We try the next room," Michael said. "Did you think we'd find him in the first place we looked?"

"No, but I had hoped to," Alex answered and turned to

Kharon. "Have you tried Merlock, or my mother? She's the one who told me they took my father."

Kharon looked up. "Victoria, are you here?"

No one moved, watching Kharon for any sign of success. Just as Alex was about to give up hope, her mother materialized near the door.

"Mother!" Alex said. The panic on Victoria's face made Alex's stomach heave.

"Hide! He's coming!" was all she said before she vanished. They could hear footsteps outside the door.

Michael rushed around the room, then dropped to the floor and slid under the bed. Kharon had no experience hiding and his ghostly pale appearance gave away his panic. Alex went to help them, but slipped and her hand hit the wall beside the fireplace. She heard a soft rustle and fell through it, landing hard on shiny stone, wind knocked out of her. As her breath filled her lungs, the pain hit, and the metallic tinge of blood covered her tongue. She wiped the blood off her lip with the back of her hand and struggled to her feet. Alone in an unfamiliar room with a desk and the reverse side of the same fireplace.

If pushing against the fireplace had let her in, maybe it would let her out. But nothing happened.

"No. No. No!" Alex begged as she struggled to hold back her tears. She pushed and prodded every part of the fireplace she could think of, but still nothing. From the next room, she heard a loud *thunk* and threw her hands over her mouth to keep from crying out. Her heartbeat drummed in her ears. It grew so loud that it drowned out everything else. Alex shook her head to force herself to breathe normally. When her heart finally slowed, she placed her ear on the wall and found only silence.

Terror filled her as she thought of being trapped in this doorless room. *There has to be a key somewhere, or a secret door.*

She went over to the desk on the far side of the room and opened the first drawer. Empty. She tried the second. It didn't budge, so she produced her dagger, pushed it into the lock, and struck the hilt of the dagger as hard as she could, breaking open the lock. Re-sheathing it, she dug through the drawer and found a journal. No keys in sight, she opened it to a random page.

February 3rd, 1543

IF MY SON turns out to be an idiot, it is entirely his mother's fault. We all felt the shift of power, but only Imelda was stupid enough to investigate. The witch went against my explicit orders and found Victoria's daughter. It seems the child survived the attack that killed her mother, and has become a returned one. Imelda did not expect the little one to have any powers and failed to catch her. That a child could defeat such a powerful sorceress has given me a great deal to think about.

GARRICK'S ROOM, eerily similar to Gryphon's, held few possessions. Bookshelves, the odd bobble. His simple bedspread was black with the Head crown stitched on it. Alex flipped to the front of the book.

July 13th, 1530

I warned her, but they wouldn't listen. He failed because he's weak. Birch ruined my boy and now he'll never be the proper Ares Titan and Head he was born to be. I gave him the simplest task imaginable, to kill a worthless mortal infant, and he failed. He doesn't even know that now he's in for a lifetime of heartache, and being second to another man. That's a pain I know all too well, but he brought it upon himself, mine was forced upon me. Regardless, I've found a spell that will ensure Birch is punished for her crimes. The day my son takes power, she'll be ripped from him for the rest of his life. Her and anyone else treacherous enough to influence a future Head.

Alex flipped through the journal scanning page after page until she found one that made her heart stop.

March 15, 1551

Months of torture and he won't utter a word. It's as if he's blocked out everything he learned about them, and about her, to protect her from us. It's unnatural! He should want her here, with him, and not there where she grows more attached to the mortal prince every day. I've had my doubts for some time now, but after hearing of her power from Lygari and seeing how much Gryphon will sacrifice for her, and only for her, I believe my greatest fears are realized.

Gryphon is the Heart, and Victoria's daughter is the Head.

· · ·

ALEX THREW the journal to the ground as if it had burned her. She shook her head. "No. I can't be the Head. I'm a sorceress. There's never been one."

A small voice inside her spoke back. *That doesn't mean you aren't the first.*

"I'm not powerful enough. Gryphon is much more powerful than me."

You are still young. Wait until you have all your powers.

"I have the weaker powers. It can't be right."

You have Merlin and show abilities in all ten powers. No other Head or Heart has had all ten.

"I don't want to be the head."

What you want and what you are do not always agree.

Alex went over to the mirror on the far wall and looked at herself. Her eyes were black, the telltale sign of her passenger.

"Go away," Alex snarled at her image.

I am as much a part of you as your gifts are, little Cassandra. But you are the first who has given me the freedom to speak to you, and soon you will release me.

"No. I'll never let you free. I'll die before I do."

You may take your own life to protect them, but will you take his life?

Alex smashed her reflection and the mirror shattered and fell into pieces on the floor. Hundreds of her face now stared back at her, mocking. There was no way to escape herself. Biting back tears, Alex wiped her bloody hands on her cloak. A colored piece of parchment jutting from the journal caught her eye. It was a painting of her mother. Alex turned it over and recognized her mother's handwriting.

MY DEAREST GARRICK,

. . .

I'm sorry that I had to leave you. I hope this small token of me will help you when you feel alone. Marry Imelda and have the son I've seen. He will grow up to be powerful and strong, and will find my daughter when she is grieving and alone, just as you found me after I lost my parents and I was feeling that my world would end. He will lift her up as you did me and teach her how truly amazing she will be.

Together, they will accomplish what we could not. They will find a way to be together, despite generations of hate, and they will bring a new sorcerer into the world who will be better than all who came before.

Take care of him, so that he can take care of her.

All my love,

Victoria

"You loved Garrick. You really loved him—he loved you." The painting sent a shiver down her spine. "I need to get to Aaron. I need to make sure Garrick doesn't do something to him, so Gryphon won't have to go through what his father did. He'll kill my father as revenge for losing you, and then kill Aaron to make me join with Gryphon sooner."

Alex stuffed the journal into the pocket of her robes and marched to the fireplace. She threw herself against the wall with all her might, and this time it worked. She ended up on the hard stone floor again and winced as more pain shot up her leg. Pushing herself up on her elbows, she took in the empty room.

There was blood on the floor.

CHAPTER 10
AARON

aron passed door after door made of wood, stone, and steel. Each bore a pair of line marks carved into the material. He passed one made of scales without line marks. Aaron felt drawn to it. He reached out to touch it, but Birch stopped him.

"Dragon scales are very dangerous, even for us. This cell was made to hold the most powerful of us."

"You mean a Head?" Stefan asked.

Birch nodded. "For my sake, please don't touch the dragon scale door. Dragon's blood is toxic to sorcerers. It's what made red steel. I don't even know what would happen to a mortal if you cut yourself on it."

Aaron backed away from the door and they continued onward in their search for one with Celtic and Poseidon symbols. He searched room after room for any sign of occupants, but kept finding himself entranced by the shimmering door made of dragon scales. He tried to shake away his curiosity.

He heard Stefan groan. "How many dungeons are there?" he asked.

"Eighty-two," Aaron replied.

Stefan crossed his arms and scowled. "That cannot be right."

"He's correct," Birch said. "There are nine lines, with each door having two lines on it. There can be double lines—I'm double Celtic. Plus, there's the one dragon scale door."

Stefan grunted. "How many have we checked so far?"

"About sixteen," Aaron replied, turning the corner to start on the next hall. The sounds of Stefan cursing to himself died out as Aaron counted the doors.

Celtic Mystic. Celtic Salem. Celtic Cassandra. Celtic Poseidon.

"I found it!" Aaron shouted back down the hall. The solid stone door had no window.

Birch and Stefan hurried around the corner. "Is he in there?" Stefan asked.

"I'll tell you when I figure out how to get in," Aaron said. He felt around where the handle should be but there was smooth stone.

"Let me try," Birch said and Aaron moved aside. "This room keeps an Ares, Salem sorcerer inside, so a little nature magic might do the trick."

Birch placed her hand on the door, and at first, nothing happened. But after a moment, a wooden handle finally appeared as if it had grown out of the door.

"I suspect this will set off a lot of alarms upstairs, so we'd better be right." She twisted the handle and the door popped open. Aaron touched Birch's arm, and she stepped back to let him and Stefan head in first. The dark room reeked of mold and dampness. Birch produced a small fire orb. It wasn't as bright as Alex's or Gryphon's was, but it allowed them to see inside the room.

A huddling figure in the corner coughed, revealing himself. When they slunk closer, he stood with a metallic rattle. Large chains snaked across the floor.

"I won't help you." Edward's voice was rough, as if he hadn't had a drink in days. "Nothing you say will make me betray my daughter. I would give my life to protect her."

"Well, that makes three of us," Aaron said.

Edward slowly looked up. "Aaron?"

"We're going to get you out of here," Stefan said.

Edward shook his head. "No. You shouldn't have come."

"Of course, we came," Aaron said. "What have they done to you? Why would you even consider that we wouldn't come to free you?"

"No," Edward shouted this time. "You don't understand. They took me to lure her here. If she's here, they won't let her leave. We are going to lose her because you let her put my life above hers."

"We aren't going to lose her," Birch said. She produced a large brass key out of her robe and unlocked the shackles on Edward's arm. Birch paused when she noticed the men staring.

"When we become the titan of a line," she said, "the only key to those dungeons just finds us. It leaves the old titan upon their death, or if they step down, it's passed on. I only have the key to the Celtic dungeons."

Edward pressed himself into the corner. "Leave me here. Just get Alex out of here."

"We will not abandon you to this room, Edward. We'll get her and get out. You'll see. Everything will be fine."

"No," Edward whispered. "*You'll* see. You've ruined us all."

CHAPTER 11

GRYPHON

Orion groaned, but stopped when Eris shot him a look Gryphon knew all too well—one he never wanted to see pointed in his direction. Orion had just left when the throne room doors flew open again. Edward marched into the room, dragging Alex behind him by her arm. He threw her to the ground.

Gryphon shook his head hard, and when he opened his eyes, Garrick and Eris were walking calmly toward Edward.

"Gryphon! What's going on?" Harold whispered.

"It's not him," he said without moving his lips.

"Well done, my boy! You've caught us, our little Heart." Garrick gloated to Gryphon. "I guess we won't be needing your help after all." To not-Edward, he said, "And the others say you're useless."

Eris produced a bottle of thick green sludge and removed the stopper. The stench of rotten fruit made it all the way to Gryphon, forcing him to swallow back the breakfast that didn't want to stay down.

Edward growled at Alex, then took the vial and gulped its

46

contents. He shook his head, and in moments his blue eyes and auburn skin vanished, replaced with golden eyes and skin as pale as the full moon. Only the black hair remained, and Lygari's visage twisted into a sick smile.

Gryphon cursed under his breath. Harold and Megesti were both gawking, their mouths wide open. Megesti came to his senses first and hurried toward Alex. Realizing what he was going to do, Gryphon motioned for Harold to stay and went after him.

"I'm impressed," Gryphon said, breezing past Megesti. "I never would have thought Lygari would be useful for anything besides lighting candles, and maybe opening a door or two. But even then, he'd have to know which way to open the door, and that's very challenging."

Lygari lunged at Gryphon, giving Alex the time she needed to back up out of his reach. Gryphon cracked away, and Lygari stumbled and fell to the ground. Enraged, he whipped his head around, looking exactly like Moorloc. The memory of him at Moorloc's castle—the day he killed Alex—made Gryphon burst into orange light as his Ares powers erupted.

The other sorcerers backed up, but one of them rushed to Lygari, a pregnant sorceress with cropped, strawberry blond hair. It took Gryphon a minute to recognize Stella, the daughter of Ember and Phobos. She helped Lygari to his feet, and he kissed and moved his hand to her belly.

Lygari? A father? Gryphon felt the chaos inside of him rising.

"Enough, Gryphon!" Eris shouted at him.

Orange rage emanated from Gryphon. He didn't like being challenged when in his Ares form, least of all by his hexa.

Despite her age, she moved quickly and slapped him. "Don't look at me like that, boy," she snarled. "I'm all Ares, and your blossoming Head powers do not scare me."

Don't explode. If you drain yourself, you'll be of no use to anyone. But that doesn't mean you take that. Gryphon lunged at his hexa, shooting fire. She didn't even flinch as the flames licked her clothes and skin.

"Are you finished?" Garrick snapped. "I, for one, would prefer to welcome the Heart into our home rather than listen to you all bicker like worthless mortals."

He took in Alex cowering on the floor for a long moment, and the room fell silent. Gryphon felt every painful beat of his heart as he waited for his father to do or say something. Finally, Garrick stepped up and held his hands out. She accepted them without hesitation, and he helped her from the ground. For a moment, she almost smiled, seemingly relaxing. But then Garrick spun her around so her back pressed against his chest. Fear ripped through Gryphon as Garrick raised his hand, and gave it a small shake, setting it on fire. Hand engulfed in flames, he wrapped his bony fingers around Alex's neck and squeezed. Immediately, she sputtered and coughed, but no water came to protect her. Alex choked.

"We have an impostor," Garrick shouted. "Fenrir! Get in here and tell me who I have in my clutches."

The former Titan of Tiere appeared, and his eyes widened. "My Head, you have that witch I call a daughter. Not only is she treacherously dressed as the Heart, but she also reeks of her. She's shamed our family enough. You're free to do with her as you see fit."

Garrick laughed. "I had set a trap to deal with the traitor titans and keep them out of my hair once and for all, but I suppose I can handle this one on my own." He squeezed Lynx's neck so hard it gurgled, and Gryphon couldn't take it anymore. He closed his eyes, threw open his well, and exploded his chaos into the room.

His father stumbled back from the force of it, releasing

Lynx. Megesti and Harold seized the opportunity and pulled her to them before anyone else could move. Gryphon's chest swelled up and down as he surveyed the surrounding sorcerers, all eyes on him.

This was not how this was supposed to go.

"It would seem we have more than one traitor in our midst," Eris said.

"Ridge," Garrick called into the crowd. "Sound the alarm."

CHAPTER 12
ALEX

Alex scrambled backward away from the pool of blood. *Which one of them was hurt? I have to find them.*

A shrill sound pierced the silence. Part dying cat and part sword scraping on stones, it was loud enough that Alex had to cover her ears against it.

"What *is* that?"

The shriek continued to sound every few seconds. *It must be some kind of alarm.* It was harsher than the bells of Datten or Warren. Alex crept up to the door and pressed her ear against the cold stones. It must have been enchanted, because she could hear everything in the hallway as if she were outside. As soon as the hall was quiet, Alex peeked out.

All the torches had gone out, and the hall was dark. Trying to remain silent, Alex crept into the hall and felt her way toward the stairs they had used to get up here. *They must have caught Michael and Kharon. But what if that's not all? What if they got more of them? If anyone gets hurt here, I don't know what I'll do.*

The stairs were empty and silent. She padded down them as quickly as her pained legs could take her until she emerged in a hallway on the main floor. *Where am I?* Her gray Hades robe would keep her out of most sorcerers' periphery, but she was terrified of running into Ember again. Swallowing hard, she proceeded down the hallway.

The horrible noise stopped as abruptly as it began, but it took a minute for the ringing in her ears to die out, only to be replaced with the sound of her heart pounding hard and fast in her chest. Trying to get her bearings, she searched the wall in front of her—it didn't quite match the others. It had been patched. After checking the hallway for sorcerers and finding none, she placed her palm against the wall. *Gryphon has been here.* This was the outer wall of the library—the one he'd exploded to get them out. Smiling for a moment, Alex tried to summon an image of Gryphon to her mind so she could find the strength and courage he always gave her. Once she was ready, she left in the opposite direction they had fled on their last visit, toward the entrance to the library.

Once inside, with the door closed tightly, Alex let out an enormous sigh. Feeling safe for the moment, she took the time to catch her breath and come up with a plan. Leaning against the large door, Alex took deep breaths until she wasn't shaking any longer. One side of the room was the huge lab the Head used, and the other had rows and rows of bookcases that held all the titan journals, except hers. She left the door and paced the open space. "All the knowledge in the sorcerer world, and no time to read it."

She wanted to light the fire to push the cold from the room, but using her magic here was strictly forbidden. Under her robe, she rubbed her arms to warm herself while she walked. Her fogging breath gathered around her head, obscuring her vision. When it parted, a figure blocked her path.

Her own face looked back.

"Who are you?" she asked.

CHAPTER 13
AARON

The alarm blared through Edward's cell.

"What is that?" Stefan shouted.

"Someone's been caught!" Birch yelled back. "They know we're here."

"I told you!" Edward shouted over the piercing sound.

Birch took Aaron's face in her hands and got up close to make sure he could hear. "You have to find them and get out," she said. "*Now.*"

"What is it?" Stefan asked.

"I'm being summoned. Garrick didn't just sound the alarm; he's calling the titans to him."

"Then help us," Aaron pleaded.

"I can't ignore the summons, and I can't do any magic other than go where I'm called. If I try, I'll be drained." Birch doubled over in pain. "Get Edward out through the tunnels I showed you! We'll get Alex out. You go!" With a loud crack, they were alone.

"We are not leaving this building without my daughter!"

Edward screamed, his voice starting to crack. "They plan to kill us all and keep her here. I'll die before I leave her behind."

"I'm with Edward!" Aaron said. "Let's find her."

Stefan nodded. He removed his second sword and passed it to Edward, and they hurried out of the cell.

CHAPTER 14
GRYPHON

The alarm screeched around them. The sight of Garrick's smile sent a chill down Gryphon's spine and sent his stomach into somersaults, as if he were a boy again. Exhausted, he placed himself between his friends and his father and hexa.

Garrick's eyes flashed blue for a moment, and he clapped his hands above his head. "Come forth, titans. I require your assistance."

A sharp pain hit Gryphon, then faded when he burst into his blue Mystic light. A moment later Lynx burst into her forest green, and her Alex disguise vanished. Pearl and Ridge were next, and stepped behind Garrick to await his orders. In succession, Ember, Phobos, Birch and Kharon appeared, all glowing in their line's color. Kharon and Birch hurried over to Lynx. All eyes in the room turned to see who would glow violet, and the instant Megesti's color erupted from him, Lygari screamed like a spoiled child. Penelope stepped forward —and nothing happened. No gold light appeared on her, and she turned as pale as Kharon.

"The little witch is here!" she shrieked.

"Quiet!" Garrick bellowed, and the former Titan of Cassandra snapped her mouth shut and pouted as she slipped into the crowd of sorcerers.

"What is taking Orion so long?" Eris asked. As if summoned, Orion appeared and Gryphon's heart froze in his chest. Orion held a sorcerer dressed in Hades apprentice robes. *It has to be Michael. Alex would be glowing gold.*

Orion shoved his prisoner into Garrick. The Head snatched him and ripped his hood from his head, then laughed again. "You're the boy the Heart is so fond of—the one she thinks of as a brother. You'll be a delightful addition to our prisoners! Take him to the other side of the room, away from the rest of his little friends. We can't have them planning anything."

Orion dragged Michael to the back wall. Gryphon did a quick head count of the ones not present. *Alex, Edward, Aaron, Stefan. It could be worse. I hope she isn't wandering around alone now. It would be hard to stay hidden with her glowing gold.*

Harold strode to Garrick and faced him squarely. "Do you have an answer for my request?"

Garrick laughed. "There will be no negotiating. I already have everything I need to trap Alexandria. I have her father, her cousin, her closest friend, and that means her prince and other brother are here too. She will come for them, and she will give herself to us to save them. She is her mother's daughter, after all."

Gryphon weighed his options. He could probably get to her before Garrick did. But he knew what would happen. His father would kill Aaron, Edward, Birch—everyone—without a second thought. That made his options exactly zero.

CHAPTER 15

ALEX

"That's a stupid question," the apparition replied.

Alex frowned. "I meant which *one* are you. I can see you're a daughter of Cassandra."

"Not 'a' daughter," she replied. "*The* daughter. The one and only daughter of Cassandra."

Alex's heart seemed to stop. "Why are you here?"

"Because little one, you are the first Head who is also a descendant from the most powerful line."

"If we're so powerful, why were we saddled with the furies?"

"To protect us. After my mother abandoned me, I was given the fury to ensure I wouldn't be hurt again. With the monsters of revenge inside us, no one would ever cross us."

"Until everyone forgot about them," Alex replied.

"A small price to pay for power."

"Why are you telling me this?"

The original daughter crossed her arms. "You need to be reminded of the power you hold. You have walked around this world allowing others to control your destiny, when they should serve *you*."

Alex opened her mouth to reply when a sharp pain shot through her head and she burst into golden light.

"What's happening to me?" she asked.

"It's a summons. The current Head is calling all the titans to him. Most likely, he's found your friends and is using this to force your hand. If you fail to reply to a summons, the pain will only become more intense."

"Is there a way to fight it?" Alex asked.

"Yes. You can kill him."

"I can't kill Gryphon's father!"

"Gryphon would kill *your* father to protect you. He'd kill anyone for you. Kill Garrick, and then his Head power will transfer to you. Then you and Gryphon will be able to control the other sorcerers and keep your mortal family safe. Attacking anyone the Head holds dear is a death sentence."

"What if something goes wrong?"

"Then your friends will get you through it."

Alex tugged on her shirt and felt a light shine on her face, coming from somewhere on the wall of ancient weapons. She moved to it, drawn to a polished bow that stood out from the rest. It was a little large for her, but skillfully crafted. When she picked it up, it shrank.

"It adjusts itself for the user. It will always be the perfect size and draw weight for you."

"It's amazing," Alex whispered. She opened her robe, discarded the bow she'd brought with her, and slung the new one on her back.

The original daughter paused. "You should go."

"But—"

"Trust me. You are not only a daughter of Cassandra. My father had power too, and it's time you harnessed it."

CHAPTER 16
AARON

Aaron, Stefan, and Edward had crept carefully through the halls of the castle, but after the alarm stopped, they no longer saw any sorcerers. *I need to find them and get out of here.* Aaron dashed up the stairs, the others following behind him. They rounded the last step into a cavernous hallway with peaked ceilings.

"Do you think this is the main floor?" Aaron asked.

Edward looked up at the ceiling and down the hall. "I think so. I can't remember if this is where they brought me when we arrived, but this space is larger and nicer than the lower floor."

"There are also very few doors," Stefan noted. "Larger rooms usually mean fewer doors, and the largest room in a castle is the throne room."

"Except in a sorcerer castle," a strange voice said from behind them.

Aaron whipped around, ready to fight, but Stefan was already running toward the speaker. When Stefan flung his arms around the figure in a bear hug, Aaron caught a glimpse of a Hades robe and a golden glow.

"Put me down, you overprotective oaf!" Alex squirmed in Stefan's embrace, but he didn't let go.

"Alexandria!" The moment Edward spoke, Stefan released her and Alex ran to her father and threw her arms around him. Edward clung to her.

Alex squeezed her father tightly. "Are you all right?"

"Sore, and rather hungry, but nothing being home in my own bed won't fix."

Her body noticeably relaxed, and Aaron felt her relief wash over him.

Aaron blinked and Alex moved like lightning, her lips on his. Aaron willed his mouth to open but they wouldn't cooperate.

Alex pulled away and watched him scratch his cheek in an attempt to surreptitiously wipe his lips with his finger. She narrowed her eyes at him. "Is it the stubble?"

Aaron swallowed a laugh and nodded.

"You shouldn't be glowing," Stefan said. "You'll draw attention to yourself."

"That's the point," Alex said. "I didn't do it. Garrick has summoned the titans, and that includes me."

"Doesn't it hurt?" Edward asked.

"Nothing I can't manage."

"Interesting," Aaron said. "Birch was in agony."

Alex shrugged. "Maybe it's a Head thing?"

"So, what do we do now?" Stefan asked. "My father would demand Alex take Edward and leave while Aaron and I go retrieve the others. But I already know Alex won't listen."

"I don't know how long I have before the summons pulls me to where everyone else is," Alex said. "I'm open to ideas."

"If you were summoned, then all our friends were too," Aaron said. "They're all titans in their own right."

Stefan nodded. "That means you have the Titans of

Cassandra, Mystics, Celtics, Tiere, Hades, and Merlin on your side. Wouldn't six against four win?"

"I don't know. They have Ares, Poseidon, Mire, and Salem. Those are the most powerful, and we have the younger, less experienced sorcerers."

"Don't you dare sell yourself short Alexandria. You're the only one of them who has military training," Edward said, and Stefan nodded.

Aaron put his hand on her shoulder. "Plus, you and Gryphon are the next Head and Heart. That has to count for something."

"All right, I agree," Alex said. "We have more power on our side than I thought, but we have to decide right now what we're going to do."

"We don't have the luxury to debate this," Aaron said.

"You sound like my father," Stefan said.

Aaron grinned at Stefan. "That's where I got it from."

"How would you feel about marching into a throne room of sorcerers with the full force of your powers on display?" Stefan asked.

Alex hesitated for a moment, confused, then it clicked. "Do you mean like I did in the camp when I found out Graham punched Michael?"

"Exactly like that."

"Huh." A wicked little smirk spread across Alex's lips. "I think I could manage that."

CHAPTER 17

GRYPHON

Gryphon's heart pounded and he struggled to breathe. "Don't do this. Please. I'm begging you, as your son. Please don't hurt her."

"Aww. He's begging you, Garrick," Orion said. "It's been a long time since one of your own begged you for anything."

"You will thank him for this, Gryphon," his hexa said. "When you have your sorceress in your arms, you will appreciate this."

"No," Gryphon shouted, drawing glares from both his father and hexa. "If you do this, I will never forgive you. I know you don't care about me or my feelings, but you both know better than to incur the wrath of the next Head."

Garrick laughed and then sighed. "But you're *not* the next Head, son. You are only the Heart. Something you clearly figured out for yourself. That's why you're here begging for the girl's happiness, even if it costs your own."

Gryphon had never hated his father more. The punishment, the neglect, the failed attempts to make him into the man his father wanted him to be? They paled in comparison to what Gryphon felt when his father threatened Alex. He hid his shaking hands, not wanting to reveal his rage.

Garrick glared at him. "But *I* am the Head, and I don't have the love of anyone holding me back."

"Well then, it's lucky for Gryphon that I like him just the way he is." Alex stood at the entrance, her Hades hood pushed back, wearing her emerald chain around her neck. Her skin glowed so brilliantly; it reflected off the vaulted ceiling.

Garrick's features contorted in confusion as he scrutinized the unfamiliar sorcerer. "Who are you?"

"The sorceress who's come to take back what's hers. But if you're confused, that's because all of you forget what my hexen was capable of." Alex removed her chain, and the green fog revealed her true appearance. She marched over to Birch and Lynx.

"We played your little game, Garrick, but we have six titans to your four, as well as the Usurper and the future Head and Heart. So. We could stay here and fight, but it's in your best interests to simply let us leave." Alex stood tall and used the same queenly tone Gryphon had heard her use to cut down the Rassgats. "Besides, I can heal anything you may do to my friends, but you would spend weeks recovering from what we'd do to you. *If* you recovered at all." Without taking her eyes off Garrick and Eris, Alex unclasped her Hades robe, tossed it on the floor, and crossed her arms.

"Someone certainly found her voice." Orion chuckled.

"Being queen suits you," Eris added. "A little power brought out a side of you I will enjoy getting to know."

"I'm sure my fury would enjoy getting to know you too, Eris." Alex closed her eyes, and when she opened them, they were black. The sorcerers closest to her leaped back as if licked by fire.

"I'll only ask one more time. Give me what's mine, and I'll let you live."

Ember, Phobos, and Lygari laughed. Alex's face contorted in a rage that Gryphon had not seen since her time at Moorloc's castle. Gryphon shoved Harold behind him. Something bad was going to happen, and he needed to keep the mortal safe. Alex held a bow and drew an arrow out of her quiver.

She's the distraction. Gryphon spotted Edward, Aaron, and Stefan creeping into the room through a side entrance. *Can't the ferflucsing mortals just stay out of the way one time?*

The moment Alex let her arrow fly, time caught up, and Ember let out a scream as an arrow ripped through her chest. The sound echoed through the cavernous throne room.

Phobos burst into orange light and roared at Alex.

She drew another arrow. "Did I forget to mention that I have red steel arrows?"

Phobos took a step back. Gryphon had never seen him retreat from anyone. Stella dropped to her mother's side, but from the pool of blood spreading across the floor, Gryphon knew there was no saving her. Even Alex wouldn't be able to.

"You're insane!" Pearl shouted. "They'll wound you too, the same as us."

"No, they won't," Alex said. "Cassandras are immune to it."

"That can't be true!" Pearl said, throwing Garrick a questioning look.

Gryphon's father hesitated, taking in Alex and questioning Eris, Orion, and Fenrir. "Is she correct?"

Eris clenched her jaw and muttered, "Yes. Ares used Cassandra powers and dead dragons to create red steel."

Alex pulled her arrow back and aimed it between Gryphon's hexa and father. "Now tell them where he got the Cassandra magic from."

"Obviously from the daughter, since her mother was gone," Fenrir snapped at her.

"Very good, except you forgot one part," Alex said as she whipped the bow around to point at him. "The daughter was his, too. *Ares* is the father of the daughters of Cassandra. It's why we're powerful enough to handle a fury, and why we're all a little mad." Alex released the arrow, and it embedded itself into Fenrir's shoulder.

He screamed, ripped it out, and shifted into his wolf form.

"Ferflucs, that one was a normal arrow."

Fenrir roared and charged. He veered past Alex straight for Stefan. Everyone else spun around to face the intruders. Lynx slammed into the beast's side, knocking her father to the ground. The sounds of hissing, howling, and snarling filled the room as the two beasts went for each other's throats.

"You little witch!" The walls rattled as Phobos' orange glow filled the room.

Alex's cocky expression wavered, and she backed away.

Gryphon threw the lid off his well and sent his full Ares force surging across the room. It crashed into Phobos, sending him flying away from Alex and shoving Garrick to the opposite corner. The surge kept going, and it took every ounce of control he had to stop it from hurting his friends. He managed to redirect it into the walls. The entire room shook from the brute force of it, and large chunks of the stone ceiling crashed onto the floor all around them.

"Alex, *go!*" Stefan shouted, and she sprinted toward Gryphon.

CHAPTER 18
AARON

Alex weaved around a few sorcerers Aaron had never seen before and dodged a piece of the ceiling that came crashing down beside her. When she reached Gryphon, he took her into his embrace. Relief flooded Aaron, surprising him a little. *She'll be safe with him. Now it's time to pay these sorcerers back for everything they've put us through.*

"Aaron, let's go!" Stefan shouted. He was already running toward Harold and Edward to help them keep Phobos at bay. Aaron drew his sword to join the other kings, but a shout from Megesti drew his eye. He and Lygari were engaged in a fierce battle. Aaron froze mid-step, wishing he could split himself in two.

"Go to Edward!" Aaron called after Stefan. "I'm going to help Megesti."

Aaron leaped around the crashing stones and made his way to Megesti and Lygari. Lygari shot fireballs, and Megesti lobbed his own back, dousing his cousin with water in between. When he got close enough, Aaron grabbed a rock from a pile of debris on the floor and hurled it at Lygari. He missed, but it made the sorcerer stumble back.

Megesti's head spun toward Aaron. "Get over here!" he shouted. "Let's finish him together, and quickly."

As Lygari righted himself, Aaron nodded to his best friend and gripped his sword.

CHAPTER 19
ALEX

Alex managed to avoid all the debris and chaos around her as she made her way to Gryphon. The moment their hands touched, he yanked her toward him, and she felt her powers expand within her as if Gryphon were pouring his own power into her well. Momentarily safe, she searched the hall for her friends.

Lynx had transformed into her animal form, and snarled and snapped at her father. A large scratch ran down her face, her beautiful sandy fur matted with dark brown blood. Fenrir was in much worse shape, with multiple patches of deep red that spread as Lynx continued to attack.

Birch and Kharon kept Eris and Orion occupied on the other side of the hall. The Celtics Titan grew vines to hold them in place while Kharon threw pieces of debris off the ground toward their faces.

It took her a minute but Alex found her father with Stefan and Harold, going up against Phobos. They outnumbered him, but Alex saw the deep orange glow coming off the enraged sorcerer and fear enveloped her. She started toward her friends, screaming out a warning, but it was too late. Phobos exploded, unleashing his powers even more violently than Gryphon had. Alex watched in horror as her loved ones were sent flying across the room. Stefan landed flat on his back, while her father slammed into a wall with a sickening thud.

No, no, NO!

Painfully, Harold struggled to his feet, favoring his right side.

Gryphon, we need to go help my father and Stefan. They need us.

Gryphon nodded, but before they could take a step, the ground shook, and they had to brace themselves to keep their balance. It took Alex a moment to realize the tremors were only impacting them.

"Now children, you're not going anywhere," Garrick dripped.

All of Alex's bravado died. She didn't make a peep when Gryphon pushed her behind him to shield her from his father.

"Still protecting her? I told you we wouldn't hurt her," Garrick said, taking a step closer.

Gryphon scoffed. "You'll forgive me if I don't trust you. I only have decades of experience with your lies."

Alex slid her bow off her shoulder, but Garrick's voice echoed inside her head.

Drop it, or I'll make sure your father leaves here in a casket.

Alex dropped her bow and felt Gryphon's body shift to look at her, but she kept her eyes locked on Garrick.

The arrows too.

Without even blinking, Alex unbuckled her quiver on her back and let it fall to the ground.

Garrick's smile made Alex want to retch. "That's better. Now, let us converse as sorcerers would." He motioned toward the anteroom.

"No," Gryphon said. "We're not leaving with you to have a little chat while you murder everyone we love in this room. We'll be staying right here."

Alex nodded and felt around for Gryphon's hand. When she brushed it, he gripped hers so tightly it hurt. Too frightened to complain, she squeezed back and let Gryphon's raw power flow into her and out again, now enriched with her own.

"It's a shame that the next Head and Heart won't give the current Head a few minutes to educate them on certain important matters, such as what will occur when you take your places as the rulers of our world."

"It isn't as though you're going to die anytime soon," Alex grumbled.

"That's true, Alexandria! And yet there is much you don't know. You need proper training beyond what my son can provide you with. You need to be taught to wield your talents by the titans of the lines. Your Salem, Poseidon, and Ares are sloppy at best. You haven't even started your Mire or Mystics training! You've had your powers for almost a decade, but you're still young. There's plenty of time, but only if you start with the proper tutelage now."

"I'd rather kiss Wesley than be *taught* by you and your lackeys. I decline," Alex said. Gryphon gently nudged her a step behind him and released her hand.

"It seems you misunderstood me," Garrick said, bursting into flames. He dove for Gryphon, throwing him to the side as if he were a rag doll, then stalked toward Alex.

She screamed and stumbled back. Her hands landed on the cold floor, now littered with rubble. *There must be something I can use to fight him.*

"I wasn't asking, Princess. You'll be staying here from now on."

No man will ever hold me prisoner again.

Alex held Garrick's stare, searching the rubble until her fingers closed around something straight, sharp—and familiar. He lunged toward her, and she jammed the broken arrow shaft into his throat.

CHAPTER 20
AARON

"Will anything happen to you or Alex if we kill him?" Aaron asked Megesti, jerking his head toward Lygari.

"Nothing. I'm already Titan of Merlin, and Alex is Titan of Cassandra. He has nothing we would need to take."

"So, he's the useless one. Interesting."

"I was useful enough to do away with your brother," Lygari snapped. Daniel's face the day he died swam before Aaron's eyes, and he felt his temper bubbling. Lygari turned his attention toward Megesti. "And the only reason *you* have any power is because of your mother. Your father was worthless."

"Where my power comes from doesn't matter," Megesti said calmly. "I have them, and you can't stand it."

Lygari lowered his hands for a moment. "The only reason my father let you and your useless father live was because of Victoria. If she hadn't made him promise never to hurt you, I wouldn't be dealing with you now."

"But here you are," Aaron replied. "And you killed my

brother. You'll be dealing with Alex and me the rest of your short, miserable life."

Lygari exploded in flames, and Megesti responded by throwing snow on him. Screaming in frustration, the sorcerer lunged at Megesti, but Aaron was too fast. He punched Lygari in the face, sending him reeling backward. As the sorcerer struggled to regain his balance, Aaron attacked again. Wanting to make sure Lygari suffered as long as possible, Aaron threw his sword to the ground and swung a left hook that connected with Lygari's face.

Blood flew from Lygari's nose, and he screeched in pain. "You stupid mortal." Lygari threw up his fists, set them on fire, and went after Aaron.

Aaron dodged the first two punches, but the third made contact and set his shoulder ablaze. He focused on extinguishing it, only stopping when he heard Megesti cry out.

Warmth ran down Aaron's abdomen and Megesti's eyes went wide. The hilt of a sword—*my sword?*—stuck out of his belly at an odd angle. While he'd been distracted by his shoulder, Lygari had snatched Aaron's sword and stabbed him. Megesti erupted in violet light and sent a gale wind at Lygari, throwing him back into a wall, where he vanished.

Aaron dropped to his knees, clutching his wound.

Megesti looked around and finding no one else, curtly said, "Alex is busy. You'll have to let me keep you alive until she's available to fix you up properly."

Aaron nodded at his friend. All the color had drained from Megesti's face, and his hands shook as he helped Aaron lie down on his side. Aaron grabbed his hand. "I trust you, Megesti. You can do this."

Despite the noise and chaos around them, Megesti focused on Aaron. His hands hovered over the wound, and then he quickly gripped the hilt and wrenched it from Aaron's abdomen. Blood poured from the wound, and Megesti's hands slammed over it. Aaron almost passed out from the pain as Megesti put pressure on the wound, and in seconds, Aaron's midsection glowed gold. Aaron had to shut his eyes against the blinding light. A few moments later, Megesti removed his hands, and Aaron sat up to examine himself. His tattered shirt dripped with blood, but his skin was perfectly healed.

"Thank you."

Megesti didn't hear him, otherwise occupied by shock and confusion. Aaron wanted to ask what the problem was, but then he heard the screams.

"Alex, *no!*"

CHAPTER 21

ALEX

Gryphon's cry sounded far away.

The red steel tip of the arrow shaft Alex held was buried in Garrick's neck, and his eyes were full of rage and shock. Hot blood spurted and flowed along the shaft, drenching her hand and sleeve. She choked back a breath as the metallic stench filled her nostrils. Then, before she changed her mind, Alex ripped the arrow out, taking a chunk of flesh with it. Garrick dropped to his knees, and his hand went to his throat.

"It's over now," she grumbled. "You're dead, and can't hurt us anymore."

"And you're ... trapped." Garrick slouched forward and made a sound that could have been a laugh through the gurgling blood.

"Alex!" Gryphon's voice barely registered behind her. "If he dies, you and I will be stuck here!"

Stuck?

"We can't leave! We'll be trapped here!"

"No!" Alex dove toward Garrick's lifeless body. Her hands

were slick with his fresh blood as she erupted in gold light and tried to force her healing magic into him. But the light merely left through one hand and flowed back into the other, and nothing happened.

Aaron was already running toward her. She scrambled to her feet and made a mad dash across the room. As she ran, she heard faint popping sounds. She ignored them, afraid she'd trip if she looked away.

"It's okay!" Aaron said as they got closer. "I've got you!"

Alex had nearly reached him when Aaron vanished with a loud pop. Alex couldn't slow down in time and slammed into the wall. *Aaron!* Mortal and sorcerer alike, all of her friends except for Gryphon had vanished, and the only ones left were the terrible sorcerers she wanted nothing to do with.

Gryphon? Gryphon, help!

Alex's emotions ripped through her like a hurricane. They took over, and something deep and primal within her reared up. Pain surged through her gut as this new part of her made its presence known. Her breath sped up, and the entire room rumbled. Sorcerers around her screamed as stones fell from the ceiling. The force of the floor stones moving knocked Ridge to the ground. Alex struggled to keep her balance. Then the homey smell of a campfire encircled her.

She collapsed on the unsteady ground. Gryphon caught her and pulled her tightly against him. Sorcerers fled the room. Alex clung to Gryphon, desperate to stop spinning.

Get us out of here, please! she shouted at Gryphon from inside her head, hoping he heard her. All of her energy was being zapped away. She blinked and found herself on a semi-circular balcony overlooking an endless forest.

Fresh air found her lungs, and she gasped as if her body suddenly remembered how to breathe. A warm hand rubbed her back, sending calm through her. Then came the nausea, and she leaned over the thick stone railing and let herself be sick. "What just happened?" she asked weakly.

"When you killed my father, his power transferred to us, and we became the current Head and Heart."

"Does that mean I'm going to want to kill you now?"

"Not any more than normal. We're different."

"But where did everyone go? Why did the room start crumbling around us? What did your father mean when he said we were trapped?"

"The castle is recreating itself," Gryphon said. "Every Head gets to shape their castle how they want it. And..." Gryphon turned her to face him. "After the great sorcerer and human war that cost both sides so much, Tabitha made a spell to protect the mortals from us. When a new Head or Heart takes over, they cannot leave the Forbidden Lands to enter the mortal world. It lasts until the day that they no longer want to go."

Alex's stomach roiled. She pulled away from Gryphon, but didn't make it to the edge this time before she retched on the ground.

"Are you all right?" Gryphon asked as he helped her up.

"No, I'm not all right!" Alex shouted at him as her body burst into an orange glow. "I'm terrified, and exhausted, and trapped in this horrible castle that wants to move everything around, and I just want to go home!" Alex cried, and her entire body shook. Gryphon moved to hold her, but she shoved him as hard as she could.

"Don't you dare touch me! You knew this could happen, and you didn't warn us!"

"How could I have known you would kill my father?" Gryphon shouted back, losing his temper.

"It didn't have to be me," Alex snapped back. "We brought

red steel. Aaron, Stefan, or my father could have killed him, too."

"They never would have gotten close enough."

"Even more reason for you to tell me then." Alex covered her face with her hands. She could feel her heart beating so fast she worried she might pass out. She moved her hand over her abdomen and tried the breathing techniques that Emmerich and Jerome had taught her.

Gryphon moved closer, the regret on his face clear. "I'm so sorry. You're right, I should have told you. I just didn't think he'd ever die."

Alex's breaths slowed. "It's not fair."

"I know. I should be trapped here … not us."

"That's not what I meant. I mean it's not fair that I don't get to stay mad at you because you're the only person on this entire island that I trust."

"We'll figure this out. So far, there hasn't been anything we couldn't solve together."

"I can't stay here. I have to go home," Alex said. Her entire body began to shake, and when Gryphon held out his arms, she let him hold her.

"I'll get you home. Whether it takes a week, a month, a year—"

"It can't be a year. I need to be home as soon as possible. I can't let Aaron miss everything."

"Miss everything?"

"I was going to tell him after we got my father back. He'd never have let me come if I had."

"Tell him what?"

PART TWO

A HEART NEEDS THEIR HEAD

CHAPTER 22
GRYPHON

"*I'm pregnant.*"

Gryphon wrenched away, leaving her startled. The words hit him like a blast from a Salem explosion. "Pregnant ... how?"

Alex rolled her eyes. "Gryphon."

"That's not what I meant. I meant ... Why?"

"It just happened," Alex snapped. "Despite all the chaos around us we weren't doing anything to prevent this. We're supposed to be making a bunch of heirs, but it figures it would finally happen at the worst possible time."

"You have no idea bad this is."

Alex crossed her arms and stepped back again. "I know the curse made Aaron jealous and messed things up between you two even more, but you could at least pretend to be happy for *me*. I want this." Alex wiped away the tears and turned to leave the balcony.

"Stop!" Gryphon shouted more harshly than he meant to. Alex stopped moving but the rage on her face made it clear he

81

had to talk fast. "In any other circumstance, I'd be ecstatic for you if this is what you want. But here it's dangerous—life-threatening even. Lynx can smell when you're different. The other Tiere sorcerers here ... they'll know you're pregnant in no time, and worse, they'll be able to smell that the baby is mortal."

Alex's hands moved to her belly, as if to shield her child from what he was saying. "How?"

"All sorcerers give off a magical essence, and it starts as soon as we are created. Those Tiere sorcerers who are more perceptive will know the truth, and if you think they will tolerate their Head birthing a mortal child ..." Gryphon frowned and shook his head, unable to speak.

"No," Alex whispered. "I won't let them hurt him. They took one child from me. I will not lose another to their callous disregard for mortal life."

"And *that* is why we are trapped here. To protect your loved ones from the terror our kind can reap."

Alex took a step back and stumbled. Gryphon rushed to her. She tried to push him away, but he wouldn't let her, so she pounded on his chest as he held her upright.

"You would have killed Aaron as a baby if my mother hadn't stopped you. I will not let you hurt our son!" Alex's strikes became softer, and her breaths more rigid.

By the time he'd carried her to their bedroom, she'd practically fallen asleep in his arms. Seeing their room for the first time, Gryphon smiled. It was exactly how he'd always imagined it would be. Across the room from the balcony, a pair of elaborately carved doors stood with large stones around them. Each of the stones had one of the ten-line marks etched into it, and the doors had a crown and heart merged together. The opposite corners were filled by two giant stone dragon head carvings. Gryphon lit fireplaces inside the mouths, making the dragons appear ready to breathe fire across the room.

Each fireplace had taken after Gryphon and Alex, with the left one carved from a strange dark red stone Gryphon couldn't identify but reminded him of dragon's blood. The opposite one was cut from sandstone with amethyst for the dragon's eyes. Stepping further into the room, Gryphon found a bed large enough to sleep at least five people, with a dozen oversized pillows and mystics-blue bedding. Trees grew from the floor, serving as the bedposts. Gryphon lowered Alex onto the magically soft bed, softer than anything he'd ever touched. A vast wardrobe, several bookcases, and two couches faced the larger, red fireplace. Gryphon examined Alex, covered in dirt, sweat, and blood. He leaned down and gently stroked her temple, searching for her feelings after the last time he faced this choice.

"Well, you didn't hate me at Moorloc's when I cleaned Tristan and Doyle's blood off you, so I hope you'll forgive me for removing my father's." He crossed the room to the wardrobe and opened it, revealing his clothes. He selected a blue mystics shirt and got to work cleaning her up. As soon as he got her out of the blood-soaked clothes, he put the shirt on her and tucked her into the bed under the large quilt.

After settling Alex safely in their bed, Gryphon's own exhaustion hit him. As tempting as it was to go explore the castle and see how it all had changed, he couldn't leave Alex alone, not after learning about the baby.

... Ferflucs. How are we going to hide this? If Kharon, Birch and Lynx haven't come back yet, my father clearly did something to keep them away. Leave it to him, to make sure the only support I have in in this world is ripped from me when I need them most. Well not everyone. I still have her, and ... now she's going to have a much

harder time adjusting here, especially once the pregnancy interferes with her control. Ares help me.

Alex slept quietly on one side of the bed. "I'm risking your temper." He placed pillows from the headboard in a line down the middle of the bed. She didn't even stir as he settled in on the opposite side and pulled the blanket over himself.

CHAPTER 23
AARON

Aaron landed in the Datten throne room with his arms outstretched, ready to catch Alex. Immediately, the room filled with the clanging of metal as his knights leaped into action. Jerome appeared, and it took Aaron a moment to register that the others were popping into the room all around him.

"Where are they?" Michael's voice was high with panic.

"We're missing Alex, Edward, and Harold," Stefan said, his voice getting louder as he hurried to Aaron and Jerome. "Could they have gone home?"

"Aaron, where are you going?" General Avery asked while Jerome shouted for Aaron to wait.

Terror and rage threatened to overwhelm him as Aaron threw open the door and charged into the hallway toward the king's suite. He ran into the room, screaming Alex's name before dashing up the stairs to the second floor. When there was still no answer, he dashed back into the hallway to try his luck in the library. He slammed his fist into his door and leaned his forehead against the wood to calm his breathing.

A throat cleared behind him, too gentle to be a Wafner. Lynx's clothes were covered in blood from the fight with her father, but her face was virtually spotless.

"Did you know what would happen? Did he?" Aaron asked. "Was this his plan all along?"

Lynx exhaled loudly, apparently unable to form more words right away. "When I became a titan," she began after several long minutes of silence, "I was taught that when a new Head takes over, the Forbidden Lands reforms itself to please the new master. But I never thought it would banish sorcerers, let alone titans. I think Garrick or Eris found a way to keep *us* from helping Gryphon and Alex."

"Can I get them back?" Aaron asked.

"Them?" Lynx asked, swallowing as she stepped closer to Aaron. "You'd allow Gryphon to return?"

"Part of me wants to punish him if he was misleading us about these risks, but I know Alex still needs his help, especially if I take a while to get her back." Aaron swallowed hard and ran his hand through his hair. "Tell me we'll get her back in my lifetime, please."

"We'll do everything we can," she whispered and reached out to Aaron.

"I'll never stop trying," Michael said as he and the Wafner men arrived from the throne room. "You remember what I told you when we went to get her back from Moorloc, don't you?"

Aaron nodded. He turned to face them all, arms crossed, and leaned against the door to his room. "One friend. She needs one person to trust and lean on to survive. In the forest, growing up, it was Stefan and you. She had you both here too, along with her ladies and me. At Moorloc's, it was Gryphon, and she got through it."

"So, she'll keep fighting and pushing forward, because he'll be there," Michael said.

Megesti and Birch cracked into the hall with Harold in tow. "They're safe," Megesti said.

Harold shrugged. "Somehow, I ended up at home."

"And Edward?" Stefan asked.

"The same," Kharon replied. As usual, they'd blended into the background. "He wanted to clean himself up and find Matthew before coming here."

"I think that's a good idea," Aaron said. "Everyone clean up, and we'll meet in the dining hall. Jerome will have the kitchen bring up whatever they have. Even if no one is hungry, I want the option there." As everyone left, Aaron pulled Kharon aside and asked them to retrieve Guinevere from her visit to Warren. He wanted her safe and in his sight.

Aaron marched into his room and froze when he opened the door. They'd been so preoccupied before they left to get Edward back that no one had asked the staff to come in here and tidy up the mess they'd made preparing their disguises. Reaching down, Aaron grabbed the first gray belt the seamstress had made for Alex. Kharon had declared it too fancy for a Hades sorcerer, so Alex had left it on her reading spot on their couch.

Unable to get Alex out of his mind, he headed into the bathing suite to clean up. A copper trough held the water he used for bathing. The maids hadn't known he was coming, but the chilly water didn't bother him. He'd had to bathe in icy mountain water before, and he needed every trace of the sorcerers off him. By the time he finished, the water was so muddy he could no longer see to the bottom.

Aaron took the steps two at a time to their bedroom. Alex's nightdress was tossed onto their bed from when she'd dressed in her Hades robe. Aaron picked it up and ran his thumb across the soft fabric, bringing it to his nose and inhaling her scent. An icy chill surrounded him, and he turned to look for

Alex's expression on instinct to see who visited, but he was alone.

"Father, or Daniel—whoever it is—help me get her back. I can't handle everything on my own without her."

There was a frantic knock, and his door flew open. "Aaron?"

"I'm here, Mother."

Guinevere rushed across the room and pulled Aaron into a hug. "I'm so sorry, dear. We'll get her back. I know we will."

He gave her a hug and took the hand of his uncle Bernhard, and Cameron, his cousin. "Thank you for accompanying her," Aaron said, as his mother finally released him.

Bernhard nodded. "Edward came with us. He's with General Bishop in the dining hall, where you asked everyone to meet. I'm happy to join you or stay with your mother. Whatever you need."

"No one is staying with me," Guinevere declared. "You'll all attend. The more ideas we have, the better."

Aaron hugged his mother tightly, and she whispered, "They'll push you, Aaron, and you're going to have to put your pain aside to manage theirs. You can't just be Alexandra's husband right now … you have to be their king." As she released him, Guinevere kissed his cheek, and Aaron left with his family for the dining hall.

As they walked, Cameron looked at him expectantly. "We only got part of the story. What happened this time?" he finally asked.

"It all happened so fast, but Alex somehow killed Gryphon's father. He was the Head, and apparently when a new Head and Heart take power, they're forced to stay in the Forbidden Lands."

"So, she's stuck there … with Gryphon?" Cameron sucked his breath in.

"I don't like the idea of her being trapped anywhere. But to be in the Forbidden Lands, with *him,* for who knows how long …" Aaron paused and slapped the stone wall beside them. "Cameron, I was barely holding it together after my father's death, along with becoming king, and getting cursed. But now … I'm going to lose my mind."

Cameron shook Aaron. "You are not. You are King Aaron of Datten. You're as tough as your father, as thoughtful as your mother, and as brave as your brother was. Plus, you are smarter than the last five Datten kings put together. You will figure this out."

"What if I can't do it? What if I fail to get her back?"

"Then she'll figure out how to get back to you."

"Cameron's right," Michael said, coming up behind them. "If anything, Alex will fight harder to get back here."

"And if she forgets about me?" Aaron whispered.

"Stop it," Michael grumbled. "We only lost her, but she lost all of us. She won't stop fighting, ever."

The dining hall rang loud with the chatter of their friends who'd been in battle updating those who'd been left behind. Jessica and Edith were distraught. Macht, Jerome, and Avery sat beside them, asking a few questions and listening quietly. Jerome's eyes moved from person to person as he caught details of each story.

Aaron took a seat beside his general. "Taking all the versions and putting them together will provide you with the actual truth. Isn't that what you always said?"

"Listen to what everyone else says they saw, and we'll figure out where we went wrong and to fix this."

"There's no quick fix to this," Aaron said. "She's stuck there, and there isn't a *ferflucsing* thing I can do."

The chatter stopped abruptly, all eyes on Aaron. Cameron and Stefan looked as horrified as Aaron felt, but Michael's expression shocked him. The Veremund heir's face twisted in rage.

"Are you really so arrogant to think that just because *you* don't know what to do, we can't get her back?"

"It's not arrogance if it's true," Aaron snapped.

"You are not allowed to just give up on her," Michael spat at him.

Stefan steadied Michael, but he shook him off, brushing past Jessica and Harold to confront Aaron.

"I'm not giving up, Michael," Aaron snapped back. "But I'm allowed to feel hopeless at having lost my wife, again!"

Michael rubbed his stubbled chin, considering his words. He wagged his finger at Aaron. "I thought you were supposed to be a king now. When you were crown prince and Alex was taken, you didn't give up. You rallied an army in a day and crossed the Ogre Mountains to save her. But now, as her husband and king, there isn't anything you can do?"

"Michael—"

"No. Stop whining and listen to the people who have gathered here to help *us* get her back."

Aaron stood up and slammed his hands on the table. "It isn't the same as when I saved her from Moorloc."

"Clearly. Prince Aaron wouldn't give up, but King Aaron can't even hold a meeting without thinking it's hopeless?"

"Michael," Jerome growled through clenched teeth.

"What can I do against the entire sorcerer world?" Aaron replied.

"That's your problem!" Michael snapped. "You think it's all on you. Try asking Lynx or Kharon or Birch. I'm sure they know a little something about the Forbidden Lands. Use your generals, your friends, the three immensely powerful titans, including one who speaks to the dead. We are all here to help get her back."

"Michael—"

"It's not Michael. It's *Earl Veremund* to you, Your Royal Highness. Because if the Crown Princess of Warren is not here to plead with you to come to your senses and use the resources you have to come up with a plan to rescue her, then your uncle and I will."

Aaron chuckled and shook his head. "You think that's how this works?"

"He's correct," Bernhard said. "If Alexandria isn't here, and Edward is not available, then it falls to Michael, Matthew, and myself, as the highest-ranking men of Warren nobility, to speak on behalf of the royals, and the Veremunds have advised the kings for centuries."

Stefan gently placed himself between Michael and Aaron. "Squabbling won't help. It'll only make us lose sight of what we need to be doing. We all need to share what we learned of the castle, the sorcerers, and the magic we witnessed. Then Kharon, Birch, and Lynx will tell us everything they know about the spell and the magic keeping us apart. From there, I'm sure we'll come up with several plans."

"Such as?" Aaron crossed his arms and glared at them both.

Harold growled. "I'll send my entire fleet to the island. They can bring her back."

"Or the Warren ships," Cameron added.

"Lynx, are animals able to get through?" Jessica asked.

"I don't know," she replied. "But I'll find out."

"If the Nials still have our pearl, we could try that," Edith said.

Michael turned to Aaron and crossed his arms. "See?"

"When did you become so pushy?" Aaron asked.

"The moment you tried to give up on my best friend!"

"Feeling frustrated is not giving up," Aaron replied.

"It is if you're a king," Michael replied.

Aaron stomped toward Michael, but Stefan held his arm out. "Michael, stop it," Stefan said. "The last thing Alex would want is you picking a fight with Aaron. It helps no one."

"You're only saying these things because you blame yourself," Aaron said.

"Why would I?"

"You were the one with her. You were supposed to be protecting her."

Michael's face went ashen when Megesti stepped between them and pushed Stefan and Michael apart. "That's enough."

Birch turned to Michael. "I'm glad you are so insistent that we fight for Alexandria, but you have to realize that no matter how much you love her, this is going to be the hardest on Aaron and Edward. They didn't spend her entire life with her already."

Michael huffed, then sat back down, avoiding Aaron's gaze.

After a moment, Jerome broke the silence. "I think it's best if you take turns telling us what happened while you were there."

"Agreed." Aaron sat back down at the table and allowed Megesti and Harold to speak first.

CHAPTER 24
ALEX

Everything hurts. Why does everything always hurt?

Alex slit open her eyes, then shut them again. The morning sun somehow shone all the way from the balcony onto her face. She forced herself to look over, then bolted up in bed. *This isn't my bed. This isn't my shirt. This isn't even my room!* Her scream rattled the walls, something she knew she had to work on, but right now she didn't care.

A loud thump followed by a groan came from the opposite side of the bed. Alex tentatively raised her head and peeked over the pillow barrier that had been erected. The sheets were ruffled, but empty. From the floor, Gryphon rubbed his shoulder, grumbling. Not sure whether to be angry or scared, Alex decided not to scream again until she knew more.

"Gryphon?"

"You're awake." Gryphon scrambled onto the bed, being careful not to cross the pillows.

"I thought my scream gave that away."

"I assumed it was a nightmare. It wasn't your first scream tonight."

"Where are we?"

"How much do you remember from yesterday?" Gryphon moved a few of the pillows away, then shifted into a sitting position on his side of the remaining barrier. He wore only sleeping pants that matched her shirt. Alex had seen him shirtless so many times now she'd lost count, but looking up at him from the bed, she felt warm all over.

"I remember everything except this room. I ... I killed your father, and it trapped us here. And then I screamed at you for not telling me it would happen."

"Accurate. What else?"

"Ember is dead. My friends were all cast out, and I didn't even get to say goodbye. And somehow you're the Heart, and I'm the Head. Where are Birch and Lynx?"

"They haven't returned, so I suspect they can't. You also told me about the baby."

"Which you were very upset about."

"I'm not upset you're pregnant by Aaron," Gryphon said.

Alex snorted. Gryphon ignored her and continued. "I knew it would happen eventually ... I'm just worried about how we're going to hide that baby from the sorcerers here. Yes, Ember, my father, and my mother are gone, but Eris, Orion, and Phobos are all still alive, and while we are the Head and Heart, we cannot defeat every sorcerer if they turn on us."

"Because we don't have our titans?"

"Correct. Megesti, Lynx, Birch, and Kharon appear to be stuck in the mortal world. I believe others have come back in the past, so we just have to find out how."

"You mean ... we could leave?"

"Perhaps. I can't say for sure, but even if we manage to figure out how, it's going to take time. You cannot get your hopes up. There are thousands of books in the library, but I don't have any idea where that spell would be. My father wasn't exactly the sharing type."

"But there *is* a spell?"

"I assume so. Magic set that spell, it should be able to break it."

"Okay, so we start now." Alex hopped off the bed and felt the hem of her shirt graze her upper thigh. Her cheeks heated at the scant coverage it provided. "Did you dress me?"

"I did." Instantly, her embarrassment was replaced by rage, and Gryphon held his hands up in surrender. "Before you get angry, I checked your memory from Moorloc's to see how you handled me washing you there. You weren't angry then. Plus, I didn't think you would want to wake up soaked in my father's blood. If I overstepped, I'm sorry, but I wanted you to be okay when you woke up. Well, as okay as possible."

Alex crossed her arms, considering his expression. *I'm terrified of being stuck here forever, but I'm also nervous about being alone with you for so long. I can be miserable, or I can make the best of it. Trying to live as normally as possible will hopefully make it hurt less.* At least she'd get to read all the books and learn about how sorcerers used magic in everyday life. She might even be able to get extra lessons while trapped here. And she trusted him to behave. "You're supposed to be another Michael or Stefan ... right?"

Gryphon nodded.

"Then I have to treat you as one. I wouldn't scream at them for it, but please only do what you just did when it's absolutely necessary. I can handle it if I wake up covered in blood. I am a woman, after all. It happens regularly."

"Anything else?"

"I want proper clothes."

"Of course." Gryphon climbed out of the bed and went over

to the wardrobe. He opened it by the handles and pointed. Alex crept over and peeked inside. It was full of his clothes.

"That's not what I—"

Gryphon released the doors, and they swung shut. "Now you open it."

Alex scoffed but decided to humor him and opened one of the doors. The clothes had changed. She flung open the second door with so much force that it flew back toward Gryphon.

He managed to catch it. "It's enchanted," he teased. "It'll show your clothes when you open it and mine when I do. I couldn't get you a proper nightdress, and for that I apologize."

"Well, I can't very well be angry with you now." Alex groaned. "You looked inside my head for consent and you dressed me in the best you could, even if I hate blue."

"I figured between the Mystics blue and Ares orange ..."

"Definitely the right choice. Turn around."

"What?"

Alex grabbed a pair of training pants and a gold tunic. "I need to get dressed."

"Right. Sorry." Gryphon swiftly exited toward the balcony doors and slipped outside, closing them behind him.

Alex took off Gryphon's shirt and dropped it on the floor, quickly pulling on her pants, and tunic. "This is surprisingly soft."

"Did you think we don't appreciate nice things?"

"You're supposed to stay out there until I call you." Alex turned to scold him, but he had stayed on the balcony with his back to her. "How did you hear me from out there?" Alex walked the length of the room and threw open the doors.

"Can I turn around now?"

"Obviously."

Gryphon spun on his heel. "It would seem, Princess, that our bond is significantly stronger now that we're the Head and Heart. I could hear you as clearly as a bell despite the walls."

"I can't decide if that is good or bad."

"For now, take it as a good thing. If you run into trouble, I'll know."

"You keep saying that as if you expect every sorcerer in the Forbidden Lands to attack me on sight, and yet no one has set foot in here."

"That's because in here, we're protected."

"Explain," Alex said.

"While the castle reshapes itself for each new Head, there are certain elements that remain. The dungeon wall locations change, but the number of rooms and their properties do not. The entrance doors from the territories stay the same, since the territories are unaffected. Finally, the bedroom of the Head is protected. Only those most intimately connected to the Head can enter the room."

"Such as their bonded partners?"

"Not always. My mother couldn't enter my father's room."

"That's absurd," Alex said.

"If my father wished to visit her, he had to go to her room. As far as I know, no one ever entered his room."

"I did."

Gryphon froze. "What?"

"Yesterday. Michael, Kharon, and I found Eris' room, and I fell through a wall and ended up in your father's room. I think I have some of his things." Alex brushed past Gryphon and found her robe on the ground by the bed. Somehow, it had come with them to the room despite Alex tossing it aside in the throne room. Clearly the new castle wanted her to have it. She dug through the pockets until she found the journal she'd been reading and handed it to Gryphon.

"How could you get in when I couldn't?"

"Because I'm the Head? Or maybe because of my mother." Alex tugged the portrait of her mother out of the back of the journal and Gryphon took it. He held it beside her face and smiled.

"You're prettier."

"We're identical, Sunset."

Gryphon smirked. "Not to me." He strolled to the closest fireplace and stood the painting in the center of the mantle. "We'll get a frame for it as soon as we can."

"Thank you." Alex tugged on her shirt, trying to figure out the right words to say.

Gryphon nodded. "Well, Princess, I think we've hidden in here long enough. We should take a tour of the new castle and see if we—"

"—can find the library?"

"I was going to say, find you something to eat."

Alex moved a hand to her mouth and shook her head. "No. I'm not up to eating in the mornings."

"Well then, we'll find you something to bring along for later."

Gryphon opened the door. When Alex nodded, he stepped into the hall, and she followed.

CHAPTER 25

GRYPHON

When Gryphon entered the hallway, he had half-expected the titans to be waiting to attack them, but it was empty. He held his hand out to Alex, and they crept out of the room to find a simple, bare hallway. A large staircase across from them led down. Alex dragged Gryphon toward a large door of the same dark oak as the one leading to their bedroom. He tried to stop her, but she kept moving toward the end of the hallway.

"Let me go first," Gryphon said, and though Alex rolled her eyes, she relented. Alex was astonished when the door swung open before he even touched the knob.

"It seems the library came from your dreams, because I've never imagined anything this grand," Gryphon said. Alex stepped over the threshold into a room that held nothing but bookshelves. They ran along every wall up to the ceiling, which was twice the height of a normal castle room, and in the middle were more rows of bookcases than Gryphon could count at a glance. A sturdy-looking ladder provided each access to the higher books without magic. Alex raced and disappeared into the bookcases, bursting into a high-pitched squeal of delight.

"Alex, wait for me! We don't know what's in here."

"Books, Gryphon! Books are in here. All the books in the world."

Gryphon chased the soft echo that gave away her location among the stacks. He found her in the back corner, in front of a spiral stone staircase that disappeared into the ceiling. Unlike the plan hallway stones, these sparkled like the outside of his father's castle had.

"I'm going to guess that's the lab," she said. "It smells like the forest mixed with my satchel after a trip here."

Gryphon motioned for her to go, and she dashed up the stairs two at a time. Indeed, the floor above held the lab. As large as any of the mortal throne rooms, it seemed to be set up to teach lessons, and from the looks of some of the simpler exercises, not only to Alex but to anyone who needed help. Alex walked among the endless inset stone shelves of jars, powders, animals, and plants. Gryphon couldn't help but marvel at how comfortable she looked examining a jar to decipher which powder it held. Watching her, he felt a need deep inside himself awaken. It was a strange feeling he'd never had before —a combination of desire, protectiveness, and needing to touch her so he didn't explode. Not wanting to spook her, he slowly slid his hand onto her hip, preparing for her to growl, but she was so transfixed she either didn't notice, or didn't mind. *Would you let Stefan and Michael touch you like this? Is that why you don't mind, or ... is it me?*

"What have you got there?" he asked, and she jerked a little at the sound of his voice.

"You scared me." She held up the jar. The powder inside was red with a few flecks of green and black.

"That's dried dragon liver," he told her.

"How can you tell?"

"Red powders are usually a body part, but only dragons have two color flecks in them. The black is from the mineral they consume that lets them breathe fire."

Alex nodded and replaced the jar. "I have so much to learn."

"You have a lifetime to learn. Remember, despite my youthful good looks, I've been studying this for decades."

Alex wrinkled her nose at him and shook her head. "I forget that you're so much older. You're old enough to be my grandfather." Alex snickered and went back to perusing the powders.

"I believe we were hunting for the kitchen and food."

"Uh huh," Alex said, ignoring him.

"We need to eat, Alex. If you want to read and try spells, you'll need energy."

"I know."

Gryphon sighed. "If I leave you here to find food, do you promise not to go anywhere?"

Alex nodded eagerly, but when Gryphon stepped toward her, she backed up to the shelf and swallowed. Her cheeks grew pink and her breathing quickened under his stare. *Strange reaction from you. You normally push back when I come close. We're going to have to be extra careful around each other while we adjust to our new powers.* "I'm serious," Gryphon said. "Do not leave this room. I have no idea who is in here or what they are up to. Understood?"

Alex nodded, and Gryphon was about to give a stronger warning when she placed her hand over her belly. "I won't leave here, but please hurry back. You're making me nervous about being alone here."

Satisfied, Gryphon nodded and hurried back down to the library. The second floor was filled with guest rooms and storage space, but at the end of a small hall, he could see through an interior window down into the colossal throne room, which comprised much of the first floor. It was yet another thing the castle took from Alex, mimicking Datten and Warren's halls. Gryphon found his way down and discovered a dining hall and an enormous kitchen. He had never seen such a large kitchen, and it took him by surprise. He'd never considered what the kitchen in his castle would look like, and the castle noticed, choosing Alex's vision.

It reminded him of one of the sorcerers' labs in its layout, with ample work benches and supplies on display and out in the open. It only took a minute to find the pantry stocked with fruit, dried meat and cheese, and more of Alex's favorites. Not sure what she could stomach at the moment, he took a little of everything, along with a whole baguette and two of the giant green apples she'd enjoyed so much when he'd brought them to her at Moorloc's. Satisfied that he could at least keep her energy up, he cracked back to the lab.

Seeing she wasn't there, Gryphon panicked and practically threw the food onto the table, his heart pounding. "Alex!" The walls shook with each yell. "Alex, where are you?"

"Out here."

Gryphon spun, searching for her voice, until her face appeared at a door he hadn't noticed.

"There's a roof garden, like at my mother's!" Alex smiled so broadly that Gryphon's heart stopped for a moment.

"How are you smiling?" When Alex blushed, he added, "I'm sorry. I'm tired and saying things I meant to think."

"Thinking things doesn't always hide them from me."

"True." Gryphon picked an apple and went to join Alex on the roof. The garden boxes were exactly like her mother's, but the roof had a few additions. At the end, a large fire pit allowed foul-smelling potions to be made outside. A huge rain barrel on the other side made him chuckle. Considering Alex's ability with water, it seemed like a waste of space. *Unless the castle knows something I don't and she won't stay with me here.* The thought stilled his mirth.

Alex sat cross-legged in a fabric swing that hung between two apple trees, gazing into the distance.

Gryphon twisted off an apple from a branch and handed it to her. "What are you looking at?"

She grabbed it with both hands and idly turned it, searching for the little spot that curved in before taking a bite. "I'm watching the wind blow the leaves of the plants in the boxes. It soothes me."

"Birch and Lynx do that too. They claim that plants sing to them. They have been telling me that since I was a boy, but I know they're just playing with me."

"I can promise you they aren't." Alex patted the fabric beside her. "Sit."

Gryphon lowered himself next to her, but as he put his weight down, he fell into Alex, and the whole thing rocked. "What is this abomination?"

"It's a hammock. We had them at the camp for the summer nights when it was too hot to sleep in the huts. Have you really never seen a hammock?"

Gryphon struggled to balance himself without falling onto Alex's lap. His earnest squirming made her laugh.

"It's not funny," he protested. "I'm trying not to fall onto you and you're laughing."

Alex took his hands, stilling him. "Stop moving, and focus."

"On what?"

"The plants."

Heat coursed through Gryphon when Alex intertwined

their fingers. All he could hear was his blood pumping through his ears, but he held his breath a moment—and then he heard it. The garden hummed a gentle tune he'd noticed before. "I know this song. Birch would sing me to sleep with it when I was a little boy."

Alex smiled. "I think she'd sing to you, and once you were relaxed enough, the plants would take over for her. It seems your chaotic mind is capable of quiescence."

Gryphon playfully pushed Alex with his shoulder. "My mind is only calm around a select group of people."

"You mean a select group of sorceresses. Birch, Lynx, and I."

"Birch and Lynx," Gryphon corrected. "You have the opposite effect. You calm my violent chaos, but you cause a whole slew of other chaos inside me."

"Oh." Alex released his hand and moved to stand.

Gryphon stopped her. "I didn't mean it in a bad way."

"Then how did you mean it?"

She struggled to hide her emotions, confusion and hurt clear on her face. "I mean, that you bring up feelings in me I'm not used to," he said. "I'm normally a very cocky Ares male, but that doesn't work with you. I'm torn between being myself and being protective about all the chaos that seems to follow you around."

His awkward confession made Alex smile mischievously. "I like that I keep you on your toes, but for the record, just be yourself. I became friends with the cocky sorcerer and stayed after seeing your Ares chaos on full display. So I'm not going anywhere."

"Good. Now, can you help me out of this contraption so we can go eat?"

Alex giggled and held out her hand so Gryphon could wiggle and finally fall out of the hammock. Alex tried very hard, but the moment he turned his back, she lost her hold and erupted into laughter. Gryphon spun around and lunged toward her. She attempted to evade him, but he grabbed her and threw her over his shoulder to carry her kicking and screaming for him to put her down.

Back inside, Alex ate her food while perusing a book she'd found on Poseidon powers. Gryphon watched her sniff one of the dried meats suspiciously. "What is this?"

"Dried goat. Do you not have goats?"

"Not ones with orange flesh. It smells weird, like the purple fish Moorloc made me eat." Alex dropped the dried meat and pushed her plate away, covering her mouth.

"Lost your appetite?"

"Yes." She sipped her tea and went back to reading the book.

"Alex, we have to talk."

She looked up from her book and batted her eyes at him. "Yes, Gryphon?"

"I'm concerned about how well you're handling this, and how calm you are."

"Why would I not be? You said there's a spell and we just have to find it."

"Yes, but I also warned you, there are thousands of books."

"In total. How many Titan journals can there be, or Head journals for that matter?" Alex asked.

Gryphon exhaled sharply. "There are nearly two thousand titan books and over thirteen hundred head books. Heads typically write one a year at minimum, and that's what has survived."

"Thirteen hundred?" Alex's mouth dropped open. "How are we ever going to find the book we need?"

Gryphon reached over to take her hand. "We can do this. It'll just take time."

"I can't have this baby here. I need Aaron. And Jessica and Guinevere. I have no idea what I'm doing." Tears filled her eyes.

"You've got me, and I'm going to do everything I can to make sure you get home." *Even if it means I have to stay here alone.*

CHAPTER 26
AARON

Aaron's sword whistled through the air until it met Caleb's sword with such force that Caleb stumbled back. Before he could recover, Aaron swung even harder and sent Caleb's shoulder armor flying off. He kicked his friend to the ground, and Caleb lifted his hands in surrender. With Caleb down, that left Hunter and Lucas. Aaron stilled long enough to hear Lucas' nasally breathing to his right and spun to face him. Aaron shifted to a two-handed hold on his sword for a barrage of attacks against the youngest of his friends. In less than a minute, Lucas joined Caleb on the ground, moaning in pain, and Aaron stalked toward the woods to face his final opponent. Hunter wasn't the most skilled swordsman, but he was an exceptional tracker, so finding him before he found Aaron would be the challenge. Aaron crept into the tree line, but all he heard were the branches moving in the wind, so Aaron stood still and waited for Hunter to come to him.

When the knight finally made his appearance, Aaron

dispatched of him quickly, and Hunter soon joined the other two on the ground.

A deep voice bellowed. "You're released from sparring duty. We'll take it from here."

Aaron turned to demand that Jerome explain himself, but seeing Stefan dressed in armor was the only answer he needed.

"It seems both you and my son need to work out your frustrations. I thought you could help one another out in this matter." Jerome handed Stefan his sword. "Try not to kill each other."

The general turned and walked away, leaving Aaron and Stefan to face one another.

Stefan wore his Datten armor, not the lighter Warren one, making them equally weighted, and while Stefan was larger and stronger than his previous rivals, Jerome had trained Aaron to fight above his weight class.

Aaron nodded. "I accept your challenge, Sir Wafner."

"Thank you, Your Royal Highness." Stefan bowed low to Aaron, and as he rose they both took the starting position.

Stefan's stance was similar to his father's. *What other fighting traits might they share?* A wicked grin filled Aaron's face. He waited for Stefan to come for him, and when he didn't, Aaron attacked. He slashed his sword down toward Stefan's thigh, but the younger Wafner deflected the blade with enough force that Aaron stumbled.

"Are you tired from knocking your friends around? Shall I go easy on you?"

Aaron glared. "Would you go easy on Alex?"

"Never had to," Stefan bit back, and Aaron lunged again, this time going for the shoulder, but Stefan was faster. He deftly twisted his sword and knocked Aaron back again.

Aaron saw spots. The Datten temper in him rose dangerously close to the surface. Stefan's expression made him call out, "You can see it, can't you?"

"See what?" Stefan asked calmly.

"You can see me losing control."

Stefan lowered his sword and nodded. "You and Alex have a similar tell."

Aaron nodded and waited for Stefan to move back into position. Their fight lasted for over an hour. Each time Aaron thought he'd gained the upper hand, Stefan knocked him right back. By the time they'd finished sparring, both were bruised and exhausted. They slowly dragged themselves back to the castle.

"Thank you," Aaron said.

"I could tell you needed to burn off some rage, and I was worried for poor Lucas and Hunter. I sparred with Alex whenever she needed it and would be happy to help you."

"You just enjoy hitting me."

"That, too."

AFTER A QUICK CHANGE OF CLOTHES, Aaron headed to the library to meet Lynx, who'd been trying to communicate with some animals to see if they could help get a message to Alex. Aaron was disappointed to learn that all the animals she'd sent out were unable to locate the Forbidden Lands. Aaron thanked her for trying and bid her goodnight.

He left the library with all its reminders of Alex and distracted himself by checking on Megesti to make sure he wasn't overworking himself. A few minutes later, Aaron knocked once and opened the door to the Datten lab. Megesti read an enormous book in the dim light provided by the fireplace and a cluster of candles on the table. He held his head up with his fist. Trying not to startle him, Aaron closed the door softly, but Megesti's head snapped up.

"Megesti—you need to get some rest."

"I'll rest after I figure out how you healed from that wound."

Aaron touched his midsection, where a few days prior, Lygari had run his own blade right through him. The wound felt completely gone, as if there had never been a wound at all. "*You* healed me, Megesti. Didn't you?"

Megesti slouched in his seat. "I didn't, Aaron. I don't have that kind of healing power. The only reason I can heal Alex when she's hurt is because I can take her healing magic and focus it on the injured area. I don't know how you were healed, but I promise you, it wasn't me."

Aaron sat on the stool across from Megesti. "Are you sure?"

Megesti nodded.

"But if it wasn't you ... then who? How?"

"My best guess is that your bond with Alex has somehow moved some of her magic into you. The only other example of a sorcerer married to a mortal is Victoria, with Edward. My uncle Moorloc must have had a woman at some point to bear Lygari, but no one knows anything about her."

Aaron rubbed his hands together, mulling over what Megesti had said. He was right that they didn't know much about the lives of sorcerers and even less about how bonds with a mortal changed them. *If I had any of Alex's magic, wouldn't I have felt something?* He'd never asked Alex what it felt like to glow gold—it was always just something she could do, another part of what made her *his* Alex. He worried over her safety again and hoped Gryphon would help her find a way home. Without him, who knew what kind of risky ideas she might be entertaining? Thinking of that led his mind to a forgotten sorcerer, mortal pairing, and Aaron couldn't help but chuckle.

"What is it?"

"I was just thinking, we'll know for sure if a sorcerer's magic can transfer to their mortal spouse if Stefan starts growing fur."

Megesti seemed to actually consider this for a moment, until a smile spread across his weary face.

Aaron kept going. "Do you think he'd have sandy fur like her, or Wafner red?"

Megesti laughed so hard he snorted like Alex. "It would depend on the animal he got!" They continued on like this for a long time, countering each other with more and more outlandish examples of the kind of animal Stefan might turn into. Eventually, they both had tears in their eyes.

When they finally calmed down, Megesti closed his book and slid it across the table. "I'll make a deal with you."

"All right."

"I'll stop working and go to bed right now, if you answer one question honestly."

Aaron waited.

"How are you doing? And before you tell me the usual lie, know that I can see right through it!"

Aaron picked at a piece of ink-stained parchment. "How do you think I'm doing? Alex is trapped in a place I can't get to— that nobody can get to, so far. It's filled with violent monsters and evil sorcerers that I couldn't protect her from even if I *were* there. I'm so grateful she's not alone. But I hate that I still feel jealous. I'm afraid of what will happen between them and what it would mean for us, especially the longer it takes us to get her home. I'm scared of what I might do. I'm overwhelmed, and angry, and Megesti ... I'm so tired of fighting. Why can't anything ever be calm for a *ferflucsing* minute?" He could feel the turmoil inside him start to bubble into rage, and he took a shaky breath.

Megesti listened quietly and nodded along. Finally, he said, "You know, it takes an incredibly strong connection for a sorcerer to bond with someone as a child, the way Alex bonded with you. It's not something that happens very often."

"Really?"

"According to Birch, it's extremely rare. You and Alex are a set. You've always found your way back to each other, and you always will. It's okay that you feel lost and angry at the situation, but you need to remember, when you let those feelings take over, you're not giving Alex enough credit for how stubborn she is."

Aaron sighed. "I know. I know! I just need her to find her way back to me before ... I don't know."

"Yes, you do. You know Alex's heart is huge," Megesti said. "Gryphon already has a place there, and there's more than enough love to go around for you, Gryphon, and all the rest of our friends. What are you really trying to say?"

Aaron slammed his hand onto the table. "What if he talks her into bed? Or what if something awful happens, like at Moorloc's? What if they bond over some crazy trauma we can't even imagine from here? He's reminded me many times that sorcerers are not monogamous. What if being in the Forbidden Lands brings out a side of her we haven't seen? What if she realizes she belongs there?" At this, his voice cracked. "What if... what if she decides to stay?"

Megesti took a deep breath. He laid a hand over Aaron's, thinking. "Okay. Well, yes. What if? If anything like that happened, what would you do?"

"I'm honestly not sure I could handle it again."

"Would you try?"

"I ... I would *want* to try. But we don't even know what we're talking about here. How can I say I'd be okay if I don't even know what she might be doing over there?"

"Well, you figured out a way to work through what happened at Moorloc's castle together. And as a sorcerer who's also come into a great amount of unexpected power in a short time, I can tell you—it really isn't easy. And Aaron, you know how most of the Datten kings—not your father, of course, but most of them—were always having extramarital affairs?"

"Alex and I are not like those former kings and queens," Aaron snapped. "We are doing things differently."

"That's exactly my point. You're not destined to act a certain way just because your ancestors did, and neither is Alex. It's okay to be scared and angry, but just because you have nightmares doesn't mean any of those things are going to happen. Have you ever known Alex to do anything she didn't want to do?"

Aaron ignored this last part. He leaned forward. "How did you know I've had nightmares?"

"Your father and brother told Kharon, who told Birch, who told me. She was hoping I might be able to help."

Aaron nodded. "Did they tell you what the nightmares were about? Can they even see those things?"

"They didn't have to. I know you, Aaron. It's not just what might be happening in the Forbidden Lands that's got you acting this way. It's how you'll react to whatever she comes home having to tell you. You're more scared of that than anything else."

There was nothing more to say.

Megesti eyed him for a long minute, then heaved himself out of his chair and went to a large shelf containing colored jars, heavy growlers stopped with thick corks, and nubby mortars and pestles. Megesti scanned the shelf until he landed on a growler filled with thick, dark sludge. He uncorked the jug and took a sniff.

"Ugh! That's it! Birch's sleeping draught." Coughing from the stench, he replaced the cork and found a clean wooden mug. He set both the growler and the mug in front of Aaron, who groaned in disgust. At least he would sleep tonight.

CHAPTER 27
ALEX

Alex sighed and closed her book. They were each getting through about five journals a day, six if they really pushed, but with thousands of books in the library, Alex was getting discouraged. They wouldn't be able to keep reading at this rate, and when they slowed down, it would only take longer. Gryphon encouraged her to keep going in an attempt to lift her spirits, but he could feel her worry.

They hadn't seen any other sorcerers yet. Gryphon was hiding her until they figured out what to do. He'd locked down the castle, so the two of them were left alone to wander the endless halls and chambers. Neither of them had much cooking ability, so they had some inventive meals scrounged from the kitchen's stores. Luckily, this magical castle had a magical kitchen, so there were apples and bread aplenty.

After four days locked in the library, Alex was crawling out of her skin. Her legs, used to daily runs and grueling training with Jerome, felt weak and achy. Her skin missed the sun. Her shoulders and arms felt listless. She needed to spar someone, to sprint, to ride—anything.

"Can we *please* go outside today?" she asked.

"Sure, we always go into the garden."

"I'm tired of the garden. I want to go for a walk."

"No."

"Why not?"

"Did you forget that you're carrying a future *mortal* king?"

Gryphon had been using this argument on the grounds that Alex's mortal child would be at grave risk if they even set foot outside the castle. *He might be right, but I'm going to go out of my mind if I don't get some fresh air. This can't be good for the baby either.*

Gryphon groaned, finally relenting. "We'll go on one condition. You do exactly as I say, when I say it, and *no* arguments. Deal?"

"Deal."

"Good. Now grab that leftover jerky. I'm sure Echidna is hungry."

"Who?"

GRYPHON CRACKED them into the yard of a burned-out house in the Celtics territory. Alex could sense Birch all around them. The trees and bushes surrounding the house had rainbow-colored flowers and leaves that reminded Alex of butterflies, though there were far too many and in too great variety. Flowering vines grew in spirals up the trunks of the trees. Birch's magical essence was all over the plants, the earth, and everything. When the wind encompassed them, Alex could hear her voice whispering to the plants. Moving closer to the sound, Alex realized the large, multihued bush was not covered in flowers, but actually butterflies, unlike anything in the mortal world.

When she reached out, they took to the sky in a whirlwind

of colors, and a pair of them fluttered toward Gryphon, landing on his back. Trying not to spook Gryphon and scare away his new friends, Alex crept over to a pile of burned pieces of wood that she assumed was the door. Movement caught her eye. A pile of leaves rose and shook itself. When it finished, a sentient plant towered over her. Where a flower should be, a mouth full of teeth snarled. Alex stumbled backward, and its mouth revealed a long snake-like tongue. Her scream stuck in her throat and her eyes darted from the dark brown stalk of the plant, thicker than Stefan's thigh, to the large emerald green leaves that could easily wrap around her entire head. The tongue came closer, as if sniffing her, and Alex finally managed a little squeak.

"Echidna, you're all right!" Gryphon shouted, and the plant whipped away from Alex to face the sorcerer.

"*This* is Echidna?" Alex whispered, staring at the creature.

"Yes. He's Birch's pet. She said he's a Venus flytrap." Gryphon arrived and held out the jerky. "You wouldn't know it to look at him, but he's over a century old."

"He isn't dangerous, is he?"

Echnida snatched the meat from Gryphon's outstretched hand with his tongue and sent it back to lick every bit of seasoning and grease off Gryphon's palm.

"He can be, but he's sensed your Celtic gifts. I think he'd like it if you grew back Birch's garden."

"Happily," Alex said, composing herself and glancing around them. "But I don't recognize these plants. How can I grow what I don't know?"

"I'll show you what was here, if you can handle looking through my mind a little."

"Just warn me before we stop."

"Of course." Gryphon held his hands out, but before she could take them, a weight hit her stomach, and she paused, overcome by the feeling that everything in their lives was about to change. Sensing her anxiety, Gryphon rubbed her arms up and down. She felt calmer, and then a rush of warmth made her shudder in surprise.

"Something here is really weird," she said.

"It could be the fire. Someone with Celtic powers as strong as yours would feel the pain from all the plants that were burned here."

"That's possible?"

"You heard them sing," Gryphon said. "I've only known a few Celtics who could."

"But you could."

"Only when Birch lets me. Or you, now, I guess." Gryphon smiled and they held each other's gaze for a second too long. He released her, looking guilty. Alex took his hand.

"Show me."

Gryphon nodded and Alex opened her well to release her Celtic powers. She let Gryphon place her hands on his forehead and pull her into his mind.

At first, it was mostly dark, but then an orb of light brought the world into view. Gryphon bounced down a path, sending foxes and rabbits scurrying. His eyes were fixed on the stones of the path, and soon Echidna appeared. He followed the plant to an old wooden door the color of the acorns she used to collect in the Dark Forest. Its frame was surrounded by moss and vines, similar to ivy, except the leaves were red with yellow veins running through them. Gryphon pushed the plants to the side and burst through the door.

"I'm home, Auntie Birch. I brought you another book." A bright green journal came into view, and Gryphon examined the cover. "This one's from your mom."

Birch stepped into the room wearing a brown apron over her light green tunic and a long brown skirt. She dried her hands, then dropped them to her hips, smiling and shaking her head. "You're a mess."

"It's not my fault. Salem explosions are messy. Should you need some more red clay, visit the mountains in the Salem territory. Specifically, where they meet the trees near the sea."

"I will do that. I take it lessons are going well."

"It would seem my extra powers are coming in nicely. Father is pleased, though Mother is angry my Tiere ones aren't stronger. Talking with over a dozen species isn't enough for her."

"What do you intend to do?" She had a hint of nervousness in her tone.

"I found a spell that will help me take an animal form, despite not being a pure Tiere. I intend to try it."

"You're brave, considering what the animals decided for you," came a voice from behind him.

"Naturally," he said, turning around to face Lynx. "But it's a secret, remember."

"Well, as long as it's not your namesake, you'll be fine." Birch narrowed her eyes at him, and Lynx covered her mouth to hide her smile.

"You aren't," Birch said. "Are you?"

Gryphon scoffed. "What a wild idea."

Birch retreated to the other room. Gryphon and Lynx followed her through the living area, past some lovely green couches, and into a small kitchen and lab. A cauldron sat over a fire, bubbling away. Lynx took a stool at the small table. Gryphon dropped the journal in front of her, then peeked into the cauldron to see a roiling green and blue-streaked liquid. Thick like porridge and smelling so potently of peppermint, one sniff was enough to make Alex feel like Gryphon had shoved an entire garden up his nose. It overpowered her, even in the memory.

"What are you making?" he asked.

"It's an ointment for pain. I figure you'll need an extra strong batch once you start on explosions. You might be the future Head, but you're still only twenty," Birch said.

"Don't remind me. I would prefer if everyone believed I'm older."

Lynx chuckled. "Then grow some facial hair. I'm sure Birch could make you a potion to help. Or I could get you some fur to attach to your face."

Gryphon muttered under his breath and left the kitchen.

"What was that?" Lynx shouted after him.

"Nothing," he replied quickly.

"Thought so," she called back.

He retreated down a narrow, homey hallway adorned with vines and flowers, except for a few places where a painting hung. Gryphon glanced and moved on, but a moment was all Alex needed to recognize a young Merlock and her mother. Alex wished Gryphon would go back so she could examine the painting further, but memories didn't work like that.

A door flew open, and Gryphon marched into a bedroom that reminded Alex of the one they shared in the castle. The bed was made of a tree, and the bottom was a little like a nest. A knitted blanket hung half out of the bed, and half on the floor. Books, trinkets, and papers overflowed from a bookshelf. A wardrobe with a mirrored door had been shoved into one corner, and a table sat below the one window. Gryphon looked at himself in the mirror, rubbing his chin, and huffed. Normally, Gryphon only looked around twenty-four, but in the mirror he could have passed for sixteen. The most powerful sorcerer alive at the moment was a late bloomer. He took off his dirty tunic and opened the wardrobe to select a clean one.

It's not blue or orange.

Gryphon wore gray, like Kharon would, and kicked off his

boots. At the bookcase, he removed a little fox figure that had been whittled out of wood and a jar of red sand. Behind them was a weathered and well-loved book. He grabbed a pencil, climbed into bed, and after flicking an orb above his head, he opened the journal and began to write.

Alex pulled back and nausea rushed through her. The burned building reappeared. She felt dizzy, and Gryphon caught her again.

"Are you all right?" he whispered.

Alex nodded, but another wave of nausea hit her, and she fell to her knees and threw up into the grass. She wiped her hand across her mouth while Gryphon held her hair back for her.

He looked stricken. "I didn't know what else to do. I hope it's okay."

"Thank you." Alex stood up and rested her hand on her belly, studying him. She wanted to laugh, but his concerned expression made her hold her tongue.

"Is it the food here? The constant nausea."

Now Alex did smile. "No. The exhaustion and nausea are all thanks to this little one. You've never been around a pregnant mortal before?" Gryphon shook his head. "Do you have any plants that help with nausea?" she asked. "I only know the ones from home."

"We do," Gryphon said. He motioned for Alex to go ahead of him.

The plants moved out of her way, forming a path for them. To most, it would look as if a wind had blown down the line, sending them to the side, but Alex knew better. She smiled and Gryphon said. "Tell them what you're looking for."

Alex scoffed, but Gryphon looked incredulous. "That works for Birch, but not me or Lynx. You should try."

Alex softly ran her hands along the tall grass. "Umm ...

hello, little plants. I need to find something to help me with nausea. Please."

The smell of peppermint and apple blossoms encased them, and a path branching to the side revealed itself on the parted grass. "I suppose we follow it," Gryphon said.

Alex lifted her leg much higher than necessary to step over the few blades of grass that hadn't moved over with the others. On they went down the path, and she continued to look around at the plants lining their way, even stopping to ask questions about a particular one. Gryphon would smile and share what he knew about the plant and they'd keep going. After a while, they ended up in a vast field of peppermint.

Alex felt her mouth drop open at the sight of the plants. The mortal version was deep green with small leaves, but here, each leaf was the size of Gryphon's entire hand, and they were bright green with purple splashes. Here was the reason for the purple hue of some of Birch's concoctions. She picked a leaf and examined it. "They're huge."

"Makes it easy to pick them." Gryphon stepped off the trail and plucked as many leaves as he could fit in his hand. He handed them to Alex and went to pick more. Once they had gathered enough, he cracked them back to the kitchen.

"Will they taste the same as mortal peppermint?" Alex asked.

"The taste will be stronger because the plant is more potent. So it will help you even more. If it doesn't, I'm sure there has to be a spell book with some other options."

"Have you come up with any ideas on how to hide the baby?" Alex sensed Gryphon watching her intently, but ignored him and softly rubbed her belly.

"Actually ... yes. I think I have a solution to hide him from our kind."

"You do? When were you going to tell me?"

"Today. It's the reason I agreed to let you get out of the castle. I hoped the Celtic territory would calm you."

"And just why would I need help to remain calm?"

"Because the best way to hide him—is with another baby."

Alex blinked. "I don't understand."

"You and I are going to make a baby, and he will give off enough magic to hide Aaron's mortal child."

CHAPTER 28

GRYPHON

"Don't touch me," she shouted. She'd jumped away so quickly she knocked the kettle off the counter, sending hot water all over the floor.

"I won't hurt you."

She took another step back.

"Alex, listen to me. It's not what you think."

Alex checked behind her, preparing to bolt. The stench of fear was so strong Gryphon couldn't smell anything else, so he cracked behind her. She ended up running into him, and Gryphon held her against him with one arm to keep her from barreling through him. With his free hand, he reached up and ripped his palm open on a nail holding some dried herbs. As soon as Alex stopped struggling, he took her hand and scratched it on the same nail, then locked their bleeding palms together.

"Alexandria, daughter of Cassandra, and Head of this generation," Gryphon started. She stopped struggling, as if sensing what was coming. "I give you a blood oath that I will never put my hands on you in a way you don't want. I will do so to only protect you, but not for my own desires."

When their hands separated, their palms were glowing a soft gold color. "*Listen to me.* This is how sorcerers have made babies for centuries. We'll perform the formal bonding ceremony and then decide the lines we want our son to have, and make sure he inherits what we need him to. All of our clothes shall remain on. In fact, let's wear extra."

"Is this why you brought me to Birch's?" she asked.

"Yes, and no. I knew you needed to get out and move. You've never been one to sit still for too long—even when you were held prisoner, you were still wandering. I figured talking about my plan in the most peaceful territory would be for the best. Plus ... I wanted you to see how I really grew up."

Alex smiled at the memory of young Gryphon and how much he and Lynx had reminded her of herself and Michael.

"I wish I could have seen more of that painting Birch had."

"The one of your mother and uncle? Picture it when we get back to the library, and it will appear there."

"Really?"

"That's how the castle works. But if you plan to create a life-sized portrait of your princeling, let's keep it in the library. We don't want the other sorcerers to get suspicious."

Alex rolled her eyes. "How long will we have to keep tiptoeing around them?"

"Until I can't smell Aaron on you." Exhaling, Gryphon explained how potent the scent of Aaron on her would be to the other sorcerers, now only magnified by their child. He reminded her that sorcerers were not monogamous and that their relationship would not prevent her from being considered the highest conquest alive, the only sorceress Head to ever be born.

Annoyed, Alex scowled and crossed her arms, but Gryphon

went on to remind her that sorcerers were not men, and while she could handle herself with mortal men, she was not powerful enough to protect herself from their kind yet. In the end, Alex agreed that having a jealous, possessive Ares male for a partner would make it clear to the other sorcerers that, should they attempt to even get near Alex, Gryphon would make sure they regretted it.

"Some sorcerers will try to woo you, some will try to prove their worth as a lover, and some will try to take what they want. That's where we differ from the nobility you're used to dealing with." Alex tugged on her shirt hem. "You're experienced with the first two. I'll deal with the others. If anyone makes you uncomfortable, you tell me. If even one sorcerer is allowed to get close to you, the others will get more aggressive."

"So, for my sake—"

"For *both* our sakes, and Princeling Junior."

"Excuse me?"

"That's what I'm calling the baby."

CHAPTER 29
ALEX

Alex wrapped her cloak around her shoulders to fight off the icy chill coming from the seawater rushing past her calves. The Oreean Sea summoned images of Warren and Aaron, so far away and still connected by the ocean. It had been a week since Gryphon suggested the solution for protecting her and Aaron's son. Alex rubbed her tiny bump affectionately, a habit she'd developed over the last few days. Looking at her, no one would know she was with child yet. She'd regularly had a larger bump from eating her fill at a royal banquet. But knowing that the sorcerers would want to hurt the baby made her extra protective.

Breathing deeply, she glanced back at the blanket on the beach. She'd already eaten the bread and cheese she brought, leaving only her apple and the bottle of cider. But despite the food being delicious, it sat in her gut like a rock. Alex lifted her cloak and walked toward the closed satchel beside her food.

Gryphon had given her one of his when she'd taken to carrying her books between the lab, library, garden, and bedroom. But today, the bag was almost empty. Brushing the sand off her feet, Alex kneeled on the blanket and retrieved the Tiere spell book. She checked that Gryphon was nowhere to be seen. He'd sensed her anxiety and had been keeping his distance for the last few days.

Alex dumped the pearl onto the blanket and flipped through the book that Gryphon had discovered. She flopped onto the sand and reviewed the spell they'd need to perform for the twentieth time that week. It wasn't a complicated spell. If all went well, it would allow her to conceive and carry a second baby, while already pregnant with her first—but they were running out of time.

Gryphon had only mentioned it once, not wanting to put pressure on her, but Alex had heard the urgency in his voice. The spell was clear that she had to do it in the next few days, or she'd risk the new baby not being able to catch up to the first baby in size, and it would be born too early.

"Why aren't you here?" Alex whispered, fighting back tears. "Emmerich and Daniel I understand. They're human, clearly they'd be kept away. But of all the times to abandon me, Mother, why now? I need you."

Squeezing her eyes shut, she felt the tears slip free, and she wiped her sleeve across her face. Alex dropped her cloak and stepped into the surf. Already the pearl heated in her hands. "Show me the future if I say yes. *Please.*"

Unsure whether it would even work for a Cassandra but willing to try anything, she silently pleaded with the future pearl, desperate. An intense fire rushed up her arm, spreading through her core and exploding into her entire body. Alex refused to let the pain stop her and squeezed the pearl even harder.

Fog appeared on the water, revealing a small blond head peeking out from behind a tree. Alex smiled. An oversized royal Datten tunic hung from the small boy's frame as he searched for someone. A moment later, a figure moved through the fog and jumped onto the boy, their tousling surrounding them both in a dust cloud. As the dust settled, the children both screamed, *Daddy!*

The pearl was becoming unbearably hot, but Alex ignored it and turned to see who the children called to. They raced toward Aaron and Gryphon, each being scooped up by their own father.

It works out? Alex stepped closer to the figures and examined Aaron's face for any hint of anger or resentment, but there was none.

You accept both twins? Both of you?

Gryphon laughed, and Aaron reminded the twins they were supposed to be at their lessons and not running wild in the woods. He exchanged a quick glance with Gryphon, and the sorcerer cracked them away.

The pearl grew too hot, searing her skin. Without thinking, Alex threw it, shrieking, and watched in horror as it splashed into the sea, bobbing for a moment before vanishing.

Biting her cheek, she swallowed roughly. *I won't mention that to Gryphon.*

CHAPTER 30
GRYPHON

Gryphon peeked around the corner of the kitchen, holding his breath. Part of him felt stupid for avoiding Alex, but ever since they'd returned from Birch's cottage, he couldn't help it. His suggestion—creating another baby to protect Aaron's—had been a lot for her to process, and she'd been in a strange mood since. Being around her all day was harder than it had been at Moorloc's castle. Without Aaron or any of the other mortals around, he felt a stronger urge to touch her, to comfort her when she was upset, to hold her tight. He knew they'd figure out a way to get her home sooner or later, and when they did, he'd have to give her up all over again. And he hadn't even told her about how things would change between them if she decided to move forward with his plan. So, he was hiding.

Gryphon? I need to speak to you. Could you come to the roof?

Well, so much for hiding.

Gryphon closed his eyes and felt for Alex, stopping at a warm breeze and the fresh smell of earth. He cracked to the rooftop garden, and saw something he'd never expected.

The entire area had come to life. Alex had coaxed all the plants into bloom and grown a giant vine arch that spanned two plant boxes. Burnt orange, cobalt, gold, and violet flowers surrounded the green leaves. Floating around the air were little fire orbs, fireflies, and butterflies.

"What's all this?" Gryphon asked. Alex clutched her necklace, an unconscious tick that gave away her nervousness. The long, flowing sleeves of her simple gown spilled down from her worried hands. A typical sorceress gown with matching flowing skirts, it was free of embellishments, and Alex's true beauty took over. Gryphon looked at her in awe.

The longer he stared, the more Alex fidgeted.

Gryphon walked up the row of plants until he stood under the arch with her and smiled to put her at ease. "I feel underdressed." He gestured to his usual black pants, which of course were covered in dust, and his orange tunic.

"Maybe a little," Alex replied.

Gryphon smirked. He ran his hands through his hair, and it immediately fell into place. He shook his hands three times, and on the last shake, he swapped his outfit for his formal Mystics robe.

Alex shook her head at his choice.

"What?"

"That's the wrong color."

"But you hate orange."

"But you love it. So, orange, please."

Suspicion crept into him. He hesitated, rubbing the back of his neck. Gryphon made himself address her. "What exactly is this, Alex? Why do I feel you're ... what is the mortal word?"

"Proposing?"

"Yes."

"Because I am. It's clear we aren't getting out of here

anytime soon, and you need to protect me and my son. So, I'm asking you to formally bond with me."

You're asking me? That explains your mood the last few days. That decision could not have been easy. Gryphon shook his hands roughly one final time, turning his robe orange. "I, of course, say yes, but why the setup?"

Alex's face went pink. "I'm sorry. Is this not how it's done? I'm being mortal, aren't I?"

You're being beautiful. "I'm not complaining. I just didn't expect it. Most bonds are transactional and done to create a child, and nothing more. I assumed ours would be the same."

Alex's cheeks grew from pink to dark red. "I always expected our bonding would happen in a century, and we'd have our friends here, but if we're going it alone, I think you deserve a special event."

"Me? Isn't it the bride in the mortal world who wants a special day?"

"I had mine. This one is yours. To mortals, it's a very special occasion. One to be treasured."

So, you did this just for me? At that moment, a butterfly fluttered past them, and he grinned back at her. "It's perfect."

Alex swallowed. "Then we can begin."

Gryphon interlocked his fingers with hers. He focused on his well, and his hands lit up—the right in burnt orange and the left in cobalt. She closed her eyes and trembled. Her nose and lips twitched, a sign she was focusing on her well. Slowly, her left hand lit up in golden light, and then her right one went violet.

"Well done, Princess."

Alex smiled at her glowing violet hand. "Thank you, Sunset."

Gryphon cleared his throat and focused on her face. "I,

Gryphon, Titan of Mystics and Ares, Heart of the Generation, bond myself to you, Alexandria, Titan of Cassandra, daughter of Cassandra, Head of the Generation. Together, we will bring about the next evolution of sorcerers. We shall birth the strongest sorcerer to walk our world."

Their light grew brighter with each word, and his bond mark itched. To distract himself, he tried to memorize every part of Alex's face. "Your turn," he whispered.

"I, uh, Alexandria, Crown Princess of Warren, Queen of Datten, daughter of Cassandra and Head of the Generation, accept you, Sunset—I mean Gryphon—Titan of Mystics and Ares, Heart of the Generation."

Her hands now glowed so brightly he had to look away, but the itching had stopped. Gryphon was now so close their bodies nearly touched. He let go of her hands and was about to speak when Alex grabbed the front of his robe and pressed her lips to his.

Every part of Gryphon awakened at once. His magic frothed out of his well, shooting fire through his blood and awakening his insides as if the butterflies fluttering around them were trapped. His heart beat so hard, he didn't know if it would ever recover.

Over the decades he'd kissed dozens of sorceresses, but not one of those instances could even come close to what Alex's kiss did to him. His hands slipped around her waist so he could savor the moment for as long as possible. Surprisingly, Alex opened her mouth, and Gryphon responded. His tongue tickled hers, and in response, Alex snaked her arms around his neck. Her fingers plunged into his thick hair, pulling him closer. It felt as if she were trying to meld their bodies into one.

More of him came to life, now. Magic poured into parts of him that had never known it. Even the darkest crevices of his pain were alight in gold and violet, suffused with Alex's loving magic. After a few minutes, Gryphon felt he should put an end to it, since a kiss wasn't required for bonding. He stepped back, gasping for breath.

"That was it?" Alex asked, panting to catch her breath.

Gryphon nodded.

"I don't feel any different."

"Did you change after you married Aaron?"

"No, but that was a mortal wedding. This is magic."

"That kiss changed me."

"Stop it," Alex said, looking away.

"I'm serious." Gryphon smiled. "I don't think anyone will live up to that."

Alex's cheeks reddened and Gryphon held her against him to keep her from fleeing.

"Now let's protect your little princeling."

Alex nodded, and they stood straight, looking at one another. Gryphon held his hands in the air with his palms out, and Alex placed her palms against his.

"Ares," Gryphon said, and his left hand lit up in burnt orange again. He nodded.

"Merlin," Alex whispered. Her left hand lit up in violet light.

"Son," Gryphon said.

Alex nodded, her eyes closed, and her lips moved too softly for him to hear. When she opened her eyes again, their glowing hands had turned into small balls of light. Gryphon stepped back and Alex turned her palms up. The light spheres melted into her hands and rushed up her arms. They joined together in her chest and moved down to her lower abdomen, where they glowed brightly before finally disappearing.

"Now what?" Alex asked.

"Now we feed you and get you some rest. Sorcerer pregnancies take anywhere from seven to ten months. I expect our baby will grow quickly to catch up to the little mortal one, so you'll be exhausted for at least the next week."

CHAPTER 31
ALEX

The Titans were late.

"Do they know you're the Heart and I'm the Head?" Alex asked Gryphon who untied the knot she'd made in her belt by mistake in her rush to get ready. Both of them had chosen to wear black robes embroidered with a gold crown and heart rather than the robes of their line marks.

"They should. It was shouted at our fight to get your father back, and sorcerers love gossip."

"I wish we didn't have to replace our friends."

"It's only temporary. Birch, Kharon, Lynx, and Megesti are still the Titans of their lines, but this is like when a titan is injured. We need someone here to perform their roles until they're back."

Alex rubbed her belly. "The idea of facing them all makes me feel queasy."

"Everything makes you feel queasy. Once it's over, you can hide in our private chambers and read for the rest of the day."

Her belt fixed, Gryphon held his arm out, and Alex accepted it, properly taking in the throne room. Like the rest of the castle, it had changed since they'd taken over. Gone were the blood-soaked stones, and in their place was a mosaic of square quartz and marble, in the various line colors. The room had reverted from a circle to a decagon—where each side contained a wooden door. They were made of all different types of wood, and each had a line mark carved into it, enchanted to glow the color of that line. A carpet matching the color of the line led from the doors to the center of the room. Gryphon gently tugged her toward the space where the carpets all met. Sure enough, carved into the stone floor were the ten-line marks, along with the Head and Heart marks.

Gryphon stepped into the center and spun around. "This is new. I like it."

Garrick had built a giant dais and thrones in the center to remind everyone of his superiority, but in Alex and Gryphon's version, it was gone.

"It's set up for conversation, not orders," Alex said. She walked over to the Merlin and Cassandra marks and stepped on the sun, but nothing happened. Confusion crossed Gryphon's face, and Alex's own nose wrinkled in annoyance. Without a word, Gryphon crossed the circle and stepped onto the heart, signifying the Heart of the Generation, and the mark glowed white. Alex groaned and followed him until she stood on the crown and it lit up too.

"It seems we cannot hide from our duties," Gryphon said.

"As it should be," Phobos said.

"You!" Alex spun to face him. The day in the market was burned into her memory, and she would have her revenge. She stormed toward the powerful Ares sorcerer.

"Gryphon, call off your witch. She seems to have forgotten her place."

Alex stopped walking when a wicked voice whispered to her.

Let me take care of him, little one. We both know I'm more suited to this sort of thing.

Alex shook her head to silence the invasive voice and turned her attention back to Phobos. *I could throw him into the wall, or let my vines string him by his ankles.*

A comforting warmth filled her.

You handle him how you see fit, Alex. But if you want me to, simply ask.

Alex rubbed her hands together. *Fear is the best option.* Ignoring the murmurs from the crowd that had arrived to see the Titans retake their oath, she strode up to him without blinking.

At first he chuckled, but the longer she stared at him, the more uncomfortable he appeared. "What do you want, little witch—"

Phobos never got to finish his sentence because his mouth slammed shut, and no matter how hard he tried, it wouldn't open. Even his hands couldn't break the seal.

"I've heard enough from you. It will release when you leave this castle." Alex returned to Gryphon, pausing halfway to say, "Next time, it'll be permanent."

Alex took Gryphon's arm when she arrived at his side.

Showing mercy and viciousness all at once. Impressive, Princess.

After Kruft, I swore I'd never let another weak or worthless male hold power over me.

"You'd all do well to remember," Gryphon projected across the hall, "that while Alexandria may be young, she's still our Head, and clearly holds the power we expect to see from a Head. I suggest you all show her the respect she deserves."

More murmurs ran through the growing crowd. Alex narrowed her eyes at them, and over a few seconds, they all bowed. She glanced at Gryphon, unsure of how to respond.

He leaned down to her ear and whispered. "You can respond however you wish. You can even do nothing."

Alex pointed to the line marks on the stone floor. "Titans, take your places. If the line mark doesn't glow for you, then you are not worthy of being *my* titan."

The sorcerers hesitated, confused, until Gryphon stepped onto the heart, making the carved symbol light up. He held his hand out to Alex, and she accepted it and let him pull her to the crown. After it too lit up, the sorcerers moved. Fenrir pushed Kit toward the Tiere line mark. The moment his foot hit the ground, the fox head lit up.

I'd rather have Kit sit in for Lynx than her father.

Alex nodded at Gryphon.

Ridge brushed pretend dust from his shoulder and confidently took his place on the Mire line. Pearl moved to her spot without looking at them, but Phobos stared at Alex as he stepped on the ax. It lit up, and he flinched. *Good.* With Ember dead, Stella stepped out of the crowd to take her mother's place. She walked a little strangely, and—*no*—she was pregnant too. The idea of Lygari being someone's father made Alex feel sick. The remaining marks were filled quickly. Glenn made the Celtic leaf light up, and a young sorceress named Morana made the Hades mark glow. Gryphon whispered that she was a distant cousin of Kharon's. *The Mystics and Merlin marks ... No!*

Lygari left the crowd and stepped onto the Merlin mark, and it glowed. Alex could feel Gryphon's rage. His eyes were fixed on a tall, slim sorcerer with white and blond hair. He was older than Gryphon, looking closer to one hundred fifty. His eyes, the same shade of blue as the Mystics robe he wore, stared down Gryphon, stepping onto the engraving of the moon. Alex craned her head to see his line marks—he bore only the Mystics mark.

Who is he?

Not here.

Can he hear—

Yes.

The group was wrong—all wrong! All the marks were glowing, but this was nothing like her premonition. In her dream, the Titans had been her friends, and she'd been thrilled to have them. Today, the people staring back at her, aside from Morana, were all her enemies, and Alex didn't want any of them here.

"As is customary," Gryphon began. "You may now swear your oath to us. Failure to do so will single you out as a traitor."

In unison, the Titans raised their hands, palms up. Alex opened her mouth to ask, but Gryphon simply whispered, "Watch."

Alex gasped when a tiny light appeared on each of their chests. Slowly the light moved up their bodies until it wound up their arm and a small glowing orb sat on their outstretched palm. Once all the orbs were ready, the Titans flicked their fingers, and the orbs danced through the air like fireflies until they gathered in the center of the circle, rotating around each other and forming a larger glowing mass. Gryphon smiled and held his hand out. Alex felt a flutter in her stomach, but did the same.

The Ares orb left the mass, and when it neared them, it split into two smaller orbs, and one landed on each of their palms like a butterfly in the forest, before it was absorbed into their skin. Quickly the remaining orbs followed, and once they'd all been absorbed, Alex felt drained and tired.

"Very well," Gryphon said. "We accept your pledges. You will rule your own kind and help teach the young of your lines. You will stand by us and come whenever we call."

"What of your secret?" Fenrir asked, and everyone in the room turned to him. "I can smell it on you, my young Head.

You're expecting, and a very powerful pup at that. It would seem our Heart isn't as incapable as his parents believed."

The entire room burst into cheers. Alex gripped Gryphon's arm tightly, and he cracked her to their room.

What is going on?

They want to celebrate. Our child is supposed to be the next evolution of sorcerers. But I didn't think you'd want to be here for that.

"I don't," Alex replied out loud.

I'll get rid of them as soon as I can. You can hide in the library. I left some bread and cheese in there for you earlier.

Thank you.

Alex headed to the library to find her snack and read the next shelf of books. Her love of reading never waned, but at that moment she would have accepted any distraction from the sorcerers and their hungry eyes. Luckily, her books welcomed her like an old friend, even the new ones. She was starting her sixth book when she paused, reread the paragraph, and flipped to the cover.

"This book doesn't make any sense. It's as if words are missing." As soon as the words left her mouth, Alex realized what she was holding. "The journals Cassandra told Michael and I to find. The ones that don't match. If I find the other one ..."

CHAPTER 32
AARON

Despite the warm weather, the Oreean Sea air sent a frigid chill through Aaron, and he shivered. Harold patted his back while Megesti finished assembling the eye pieces Macht had given him. Aaron barely listened to Harold explain how to secure the curved glass pieces inside the long tubes so that they could see ships far out at sea from shore. The glass smiths had worked tirelessly to find the right curve of glass to let them see farther than ever before. Megesti gasped when he turned the eyepiece toward the sea, grabbing Aaron's attention. The three of them stood together in the observation area in the central, tallest tower in Moorloc's old castle, where they thought they'd have the best view. Harold had sent Betruger ships the first week they'd returned home. Weeks had passed, and the first ship had arrived back two days ago with devastating news, so Harold hoped to spot his other ships farther out.

"How does an entire island just disappear?" Megesti asked.

"Could it sink?" Harold suggested, holding up his eyepiece

to search the horizon. "On a clear day, Macht and I have seen it from here before with our eye glasses."

"I've only seen a little of it, but it's not a small island," Aaron replied. "From what the sorcerers have told us, it's nearly as large as Warren's territory."

The three of them searched in silence for a sign of Harold's ships, since the Forbidden Lands were eluding them.

"Nothing yet," Harold said. "If our first ship has returned, others can't be far behind."

"How many Warren ships did Edward send?" Megesti asked.

"A dozen of the largest in his fleet," Aaron replied.

"They were finely crafted. Alex and I have discussed these ships many times," Harold said.

Aaron put down his eye glass and rubbed the back of his neck. *Neither the Warren nor the Betruger ships can find any trace of the island. The sorcerers who were with us can't go back, the Nial's blue pearl was useless, and Kharon can't seem to get any of the dead to talk to him. What am I supposed to do?*

"We keep trying," Harold said, answering the question Aaron hadn't dared to speak.

"Alex wouldn't give up, so we won't either," Megesti said.

"Easy for you to say. You've got magic. I have to sit here and worry about what those monsters are doing to my wife."

"Alex means a great deal to all of us. She's my cousin—the last connection I have to my father."

"Edith misses her a great deal," Harold added. "She often stands on our balcony and watches the sea. I don't need to have magic to know she's worried for Alex."

"What can we do?" Aaron asked Megesti.

"What do you mean?"

"Magically. There has to be a spell or a potion or something we can try," Aaron heard the anxiety in his own voice.

Megesti fidgeted. "Lynx is trying something. But we don't know if it'll work. She didn't want to get your hopes up."

"I thought she exhausted her Tiere abilities when none of the animals could find the Forbidden Lands."

"The animals she can communicate with cannot, so she wants to try herself."

"But lynxes cannot swim that far!" Harold protested.

"Right. Tiere sorcerers can usually turn into one animal. The best of them can manage two, but only if the second animal species accepts them. Lynx has only ever been a lynx. So she's trying to force another animal form—one that can swim or fly."

"Can she? Force one, I mean?" Aaron asked.

"Apparently as a Titan she can, but it's painful, which is why it's taking so long, and there is no guarantee she'll succeed."

"Is she still a titan if she's stuck here?"

"Kharon said they're still titans as they haven't given up the title or position. But another sorcerous has to be chosen in the Forbidden Lands to do their duties until they can return," Megesti said.

"I put Jerome or mother in charge when I'm gone," Aaron said.

"Is there anything we can do to help?" Harold asked.

Megesti shook his head. "It's complex magic even for me. To get the spell, they had to summon one of the Tiere line founders."

Aaron remembered the night Megesti and Alex summoned Daniel and Victoria to ask where their family journals were. Merlock had been livid with them. Aaron would never forget how upset Alex had been after being scolded by her uncle. "Isn't that dangerous?" he asked.

"Summoning anyone is dangerous, but a line founder is

even worse." Megesti picked a small pebble off the ground and threw it off the tower. "Very few of them seem to be helpful, usually choosing to talk in riddles or outright threats. But right now it's even harder since Kharon can't reach out to the dead as easily."

"Why not?" Harold asked.

Aaron replied. "He sees the mortal dead in our castles, but they can't go anywhere either. It seems even the dead are stuck in their places."

"And Daniel is not happy about it," Megesti said. "He was usually with Alex, but he can't leave Datten now. Megesti patted Aaron.

Aaron stopped on the final step and turned to Megesti, open-mouthed.

"It makes sense," Harold said. "He protected her so she could marry you. Now it's your job to watch her, and his to take care of your father."

And I can't even do that right. Aaron shook his head, silencing the creeping little voice. "Who can we help? Kharon? Lynx? Whatever they need, we'll do it."

Megesti scratched his chin for a moment and smiled at Aaron. "Well, we need some herbs. With all these failed potions, Birch is running out. Some are so complex to grow that she can't do it, and they have to be collected manually on the far south end of the Dark Forest."

"Harold, care to accompany me to visit my southern lords and search for—What are we even looking for?" Aaron asked.

"Dragon thistle."

Aaron groaned. "That's the one made entirely of thorns and burns if you get it on your skin, isn't it?"

Megesti nodded. Aaron tried to smile at Harold, but it felt like a wince. The Betruger king laughed and clapped him on the back. "I'll get some gloves from my blacksmith."

CHAPTER 33
GRYPHON

Gryphon pretended to be asleep while Alex cried softly into her pillow. It had been six weeks since they'd become trapped here, and the longer they remained, the more Alex struggled, becoming more agitated and restless than when Gryphon had trained her at Moorloc's castle. Watching the energetic and loving Alex slip away tortured Gryphon.

On top of being overwhelmed from the pregnancy, she's terrified she'll never see them again ... how can I make that easier? I can't lie to her, and we both know that is a real possibility. But ... what if?

It was still dark outside, but the summer nights were shorter. Gryphon threw the blanket off and padded to their wardrobe.

Alex bolted upright in bed and wiped her eyes and cheeks. "How long have you been up?"

Gryphon dug through the wardrobe until he found the clothes he wanted. He went over to Alex and held out a simple knee-length robe and training pants. "Long enough," he replied softly. "Come on. I have a fun idea."

Alex twirled her nightgown in her fingers but Gryphon would not be deterred. He shook the clothes at her until she took them.

"Gryphon—"

"Not a word."

Alex stumbled when their feet landed on soft, squishy sand, but Gryphon steadied her. Alex clutched his shirt and trembled, her face washed out in the light of his fire orbs flitting above. Her fear slammed into him, knocking the air from his chest. Since they'd completed the spells to bond and make her pregnant with his child, he could feel everything she felt. *I'll have to tell her soon, or risk her anger.* A sorceress lost much of her control over her magic while she was pregnant, so the baby's father was tied to her needs, allowing him to protect her but more importantly anticipate her bodily needs and provide for her. Gryphon had enjoyed the impressed looks Alex gave him when he knew she was hungry and exactly what she wanted to eat, but he hadn't considered that her emotional pain would come through too. Now her loneliness flooded through him every single day, and he knew he had to do something.

The fear she radiated now didn't faze him. "Can you feel where we are?" Gryphon asked.

Alex stopped. "My magic is tingling. Are we in Merlin territory?"

"Close. We're in the land of Cassandra. Just up the beach is the Tiere territory. Merlin connects to Cassandra on the other side. I brought you here because this land faces east, and I wanted you to see the sunrise over the sea, the way you do in Warren."

Alex's eyes widened. "How did you know I've missed that?"

"You send me your feelings." Gryphon admitted everything

he'd been keeping from her. He'd expected anger, but now he sensed only sorrow.

"I'm sorry. I've been trying to be at peace here. I really have."

Gryphon took her into a tight hug. "It's all right. This whole situation is complicated. I know you're worried about Aaron and what he'll think. And none of us thought to teach you what to expect while pregnant with a sorcerer baby because we didn't think you'd need to know for decades."

"Would Aaron be able to feel things too?"

"I don't think so."

Alex wiped her cheeks and her expression changed to a cold, stoic stare. She placed her hands on her hips and narrowed her eyes at him. "What am I feeling now?"

Gryphon cocked his head and smirked. "You're feeling loved and appreciative of this."

"Fine. I believe you."

Gryphon chuckled and spun her to face the east, a comfortable silence settling around them.

The sun rose across the Oreean Sea. Red light danced across the water toward them, growing orange, gold, then yellow until the sun peeked above the horizon, rising into the sky. Alex slipped out of Gryphon's hold and pulled his thick shirt over her head. When she handed it back, he cracked the shirt back to the castle.

"Can we explore a little?" she asked.

"Of course. This is the territory of Cassandra's line, and you are her living daughter. If Victoria hadn't left, this would have been your home." Alex seemed at home here by the beach and the sea, filling Gryphon with peace for the first time in weeks.

"I'd like to come watch the sun more often," Alex said.

"I can arrange that. But only if we watch it rise over the sea. It's not the same if we do it from the castle."

Alex nodded, and Gryphon bowed playfully at her. Her laugh, so genuine, made his heart melt. She yanked him toward the trees. "Come on, Sunset. You have a forest to show me."

Gryphon grinned. "Clearly, I should lead the way, because you're heading right into the Tiere forest."

Alex laughed again, shaking her head, and let Gryphon lead her in the other direction.

They spent the entire day walking and exploring the Cassandra territory. At one point they made it to the Merlin border, but Alex said she wanted to keep it for another day so she'd have something to look forward to.

In the coming weeks, they repeated their excursions, always watching the sunrise and going on long walks. The more time they spent outside, in Alex's territories, the easier things between them became. Gryphon felt a joy he had never felt inside, and decided it was because she was so relaxed. He could still detect her loneliness and sadness, but his efforts tempered the raw pain consuming her.

One day, while reading, he sensed a pang of fear that sent him rushing to their bedroom where Alex slept.

After checking on Alex and their entire room and finding nothing amiss, he heard her whimper in her sleep.

Unconsciously, Gryphon flicked his palm up, alighted it with fire, then extinguished it. *Only one more possibility.* At that moment, he made a dangerous decision.

Gryphon lay down next to Alex and softly touched her back. He thought of her, and opened his Mystics well, hoping his magic would do what he wanted, and then he forced himself to sleep.

When he next opened his eyes, he stood on the rooftop garden of their castle. Whatever upset Alex in her dream had taken place in their home. He scanned the garden but didn't find her there, so he hurried into the lab. Empty. A crash came from the library, and he dashed down the stairs and weaved through the shelves. "Alex?"

He stood motionless, listening intently until the sound of Alex's panting filled his ears.

It's just a dream. They can't really hurt her.

He raced along the shelves, scanning through the spaces between the books until he rounded the last one and skidded to a halt. Alex sat on the table, very much naked, and Aaron, also naked, stood over her. Embarrassed at how badly he'd misinterpreted her sounds, he hid behind the shelf, ignoring the voice in his head screaming at him to peek. No, he would leave. It wasn't right to watch Alex and the man she loved. Before he made it five steps, Alex breathily called out, "Oh Gryphon."

Gryphon froze.

She didn't see me, did she? But that would mean ...

He slunk back to the end of the row and peeked. It was not Aaron. The bronze skin, and black hair with a gold streak gave him away, though Gryphon couldn't help but notice that his butterfly shaped birthmark was on the wrong butt cheek. Dream Gryphon slammed Alex against him, sending books flying off the table. Alex cried out in surprise when the whole table shifted beneath them, and she quickly stabilized herself with her hand. Unable to look away, Gryphon watched himself take Alex on their library table until she screamed so loudly the shelf he leaned against rattled.

Listening carefully, he heard them both whisper "I love you," and then his doppelgänger took Alex into a sweet embrace and kissed her.

Never in his entire life had he wanted something to be a premonition dream so badly.

CHAPTER 34
ALEX

Alex woke up with an arm resting on the right side of her belly, the side their powers had gone into. At first, they had made sure to never even touch when they were in bed together. It was only after Alex had repeatedly pulled Gryphon's arm around her that they'd given up. After years of sleeping with Aaron, Alex would creep across the bed in her sleep, looking for him. Both she and Gryphon knew she sought Aaron, but Alex slept better if Gryphon held her and he hadn't complained.

Alex yawned and rolled away from Gryphon. *With all the talks I've had about what to expect when I was pregnant, why did no one warn me how much I'd need to pee?*

After she relieved herself, Alex returned to find Gryphon awake. They'd slept in and missed the sunrise, but Alex still wanted to go exploring before it became too hot. She thought she saw him smirking, but when she caught him, his face changed back to stoic disinterest.

"Are we going walking today before reading and magic practice?" he asked.

"Yes, but Merlin territory, please."

"Of course. I'll grab us some food while you change. After you explore to your heart's content, we can work on Mystics powers. I have a fun skill for you to try."

"Oh?"

"It's called dream walking. Mystics sorcerers can visit other sorcerers' dreams."

"What?"

Leaning down to her ear, he whispered. "It's a handy skill for checking in on someone's nightmares, but sometimes the things you find can be scandalous."

Alex grabbed her pillow off the bed and smacked Gryphon as hard as she could with it. "What did you see?"

"I don't know what you're talking about."

"That ridiculous smirk says otherwise." Alex hit him again. Before Gryphon could flee, she hip-checked him and knocked him onto the bed. She sat on him, locked his right arm at his side, and conjured a huge snowball above his head. "Tell me, or I'll freeze you."

"Let me just say, for the record, that my butterfly birthmark is on my left cheek, not the right."

Alex felt the color leave her face. "You saw that?"

Gryphon abandoned his teasing tone. Taking her chin in his hand, he gently turned Alex to face him. He wanted to make his sincerity apparent. "Dreams like that are perfectly normal for a sorceress your age."

"I highly doubt that."

"They are."

"Some things I dream about feel wrong," Alex said.

Gryphon tucked her hair behind her ear. "That's the mortal world talking."

"I don't think Aaron would feel that way."

"Do you honestly think Aaron would be mad at you for

dreaming? What you do in your dreams ... do they bring you pleasure?"

Alex felt her cheeks burn, but nodded anyway.

"Then they are normal. Sorcerers your age in our world are exploring what it is they enjoy. Most of them are sleeping with at least a dozen sorcerers to figure out what they prefer. We train hard at your age, and so we play hard when the work is done. I don't know how much Lynx has told you about her past, but she often had two or three different sorcerers in her bed at a time."

"Three?" Alex moved to let Gryphon get up. "I don't know if I could handle three."

Gryphon spun around and faced her. "Wait—does that mean you've considered two? Because I'd be more than happy to share with Aaron."

Alex slammed the pillow at his face.

"I'll take that as a yes, you've considered ... or perhaps dreamed it."

Alex brought up a snowball and narrowed her brows at Gryphon.

"Simmer down. I'll get us some food." Gryphon cackled and cracked away.

When he returned, he'd brought along a large map of the different territories. They moved to the library and spread the map on the table to look over the Merlin territory. More than once, Alex caught Gryphon staring at a particular spot on the table. She avoided looking at him but the moment she did, he winked at her.

Alex stood up and smacked her palms against the table. "Fine, you caught me in a naughty dream. How long are you going to tease me about it?"

"It wasn't just a naughty dream, little Heart. It was a sex dream."

"What do you expect when my husband is trapped halfway across the world?"

"The library part isn't surprising, considering it's your favorite room, but I certainly didn't expect your dream to have me in it. Knowing that you dream about me means I'm going to tease you for some time."

Alex covered her face and looked down at the map. "Pretend I didn't ask."

Gryphon chuckled and pressed against her to point out a few places on the map that he thought would interest Alex. He avoided one area.

"Will we have to worry about Lygari when we're there?"

"He'll be busy with his own sorceress and likely be in the Salem territory with her. But if he tries to cause you any grief, I'll deal with him."

"Thank you." Glancing at the map, Alex pointed at the middle area Gryphon had avoided. "Here. I don't know why but something is pulling me there."

THEY CLIMBED over another fallen log and Alex took note of the differences here. The Cassandra and Merlin territories had both been left without a caretaker for many years, but while the Cassandra land thrived as much as the Tiere territory it bordered on, the Merlin lands were a mess. The paths had all been overgrown, and what was likely decades worth of fallen trees were left to rot in brackish ponds. While the Cassandra forests gave off feelings of peace and tranquility, the Merlin lands felt restless. Alex couldn't help but wonder if it had something to do with her grandfather's death or the lack of a proper Merlin Titan for so long. *Perhaps without a powerful Merlin descendant living in the territory, the land is dying.* A muggy breeze hit her and shook the leaves in the canopy above them. As the green leaves fluttered down to join the decaying forest floor, Alex felt a heavy pain hit her.

Gryphon shot her a questioning glance.

"I feel bad for the land," Alex responded. "That it's dying. Is that dumb?"

"Heightened emotions are normal for a pregnant sorceress."

"Have a lot of experience with that, do you?" Alex teased.

"I only want to make sure I'm doing my duty in taking care of you both. I found a few books on it in the library, and read them after we performed the ceremony."

Alex kicked the dirt beneath her foot and sheepishly glanced at Gryphon. He walked to her and kissed the top of her head. "You'll be fine. You lasted years with your magic being controlled by your emotions. What's a few months?"

Alex kept walking, but muttered, "But no one could watch my dreams then."

"What was that?" Gryphon asked with such a smirk that Alex conjured a snowball in her hand and threw it at him. He shrieked when the cold hit him, and Alex cackled, climbing over another log to scurry away before he could get revenge.

She rushed through the foliage, dodging thorn bushes, careful not to trip. She pushed into a small clearing when a strange sensation hit her—as if she'd walked into fire. Heat encased her and made it hard to breathe. The magic rushed through her body, and then the strangeness was gone as quickly as it had appeared.

"Alex! Where are you?" Gryphon screamed, tearing through the forest after her. The moment he arrived in the clearing, he took Alex's face in his hand to check her over. "Are you all right? I felt terror from you."

"I'm fine. I just felt like I was boiling and then it was gone."

Gryphon slowly crept forward, keeping himself between Alex and the trees he scanned.

Her magic drew her to a dark path between a pair of birch trees, and without worrying about the consequences, she let her magic lead her. Gryphon cursed and then gave chase after her.

Once they were both on the path, vines and leaves intertwined behind them, sealing them in. Alex felt no fear from them, and instead shrugged and pushed on. Warmth filled her when Gryphon took her hand in his and squeezed. Alex expected him to insist they go back, but he merely smiled. They hadn't walked far when the tunnel exited into another clearing.

This one was different. The trees packed so closely against one another, they seemed to form a wall, keeping everything out.

Gryphon took a step ahead of her, but they were in Merlin territory, *her* territory. She grabbed the back of his shirt and yanked him back, charging into the clearing. She spun around to take it all in, and when she faced the center of the clearing once more, a cottage had appeared.

"Is that normal?" Alex asked.

Gryphon shook his head. "Even Birch couldn't make her cottage vanish."

Alex held out her hand and he took it so they could approach the decrepit building together. The structure was similar to the huts in the camp where Alex grew up, with logs forming the walls. A pair of windows flanked the solid wooden front door, one of them broken. A small porch spanned the width of the house, with a crumbling roof above it. As they got closer, dark patches became moss growing on the logs and spreading to the windows. The tension in the air made it hard to breathe.

When they reached the porch, Gryphon wore a look she recognized from Stefan. She didn't feel like arguing with him, so she pushed him toward the door. He shoved it a few times and it creaked open. When he stepped through and found it sufficiently safe for his liking, he motioned that she could follow.

Stale, musty air assaulted her and she covered her nose. She'd expected a lab or a small library, not an ordinary one-room cottage. Along the walls, she saw a dusty old bed, a shelf with knick-knacks, and a few broken jars. A stained chair was positioned in front of the fireplace. Moths long ago devoured the sun-faded rug. Squatting down, she could see a faint color of violet beneath the layers of dirt. The only other thing in the room was a wooden table pushed against the wall.

"I'm disappointed," Alex said.

"Why?" Gryphon asked.

"I assumed a cottage hidden this deep in the forest, with a secret path to get to it like the Verlassen Castle—and being masked like Moorloc's was—would have held some great secret. But this is just a rundown home, like the huts I grew up in."

Gryphon examined the walls of the room, and when Alex seemed confused, he pressed her hand against one.

"Gryphon, what are you—"

"It knows you. It's me. I'm the problem," he said pressing his hand on hers. "Masking castles isn't a common skill in our world. We can mask small things, but buildings are difficult. Even Birch's cottage was out in the open. But your mother and Moorloc must have learned to mask their castles from some-where. Your mother's lab was locked to her line only."

"You think Merlin locked this hut."

"Exactly," Gryphon said. "We go out, and then you go in alone, and we'll see what happens."

Alex raced out of the building and stood in the grass, leaving Gryphon to close the door and follow her. The moment he returned, Alex walked back up to the house. She placed one hand on the door and the other on the knob and pressed her forehead against the cool wood. "Hello, grandfather. Please help me get home."

She turned the knob and pushed open the door.

CHAPTER 35

AARON

"Aaron, watch your step!" Jerome warned.

Aaron stopped. At his feet grew a giant batch of hog thistle. It was a darker green, smaller cousin to the plant they wanted. The southern Dark Forest grew denser than the northern part, thanks to the warmer climate and richer soil. It made it much harder to tell dragon and hog thistle apart for everyone except Jerome. Apparently he'd fallen into a rather large patch on the last day of his honor rite and learned how to spot it from a long distance away. Frustrated, Aaron stomped over the plants rather than trying to go around them. Macht chuckled and leaned over to Jerome before the generals moved ahead to scout for more thistles.

"Did you hear what they said?" Aaron asked Harold.

Harold shook his head. "I don't worry about what our generals say to one another. Why shouldn't they be friends too? It isn't as though there are many men of their military caliber for them to befriend."

Aaron scoffed. "How are you always so articulate no matter the circumstances?"

"I've been king longer than you. Edward is put together as well—when it doesn't involve Alexandria. It comes with experience."

"So I'll get better at putting on a brave face?"

"No, you'll get better at lying to yourself that everything is all right."

"King Harold's not wrong," Kharon said, finally catching up to them. "Age teaches us all a great deal, but there is only so much for us to comprehend."

"Are you saying there is a limit to how much we can learn?"

"I am."

"Don't tell Alex that. She spends all her free time in the library and would be heartbroken to know that she might never read and learn everything in all our books."

Kharon smiled at Aaron. "Our secret, then."

An icy breeze surrounded them, making even Harold shiver. "Do we have a visitor?" he asked.

"We do." Kharon smiled. "Hello, Your Highness." Their smile dropped quickly as they stared at the empty space in front of them. "I see." Kharon tugged their chin and crossed their arm beneath their elbow, listening.

"I'm sorry, Aaron," they said. "Daniel tried everything, but no mortal ghost can get to the Forbidden Lands, and no sorcerer spirit can come to us without the summoning spell."

"That makes finding this dragon thistle even more important." Aaron turned and hurried after the generals. *We have to find this* ferflucsing *plant. I need Lynx to turn herself into a bird or fish or whatever animal she picked. Alex was gone for fourteen years, and I believed she was alive that whole time, and she was. She didn't give up on me when I was cursed. I will not give up on her.*

Aaron marched ahead, when another icy breeze surrounded him. Something in him told him this wasn't his brother.

"Father?" Aaron whispered, coming to a halt. The air grew colder. Letting his breath slow, Aaron watched the fog from his exhalations hang in the air. His right arm grew cold, and frigid air gusted him toward a break in the woods. Aaron took off.

The others shouted after him, but Aaron paid them any mind, weaving between the trees to hurry after his father. In a few minutes, he burst from the thicket into an open patch and nearly tripped over an enormous rotting log. When he regained his balance, he found himself in a clearing filled with dragon thistle.

"Thank you, Father," Aaron whispered. The surrounding air became unbearably cold and then the chill vanished. "I'm over here! Bring the bags. I found the thistle."

"WELL, you certainly impressed me. I was hoping for a half bag! This will last us years." She held up the two bags of dragon thistle they had foraged.

"We wanted to ensure Lynx had all she needed," Harold said.

"How soon do you think she'll have the potion ready?" Aaron asked.

Kharon hoisted the remaining two bags over their shoulder. "Knowing Lynx, she probably has everything ready and was waiting on this." Birch nodded in agreement, and they headed into the lab in the Verlassen Castle basement.

"How *long*?" Aaron asked, unable to hold back.

Birch gestured toward the lab. "I can't say. This potion will only allow Lynx to *attempt* to take a second animal form. It could fail or the animals could reject her request. She could end up getting an animal that doesn't help us. So many things are outside of our control with this sort of magic. We just need to hope for the best."

Aaron crossed his arms. "Thank you, Birch." She descended the dark spiral stairs to the lab. When she was out of sight, he turned to Harold. "Ale?"

"Yes."

The kings headed to the kitchen to raid the ale barrels. Harold poured him a mug of Warren ale, then filled his own and watched Aaron take a swig. "I thought you only drank Datten ale."

"I prefer it, but this is Alex's castle, so she stocks what the guards want."

"That does sound like Alex. Thoughtful."

They stayed in the kitchen drinking their ale and talking. The Betruger castle had been restored and, as their new queen, Edith was trying to make her mark. Harold was thrilled at how easily she'd taken to the role. She genuinely loved the Betruger people as much as her own Warrenites.

They had just started their third cup of ale when Stefan found them. "Lynx asked me to get you. She thinks one of the batches of potion worked."

Aaron slammed his mug down and hurried past Stefan to get to the lab. He heard the others follow, but he continued on ahead of them.

The lab normally smelled musty with a hint of some potent herbs Aaron recognized, like peppermint or lavender. But today it reeked of burned hair, dragon thistles, sweat, and what might have been blood.

"That stinks," Harold said, walking in behind Aaron.

"That means it will taste even worse," Stefan said. He looked pale.

Lynx had dressed simply in training clothes with her wild blonde locks tied up in a tight braid. Her normally glowing complexion was dull and covered in ash smudges. She hunched over the fire pit, three different cauldrons bubbling.

Lynx beckoned for Birch to come over. "Which do you think looks right?" she asked.

The Celtics Titan carefully examined the three potions. "I would think the darker green one."

"That was my thought too," Lynx said.

Being here, smelling the potions, watching them bubble and froth, and seeing the look in Stefan's eyes, Aaron was overcome with a sense of foreboding. "You don't have to do this, Lynx," he said.

"Of course, I do," she replied. "I need Alex back as much as I need Gryphon. She's the only young sorceress I've ever been close with."

"Most powerful sorceresses are insufferable," Birch explained.

"And Gryphon is practically my brother. I won't live without either of them."

"I understand all that," Aaron said. "But no one expects you to do this, especially since there are risks to you. You're just as important to us as the two of them are to you."

Lynx avoided Aaron, instead searching for the eyes of her husband.

"Don't look at me like that," Stefan said. "I may not like it, but I know better than to order around a sorceress when she sets her mind to something."

Lynx squeezed Stefan's hand. "I accept the risks. At this moment, I'm our last hope."

CHAPTER 36

ALEX

Alex stepped through the door, and the musty old room vanished. In its place the most glorious lab Alex had ever seen welcomed her. Despite having been locked away for so many years, it was spotless and still smelled of peppermint. The floor was made of a stone she couldn't identify, but violet light shimmered beneath her feet, like ripples in a pond. A fireplace took up the entire back wall. Whereas the castle labs had immense fires, this one was split into three—one small, one medium, and one taking up almost half the wall. Each could hold a different-sized fire that could produce the specific, desired amount of heat. A cauldron on a hook hung over each one. A shelf built into one of the stone walls held more cauldrons of various sizes.

"But the outside is wood." Alex touched the wall, which felt like stone, meaning the logs outside were part of the illusion. She continued exploring the lab, finding a desk strewn with unfinished letters addressed to Hermes, Merlock, and Victoria, and underneath those, a few journals. On the final wall, there were at least a hundred books and jars with all sorts of rare ingredients, including dragon scales, powdered dragon tooth, and mermaid tears, some of the most difficult to source materials in the Forbidden Lands. Alex ran her fingers over the jars and smiled.

"Alex, are you okay?"

"Gryphon—it's amazing. Come see." She heard footsteps and went to the door to extend her hand to Gryphon, but the moment he stepped into the room, the rundown hut returned.

"I don't understand," Alex said. She went over and touched the wall where the bookshelf had been.

"It seems Merlin was not taking any chances," Gryphon replied. "If there's anything here you want me to see or help you understand, you're going to have to retrieve it on your own."

"I need crates. Lots and lots of crates! There were books, potions, letters—even cauldrons."

"You want to take his cauldrons?" Gryphon asked. Even if he could read her emotions, he couldn't always understand her actions. "We have an extensive selection at the castle."

"I know," she whispered. "But I don't have a lot from my family, and I'd like to use his in our lab."

"You could work here if you like it so much."

Alex bit her cheek and shook her head. "One day ... but I'm not ready for that now, especially considering my situation. I don't want to be out here alone."

Gryphon rubbed her back and nodded. "Then the cauldrons come too. Give me a few minutes to find you some crates. I'll be right back. Close the door until I get back."

Alex went back into the room and put her hands on her hips. There was so much of potential value here, and it was daunting to decide where to start. She pushed up her sleeves and sorted through the papers on the desk.

She heard Gryphon stacking crates on the porch, so she

brought them one at a time to the lab table. Merlin's table split into two halves: one the height for sitting and the other for standing. As she filled each crate, Gryphon stepped over the threshold and carried the crate out of the run-down hut. Once outside, he'd crack away, and she'd start on the next one.

It took them the entire day to take everything Alex wanted back to their castle. By the time they were done, Alex was exhausted, but the castle's lab and library tables were stacked high with crates. Gryphon went off to find them something to eat while Alex took stock of her acquisitions. She picked the crate with the letters from the desk and settled onto the library's reading couch. Pulling out the letters that were inside, Alex flipped through them. Merlock and Victoria's were only a few lines, but Alex spotted one that said Alexandria.

"How old is this letter? Merlin did know my grandmother." Alex unfolded the top, but the letter seemed to be blank. When she finished opening the page, words appeared as if they were being written.

My darling Alexandria,

From the day she married my son Hermes, your namesake foretold your arrival and everything you would do to help join the mortal and sorcerer worlds in ways I could never achieve.

Your future is one full of magic, battles, heartbreak, and so much love it is unfathomable that one person could hold all of it in their hand. The final years of my life were dedicated to recording everything Alexandria told me you would need to know, and creating the spells and potions you would need to achieve your greatness. The journals your mother and uncle took with them are

Megesti's. Everything in this cabin is your inheritance from the other sorcerer mortal of our world.

I know your weakness is not being able to rely on others, but these journals were protected, so only you may grant another the ability to read them. Place their hand on a book, cover it with yours, and tell them you let them in. The book will then reveal itself.

All the answers you seek are here—from how to overcome your fury, free yourself from your prison, and even how to keep your king at your side for longer. Remember that you cannot do it on your own, for like the forest that surrounds my home, the many standing together are stronger than the one alone.

Remember this, and you will succeed.

Your beloved grandfather,

Merlin

Alex swallowed hard and reread the letter until she heard a crash. Gryphon had dropped the food and rushed to her. It wasn't until he touched her face that she realized she'd begun to cry. Trembling, she held the letter out to him.

Gryphon slunk to his knees and put his hand on her leg. "They're here? All the books we couldn't find ... every answer that eluded you. We could even find the book that talks about getting that fury under control."

Alex nodded. She reached for the next crate but stopped when a sharp pain ran through her head. She dropped to her knees, Gryphon beside her, clutching his head.

"What's happening?" Alex asked.

"The Titans are calling *us*."

CHAPTER 37

GRYPHON

"Why does it have to hurt if *they* summon *us*?" Alex asked.

"Because it's an emergency," Gryphon replied.

He held out his hand, taking Alex in. Her pregnancy had become more visible in the last week, but that was expected with twins. Fortunately, the duration of sorcerer pregnancies varied enough that he knew they could convince anyone who dared to ask that Alex was simply having a shorter one because of her age.

Gryphon and Alex had opted for simple tunics and pants for their walk that turned into a moving adventure, and the lack of formality could put them at a disadvantage.

"Our clothes are fine," Alex said. "Our power is not in our clothes, but in these." She tapped the Heart mark burned above his line marks. Anytime she touched that spot on his neck, a shiver ran through him. Alex smirked. "Why is it my touch makes you freeze, and yours makes me hot?"

"Opposites attract," he said. Alex rolled her eyes, and he brought her close.

"What are you doing?" Alex asked, plugging her nose and pushing him away.

"Making sure you smell enough like me to hide that mortal baby."

"But you stink!"

Gryphon smirked. "Good. That means it's easier to put my scent on you."

"Gross," Alex groaned, pulling away.

"One last thing." Gryphon ran his hands through her hair to tussle it. "This will throw them off of what we're doing here. Now they'll think they interrupted what you were dreaming about the other night."

Alex's face went red, making Gryphon chuckle as he cracked them to the throne room. Around them, the sorcerers were shouting and accusing one another. Alex clamped onto his arm, trembling, so he moved his arm around her, holding her tight.

If they get violent, I'll send you away.

"He killed her!" a Poseidon sorceress whose name escaped Gryphon exclaimed.

"Killed who?" Gryphon asked.

"Why, Phobos killed Penelope," Eris said. The crowd parted to let her through, Orion and Fenrir at her side.

"She was a distant Cassandra who never managed a premonition in her life." Phobos crossed his arms. "I figured we didn't need her, now that the true daughter of Cassandra has returned to us." He devoured Alex with his eyes, not even attempting to hide his hunger.

Gryphon felt nausea and fear flow from Alex when she pushed tighter against him. Phobos' lingering gaze aroused every ounce of jealousy Gryphon had and released his Ares powers. In the blink of an eye, Gryphon darted across the room, slamming Phobos into the wall and holding him by the neck. Talons burst through Gryphon's hand as his arm shifted to its gryphon form, drawing blood.

Eris cackled, waving her hand and bringing Phobos back to her side. "Look at him! Does that quiet the naysayers? He reacted exactly as a possessive Ares male would, protecting his bonded sorceress and child."

"What of the other child?" Fenrir asked. Alex shrieked, and Gryphon whipped around to see Fenrir holding Alex by the arm and sniffing her.

Alex burst into blue light, and a gale-force wind rushed through the room, sending Fenrir and all the sorcerers away. Gryphon started toward her, but his hexa yanked him over to Fenrir.

"What do you mean, Fenrir?" Eris asked.

"I smell Gryphon all over her, but there are three heart-beats coming from her, and there is a faint stench of the mortal boy on her."

Eris squeezed Gryphon's arm painfully hard, and when he tried to throw her off, he failed. "It would seem our Head and Heart are keeping secrets."

All eyes were on Alex now, and the stench of her fear filled the room. She stepped back to put more distance between them. Gryphon wrenched his arm free and cracked to her side.

"Admit it," Fenrir growled, slinking closer. "You're carrying the mortal's bastard pup."

Alex moved faster than Gryphon had ever seen her. She punched Fenrir in the face and kicked him in the knee, sending him to the ground. The wind raced back and swirled around her, creating a vortex like the night she injured Aaron and Stefan in her mother's castle. Alex's hair flew around her face, but she slipped into her fighting stance and stared down the room of sorcerers. She took Gryphon's hand and squeezed it, drawing upon his Ares magic as it crackled through the air. They both burst into blinding orange light.

"Back up!" Alex shouted.

Gryphon squeezed her hand back, sending all his confidence into her. *You can do this. Make them yield.*

"No one touches me without my permission. Understood?"

When no one replied, Alex closed her eyes. When she opened them, they had turned black as night. Facing the sorcerers, she thrust her hands up, creating a black cloud on the ceiling. Lightning shot down, narrowly missing the screaming sorcerers. Only Eris, Fenrir, and Phobos didn't panic; instead, each of them smirked.

"Get out," Alex said in a voice that was not hers, and the sorcerers obeyed.

As soon as they were gone, Alex dropped to her knees like a stone.

Gryphon barely caught her in time. "Quite the show you put on, Princess. Did you have to drain yourself again?"

"I didn't. *She* did."

"The fury?" Gryphon scooped Alex up in his arms, and she clung to his neck letting him carry her to their bedroom.

Alex nodded against his chest. "I'm losing control of her."

CHAPTER 38
AARON

The group walked up the stairs to the Verlassen Castle courtyard. Aaron had never realized how many steps there were going up, because they had always been cracked when leaving the lab. Harold shot Aaron a questioning look but all Aaron could do was shrug. The sorcerers must have their reasons.

When they arrived in the courtyard, Aaron ordered the guards there to leave. Lynx kissed Stefan and took the first potion jar from Birch. She secured the lid and gave it a good long shake before opening it. She pinched her nose.

"You can still change your mind," Aaron said.

Lynx shook her head and chugged the entire jar of liquid. She wiped her mouth and shrugged.

"How long until we know?" Stefan asked.

"I'm not sure," Lynx admitted, and everyone went silent for a minute. Then she clutched her stomach and screamed. Stefan started toward her, but Birch stopped him.

"No," she said. "New transformations hurt. That's why it's

172

so painful for Gryphon to turn. He refuses to practice because he's afraid of losing control."

Lynx dropped to her knees, crying out in pain. Aaron could hardly stand to listen to it and did not know how Stefan could. The next time Lynx screamed, her cry turned into a screeching *kik-kik-kik*. Harold and Aaron stepped back, and feathers ripped through Lynx's arms, neck, and chest, shredding her clothes. With the next cry, claws ripped through her boots, and her legs withered into spindles that curved backward, and she shrank in size. A beak burst from her face and, finally, giant tail feathers erupted from her tailbone. The small falcon had one brown eye like Lynx, and one dark green, the color of her Tiere line. Birch squatted and extended her arm, but the bird shrieked and backed away. Only when Stefan bent down did she move closer.

"Someone's picking favorites," Harold whispered, and Aaron had to bite his cheek to hold back his smirk.

Stefan offered the small falcon his arm and she puffed up. When she perched on him, he examined her carefully. "You wouldn't know she wasn't a bird."

"That's the idea, dear," Birch said.

Aaron crept forward, making sure to keep himself in sight of Lynx as he got closer. "All right, do you remember what you need to do?"

The bird straightened, arranged her feathers, and bobbed her head up and down. Stefan held his finger and Lynx scratched her head against it. "All right, Lynx. Time to go find Alex and Gryphon," he said.

Lynx opened her wings and took off from his arm, sailing high into the air. She flapped her wings and at first she dropped but quickly she recovered and managed to soar upwards. She flew higher and the group watched her until they could no longer make out her small form.

"And now we wait," Aaron said. A comforting pat made him turn to his friend, Harold. "Training?"

"You want to train *now*?"

Stefan's eyes brightened. "Of course. Alex always trains when she's nervous and worried. Or are kings too delicate to use brute force to take their minds off things?"

Harold burst out in laughter and Aaron narrowed his gaze at Stefan. "Let's go, little Wafner. I'll show you a few things your father taught me."

CHAPTER 39
ALEX

Dust flew across the room when Alex slammed another book shut. Merlin's books were filled with so many amazing spells, potions, prophecies, and more. It hurt Alex's heart to have to rush past everything when she couldn't find the information she was searching for.

You could just surrender to your fate, little one. I would handle things for us, the fury whispered. Alex pressed her palms into her eyes and shook her head violently.

"Get out of my head!"

Careful what you wish for, Princess. If I get out, then you'll be the one trapped up here.

"Gryphon will never let that happen."

So much faith in the sorcerer. You love him, carry his child, and share his bed, and yet you won't let him touch you.

"Be quiet."

I'd let him do anything to us. Perhaps if he knew he'd help me instead.

"Enough!" Alex shouted so loud, the wind threw open the door to the rooftop garden. A minute later, Gryphon's body filled the doorway. He leaned against the frame with his arms crossed and didn't say anything, choosing instead to let her address him.

"She won't be quiet," Alex whispered. "We all have the nagging little voice in our heads that says we're going to fail, but mine is actually trying to make me fail."

Gryphon cocked his head to the side, a telltale sign he was trying to figure her out.

"What?" Alex snapped. *You better not have been reading my mind when she ...*

"What did she say?"

"It doesn't matter," Alex said.

"With how upset you are, I would say it does."

Alex opened the next book with a huff. "These two were fascinating but useless."

"Alexandria."

The table creaked and tilted toward her slightly, making the book she'd been using as a distraction slide away. She raised her eyes to find Gryphon leaning on the table, staring at her with an intensity that made her squirm in her seat. Until that moment only Stefan had been able to make her feel this way.

Her voice was only a whisper when she spoke. "She said you'd side with her when you learned she'd let you bed us."

A long silence filled the room, making Alex's stomach drop. *He wouldn't. If he loves me even half as much as he claims, he knows that would destroy me.*

A surge of heat ran through her when Gryphon clasped her hands in his. "I'll repeat what I said. You have nothing to fear from me. I have not, and will not, touch you in a romantic way without you wanting it. And I mean *you*, not cursed you, possessed you, or fury you. If you are not completely in control of yourself, it isn't you ... and I don't want her."

Alex sighed with relief so loud it made Gryphon frown. "You honestly thought I'd side with a fury so I could get between your legs?"

"No ... maybe ... I don't know what I'm thinking. I finally understand how Kharon feels with the ghosts harassing them all day."

"If I knew a spell to silence her, I'd tell you."

"Thank you." Alex took her book back, looking at him over the top of the pages. "Did you have any luck with your books?"

"Not yet."

Alex tapped the huge stack beside them. "Well at least we have more to go through. The letter Merlin left me assured us that what we need is in here."

Gryphon picked another book off the top of the pile and plopped back on the table, rattling it so hard, the stack of books toppled over. They both jumped up to catch the books, but were too late.

"I'm sorry, Alex. Let me get them." Gryphon dropped to the ground, where she'd ended up trying to catch the load.

"It's fine, Gryphon. I'm pregnant not dying. I can pick up some books."

Gryphon grabbed a few books, slamming the first one shut as if it bit him. Alex reached for an open book and stilled when she saw an ink drawing of a crib. Protecting the crib, a sorceress with long hair confronted a sorcerer. Alex didn't need to see his face to know it was Gryphon, sent to kill Aaron. The sketch made it real—irrefutably real.

"Alex?" Gryphon reached for her, and she withdrew. Hurt and confusion crossed his face until he saw the book in front of her. His eyes widened.

"Would you have?" Alex asked, feeling her voice break in her throat.

"I want to say no, but I was a different sorcerer back then. If your mother hadn't stepped in ... I hate who I was then, and what I was becoming. If I believed it would have made my father and hexa leave me alone—even for a day..."

Alex shook her head and sat back. "I'm glad I didn't know you then."

"I'm not."

"Why?"

"Because I was that sorcerer until the day I met you. You gave me a reason to be better."

Rage coursed through her stomach. "That is a terrible thing to say." She scooped up the books near her and placed them on the table, rushing to the stairs that led to the library. Gryphon cracked after her.

"Why? You make Aaron a better man and you seem proud of it."

"Aaron was always good. I don't want to be the reason you decide to be good! Do you not realize how much pressure that puts on me? What if you change your mind one day, and decide I'm not worth being good for?"

"I will never change my mind about you."

"You changed your mind about killing Aaron."

Alex turned to leave but Gryphon held her arm tight, no matter how she tried to rip away.

"Let me go," Alex demanded.

"No. You don't get to run when things are hard."

Alex slammed her hip into his stomach, knocking him off balance, and he released her. She lunged away, panting. "I'm not fleeing because it's hard," the air around them crackled with electricity. "I'm leaving because I'm angry, and my powers are not something I can control right now. I'm angry because you just admitted that the only reason you didn't murder Aaron as an innocent baby was because my mother threatened to take me away from you. And that horrifies me."

"You stand there and judge me for having to kill one child? How many lives ended because of you? How many babies will never meet their fathers because you did what you thought was *right* and it got knights killed."

Guilt soiled the food in Alex's stomach so quickly, she had to fight not to be sick.

"We are all capable of good and evil, but it's our choices that define how we and others see ourselves."

Alex's heart pounded so hard she could hardly take a proper breath. For the first time ever, she saw the truly cruel sorcerer he'd always warned her he was. Sliding her hand protectively over her belly, she stepped back.

I will always choose what is best for the greater good, regardless of what it does to me.

And I will always choose what gets me with you in the end.

Gryphon raised his hand to touch her face, but Alex slapped it away and cracked.

CHAPTER 40
AARON

Aaron ripped his crown off his head and it clanged down on the table in the library. "It isn't enough!"

"Don't let Stefan hear you say that, after what Lynx went through to become a falcon."

Aaron ran his hand through his hair, scratching where the crown had weighed on his scalp. "I'm sorry, Megesti." His friend uncrossed his arms and sat across from Aaron. "I don't mean to sound unappreciative. I'm just so worried. This isn't a single sorcerer or a person keeping us apart—it's a curse put on by a powerful sorcerer years ago."

"According to Kharon, it's a sorceress who did it. Tabitha was the last sorceress Heart, and she was a Tiere, like Lynx. She loved all living things and put the spell in place to protect the mortals from sorcerers."

"No one ever expected a sorceress to fall in love with a mortal," Aaron whispered.

"Not just a sorceress—a Head."

"So what do we do?"

"We wait. When Alex was in the labyrinth, I saw you tirelessly work on Datten. You made it a home Alex would be proud to come back to."

Aaron leaned back on his chair. "Before all this we had talked about starting a noble ladies' committee, like in Warren."

A knock at the door brought Caleb into the room, holding a letter. "King Harold sent this. He's asking if you have any news."

Aaron motioned for him to enter. "Have we heard from Warren?"

Caleb shook his head. The door flew open and Jerome marched in.

"Lynx has returned."

Aaron dropped the letter. "Where?"

"Stefan's suite. She's exhausted."

Aaron brushed past Jerome and ran down the hall toward the west stairs. In all his years in this castle, he'd never scaled the stairs that fast. He missed the last step and fell onto the stone hallway of the second floor but didn't care. He wiped the blood from his chin, threw open the solid door, and burst into Stefan and Lynx's suite.

Alex had insisted that both Stefan and Michael receive larger quarters than normal knights. Surprisingly, Jerome had agreed, probably because Michael was already married and he hoped Stefan would find someone eventually. Now, with both of their wives part of Alex's inner circle, having the entire family in the castle was a tremendous help.

Lynx panted heavily, curled up on the couch, wrapped in a forest green blanket. Stefan crouched beside her, and Birch held out a mug, trying to get the Titan of Tiere to drink. Kharon grumbled, pacing back and forth near the fire, muttering to themself.

Lynx took a sip from Birch's mug. She was even paler than Kharon.

Aaron stepped inside. "Are you all right?" The younger Wafner looked every bit the worried husband. Alex would have teased him, if she were here.

"There's nothing," Lynx said between exhausted breaths. "I flew for days. I went twice as far as it should have been. It's gone. They're gone." She buried her face in the pillow.

Aaron stepped back, leaving Stefan to comfort her while he exchanged a nervous look with Kharon and Birch. "Harold's ships have all returned now. They found nothing."

"And Warren's found nothing, and now Lynx," Stefan muttered.

Aaron stumbled back as if Stefan had punched him in the gut. "Lynx, thank you for trying. I'll let you recover in private." He turned and walked quickly from the room to avoid dealing with the Wafners' questions. Inside, his fear and grief boiled over into rage. He ran through the halls, past the throne room and royal suites, and down the stairs to the castle's lower level.

The basement halls were deserted, and Aaron couldn't have been happier about it. He stumbled through the barely lit space, trying door after door, until he found one unlocked. Throwing his weight into it, the heavy wooden door cracked open enough for him to slip inside. Aaron stood facing a room filled with old furniture and belongings of former Datten royals. A gorgeously carved desk and matching wardrobe were in one corner next to a stack of chairs. In another corner, a sparring dummy covered in a rusty suit of armor leaned against a pile of barrels, chests, and knick-knacks.

Thinking of Alex being scared and alone in the Forbidden Lands made Aaron's breath freeze in his throat. He grabbed a vase off the pile of things and threw it against the wall.

Ceramic shards hailed down and Aaron's breath returned in deep, painful gasps.

"I just want my wife back!" Aaron took a horse statue off the same pile and threw it even harder.

"I'm tired of everything always being so hard!" He swiped his muscular arm across the top of the desk, sending empty ink bottles flying across the room and floor. Unsatisfied, he ripped the drawers out and smashed them against the stone floor.

"I can't talk to my brother or my father. Harold and Jerome are busy fighting to get Alex back. I'm terrified and the only person I can talk to about that is trapped in another land!"

Dropping to the floor, Aaron let the stones rip through his pants, not caring that his knees stung. He dropped his head into his hands, and let the painful sobs erupt from him. When his breathing finally slowed to normal, Aaron's arms prickled and his breath hung in the air.

"Please don't let anything happen to her," he whispered to whichever of his relatives was at his side. When the space warmed again, Aaron went to his royal suite.

When it became clear that the footsteps behind him were actually following him, Aaron stopped outside his room.

"I'm fine, Jerome."

PART THREE

BETRAYAL

CHAPTER 41
GRYPHON

Gryphon slammed the door that led out of the castle into the space where the territories split off from his home. Without even taking a breath he crossed the line into the Mystics territory. Their land was mostly plains with some woods and scattered hills, open spaces leaving ample opportunity to practice long distance cracking. He threw a last look over behind him to make sure Alex hadn't heard him leave. But the castle remained dark and silent as a crypt. Adjusting the satchel on is shoulder, he rubbed his hands together to produce several fire balls that bobbed around him. He slapped the red steal bracelet on his wrist and ran.

Gryphon raced across his territory, orbs in tow. Not one to use mortal methods, he needed to make sure that no one could follow his magic trail. Gryphon ran for nearly an hour before he found the tree he needed. Soaked in sweat from the humid summer night, he knelt down at the base of the tree and cut his finger on a sharp rock nearby. He pushed his thumb into the bark of the tree and it lifted from the ground, exposing a small opening inside the tree.

Settling on his knees, Gryphon withdrew the treasures he'd amassed in his life. His hexen's journal—he'd never met him because Eris murdered him for giving his mother Tiere instead of Ares. Along with the journal, he had hidden a bag of all the gryphon feathers he'd lost over the years, or at least the ones he could find, and a few ordinary things like a quartz stone shaped like a heart Lynx had given him and a pinecone from the trees Birch grew the day he was born. Mementos from his real family could never be allowed to fall into his father's hands. Finally, he fished out a piece of jewelry, cold to the touch.

Looking at the emerald bracelet that gave the owner power over whomever they gifted it to, a wicked voice awoke in his head. *If you gave it to Alex, you'd never have to worry about her trying to leave you.*

Gryphon scoffed. "I will accept nothing but the real her choosing me."

Opening the spell book, Gryphon's face twisted into a sneer.

How to turn a mortal into a sorcerer.

GRYPHON'S TEMPER seeped out of him and he growled. He slammed the book shut and shoved it and all the rest back into the tree. A wave of sorrow hit him, and he removed the bracelet from his wrist, opening his well to find Alex. He couldn't sense her fully, but he could sense she was troubled. Overwhelming loss spread through him. *She's thinking of the kingling again.* Groaning, Gryphon burst into orange light.

"No." He turned back to the tree to watch it sink down into

the dirt, hiding his secrets inside. Clutching his fists so tight that his nails drew blood, he turned back to the castle. "I will be patient. I will give him his decades, but I will not give up my time with her."

CHAPTER 42

ALEX

Alex seethed at Gryphon's turned back. The first two times she'd woken up, he hadn't been there, but he was there now, fast asleep. The moon closed in on the horizon. She should wake him, tell him what she was feeling. Aaron would always want to talk things out with her even if he needed some space first. But right then, she wanted to reach into her well and freeze Gryphon into a big block of ice.

My sorceress side really is waking up if I'm seriously considering punishing you. I wish Aaron were here. I miss him and am tired of feeling alone. Not trusting herself, Alex got out of bed and dressed. She had to open the closet four times before it finally showed her Gryphon's clothes, and she stole his shirt to keep the night chill off her. For good measure, she froze the rest of his clothes into a solid block of ice. She slipped out onto their oversized balcony and leaned against the thick stone guard rail that ran around it. Watching the moon above the Celtic and Tiere territory was magical, but they were to the east, so instead she watched the moon vanish in the Ares and Salem mountains.

How long has it been since I lost them? Alex closed her eyes and listened. The forests of the Forbidden Lands sounded so different from the Dark Forest where she'd grown up. A pair of owls hooted in the distance, and some sort of enormous cat screamed. The cry made Alex think of Lynx, and immediately her eyes popped open. Scanning the treetops below, she couldn't help but wonder how many of the animals she heard were actually sorcerers in animal form. No longer comfortable standing outside alone, Alex rushed back into her room and closed the doors. She even flipped the magical latch Gryphon had put on them, remembering the night in Datten when Lygari had stood on her bedroom balcony.

She picked up the Merlin book she'd been perusing before bed from her nightstand and cracked to their lab to get an early start. She dropped it on the already-read pile, about to select another off the stack, when an icy shiver ran through her. She spun, finding herself alone.

Feeling things that aren't there, little one?

Her hands curled into tight fists as she tried to ignore the voice in her head.

You're using all your magic and energy to grow and protect those little babies. You had enough magic to grow one and keep me at bay, but with twins ... ahhh. I'm getting stronger, and soon you'll be in here and I'll be getting you the vengeance you desperately deserve.

"Or we'll both be dead," Alex replied to the fury.

You wouldn't do that to your friends, or your father. He lost your mother. Losing you would kill him.

It was late, so Alex knew she wouldn't encounter anyone. She cracked to the Poseidon territory and stood at the end of the pier. There were no ships or signs of life at the docks. Eerie enough in the daytime, at night it was scary.

Pushing her shoulders back, Alex walked to the end of the

pier. "I am the Head. I will not be afraid." The sea, black as coal, lapped the wood. She took off her pants, boots, and Gryphon's warm shirt and left them in a neatly folded pile. Placing her hand on her bump, she emptied her lungs before filling them with the icy air and leaping into the sea.

Blackness surrounded her, but unlike the other times in her life, Alex felt no fear. Water brought her peace and strength, and she needed both right now. The chilly sea embraced her and Alex wondered what her mother would tell her to do. Her throat burned, but she fought to stay under the water as long as she could, hoping some clarity would find her. When her lungs felt as if they would burst, she broke the surface of the water. Alex gasped, her lungs taking their fill. Finally, when her breath returned to normal, she searched for a ladder to help her climb out of the water. It was that moment that she heard the growl.

Gryphon stood at the edge of the pier, arms crossed over his nightclothes. Red and orange orbs floated around him, the dramatic lighting only further emphasizing a rage she wasn't used to seeing from him.

"One fight, and suddenly you're done trusting me?" Alex snapped.

"One fight, and you lose your mind! What possessed you to leave the safety of our castle and throw yourself in the Oreean Sea?"

Alex rolled her eyes and cracked herself out of the water. The aged planks creaked beneath her feet as she wrung out her sopping wet tunic. She couldn't help but shiver.

Gryphon never took his eyes off her, but he waved his hand. A warm breeze surrounded her, drying her in seconds. "Why?" he asked.

"I needed to clear my head, and feel ... less muddled. We try spell after spell. To stop the fury gaining control, to break the hold trapping us here, to help me control my powers. But nothing is working. Since I became pregnant, my thoughts have become jumbled, and I don't know what I'm doing half the time. I wanted the clarity that only the sea can give me."

"But at night?"

"I couldn't sleep, and figured fewer sorcerers would be awake." Alex slipped her legs into her pants and hopped as she pulled them up in one fast motion. Gryphon kneeled in front of her now, holding out one of her boots for her. Alex swallowed and pushed her foot in.

"You could have woken me. I would have come," he said, tying the laces.

Alex chewed on her cheek before answering. "I didn't want you to come. I'm still mad at you."

Gryphon scoffed and shook his head. "It seems unfair that you give Aaron time to clear his mind when you disagree, but not me."

"You didn't come to bed until late."

"That had nothing to do with our tiff." He moved closer. "I'm waiting years—no, decades—for my time with you, and I intend to savor every second I'm given, even if you want to spend them trying to freeze me into a block of ice."

Alex couldn't stop the smile that covered her face. "How did you know what I was thinking of doing to you?"

Gryphon brushed her hair off her face. "Because I know you. And I tried to find my cloak before following you."

Alex felt her face burn fiercely, and he stepped back, as if he sensed her nervousness. "Ready to go back?" he asked, then smirked. "I can hear Merlin's books calling you now." Despite the fight, her night swim, and his obvious terror at something happening to her, he still smiled at her, the same way he had the day he met her on the beach.

He noticed her staring. "What?"

"Nothing." Alex shook her head and held her hand out. Gryphon cocked his head to the side and narrowed his eyes. She stared back at him. *Get out of my head, you creep.*

He snorted and cracked them back to the lab. After her cold swim, the room was suffocating, so Alex opened the door to the balcony, lingering there. Something was different.

"What's wrong?" Gryphon slid his hand around her from behind, protectively covering her belly while gazing over her shoulder at the garden.

"Is it just me or are there more birds around than usual?"

She felt him tense, and he gently ushered her back inside, then stepped through the threshold. He raised his hand to stop her and walked a few steps away from the door, slowly turning and sniffing the air. Without warning, a flock of birds rose up and circled him, screeching.

Alex screamed, as a small gray and violet bird flew into the lab and the door slammed closed, trapping Gryphon outside. He fought the birds off and she could hear him trying to open the door.

Alex desperately yanked on it from her side, but it was no use. She slowly turned around at the sound of rustling and found the bird hopping along the table with the books. Gryphon cracked in front of her, ready to fry the bird, but Alex stopped him.

Just watch it.

Why?

Trust me.

The tiny bird hopped from stack to stack until it stopped and scratched at one. Alex slipped away from Gryphon and crept to the bird. It hopped off the stack of books now, and pecked at the table around them. Something inside her told Alex to spread out the books, so she did. The little bird cocked its shimmering violet head to the side, cheeped, and hopped to the books.

"It looks like it's reading the titles," Gryphon whispered. The bird pecked at one book, hopped back, cocked its head, and hopped over to repeat the same routine with another. Alex shot Gryphon a questioning look and he shrugged. While they were distracted, the bird vanished.

"Where did it go?" Alex searched the shelves to see if it was hiding on the top of one while Gryphon flipped open the two books.

"Alex?" Gryphon had gone ashen and his eyes were wide. "This journal," Gryphon placed his hand on the open book, "tells of a Head who will birth non-identical twins that will unite mortals and sorcerers after centuries of hatred."

Alex's hands went to her stomach. She couldn't help looking down at her pronounced bump and rubbing it. "What about the other one?"

A smirk spread across Gryphon's face. "I should have known. It takes a Head *and a* Heart to cast the spell."

Alex hurried to his side and took the book. "It's written by Tabitha and Grindal, not Merlin."

"She was a brilliant Tiere and valued all life. She's the reason the dragons didn't go extinct sooner, and she made sure our kind wouldn't be able to hurt the mortals. They are the ones who put the protection on the sorcerer world."

"And since it took both of them to cast it, it will take both of us to remove it. So, what do we do?"

"We follow their steps but in reverse." Gryphon looked at her clothes, and then back at his night clothes. "I should get dressed, and we need to eat something before we go."

"All right."

STUFFING BREAD IN HER FACE, Alex walked through the Tiere forest trying to find anything resembling the description the journal provided. After reading the book, they'd figured out how Tabitha had done it. Now they needed to find the place marked on the map. They'd have to perform the spell once in each of the nine-line territories, and then a tenth time at a central location. Gryphon's knowledge of the Forbidden Lands terrain had been incredibly helpful in finding the specific locations in the territories.

In Salem, they went straight to the sacred fire to cast the spell. The size of the column of flames had surprised Alex, but Gryphon explained the history of the Salem line and the witch trials in the other world that led to them fleeing to Torian. His ancestors had erected the sacred fire, and it had burned ever since. When they came of age, all young Salems swore their oaths to the Head and received their line marks before the fire.

The Ares territory had a monster-sized sacrificial altar. It shared a border with Mire, which contained the tallest mountain peak in the Forbidden Lands. Only Tacita's Peak in the mortal world was taller. In the Mystics territory Gryphon had taken her to a small cave near the beach, which held millions of crystals, ones eerily similar to the glowing crystals in the labyrinth she'd navigated with Michael and Edith.

Poseidon had been Alex's favorite. The land was flat and marshy with many beaches. Their sacred ponds ran deep into the ground and connected beneath the earth. Alex wondered if they flowed all the way to the Oreean Sea despite their distance inland.

Alex and Gryphon had to perform different spells, and Gryphon was relieved that Alex had to cast that part of the spell. The instructions were clear—they must each cast the spell in their own territories and those in which they possessed more power. That meant Alex would do Celtics, Poseidon, Cassandra, and Hades, leaving Gryphon with Salem, Ares, Mystics, and Tiere. Since they weren't sure who was better in Mire, they both performed that one. Alex finished Cassandra and Gryphon prepared for Tiere before they headed back to the castle.

More and more questions brewed in her mind with each step they took. She wondered why Merlin even had these books. Maybe he'd been entrusted with them as founder of the tenth line. Or perhaps his line simply hadn't existed when Tabitha cast the original spell.

"If Merlin wasn't here when the spell was laid down, does that mean he was immune to it?" Alex asked Gryphon.

"I've never thought about it," Gryphon admitted.

They had been walking all day, and Alex's feet hurt, but she refused to complain. Not when they were so close.

Close but not close enough. How do you know he's not doing them wrong on purpose to keep you?

Alex grabbed her head and shook it, trying to cast out the fury or at the very least silence her. Gryphon heard her groan and rushed back. Without a word, he pulled her to his chest and heat engulfed her. He gently stroked her head, whispering how strong she was and how they would get through this. Soon, the voice subsided and Alex could carry on.

"Do you know where we're going?" Alex asked.

"We have to find the Tiere's tree of life. The legend goes that when the Tiere line first arrived, they were made from the children of monsters. These children had received their parents' powers but looked mortal. They picked this tree to hold their important discussions. It's said to be the oldest and largest in all of Torian. Every child born into the Tiere line or to a Tiere parent is carved into it."

"Wow."

"Those of us with the ability to shift have our animal listed next to us."

"It's a permanent record. That's fascinating."

"Come on. I know it's around here somewhere." Gryphon held his hand out to Alex. She accepted, and he helped her over a large fallen tree, so they could continue on.

The forest of the Tiere and Celtics territories grew as dense as the Dark Forest near Datten. In some spots, it smelled dank, but usually the air felt crisp, and thanks to the warm summer weather, it smelled sweet from all the flowers in the area. After a few wrong turns that made Gryphon curse and Alex giggle, they arrived in a clearing.

Gryphon pointed to the largest tree Alex had ever seen. "They picked an oak because the acorns are like the sorcerers being scattered around."

Alex craned her neck back to look straight up at the tree that grew as tall as the castle towers in Datten. She could have stood there in wonder forever.

Gryphon broke her trance. "I found my hexen."

Alex walked around the tree, scanning names as she went. Many names were those of animals. Tabitha's was the highest, and Alex had to stand on her tiptoes to see it. Alex traced her name with her finger. "Gryphon," she asked. "What animal did Tabitha become?"

"A fox. Why?"

"She had two animals."

Gryphon walked around the tree to where Alex pointed. *Dragon.*

"I thought you weren't supposed to pick mythical animals," Alex said. Gryphon shot her a look, and Alex playfully bumped him with her hip. "I'm aware you're a Gryphon, but you're difficult."

Gryphon chuckled. "Tabitha was the last to get a mythical

creature. It's said only a Head or Heart can handle them. That's why I could take it along with a fox."

"You have two animals, too?" Alex asked.

Gryphon grinned. "It's not unheard of, especially for a Heart, though most titans can manage it too."

Alex stepped back and continued scanning the names carved into the tree. "How do you explain Lynx then?" she asked.

Gryphon's eyes widened. "She's only ever had one."

"Well, now she has two."

Gryphon stared at the tree for a long moment.

They want us back as much as we want to get back.

<h1 style="text-align:center">CHAPTER 43
AARON</h1>

" **I** 'm fine, Jerome," Aaron said.

"Wrong Wafner," Jessica said. "And you're not fine. How could you be? I'm not fine. Michael's distraught, and Stefan is beside himself with guilt." A sob escaped Jessica and she clapped her hand over her mouth to hold it back.

Aaron marched up to her and pulled her into a hug. "Don't hide your pain from me. You're trying to be strong for them, but I'm not just your friend. I'm your king, and I will help you carry this burden."

When Jessica relaxed into him, an even louder cry escaped her lips. He couldn't help remembering the first time she cried in his arms. It had been the first anniversary of the fire. Both their fathers were off fighting the Betruger, and his mother was busy running the memorial, leaving the two of them on their own for most of the day. They'd remained strong through the celebrations of life, but afterward, in the schoolroom, they'd held each other and cried, since their tutor had been off that day.

When Jessica quieted, Aaron asked, "Where is Michael? He wasn't in the room with Stefan and Lynx."

Jessica wiped her eyes and fixed her dress. "He's helping Kharon review the books again. Veremunds are known for being cleverer than they're given credit for, so perhaps he'll find something."

"No doubt Edith is scouring every book in the Betruger kingdom."

"Or having Harold read them to her." Jessica sighed.

"I miss her," Aaron said quietly.

"I know. It's been longer than when they were at the labyrinth now."

"But not as long as Moorloc's, so why is it harder?"

"Because *you* aren't in control this time," Megesti said, coming down the hall toward them.

"He's right.".

"What if we can't—"

"Don't say it," Megesti said. "Kharon always says if you say it out loud, you're inviting the fates to enact it."

Jessica patted Megesti's arm. "You're learning a lot from our new friends."

"I'm trying. I spent decades with only my father to teach me. And as much as I loved and admired him, he really wasn't a powerful sorcerer. But now, surrounded by Titans of all the lines I don't have powers in, I've learned so much!"

"I know we don't say it enough, Megesti," Aaron said. "But we're proud of you."

Jessica nodded in agreement. "And Aaron—don't think we haven't noticed how hard you've been working on your temper."

"I expected to find you destroying a room right now," Megesti said.

"I already did that. I wouldn't recommend going into the royal storage rooms anytime soon."

"Better some old furniture than your room," Jessica said, smiling softly.

"Destroying a room made me feel better for about five minutes. Now I'm just full of regret and self-loathing. My temper is only good for battle. Here, it serves no one."

"It would seem that whenever Alex leaves," Jessica said, "you age a decade in maturity in the meantime."

"Are you sure you aren't part sorcerer?" Megesti teased.

Aaron chuckled. "Very funny."

They heard footsteps, and they turned to see Caleb striding over to them. "Pardon the intrusion, Your Royal Highness. I need to speak with you about a personal matter pertaining to the Rassgats."

Aaron groaned, making Jessica cover a sheepish smirk with her hand, while Megesti covered his laugh with a cough. Jessica patted Aaron's shoulder. "He's all yours, Caleb." Megesti bowed to them and followed Jessica down the hall, whispering something that made her snort.

Aaron crossed his arms and turned to his friend. The usually chipper knight looked more distraught than he had on their honor rite when Aaron had informed them that Lucas had picked the poisonous bush mushrooms. "Caleb, you can speak freely."

"Not here."

Aaron sighed and opened the door to the king's suite he shared with Alex. Caleb barely closed the door when he started shouting. "You have to stop Nathaniel. He's trying to force my father to marry Ruby to Wesley."

Aaron's mouth dropped, and he wondered if he'd been cursed again. "I'm sorry, I don't think I heard you correctly."

"My father owes Nathaniel money. My grandfather

borrowed a large sum from him without telling anyone. Now that he's died, the debt was passed to my father, and we don't have the money to pay, so he's demanding my sister's hand instead."

"Ruby's twelve. She can't marry anyone. Anyone younger than sixteen needs royal approval and I'm never giving it."

"Betrothals can last for years. They'll wait. But I refuse to let my sister marry that idiot. I don't care if I have to work for you every day for the rest of my life without being paid anything. You have to put a stop to this."

"I have no authority to break this contract between your families," Aaron said, making Caleb groan in frustration. "But that doesn't mean I can't give your father the money to repay them."

Caleb's face lit up. "Then we have to go now. They're talking in the throne room, since the Rassgats have no respect and ambushed my father at work."

When Aaron and Caleb arrived, Hunter opened the doors for them, giving them a nervous glance that told Aaron the argument was not a quiet one. Entering the room, Aaron found Wesley sitting upon his throne. *Has he lost his mind? No one but the king sits in his seat. Even my mother sat in her seat while my father was away. The only person besides me who will ever sit in that seat is Alex and our children.*

Aaron stormed toward him, letting his temper, which had so long been in check, rage. "Get off of my throne!"

"Temper, temper, cousin." Wesley laughed and didn't move.

"You have ten seconds to remove yourself from my seat before I have one of my generals do it for you."

"You wouldn't," Nathaniel said.

"You both complain I don't have enough Datten in me. Perhaps I should start behaving like the older Datten kings."

Wesley jumped up and strutted down the dais to meet Aaron. "This would be the perfect time for that. The older kings were much better at handling disputes between nobles, and forcing debtors to pay up."

Aaron crossed his arms at his cousin.

"I'm sorry for the disruption, Your Royal Highness," Avery began, but Aaron held his hand to silence him.

"Caleb's brought me up to speed, and I can say that I under no circumstances will ever approve of this marriage, so if you want something from the Reinharts, you'll have to find something else, Nathaniel."

"Ridiculous," Wesley spat, joining his father. "The late Earl Reinhart agreed that if—"

"I don't care," Aaron snapped. "I'm king and my decision is final. You have one minute to decide what else you will accept."

"Fine," Nathaniel replied.

"I want a new rank. Higher than the Reinharts. Something worthy of, say, a Wafner." Wesley adjusted his tunic and stood taller, full of bravado.

Rubbing his temples, Aaron turned to Nathaniel. "And what—do—you—want?" He spoke slowly as if he were talking to children.

"As Wesley's request is so minor. I want to bury my brother in the family crypt. I'd like you to have the Reinharts dig Kruft's body up and return him to us. After what you did to him, it's the least you can do."

Aaron laughed manically. The very idea was insanity.

"What is so funny?" Wesley demanded.

"You. After everything he did, Kruft can rot where we buried him. I will die before I even tell you where he is."

"I have a right to bury my brother wherever I wish."

Rage took over. "You lost that right the day he betrayed us!

He lied to my father and tried to hurt Alexandria. My only regret is that I killed him then and can't do it again."

Nathaniel opened his mouth and closed it several times, grumbling. He looked like a fish out of water. "I will not stand for this disrespect! You will either give us what we demand or agree to the betrothal!"

Aaron grabbed Nathaniel by the scruff of his shirt. "You think I'm disrespecting *you*? You're the one shouting at your king! Your entire family seems to forget that it was a King of Datten who gave you your lands and ranks. That means a king can take them away!" Aaron shoved Nathaniel away. "Now, get out of my sight. Your requests are all denied. I will pay the gold the Reinharts owe you, and if you ever ask me about Kruft, you'll be moving to Kirsh before you can beg me to reconsider!"

"This is not how you treat nobility, Aaron."

"That's Your Royal Highness to you. And I don't have to treat other nobles like this, because no other family is as entitled as yours! Now get out."

Wesley glanced at his father for a moment. Without another word, the Rassgats marched toward the door, scowling and muttering under their breath. While Aaron couldn't make out the words, he was sure they were slanders aimed at him.

CHAPTER 44

ALEX

"Why isn't it working?" Alex screamed.

Gryphon flipped through the spell book and groaned. "A page is missing. We only did the first part."

Rage seethed through Alex's core, and the fury laughed so loudly she couldn't hear herself think.

"No, no, no. *No!*" Alex picked up a jar of dragon's thistle and threw it at the fireplace mantel. The jar exploded, sending shards of glass flying back at them. Alex didn't flinch, not even when she felt the sting of glass slicing her cheek.

"*Ferflucs,* Alex!" Gryphon growled, picking up the glass and bits of plants.

Numbness spread through her, her emotions evaporating without warning.

"Why do I suddenly feel like I'm picking you up off the floor?"

Alex squeezed her eyes shut, fighting back the hurricane of emotions flaring back to life in her. Outside, thunder boomed loud enough that the jars on the shelves rattled. She struggled to get her breathing under control so she wouldn't pass out. *This...pregnancy...*

Warm hands on her shoulders and the brush of lips against her ear made her tremble. When she opened her eyes, he tucked her wild hair behind her ear.

"Your hand." Alex examined the cut on his palm. Cassandra powers flooded to life, replacing all her tumultuous emotions.

"I'm fine. I nicked it picking up the glass." He tried to pull away, but Alex held tight. "Alex ... let go, I'm fine—"

Gryphon froze.

"What?"

He wrenched his hand from her, her Cassandra magic already moving toward the cut. A burning pain hit her the moment his hand touched her cheek. She opened her mouth to speak, but a blinding white light burst out of her and Gryphon.

A blood spell. When the light dimmed, the burning sensation vanished.

The castle shook violently, and the other jars on the shelves fell and smashed, scattering more glass shards on the floor. Gryphon rushed to protect her from the debris with his body. The violent tremors continued after everything that could fall had, then stopped as suddenly as they'd started.

Alex and Gryphon exchanged a wordless glance and cracked onto the Poseidon docks. The moon illuminated the Oreean Sea. Alex shivered in the cool breeze, but then she spotted something. She held her hand over her eyes to help eliminate the moon's glare, and there in the distance, she could see.

"There are boats," she said.

Gryphon squinted in the same direction. "We did it! We broke the spell."

"But that means—"

I can go home! I can go home? The storm of emotions flooded back to her, sending wind and even rain through the lab.

"Alex?"

"I can go home," she whispered.

"That's what we were working for."

"I know but ... it'll change everything."

Gryphon took her hand in his, caressing her face with the other. Alex's cheeks darkened from his touch. "Change is inevitable, princess."

Alex closed her eyes to steady the tears that threatened to come. "I never get to settle anywhere. Every time I think I am, something happens. I'm scared of what's next."

"You will be an amazing mother, Alex."

She wanted to believe him, to accept the sincerity in his face, but she didn't. How could anyone know what kind of mother she would be? Least of all her. "I don't even remember my mother."

I'm being ridiculous. I had exactly the same conversation with Michael.

"You'll be exactly what these babies need. Nothing more, nothing less. Now go."

"Aren't you coming?"

"In a few minutes. I think it's best if you talk to your princeling alone."

"Aaron loves me. He'll understand," Alex replied, pulling away from Gryphon. "I've seen it."

"For all our sakes, I hope so."

CHAPTER 45
AARON

Aaron paced the throne room to calm himself, but found himself only growing angrier. *Nathaniel must have known I'd never approve that marriage. Either he really wants Kruft's body dug up from Moorloc's or he really wanted me to pay the Reinhart's debt. Either way, I can't let them continue to wreak havoc in Datten. I wish I knew what my father would do.*

He stopped in front of the painting of Daniel. At times like these, he would talk to his brother's painting, hoping that his ghost listened nearby, but usually a cool breeze was all he would receive in reply.

The door banged shut. Aaron rubbed his forehead and spun around to order the unwelcome guest to leave before he did something he regretted, but a figure slipped across the back of the hall, slowly coming into focus.

"Alex?" Aaron whispered so softly he barely heard himself speak. He shook his head and moved toward her. "Is that really you?"

"Aaron!" Alex stepped out of the shadows, hand over her mouth.

Aaron's heart pounded at the sight of her. He couldn't take his eyes off her face until she put her hand on her belly. He froze at the sight of her bump. "Are you—"

"I am. Clearly, we have some matters to discuss."

His surprise at seeing her wore off, replaced by his shock when he stepped closer and caught an unmistakable whiff of Gryphon's campfire scent. His stomach turned to stone, and he frowned. "It certainly seems that way."

"What's wrong?" Alex moved closer.

Aaron took a step back toward the wall. *Everything is wrong.* "You smell like Gryphon."

"What?" Alex stopped moving and touched her stomach protectively. "We shared a lab and a room at the castle, but that's a long story."

"You shared a *bedroom* with him?"

"Purely for safety. Gryphon was worried about how the sorcerers would act toward me."

"I understand that concern." Fear engulfed him, and Aaron could feel himself slipping under as his temper roared to life. *Ferflucsing Rassgats. Stop interrogating your wife. But she stinks like him and they shared a room. And she wasn't pregnant the last time I saw her.*

"Did you share a bed?"

Alex's face went pale. "We're getting off topic."

"No, we aren't," Aaron snapped, and the truth revealed itself. Her face shifted from joy to fear, and she inhaled sharply. A part of Aaron winced at the too-familiar sight of fear in her eyes, but another part, a stronger, older part, was buoyed by it, as if her fear were a confession. *You're deflecting the question. A very important question.* "You walk into my throne room—pregnant, after months of being away, smelling of another man. I think I'm well within my rights to question you on your sleeping arrangements." Aaron marched toward her but never reached her.

Gryphon appeared between them, glowing orange. "Back up, mortal!" Eyes blazing blue, he stepped up and snarled down at Aaron.

"Call off your dog," Aaron snapped at Alex.

"She didn't summon me," Gryphon said. "Her fear of *you* did. Something you were supposed to work on."

"Why should she be afraid of me unless something happened?"

"Enough!" Alex snapped.

Aaron ignored her. Instead, he sized Gryphon up. "Where did you *sleep*, Alex?"

"In my bed," Gryphon replied. "I had to make sure no one got any funny ideas."

"No one besides you."

Alex shoved Gryphon aside and pleaded with Aaron. "Nothing happened between us. I spent hundreds of nights beside Stefan and Michael. You never once doubted them, so why is Gryphon immediately accused of the worst?"

"Because you're pregnant!" Aaron screamed at her. "You cannot honestly expect me to believe he kept his hands off you for months!"

"Aaron, it isn't just Gryphon's child ..."

Gryphon's child. The words echoed in his brain, drowning out Alex's voice. Each echo shattered his heart, and his temper exploded forth protectively. He spun toward Gryphon and punched him. The sorcerer hadn't been expecting it and went down hard, blood pouring from his face.

"Stop it!" Alex shouted, reaching for Aaron, but he brushed her off and jumped onto Gryphon to continue his assault on the sorcerer. After three strikes, Gryphon's hands lit up with flames, and he shoved Aaron off. fire burned through his tunic to his skin, and Aaron screamed in agony.

"Both of you, stop it!" Alex cried, and the unlit torches and fireplaces burst into flames with a loud woosh.

Aaron struggled to his feet, pointing at Gryphon. "You ruined everything! Before you, we were happy, and now, because of you, I've lost everything."

"You haven't lost anything." Alex touched his arm, but Aaron ripped it away.

"Yes, I have. I can't have my queen carrying a bastard child. I want a divorce."

"Fine," Alex replied, her voice unfamiliar, cold. Aaron didn't care that he grieved her so. What about what she'd done to him?

Alex's eyes shifted slightly as if they'd momentarily gone black, but they were green again before he could be sure. Her face went ashen, and she pleaded with him, gripping his arm. "No. You don't get to throw me aside without hearing everything I went through to get back to you. You heard me out after Moorloc's but not now? What's changed?" Tears streaked her face, but Aaron wrenched free from her grasp.

"There is nothing you could say. You're having his bastard, so we're through."

"But *our* baby—"

"There is no *our* anything. Now leave, before I do something I regret."

Alex's eyes flashed black again. This time, he was sure of it. "You'll regret this." She cracked and was gone.

CHAPTER 46

GRYPHON

Gryphon reached out to find Alex, but she was keeping him out. Sighing, he shifted his Mystics powers to find Megesti, then cracked to the lab.

As usual, Megesti sat on a stool reading a book. He hadn't heard Gryphon arrive, so Gryphon clapped his hands loudly, startling his cousin so much he fell off the back of the stool.

"*Ferflucs,* Gryphon! Why would you do that?"

"Gryphon? You're back!" came Birch's voice. She tended the fire and a cauldron with a bubbling potion in it.

All Gryphon could do was nod, knowing that as soon as he filled them in, she'd be so disappointed. Birch scanned his face, set the large wooden spoon across the top of the cauldron, and held her arms out. "Whatever it is, we'll figure it out together."

Gryphon accepted her hug, letting her Celtic magic flow into him and calm his chaotic mind. When her peacefulness filled him, he told them about Alex's arrival in Datten.

"That can't be right," Megesti said. "Aaron has a temper and has been more reckless since Alex disappeared, but he'd never throw her out."

"Gryphon!" Lynx's high-pitched shriek gave him little warning before she jumped on his back, giving him a giant hug around his neck. "How dare you arrive in Datten and not immediately come to see me! I had to hear about it from Kharon's ghosts." She slid off his back and smacked him.

Kharon and Stefan arrived behind her, standing in the doorway.

"Is it true?" Stefan asked. "Did Aaron throw Alex out of Datten because she's having your child?"

"If you did anything inappropriate to my Head, I will feed you to Cerberus myself," Lynx said.

"We performed the ceremony because we *had* to," said Gryphon. "It was the only way."

Kharon gasped. "She was pregnant."

"Clearly. That's why Aaron's lost it," Megesti said.

"No." Kharon shook their head, and Gryphon sighed, knowing someone had filled them in on the full truth, so he wouldn't have to work to convince the others.

"Alexandria was pregnant with *Aaron's* child when she left for the Forbidden Lands."

Lynx's mouth dropped open. "They would kill a mortal child. Tell me you didn't let that happen."

"Of course I didn't," Gryphon said. "That's why she's pregnant with our child—to hide Aaron's. But he never gave her the chance to explain it. He saw her belly, smelled me on her, and then he kicked her out. And I ..." Gryphon didn't want to say the rest, but he did. "Well, being the overprotective Ares that I am, I made things worse."

"No," Lynx groaned.

"What?" Stefan asked.

"When sorceresses are pregnant," Birch said, "they lose control of their powers, so the baby's father becomes protective of her. Ares males are the worst."

Kharon scoffed. "Ares sorcerers have killed someone for simply *looking* at their pregnant bonded partner. If he appeared to be a threat, Aaron's lucky to be alive."

"The point is," Gryphon said, "he yelled, and I went Ares and admitted that she was carrying my child, and he heard nothing after that."

"Where is she now?" Stefan asked.

"In Warren, I expect. She's shut me out," Gryphon said.

"I'll get Michael. She's going to need us now," Stefan said.

"What about Aaron?" Megesti asked. "He's clearly upset too."

"You stay with him," Stefan said. "Of everyone here, he's closest with you. Try to talk some sense into him before he makes a bigger fool of himself."

CHAPTER 47
ALEX

Alex cracked into her room in Warren late, but she didn't care. She needed her father to know she was alive. Heart pounding and holding back tears, she burst into Edward's adjacent meeting room. He was at his table, talking to Matthew.

"Princess!" Matthew jumped to his feet at the sight of her. Edward dropped his mug, letting it smash on the stone floor. Alex threw her arms around his chest and whimpered, trying to hold back the emotions building inside her.

"Should I leave?" Matthew asked.

"No," Alex said and hugged her father harder. Edward held her as Alex told them about her twins, and then she alternated between repeating the conversation between her and Aaron, crying on her father and apologizing for being so emotional.

When she'd told all she had to tell, Edward kissed the top of her head and barked instructions at Matthew. "Summon my advisory council. I don't care what time it is. Drag them out of bed if you have to, but get them here now."

"Daddy?"

"I'm going to take care of this, Alexandria. I promise."

"Talk some sense into him—father to father. Gryphon showed up, and they got into a fight. Aaron didn't even let me tell him about our son. I know he'll understand when he hears everything."

"I know you love him. But I've had enough of his hurting you! Go to your room, and I'll come after I've met with the counsel."

Alex crossed her arms and shifted her stance, making Edward smile.

"You're welcome to come and listen to me argue with a bunch of old nobles if you want, or you can go to your room to rest, and I'll have food sent to you."

"Fresh bread?"

Edward nodded and kissed the top of her head. Alex released him and went back to the door between their suites. She entered the room she'd shared with Aaron, finding it as dark and abandoned as she felt. *What's going to happen now? Why didn't he understand? The vision I saw on the beach ... was it wrong? Did I not say the right thing? What if my father can't talk him out of the divorce? I don't want to raise our son alone.* Alex rubbed her belly. She felt exhausted, but she needed to get out of her sorceress clothing. She headed up the stairs to her wardrobe, but none of her dresses or pants would fit over her bump. Frustrated, she grabbed a pair of Aaron's pajamas and put them on. After she dressed, she heard voices below and tiptoed down the stairs.

"He said *what*?" Michael asked.

"That's impossible," Jessica said. "He loves her."

"I was there! He wouldn't even hear her out. All he heard was that she slept in my room and he immediately went to the worst place."

"What did you expect, Gryphon?" Lynx snapped. "She's

pregnant with twins. Why didn't you lead with 'She's having your baby, and the sorcerers would've killed your child if they knew'?"

Alex stepped off the last step. "There wasn't time. The moment he saw my belly, his temper took over and he wouldn't hear anything besides whatever conclusion he'd jumped to."

Stefan took Alex into a bear hug. Michael joined in a few seconds later, slipping under Stefan's arm so that Michael clung to Alex and Stefan had to squeeze them both. Gryphon, Lynx, and Jessica stood by, waiting for the trio to separate. When they finally did, Jessica and Lynx swooped in and hugged Alex almost as tightly as Michael and Stefan had.

"Gryphon explained everything," Lynx said. "Birch and Megesti stayed back to talk some sense into Aaron."

"I'm terrified he won't listen." Alex wrapped her arms around herself and dropped onto the couch, where Jessica joined her. "He was so angry. I expected him to listen. To hear me out. How could I be so stupid?"

"Enough," Stefan said. "You may not have chosen your words very well, but Aaron is a grown man and a king. He should be able to contain his temper long enough to hear what his queen has to say."

"Stefan's right," Michael said. "For months, Aaron went on and on about how badly he missed you and how he'd do anything to have you back. Then, the moment things get complicated, he throws a fit? His behavior is childish and ridiculous."

A knock sounded on the door.

Stefan glanced at Alex for permission before ordering the person in. Julius appeared and explained Earl Veremund needed to be present for the urgent council meeting. Michael rolled his eyes at being addressed with his title, but he hugged

Alex one last time and left. Julius remained and cleared his throat.

"Yes, Julius?" Alex asked.

"I need a sorcerer, too."

"A sorcerer?" Stefan asked. "Why?"

"His Royal Highness didn't say."

"I'll go." Lynx gestured toward Stefan, saying, "Try to keep him in line," and followed Julius out of the room.

To pass the time, Alex questioned Jessica and Stefan about what had happened while she'd been away. Jessica had given birth to a little boy with fiery-red Wafner hair whom they named Jerome. Stefan regaled her with stories of all the ways they had tried to reach her in the Forbidden Lands. Their effort didn't surprise her—but the fact that none of it had worked had taken a toll on Aaron.

After what felt like too long, Alex got impatient. "What do you think my father is doing?"

"I'm not sure," Jessica said. "When Aaron's father called emergency councils, it normally meant war."

"My father would never choose war. Would he?"

Stefan sat beside her and took her hand. "I doubt he's going to war, but you said Aaron demanded a divorce, right?"

Alex nodded.

"What if he's planning to give it to him?" Stefan asked.

Alex sat up sharply and grabbed her belly. "No. He knows I still love him. He wouldn't take Aaron from me, not after he lost my mother."

"He might if he fears for yours and the baby's safety," Jessica said.

Alex stood. "I need to speak to my father. I have to make sure he doesn't do anything I'll regret."

The door swung open, and Michael stepped in, securing it behind him.

"What is it?" Stefan asked.

Michael handed him a parchment. "I'm here to get your signature, Alex. After everything Aaron has put you through the last year, your father wants to be prepared. As a last resort, he'll give Aaron his divorce. The council agreed to accept his child as the official heir to Warren ... even if you go through with the divorce."

"No."

"Most of the council is livid that he wouldn't hear you out, and they're tired of his immature behavior. We could have used Randal or any Nial. It was only Bernhard and I defending Aaron," Michael said. "Gryphon, I need you to take Guinevere home. She's cutting her visit with her brother short in order to help Aaron understand the situation. Obviously she's on your side."

Michael turned back to Alex and held the parchment to her.

"No!" Alex shouted once more. She cracked to the throne room, where Edward spoke with Harold and a few of his council members. Curiously, the Bishops and Strobels were missing. She strode up to face her father.

"You can't accept this divorce! I won't allow it. I didn't fight to come home so you could let me lose him over a misunderstanding."

"Excuse us, gentlemen." Edward dismissed his council and took Alex's hands in his. "I understand you're upset right now, but we need to be prepared for the worst. You'll thank me one day."

Alex pulled away from her father, silently pleading with Harold to help. "Why would I thank you for allowing my child's father to abandon him?"

Harold looked grim. "We are all too aware that sometimes no father is a better option."

Alex waited for Harold to say something more, or even apologize. "Harold, you cannot mean that," she whispered, but the Betruger King did not reply. Alex huffed at her father. "Aaron isn't Arthur."

"Not yet." Edward held Alex in front of him, making her listen. "I know you love him Alexandria, but sometimes love isn't enough."

"Would you do this if Emmerich were still alive?" Alex whispered.

"If Emmerich were here, I wouldn't have to. He'd never have allowed things to get to this point." The door opened, and Michael arrived with Stefan, Jessica, and Gryphon a few steps behind him. "Michael, very good. You have her signature?"

"Almost." Michael held the parchment out, positioning himself between her and her father. A very convincing forgery of her signature appeared on the petition. Michael merely winked, rolled up the decree, and presented the paper to Edward.

"Thank you, Michael." Edward took the parchment and handed it to Harold. "Sir Stefan and Lady Jessica, you both live in Warren but are still Wafners. Regardless of what happens when we return from Datten, you have my permission to travel between the kingdoms. I won't ask you to abandon your father, or to leave Warren and Alex. But for now, you will need to decide which royal you'll serve, should it come down to that."

Stefan stepped beside Alex. "I'm not leaving Alex."

"Neither am I," Jessica said. She moved beside Michael and took his hand.

"I hoped that would be your choice. I'd like you to accompany Harold, Gryphon, and me to Datten. You know better than anyone where to find Alex's things so I will have you collect them from her suite while I speak to Aaron to resolve this. I was hoping you'd want the babies born in Warren."

The room began to spin, and Alex grabbed her father's hand to still it. "This is happening too fast."

Edward caressed her cheek. "I know, but I want him to see how seriously I am taking this. Hopefully, it'll bring him to his senses."

"Can't we just wait until morning so tempers can calm down?"

"I'm sorry, dear, but no."

"Promise me you'll do everything you can to make him listen. And bring him back to me."

Edward kissed Alex's cheek. "I give you my word as your father and king, that I will do everything I can to resolve the trouble between you and Aaron."

"And if he regrets his actions?" Alex asked.

"Then I'll bring him back to you and you'll have your wish."

CHAPTER 48

AARON

*I can't look back at her. I can't stop, because if I do, I'll give in
and forgive her, hear her out, and there is nothing she can say
that will fix this. Nothing will fix the betrayal of her being
with him—the thing I feared most since the moment I laid my eyes
on him.*

Aaron turned and punched the suit of armor in the hallway, sending it clanging across the floor. Shaking his bloody
fist, he stormed toward the back door and escaped into the
freezing evening air of the deserted courtyard. Aaron interlocked his fingers behind his head, covering his ears with his
elbows. He couldn't drown out Alex's voice in his mind.

"What did you do?"

Aaron spun to find Megesti staring at him. Ignoring the
cold, his friend took a tentative step toward him.

"Megesti, I'm not in the mood."

"I don't care. Someone has to knock some sense into you
and your father's not here to do it. You're making a terrible
mistake. Alex isn't perfect. She's never claimed to be, but this
isn't what you think it is."

"How can it not be?" Aaron threw his hands in the air. "She admitted to sleeping in his bed. She's carrying his child! There is no other way to take that."

Megesti waited for Aaron to stop shouting before he continued. "Sorcerers are more complicated than that."

"Megesti, I know you mean well, but I can't talk about this right now. I just need to—"

"What? Clear your head? Because that always worked so well for you in the past."

Aaron growled and marched back to Megesti. "Fine. Say whatever it is she told you to say—whatever lie you've been told to whisper into my ear."

Megesti scowled. "I'd never lie to you. But more importantly, I'd never lie for anyone. If you don't want to hear the *truth,* then let it be on your head. Just know that what you think is true isn't, and that you probably ruined the best thing you ever had in your life."

Aaron scoffed and crossed his arms. "Is that all? Can I go now?"

Megesti glared at him. "One more thing, Your Royal Highness." Megesti's voice was thick with disdain. "I resign as your royal sorcerer, effective immediately."

"What?" Aaron's pounding heart stopped.

"If you go through with sending her away, I'll be moving to Warren, to be with my cousin."

"Megesti, don't be rash."

"Unlike you, I don't have a ballroom of relatives. All I have left of my father is Alex, and I choose her. Goodbye, Aaron," Megesti said and vanished.

Aaron stood there for a moment letting the empty space sink into his soul until he heard Jerome arriving with Guinevere and Bernhard. He turned to them. *He can't be serious. He's lived here his entire life.*

"We need to speak with you, Aaron," Jerome said.

"What is wrong with you, boy?" Bernhard said, smacking Aaron upside the head.

"Ow!"

"I leave you for a few weeks, and you go to war with Warren?" Guinevere said.

"I'm not going to war with anyone!" Aaron snapped.

"That's not what Edward thinks," Bernhard said. "He called an emergency council meeting today to discuss your demand for a divorce."

"How could you demand a divorce from your queen?" Jerome said. "Honor above all, Aaron. Datten kings do not leave their wives. You know our history better than that."

"They would when that wife is carrying another man's child."

"Idiot boy," Guinevere snapped and smacked Aaron. "You spent so much time reading the Kings' journals and the generals, but you never read the queens. We spent centuries at war. Several queens were taken during war and returned with a child who wouldn't be a prince. Some of our highest-ranking families came from those 'bastard children,' as you called them."

"Such as?"

"The Rassgats," Bernhard said. Aaron rolled his eyes. *That's exactly my point.*

"That's a terrible example," Jerome said. "Although Aaron is acting just like a Rassgat at the moment. The Averys are a better example. Over six hundred years ago."

"Caleb's family?" Aaron asked, and his general nodded. "What did Edward say in the meeting?"

"He called King Harold of the Betruger and swore us all to secrecy on risk of treason, which I'm breaking to warn you,"

Bernhard said. "Edward's accepting your demands, and the Betruger will side with Warren."

"That's impossible!" Aaron said.

"It's actually not," came a voice. Aaron and his group turned to see Edward standing at the courtyard doorway with Stefan, Jessica, and Gryphon.

Seeing Gryphon made Aaron's blood boil. "You brought *him* here to talk to me? Not a great start for a peaceful resolution, Edward."

Jerome placed his hand on Aaron's shoulder to calm him, but Aaron shoved it off and marched toward Gryphon.

"Stefan. Jessica," Edward barked. "See to your duty."

"Yes, Your Royal Highness." Both Wafners hesitated before they bowed quickly and went inside.

"Edward, where are they going?" Guinevere asked.

"To fetch my daughter's things. Gryphon?"

Gryphon snapped his fingers, and a parchment appeared in one hand and a quill in the other.

"All I require from you, Aaron, is your signature, and you'll have exactly what you asked for—your freedom from my daughter."

Bernhard stepped in front of him. "What other consequences will that freedom bring?"

"For you, Bernhard, banishment. You seem to misunderstand what a secret counsel means. Cameron will be made Earl upon my return, and should you return to Warren, you'll be charged with treason against the crown and thrown in the dungeon."

"Edward, stop this. Please."

"I'm sorry, Guinevere. You'll still be allowed to see your nephew and sister-in-law, assuming Elfrieda choses to stay with her son. If she moves to Datten, she'll be allowed to return also to visit Cameron. I'll also allow your children to leave and visit you, Jerome. I won't take your family away from you after you just got them back."

"And me?" Aaron asked, crossing his arms at Edward.

"If you ever set foot in my kingdom, the first time, I'll have you dragged back to your mother. The second time, I'll take it as an act of war. Now, sign the paper."

Aaron took the parchment from Gryphon and unrolled it. At the bottom was Alex's signature. *She actually signed it? Why would she sign it if this were a big misunderstanding? Could she have been forced to sign it?*

"And if I refuse?" he asked.

"It doesn't matter. Warren's counsel has already declared Alex's marriage over and has accepted her child as the rightful heir to Warren when I die. Gryphon, go help Jessica and Stefan."

The king sneered and motioned his head toward the castle, and Gryphon cracked away.

"They're letting Gryphon's son rule? Good luck." Jerome grabbed a shield from a nearby barrel and held it up for Aaron. Aaron slapped the parchment onto it and gripped the quill.

"Not Gryphon's," Bernhard said, rubbing his forehead hard enough to leave red marks. "Aaron's."

Aaron froze. "Mine?"

"My daughter's having twins," Edward announced, and Aaron's throat went dry.

"That's what Alex was trying to tell you before you threw her out," Bernhard said. "She was pregnant when you all left to retrieve Edward. She performed some sorcerer spell and conceived a second child with Gryphon to hide yours from the sorcerers. To protect him."

"No. She would have told me," Aaron said.

"She tried to," Edward snapped. "But as usual, you weren't

interested in what she had to say and instead let your anger get the better of you. Now sign the paper."

"No," Aaron said. "I need to speak with her to see if this is true."

"You had your chance for that," Edward growled. "Now, you can sign the divorce and we'll end our truce on amicable terms, or you can refuse. But know if you do, Harold and I will take it as a declaration of war from Datten. The Betruger listen to their wives, and Edith is appalled at your behavior. And unlike you, Harold respects his wife. His loyalty lies with Warren."

Aaron swallowed hard, feeling his heart break. Jerome leaned down. "We aren't prepared for war on two fronts at this moment. You need to sign it."

Aaron turned to Guinevere. "Mother?"

"You brought this on yourself. Now you have to remember the oath you took when you became king, and do what's best for Datten, regardless of what you feel. Sign the paper."

Aaron squeezed the quill and scribbled on the parchment.

Bernhard took it and walked it across the field to Edward.

"You made the right choice, Aaron. We'll be leaving now."

"Edward, wait," Aaron's voice wavered. "Tell her I'm sorry ... that I love her and will do anything I can to fix this."

"No," Edward said, standing taller. "I'm going to tell her you said she disgusts you, and you want nothing to do with her. That even after I informed you of why she did what she did, you want nothing to do with either baby. I have no intention of allowing my daughter to hold out *any* hope that you'll come back and disrespect her again. I intend to have her remarried by the end of the month—to a proper man this time. I won't have my grandson growing up without a father. But you are dead to us."

Edward turned around and vanished into the castle. Aaron

broke out into a run and chased after him, but when he reached the hall, Edward was gone.

He went straight to his suite, finding it in shambles and half the room stripped bare. All of Alex's books were gone. So were her clothes, her favorite blanket from the couch, the bow that she kept in their room despite him telling her not to, and a painting of her mother.

Aaron fell to his knees. "What have I done?"

CHAPTER 49
ALEX

Alex lay on her bed, curled into a ball. Edith perched beside her, gently rubbing her back.

"I'm sure everything will work out," Edith whispered.

Michael paced the room. "Your father will talk some sense into Aaron."

Alex heard footsteps from the main floor. Despite her emotional state, she clambered from her bed and hurried downstairs. Her stomach sank when she saw Stefan and Jessica holding her books and dresses. A knock at the door brought Edward into the room. His stoic expression gave nothing away.

He addressed the others. "Excuse us. I need to speak to my daughter privately."

Her friends had barely made it out the door when Alex sank to her knees and sobbed. "No. Tell me it's not true. Tell me he didn't sign it."

Edward kneeled and gently held her face in his hands. "I'm

so sorry, Alexandria. I did everything I could, but he refused to hear any of it."

Alex shook her head at her father. "No."

"He doesn't care about the babies—Gryphon's or his own. He wants nothing to do with them, or you. It's over."

"He can't mean that."

"I'm so sorry, Alexandria." Edward wrapped his arms around her. "I wish I could have convinced him, but you're strong and I know you'll get through this, if not for yourself, then for your children."

Alex cried so hard she shook in her father's arms. After a few minutes, her sobs settled to sniffles, and after another minute, she looked up at her father. "I'd like to be alone, please."

"Of course." Edward kissed the top of her head and crossed the room to the door. He paused, his hand hovering over the handle. "I know it seems too soon, but we'll need to discuss a new husband for you. The people of Warren will need their future king to have a father."

"I understand."

"I'll draw up a list for you to review."

Alex nodded reluctantly, and her father departed. As soon as he was gone, Alex stood from the couch and ripped the necklace Aaron had gifted her for their wedding off her neck. Hot blood ran down her shoulders and chest where the chain snapped and cut her. She couldn't face anyone after what her father had told her. She cracked to the Verlassen Castle, retreating into her mother's lab. The darkness enveloped her until the flames on the ceiling came to life.

Alex stalked down the hallway that led to the larger workspace. Daniel waited for her. She slowed her pace and approached the ghost of the man she'd planned to name her son after.

"Please go," she whispered.

"I'm so sorry, Alex. I wish I could stop him from breaking your heart."

"I can't. Not right now. You look too much like him."

Daniel opened his mouth but closed it. "I'll try to get Kharon to let me talk to him. Convince him he's made a mistake."

"Don't," Alex shook her head and moved her hand to her stomach. "If he doesn't want us, then I'm done."

"He's just upset."

"I know, but I deserve better. Our son deserves better."

Daniel lowered his head, nodded once, and vanished. Alex put her hand on the table for support and breathed deeply, trying to hold back the onslaught of sobs trying to free themselves.

"Dry those tears, little one."

In the mirror, she could see a figure standing behind her, but when she turned, no one was there. The pale face reflected back was hers, but the eyes weren't. She froze, but her reflection reached up to touch her face and Alex jumped back.

"You know who I am, so don't act so frightened."

Alex returned to the mirror. Her face morphed. Her cheeks filled out, her emerald green eyes darkened until they were black, and her brown locks became an iridescent silver. Her expression contorted into a twisted, murderous grin.

"You're just a voice in my head."

"Not anymore. Hello, Alexandria."

"Go away."

"I can't. I'm your fury."

"Which one are you?"

Her smile grew. "I see you've been talking to Kharon. My name is Alecto. I am the goddess of vengeance, dear, and I'm here to set you free."

Alex scoffed. "You don't want to help me. You just want to use me. You want to be set free so you can kill everyone I love."

"Not everyone. Only everyone who's ever wronged you."

"No. I will never let you out."

"That will only work for so long."

"Gryphon and I found Merlin's books. We'll figure out how to keep you in there."

"Then why come here, if not to free me? Why did you flee from your loved ones?"

Alex felt sheepish. "I wanted to see my mother."

"She's not coming, little one. You're a disappointment to her. The only hope you have of making a parent proud is to marry whichever stupid mortal your father chooses for you so he can raise your mortal babe. Come to your senses and stop fighting me, because you've been betrayed by the man you love, and now I shall be freed."

CHAPTER 50
AARON

Aaron stood in the queen's suite, holding the gold training shirt they'd left behind. It had taken him hours to figure out just how much Stefan and Jessica had taken. Between the two of them, they knew every little thing Alex valued. Seeing the crib he'd used as a baby, and knowing his own would never sleep in it, broke Aaron's heart.

It's my fault. I let my temper get the best of me because of those idiotic Rassgats, after all the times I swore I'd never hurt her again. If our child is anything like the Strobel side of the family, he should grow up in Warren, away from me and Datten's influences.

A breeze ruffled his clothing, and he expected his mother ready to lecture him—but she wasn't there. His room was equally empty. Another icy breeze hit him, and Aaron followed it to the desk he shared with Alex. He opened the drawer and found a letter with his name on it. He recognized Jessica's handwriting, so he pocketed it. Another drawer rattled. Inside lay Alex's queen's journal. Aaron took it too and slammed the drawer shut.

Ridiculous. I'm worried she's going to catch me reading her journal, and she's in Warren.

Aaron opened the letter from Jessica, then rubbed the back of his neck as he read it. He was right—she had a few things to say that he didn't want to hear.

YOU SPOILED, *stuck-up, royal.*

WHAT WERE YOU THINKING? *How dare you accuse Alex of infidelity! She spent months in the Forbidden Lands working day and night to get home to you. Did that require her to do something extreme to protect herself and your child? Yes. Does that give any of us the right to judge her? NO! We can barely manage the few sorcerers we've encountered. I can't imagine what being surrounded by them was like, but unlike you, I will hear the entire story from her when she has the strength to tell it.*

You hurt her so much, I don't think she'll ever recover from this. Michael told us what the council decided about you not being allowed in Warren. Frankly, it's a blessing for you because Stefan is furious with you and will make you pay for this the moment he gets his hands on you. Megesti and Gryphon will do far worse.

I grew up with you and never thought you capable of such cruelty. I'm ashamed to say you were my friend, and if my father weren't in Datten, I would never set foot in that kingdom again.

JESSICA

AARON DROPPED the letter back on the table and took the journal to his seat. He opened it to the last page and found exactly what Gryphon had told him. Alex had confessed to finding out she was pregnant, even having it confirmed by their royal physician, and was waiting for the right time to tell Aaron the exciting news. He remembered the night she fell asleep on the couch across from him and he'd brought her to their bed. She'd had something important to tell him. *Why didn't you just tell me? It would have saved us all so much trouble.*

Aaron leaned back and watched the fire crackle.

"What do I do? Alex needed me to listen to her, but Edward made it clear she would never know."

Aaron hurried to his desk and scribbled out three almost identical letters.

I NEED YOUR HELP. Edward is lying.

I begged to be allowed to speak to her and make things right, but he refused and said he'd tell her I wanted nothing to do with her. I am coming to Warren. I need you to help me see Alex and make things right with her.

Please, I just need a chance to fix this. She is my queen and has my heart. I accept the mistake I made, but I need to make it right.

HE ADDRESSED THEM TO JESSICA, Harold, and Megesti and sealed each parchment. Hunter was on duty, and Aaron ordered him to summon Lucas and Caleb. Running up the stairs, he threw open his wardrobe and tossed his warmer Betruger clothes into a pile on the bed.

When they arrived, he let them in. "Lucas, I need you to send these letters, but send Jessica's to the Veremund estate, Harold's to the Nial estate, and Megesti's to the castle."

"Are you sure? It might take a while for Harold and Jessica to get theirs," Lucas said.

"Late is better than not at all. Edward isn't just angry with me—he's trying to take our queen from us."

"What?"

"Alexandria loves it here. She loves you!" Caleb said. "Why would he do that?"

"Because," Aaron said, laying a hand on Caleb's shoulder, "I lost my temper and Edward is finished forgiving me."

"How can we help?" Hunter asked.

Aaron could rely on his friends to help him when everyone else had abandoned him. *No, the others didn't abandon you— they stood by Alex. But with Edward outright lying to her, they're my only hope of getting to see her.*

"Lucas, you'll send the letters. Then you and Hunter will stay here. Your task is to keep Jerome, my mother, and Bernhard from learning what I am up to for as long as possible.

"And what is it you're up to?" Caleb asked.

"Get your riding clothes, Caleb. We're going to Warren to get my wife back."

CHAPTER 51
GRYPHON

Gryphon paced in front of the fire in Alex's suite.

"You're making me dizzy," Lynx said. "Sit down." She pulled Gryphon onto the couch beside her.

"I can't help it. I can't sit still. She hasn't moved in three days!"

"This is nothing," Michael said.

"When she's really being stubborn, she can easily go a week," Stefan said.

"This is different," Jessica said. "She's with child—no, children. She has to take care of herself. If not for her own sake, then for theirs."

Edith stood and flattened her skirts. "Gryphon, bring some apple cider and bread for her, please."

"What are you going to do?" Harold asked.

Edith moved from her husband to Michael. "Michael and I are going to have a conversation with our Warren."

"Michael, check on that fury too?" Gryphon asked. "I

"

expected it to come tearing out of her as soon as this happened, but it hasn't."

"Maybe one of the spells you tried in the Forbidden Lands worked," Lynx said.

"I'm not that lucky," Gryphon replied. "It's more likely she's toying with us."

Michael nodded and followed Edith up the stairs. Gryphon retrieved the food and immediately resumed pacing, being careful to stay out of Lynx's reach. After some time, he heard footsteps and Michael appeared on the stairs again.

"What happened?" Gryphon asked, but Michael held a finger to his lips.

"The fury's in there," he whispered. "It hasn't changed from what I can tell." A minute later, there were more footsteps, and Alex stepped off the last step with Edith in tow.

"I'm up. You can all leave now," Alex said.

"We already told you, no one is going to leave you alone," Michael said.

"I'm not a danger to myself," Alex snapped.

Gryphon crossed the room to her. "No one thought you were."

"Liar," Alex replied. "You are convinced the fury is going to come out and murder everyone."

"We're worried because we care," Harold said.

And Lynx added. "And we don't want you to feel alone right now."

"I am alone. The man I gave everything to didn't even have the honor to listen to me."

"We're here for you," Jessica said.

"Until Michael abandons you and little Jerome, you do not have the right to say that to me." Alex snapped her head toward Stefan and locked eyes with him. "Are we done here?"

"They are, but we aren't." Stefan nodded his head toward Gryphon.

Alex huffed and clenched her fists at her sides. The concerned faces of her friends only reminded her how alone she truly was. "You heard Stefan. You're all done now."

"Alex—" they began but she cut them off.

"Get out!"

Harold rubbed Edith's shoulders and led her to the door. Michael kissed Jessica's temple, making Alex growl. Lynx nodded at Gryphon and Stefan and closed the door behind her, leaving Gryphon alone with Alex and Stefan.

"If you're going to lecture me then get it over with so I can go back to bed."

Stefan crossed the room and hugged Alex. Her shocked expression would have made Gryphon laugh had he not been so worried about her.

"Stefan ..."

"Because I love you, and I'm terrified for you. We all are." The emotion dripped off Stefan's every word. In the past, it might have made Gryphon roll his eyes, but whether he liked it or not, these mortals had taught him his emotions weren't the enemy.

"Not everyone."

"Everyone who matters," Stefan replied. "And Gryphon more than anyone."

"More than you?" Alex asked.

Stefan pressed his forehead to Alex's. "You're carrying his child along with Aaron's, but he's not your husband, so he doesn't have the same claim to you that Aaron does ... did."

Alex peeked around Stefan at Gryphon. Her face was stoic when she held her hand out. Still, he placed his hand into hers, letting her guide it to rest on the right side of her bump.

"Our baby is fine," she said.

"You know which sides they're on?" Gryphon asked.

Alex nodded. "Yours kicks Aaron's."

Alex held her hand out to Stefan, but he shook his head. "I've felt a baby move before. Jessica let me."

Alex thrust her hand at Stefan, and when he obliged, Alex put his hand on the other side of her belly. "I may not have Aaron," she said, "but I have you both, and the rest of our family. I'll try to remember that."

"You can still grieve for what you lost," Gryphon said. "It's never easy when you expect your life to go one way and it goes in another direction."

"I know. It's what you do with that change that shows your true character," Alex whispered.

"Who told you that?" Stefan asked.

"Emmerich."

Alex's stomach gurgled loudly, breaking the silence that hung between them.

Gryphon smiled. "Are we hungry?"

"I suppose if I'm up anyway, I should eat."

"Dining hall it is," Stefan said, holding his arm out to Alex.

"I have one request for you both," Alex said. "Well, two for you, Gryphon."

"Anything," Gryphon said.

"I want my grandfather's journals to see if there are any more spells to strengthen me against the fury. I can't say for sure why she isn't in control of me yet, but I'm hoping something we did there worked, so I can do it again."

"Journals?" Stefan asked.

"I'll explain later," Gryphon said.

"Second, my father intends to have me remarry as soon as possible. I want you both to ensure whoever I marry will fall in line and behave accordingly."

"Behave accordingly?" Gryphon asked.

"I don't care that Aaron signed divorce papers. So long as he breathes, I consider myself his wife. I won't be with anyone else."

"Understood," Stefan said.

CHAPTER 52
ALEX

"What's wrong with Prince Jessie?" Edward asked.

"He's a pig. I won't have him around my son."

"Alexandria, you are being purposefully difficult. I've given you a dozen qualified men, and you've rejected them all."

"That's because you have terrible taste in men."

Edward narrowed his eyes at Alex and then sighed.

"Say it," Alex spat through her teeth. "I dare you."

Edward stood up, slapping the table. "If you think my taste is terrible, then you can bring me a name."

"Fine." Alex sat back in the chair and crossed her arms.

"Tomorrow."

"But that's too soon!"

"I said I wanted you married as quickly as possible."

"And I'm trying to give Aaron time to change his mind."

"You have a day, or else I'll choose for you." Edward walked around the table and kissed the top of Alex's head. "I know this is hard for you, but you need to appear strong for our people, and they will want their crown prince to have a father."

"I am strong," Alex groaned. "But I won't choose a man with no honor to be my son's father."

Edward bent down and hugged her. "I understand, but Aaron made himself very clear to me, so we have to accept that and move on. Clearly honor isn't everything." Edward released her and went to open the library door for her.

Stefan waited in the hallway. "Ready to go back to your suite?"

Alex nodded and left the library to follow Stefan. Michael and Jessica were settled onto the couch, waiting for them.

"Jessica, you should be with your baby, not here picking up my mess," Alex said as she sat across from them.

"Lady Bishop is watching him. Between her, Cameron's mother, and Edith's mother, I never have to worry about having help."

"The noblewomen of Warren love babies," Michael said.

Lynx cracked in beside Stefan and thrust a mug toward Alex. "I have your tonic from Birch." Stefan backed away slightly and covered his nose.

"Tell Birch thank you for me." Alex downed the mug's contents in three gulps. "It tastes less like dirt today."

"Gryphon told her you enjoy peppermint," Lynx said.

Alex groaned up at the ceiling, updating them on her meeting with her father and her rejected potential husbands.

"Have you considered Gryphon?" Jessica asked. "He is the other baby's father."

"No," Alex said flatly, taking another drink.

"No, you haven't considered him, or no, you won't marry him?" Michael asked.

"Can you imagine Gryphon dressed in royal attire attending the events I have to go to?"

Lynx burst into laughter. "Alex is right. Gryphon would never want to be a mortal king, and … he doesn't want to be the second choice."

"I complained so much, Father has given me until tomorrow to find a man I approve of."

"And if you don't?" Stefan asked.

"He'll pick one," Alex whispered.

Michael coughed, almost choking on air. "But that's too soon. We haven't even had time to talk to Aaron and try to get him to change his mind."

"Father doesn't care. I need to be married for the good of my twins and Warren."

A knock at the door drew Stefan's attention.

Alex's hands ached—she'd been absently clutching her mug. She set it on the side table and smoothed the velvet material of her skirt. When she heard a familiar voice speaking with Michael, it dawned on her.

"Cameron," Alex whispered.

The young Earl turned away from Michael to greet her. "Evening, Princess. I trust you're feeling well."

"Cameron," Alex repeated, gesturing toward the blonde-haired royal.

Jessica mouthed his name at Alex, but then raised her eyebrows, understanding. "Cameron! Come sit with us."

Cameron had apparently come to speak with Michael. Wild animals were scaring his horses at night, and he wanted to know if they were also a nuisance on the Veremund grounds. But soon, he sat on the couches with them, learning of Alex's predicament with Edward.

"So you need to find a husband by tomorrow or else you'll be forced to marry one of the southern kingdom royals?" Cameron asked.

Alex nodded, but Stefan spoke up for her. "Correct."

"And they are truly terrible," Jessica added.

"If only there were a Warren nobleman who would fit the requirements," Michael said, elbowing Cameron so hard, the poor earl turned crimson.

"Everyone outm" Alex ordered, standing suddenly. "I want a minute alone to speak with Cameron, please."

Holding her breath as the others left the room, Alex locked her fingers together and turned toward Cameron.

He'd risen too and gently broke the silence. "You appear to be in quite the predicament."

"It would appear so."

"Anything I can do to help?"

"Cameron." Alex had once envisioned a future with Cameron. He was kind, funny, and cared for her, but after Aaron had revealed his love, their spark had faded. He took her hands in his, and she pulled away. "I can't ask you to do this."

"And if I offer?"

Alex smiled weakly. "You realize you'd be giving up your chance to find love. That you'd be tied to a princess who loves ... someone else ... who couldn't give you children because of how sorcerer bonds work."

Cameron extended his hand, an invitation. "I care about you and Warren too much to let some idiot southern prince try to ruin what we've worked centuries to build. Besides, I don't trust anyone else to raise my cousin's son. He'll be a quarter Strobel, after all."

Alex's cheek heated when she said, "You should also know that despite the divorce, I still feel as if I'm married to Aaron. I can't ..."

"And I wouldn't ask you to. I truly hope Aaron will come to his senses eventually, and if he does ... I'll step aside. But only if that's *your* wish, not his."

Alex took his hand, stood on her tiptoes, and kissed Cameron's cheek. "Then I accept."

Cameron nodded. "I will go speak to your father."

"He told me to bring him a name," Alex said.

"Yes, but Warren nobles expect the man or woman asking for your hand to go to your parents." He squeezed her hands. "Will I still get to work with my horses?"

"Absolutely," Alex said. "My father is young and healthy. I'm sure Daniel and I will handle the royal duties when the time comes."

Cameron's eyes widened for a moment, then he smiled. "Daniel is the perfect name." He went to open the door and jumped back. All of Alex's friends were standing in front of her door, obviously listening.

Alex shrugged. "And you'll need to get used to that."

Cameron grinned. "If you'll all excuse me, I have to speak to Edward." He squeezed between Michael and Stefan and headed down the hallway.

Jessica took Alex's hands. "What did Cameron say?"

"He said yes. He doesn't trust anyone outside of Warren to do the job, and he doesn't want anyone outside of their families raising Aaron's son."

"Good," Stefan said. "He's already afraid of me."

CHAPTER 53
AARON

"Do we have to ride so hard?" Caleb groaned.

"Weren't you the one who said you'd do anything to help me get Alex back?" Aaron asked.

"I did, but we've been riding for hours. I'm exhausted."

"You've ridden much harder than this, so stop complaining," Aaron ordered.

Caleb readjusted his saddle. "It's been forever since we had to ride to Warren. Why didn't you ask Megesti to take us?"

Aaron pushed Thunder on. "Because he went to Warren to be with Alex."

"How could he pick her? He's been in Datten his whole life."

"Simple. Alex is the last connection he has with his father."

"They never seemed close. I would have expected him to stick with you."

"Megesti is a private person. He interacted with Alex every day, but since he's not watched the way I am, no one noticed it outside of myself, Stefan, and Gryphon. And they only noticed because they spend their days watching Alex."

The pair carried on down the deserted Dark Forest trail in silence. Even the woodland creatures knew to stay out of their way as their horses raced for Warren. Once they'd gone as far as the light allowed, they found a clearing to make camp. Caleb set up a fire and prepared their food and sleeping mats while Aaron fed and watered their horses and ensured they were tied securely. The two settled around a small fire to warm the sausages the kitchen maids had packed for them.

"What are you thinking?" Aaron asked. "You're never this quiet."

Caleb's green eyes fixed on Aaron. He took another bite of his venison sausage.

Aaron groaned. "Caleb, I can order you if it's easier."

Caleb chewed for a long while. When he finally spoke, his voice was so soft Aaron barely heard him. "Are the rumors true?"

"Rumors?"

"That you said terrible things to Alex, accused her of infidelity, and ordered her to leave us?"

Aaron rubbed his neck and pursed his lips at his old friend. "I did. I was furious about what the Rassgats did to your family, and Alex arrived minutes after they left. I acted like a petty Datten king, rather than her husband."

"Aaron, that's horrible." Caleb's face twisted into disgust.

"I never claimed to be perfect, Caleb. Being a king doesn't make me infallible. But it does mean that I admit my mistakes and fix them."

"What if they don't let you see her?"

"Then we try again. I'll try a hundred times if I have to."

Caleb nodded. "That's a plan I can get behind. We need our queen. She's the only thing keeping our king in line."

Aaron threw a piece of bread at Caleb, and they chuckled.

Once their bellies were full, they settled down on their mats and watched the stars as they fell asleep.

CHAPTER 54

GRYPHON

Gryphon floated another stack of Merlin's journals to review beside him and walked down the empty hallway. Alex was safe in Warren, under the watch of Michael and Stefan, and they could use a few days apart. She deserved a day or two of normalcy before they worried about the fury, the Forbidden Lands, Eris ... they had a lot of magical problems that needed to be handled.

Unfortunately, tonight would be anything but normal. *She's barely home, and he's marrying her off again. Why is this kingdom so fixated on Alex being married?*

As Gryphon left the stairwell that led to his room in the Verlassen Castle, an icy chill ran through him. He stopped, expecting to see Daniel or even Victoria, but there was no one. *Don't be paranoid.* He shrugged it off and went into his room.

The aroma of damp earth filled his nostrils. *Why does it smell like the Tiere forest in here?* Gryphon waved his hand, and the journals following him dropped onto his table.

He crossed the room, glancing around suspiciously. "Who did this? I don't know how you have broken all the protection spells, but I swear, if you hurt a hair on Alex's head, I will set you on—"

Something out of place stopped Gryphon. A bundle on his pillow, brown, but not of the Tiere line. As he crept toward it, he shivered. The cursed icy chill returned. He unwrapped the box slowly, dread growing. As soon as it was open, it fell from his hands onto his bed cover. Six blood-drenched falcon feathers spilled out.

One for each of us. Fenrir was declaring war on the Head, Heart, and their sorcerer friends. *He must have hit his head harder than I thought.* He decided then and there that Alex didn't need to know about this. She had enough to worry about in Warren. He would have to set things straight on his own.

Pinching the bridge of his nose, he cracked to the giant oak tree in the Tiere territory. The setting sun set off an eerie dark shadow in the woods around him, but the giant oak tree gave off a faint green glow that matched the Tiere line color. Without any hesitation, Gryphon told all the animals within earshot to bring Fenrir to him or else he'd burn the forest to the ground. Without a squeak, croak, or caw, the creatures took off to find him.

It wasn't long before he heard a growl in the woods behind him. Gryphon peered through the dense trees and spotted a wolf. "I'm not in the mood for your games," he told it.

The wolf cocked its head and vanished in a puff of green smoke. Fenrir stepped out of the trees toward Gryphon. "I see you found my little gift."

Gryphon threw the feathers to the ground. "I think you mean *threat.* I don't like being threatened, especially not by an ancient has-been."

"I'd suggest you watch your tongue and respect your elders, you insolent brat. Just because you're the Head—" A smirk appeared on Fenrir's face. "Oh, that's right. You're not. Just because you're the *Heart* doesn't mean you can ignore all the titans."

"Now that the spell is broken, you should realize that your daughter is once again our Titan of Tiere. The same goes for Birch, Megesti, and Kharon. My father may have had issues with them, but Alex and I do not. Now, what do you want?"

"Your place is with us, not fixing some petty mortal squabbles. When the Head and Heart are absent, things smell dangerous. You and Alexandria failed to kill those who disagree with you, and that leaves an opening for those who want to make a grab for your power."

"You mean like you and my hexa."

"Of course not, my Heart. But if your thrones remain unoccupied, you realize that someone might very well sit in them and try to seize control."

"Well, you can take a message back to that someone for me," Gryphon said, closing the space between him and Fenrir. "If I learn anyone tried to take Alex's throne, I will burn them to ash, and before you make a comment on my position as Heart, you'd do well to remember that I am the only Ares in history who has been visited by our founder."

Fenrir didn't flinch. "And you'd do well to remember, young one, that I'm not afraid of a dead god. Take those feathers as the warning they are. If you do not take control of your sorcerers, then you will lose those you hold dear to someone who cares enough to be here. I'd suggest you take some advice from your Head about leading your kind."

"And I suggest you take your threats back to my hexa and tell her if I hear the slightest whisper that she's trying to take my place, I'll make sure it's the last anyone hears about her. She is only alive because I was too preoccupied with Alex's pregnancy to deal with her—an oversight I will not hesitate to correct."

"And what of my daughter?"

"What about her?"

"You let her throw her life away on that useless mortal."

"I 'let' Lynx decide for herself who she gave her heart to. Whom she picked didn't matter to me so long as he was worthy of her love and treated her better than you ever did." A snarl left Fenrir, but Gryphon ignored it. "You never hit her, but you broke her spirit all the same, and she deserves so much better than you. Now she has a family who cherishes her. It's their love that enabled her to become even more powerful than before."

"Your hexa will be most disappointed that you won't return home."

"My place is with our Head, and you know it. As long as she carries my child, I will not leave her side, and anyone who tries to get between us or force me back to the Forbidden Lands will learn just how possessive and protective an Ares Heart is."

"And the other one? The mortal bastard she carries?"

"He will be my son's brother. As I made clear already, I will ensure *both* of Alex's children are protected."

"You're a pathetic excuse for an Ares," Fenrir said, straightening his robe.

"I'd rather be a terrible Ares than a terrible father."

Gryphon cracked away.

CHAPTER 55
ALEX

Alex tugged on her dress to fan herself in the humid air, but her fitted Warren gown made it nearly impossible. Unlike her Datten dresses, this one was poofy and stuck out around her legs, making her sweat like a pot over a fire. She'd argued with her father about the style but finally relented, telling him she didn't care. "If I am marrying a man I don't love, what does it matter what I wear?"

He'd moved to take her hand, but Alex had ripped away from him and stormed off. Now she stood alone on her balcony looking over the sea, waiting to be summoned for her wedding. *Maybe staying in the Forbidden Lands would have been better.*

We could run.

Alex turned to face Gryphon. He leaned against the door frame, dressed in his formal Titan robe.

"It wouldn't help," Alex said, turning back to the sea.

"Why are you going through with this? Why let your father control you so much?"

"I'm not doing it for him." Alex ran her hand across her swollen belly and turned back to Gryphon. "My son deserves a father. I was raised without parents, and I won't put my children through that."

"Alex—"

"No," Alex snapped. "Your child will have both of us, even if we aren't together. I can't have Aaron's be fatherless, and despite what my vision showed me, it's not fair to ask you to raise his son."

"I would have said yes."

"I know." Alex wiped away the tears forming. "But you hate rules and struggled to be in charge in the Forbidden Lands for a few months. I couldn't ask you to lead a kingdom for decades."

Gryphon's lips were pursed and his nose scrunched, but his eyes were locked onto her. *You're right. I would have hated every minute, but I would have done it for you.*

I know, but I still hope Aaron will come to his senses, and if I married you ... I don't think he...

It would ruin any chance of reconciling with him. I understand.

Alex squeezed Gryphon's hand.

Don't be afraid, Princess. I'll keep the earl in line.

Julius appeared at the balcony door with a loud knock. "Pardon the intrusion, but your father is waiting."

Gryphon narrowed his eyes at the young knight. "And he'll continue to wait until she's good and ready."

"Don't kill the messenger, Gryphon," Julius replied. "I'm with you on this. Everything is happening much too soon, and His Royal Highness never even gave Aaron the chance to apologize. Without a sorcerer, he wouldn't even have been able to ride here in this time."

He's right. What if Aaron wanted to apologize?

He would have sent word, wouldn't he? At least to Cameron. Does he know you picked his cousin?

Alex sighed. *He doesn't know, so you're right.* "Come along,

Julius. You can escort me." She held out her arm, and Gryphon vanished.

Julius paused. "Forgive my impertinence, but are you sure you want to do this?"

Dropping her royal mask, Alex patted Julius' arm. "No. I don't *want* to do this. Not one bit. But my father has made it clear that if I don't marry *someone*, he'll force me to marry one of the southern princes."

At the mention of the southern princes, Julius shuddered.

"Exactly. The idea of one of those pompous idiots on my father's throne one day is terrifying. So while I wish I could wait to see if Aaron comes to his senses, I don't have the time. Cameron is kind, he's Warren born, so our people will accept him, and most importantly, I think he'll make a wonderful father."

Julius straightened his tunic and bowed low. "Your Highness, may I escort you to your betrothed?"

Alex nodded and accepted Julius' arm.

Their path took them through the garden. As they walked, Alex stretched out her hand and let her fingers run along the hedges. Everything was blooming, and seemed more colorful in the warm summer air. When her father had accepted Cameron's request to marry her, he'd given in to Alex's demands for a private wedding in the garden. After the king-dom-sized affair her wedding to Aaron had been, Alex wanted this one to be more private and personal. The hedges were so tall she couldn't see over them, but she knew her grandmoth-er's flower maze better than the back of her hand. Julius let her set the pace and walked with her until they arrived at the place she'd picked for the ceremony. It was a large circular area, off to the side of the main garden, surrounded by roses that Victoria had planted.

Julius left her and joined his father along the edge of the

circle. Edward and Cameron were standing in the middle of the space under a flowing floral arch, Birch's work. The Celtic sorceress stood off to the side with Stefan, Lynx, Jessica, and Michael. Gryphon was nowhere to be seen, but Alex had expected him to stay away.

Cameron walked down the narrow dirt path, then took her hand and kissed it. Then, his back to her father, he whispered, "You can still change your mind if you're not sure."

"Thank you, but you know we can't."

"Then for Warren, and the babies." He held out his arm, and Alex accepted it. "Your dress is lovely, even if it is blue."

Alex smiled at him, grateful for how well he already knew her, and they headed toward Edward and the judge who'd be marrying them.

Alex's third wedding was over in minutes. She'd rejected every suggestion her father made to incorporate any Warren traditions into it, and even refused the feast that would normally follow. Instead, she and Cameron returned to her quarters, intending to eat in private while her father hosted his council members. He'd asked her repeatedly to attend, and each time Alex's reply became more and more short and temperamental. In the end, her father had given in and explained her absence with a lighthearted jest about pregnant women needing their rest.

While they were waiting for the food, Stefan and Lynx joined them. Lynx followed Alex to her room to help her out of the dress and into her usual training clothes. Cameron's eyes grew wide when she came downstairs with the gown thrown over her shoulder.

"What are you doing with that?" He stood to help her and

quieted when she threw the dress into the fireplace, making the flames burn it to ash in seconds.

Stefan crossed his arms. "Are you all right, Alex?"

She stood and wiped her hands on her pants. "Perfectly fine, thank you. I just have no desire to ever see that dress again. Now, what's for dinner?"

Lynx pressed her hip against Stefan. "We should leave you two alone."

"That won't be necessary, Lynx," Cameron interjected and explained the arrangement with Alex. "Nothing is happening tonight, or any night, so please stay."

"In that case, I'd love to." Lynx dropped herself onto the empty couch across from him. Stefan motioned to the empty seats, and Alex took her spot beside Cameron.

"So, how does it feel to be married?" Alex asked Cameron and snatched a piece of cheese to nibble on.

"I thought it would feel different, but it doesn't." He rolled his wedding ring around his finger. Alex had picked both of theirs out, and she'd done her best to find something he would like, something simple and understated.

Stefan chuckled. "Everyone thinks you'll feel different, but really, nothing has changed physically for you to notice." He handed Lynx a plate of apples, grapes, cheese, and bread, then made another for Alex.

"That's true unless you wed a sorceress." Lynx smirked. "Then the bond marks burn like someone is trying to set you on fire."

Stefan rubbed his shoulder, and she giggled. She snatched her plate off the table, popped a grape into her mouth, and curled up on the couch, pulling her legs under her.

"Well, I'm certainly glad that wasn't part of our marriage," Cameron said, putting another cheese slice on Alex's plate.

She thanked him and ate the cheese immediately. "At the

rate I'm going, if I acquired a new bond mark with each new husband, I'd run out of room."

Lynx snorted, and Stefan dropped his sausage in horror.

"You really love to tease him, don't you?" Cameron asked.

"So much!" Alex giggled.

After dinner, Alex went to her room, which she had to herself. Cameron took Michael's bed in the second guard room. As she stood at the foot of the bed she'd shared with Aaron, her heart ached. Trying to push away the sinking feeling that she'd lost him forever, Alex climbed into the bed and clutched his pillow as tightly as she could. Eventually, her quiet sobs lulled her into a restless sleep.

CHAPTER 56
AARON

Aaron and Caleb made it to Warren, it early morning. The normally bustling streets were mostly empty save for the bakers and market owners opening their shops.

"Now what?" Caleb asked.

"We grab something to eat at the port and then head to Cameron or Michael's estate before anyone recognizes us. Dressed this plainly we'll look like knights off duty, but I might still be recognized." Aaron motioned to Caleb's red tunic, and his own maroon one. A glance would reveal they'd been riding for some time so Aaron felt confident that they'd be able to slip through town without being recognized. No one expected a king to be walking around dirty and disheveled. They rode their horses down to the pier and left them at a stable used by out-of-town visitors. As a precaution, Caleb paid the boy working there to keep silent about their horses and the two of them headed toward the market.

The sun rose over the Oreean sea, sending rays of light dancing across the cobblestone street. The smell of freshly-baked bread and buttered fish rolls, a Warren delicacy, wafted through the area.

"What is it with these people and fish?" Caleb grumbled. His words were muffled by the sleeve he'd pressed over his nose.

"They ask the same thing about us and venison. Now, act like you belong here." Aaron elbowed Caleb, making him lower his hand.

They wandered through the stalls, looking for anything that piqued their interest, but many were still under construction. Caleb grabbed Aaron's arm.

"Ow. Caleb, what is wrong with—"

"Julius!"

Caleb pointed, and Aaron whipped his head around to find Julius leaning against a building with his arms crossed, scanning the crowd.

"*Ferflucs!*" Aaron pulled Caleb behind a large wooden display holding buckets of flowers.

"What is he doing here?"

"He *lives* here, Caleb. You're allowed to wander around Dat —" Aaron's words died in his throat. Julius leaned against ... the bookstore. At that moment, Alex stepped out of the store, clutching her favorite basket. Jessica and Edith had made it for Alex's twentieth birthday. Julius glanced in the basket and said something that made Alex laugh.

Aaron's heart sped until he thought his lungs might explode. He could hardly breathe, and Caleb had to squeeze his shoulder to bring him back. "She's there. Right there. So close I could rush up and touch her. Julius wouldn't be enough to stop me."

Aaron straightened himself, determined to do just that, but then Stefan and Cameron stepped out of the bakery beside the book shop. Stefan traded Alex the bakery bag for her basket, and she pulled out a steaming bun. She held it up to her nose and inhaled. She offered it to Stefan, but he wrinkled his nose at it, making Alex laugh again. Cameron leaned closer, and when he moved away she ripped her bun in half, giving the other part to Cameron.

"What's Cameron doing with Alex?" Caleb asked.

"They're friends," Aaron whispered back.

A group of children rushed by their hiding spot, and Caleb tripped, knocking over a bucket of flowers. Aaron ducked behind the display, hoping Julius and Stefan hadn't seen him. When he braved a glance, the children were circling Alex and Cameron, handing them wildflowers they'd clearly picked. Some still had dirt on their roots.

"Take mine, Princess," a little girl with pigtails pleaded.

"No, take mine. It's blue," another begged.

"Mine is for the babies," a little brown-haired girl said.

Alex handed Cameron the pastry bag and collected the flowers from the children. When their teacher arrived, the children all excitedly told her which flower Alex had taken first.

"How sweet of you all," the teacher said to her students. "Now what do you say?"

"Thank you, Princess Alexandria," they replied in unison. "Thank you, Prince Cameron."

Aaron's heart stopped.

Prince Cameron?

Edward said he'd find her a husband, but she actually agreed to remarry?

And she married Cameron?

Aaron moved to take a step forward, but a hand clamped down, stopping him. Aaron whipped around to tell Caleb to let go, and found himself staring into the frowning face of Matthew Bishop. "Matthew, I can explain."

"It's General Bishop, Your Royal Highness, and I don't need

to hear it. You were warned what would happen if you showed your face here. Where's your horse?"

"Matthew—General, I just need one minute. I just want to tell her I'm sorry."

"You had your chance for that when King Edward came to Datten. Now you are to be kept away from Alexandria, for her sake, so she can move on."

"What chance? Edward never let me say a word."

"Enough," Matthew snapped, and Aaron closed his mouth. The general leaned toward a knight beside him, and the man left, returning a minute later with Julius.

Beyond the Warren men, Alex and her friends walked further and further away. Cameron's hand was interlaced with Alex's as they strolled side by side, and Aaron swallowed the massive lump in his throat.

"Aaron? What are you doing here?" Julius asked.

"It doesn't matter. Edward's orders were clear. You two will escort them back home."

"Yes sir," Julius said, grabbing Aaron's arm.

"Matthew please!" Aaron said, but the general didn't say a word, leaving to join Alex and her entourage.

CHAPTER 57
ALEX

"Jessica, I don't need quite so many for a quick trip," Alex said as Jessica stuffed another dress into her traveling trunk. "Besides, if I really wanted a specific dress, I could always crack home to get it."

"That isn't how things are done, Alex," Jessica replied.

"Stefan. Michael. Help me!" Alex threw her hands in the air, but the moment Jessica turned back to them, both men shook their heads.

From the couch where she sat cross-legged, Lynx let out a chuckle.

Cameron strode in and handed Michael and Stefan each a package, then held out a smaller one to Alex.

"What's this?" She took the package carefully, making sure not to crush the silver bow perched on top.

"We've been married a month today, so I got you a little something in town when I picked up Michael and Stefan's new guard shirts."

"Aww." Jessica stopped folding Alex's clothes and turned her attention to Alex.

Glancing at her friends, Alex felt her cheeks heat. "I didn't get you anything."

"You aren't supposed to," Cameron replied. "The monthly gifts for a new bride is a Strobel tradition—one that seemed too much fun not to carry on." As he bent down to kiss her cheek, he whispered, "You can open it. It's not embarrassing."

Alex tugged on the ribbon and took off the shimmering silver paper. Inside was a book, and she read the title out loud. "*Warren Tales, an Illustrated Edition.*"

"It was my favorite bedtime book as a boy," Cameron said. "I thought you might want to read it to the babies."

Alex ran her fingers along the words on the cover and felt herself tearing up.

"I'm sorry. I didn't think it would upset you." Cameron knelt beside her awkwardly, unsure of whether to touch her.

Lynx sprang from the couch and was at Alex's side faster than any of her other friends could manage. "It's the pregnancy, Cameron. Don't worry." She wrapped her arms around Alex and squeezed her tightly, saving him from having to figure out how to hold her.

"I'm sorry, Cameron," Alex said, once she'd composed herself. "Gryphon warned me after we put up the new protection spell on Warren that I might be a little emotional for a few days. I thought he was exaggerating."

"It's all right. As long as I didn't upset you."

"No, it's very touching and I appreciate it."

"It's a beautiful book." Jessica took it and placed it in the chest. "Do you know if they have more? I'd like to buy one for Michael to read to Jerome, since I read him Datten tales."

Cameron tapped his chest pocket and nodded his head to Stefan and Michael, who opened their new shirts to find a copy of the book tucked inside. "I figured you would all enjoy reading them."

Alex stood and gave Cameron a hug and a quick peck on the cheek. "That was very thoughtful. Thank you."

"Are you coming with us, Jessica?" Stefan asked.

Jessica shook her head. "Lynx has offered to help Alex with her dresses, so I can take little Jerome to Datten to visit our father. It's been a month since he's seen him, and I hate keeping them apart."

"Make sure you tell him hello from all of us," Alex said.

Jessica squeezed her hand. To Michael, she said, "Do make sure she wears at least one dress."

"I'll try my best."

Jessica took her leave, kissing Michael and hugging her brother.

"Julius is finishing up with Matthew and will be here shortly. Then you just need Gryphon and you can be on your way," Cameron said.

"Wait, you're not coming either?" Michael asked.

"Technically, this will be our first visit to the Betruger since everything happened, but it's not a royal visit," Alex explained. "I'm only going there to cast a protection spell on the kingdom with Gryphon. We'll just be there for one night, and honestly, I didn't even have to stay, but I wanted to give Julius an excuse to see his boyfriend. It's been hard on him since the Betruger went back."

"You could give him some time off," Lynx said.

"I have. He'll be going with us to the kingdom for this trip, and then in a week he has time off to return and visit with Edith and Fritz. Things have settled here, so I think Stefan, Michael and Gryphon can handle me."

The smell of campfire filled the room as Gryphon appeared. "I managed you solo for three months. I don't need these other two," he said.

"What were you burning before you came here? You stink," Lynx teased.

"I was working on a potion with Megesti and lost track of time. I'm ready when you all are."

Alex merely nodded, and Gryphon cracked the group away.

The moment they arrived, Edith squealed and dashed across the Betruger courtyard to embrace Alex. The sheer love coming from her was overwhelming, and Alex squeezed her dear friend even tighter.

"Welcome everyone. We're so delighted to have you here." Edith pulled away and reached down to rub Alex's pregnant belly. "How are you feeling?"

"I'm tired and hungry all the time, but everything makes me want to retch."

"You poor thing. My oldest sister had the same thing."

"Does it get better?"

"Eventually." Edith leaned closer. "Are you going to cast the spell now or later?"

Gryphon stepped away from Michael, Stefan, and Lynx. "We should do it while Alex has more energy." *That way, we can try a second time, if needed.*

"I'm all right with that," Alex said. "Who's taking us?"

"Macht and Harold will escort you to the boundaries while I show Stefan, Lynx, and Michael around," Edith said.

"Let's make sure you're all protected here," Gryphon said.

As she performed the protection spell, Gryphon's unrelenting stare bore into Alex. When she'd finished, her entire body sagged, and she let herself sit on the large rock they'd used as a marker to track the spell's distance. Harold was too polite to say anything, but Gryphon wasn't.

"I told you not to overdo it."

"I'm fine, Gryphon," Alex replied.

Harold reached for Gryphon, presumably to stop him, but the sorcerer had other ideas. He pushed past the king to confront his bond mate.

"Doesn't look like it to me."

"Then stop looking!" Alex screamed at him. Her rage and exhaustion were enough to make her tremble.

Harold gave Macht a silent order, then turned to Alex. "I missed breakfast this morning, and am feeling famished. Would you care to join me for lunch?" Harold asked.

Alex sighed and slowly got up from the rock she sat upon. "I would love to, Harold. Thank you."

After you eat, I suggest a nap. Gryphon's thoughts were barely audible even in her head, and she turned to snap at him again, but in a blink she was in the throne room with Macht and Harold, Gryphon nowhere to be found.

"Macht," Harold said. Macht nodded and left. Alex had seen her father and Emmerich both use the one-word dismissal.

Frustrated by her own disappearing act, Alex crossed her arms. "I'm sorry I snapped. I'm just ... it's a lot to deal with."

"You don't have to apologize to me, Alex," Harold said. "Royal decorum dictates that as a queen, you do not need to apologize to a king. But further, I was at your father's meeting. I know what Aaron said, and what Edward pushed on you."

Alex dropped her arms and turned to Harold. "Am I still a queen?"

"To us you are."

"Thank you. My father discourages me from trying to contact Aaron. He doesn't want me to ever speak to him again, but between us, I've tried to write to him, but I don't even know how to begin. There's nothing to say to make him forgive me. I just wish I could have said goodbye."

"Come here." Harold opened his arms, and Alex let him hold her. He was so much taller than her, it felt like when Jerome or Emmerich hugged her. "Leave it all here in my throne room, where no one will find it."

"How could he? He claimed he loved me, that he'd listen to me. I used the future pearl in the Forbidden Lands ... before I agreed to have Gryphon's child. I needed to know if this would work and it showed me this happy vision with Aaron and Gryphon. Now it's all ruined, and I don't know how to fix this, and it's all my fault."

"It's not your fault."

"If I hadn't killed Garrick, we wouldn't have gotten stuck in the Forbidden Lands." She sniffled.

Harold squeezed her tighter. "And if Aaron had controlled his temper for a single conversation and listened to you, he wouldn't have lost you to Cameron."

"He hasn't lost me, Harold." Alex wiped the tears from her cheeks. "I lost him. Even if I convinced them to let me go to Datten to see him—it wouldn't matter. He made up his mind. My vision lied."

"I know your visions aren't always accurate, but how old were your children in it?"

"Around eight."

"That means it can still happen. It's understandable that Aaron would be upset to start and eventually come around, and find peace with everything in time."

"Do you think so?" Alex whispered.

"I do, because something here feels off to me."

"What does?"

"I shouldn't speak ill of ... others."

"Harold, please tell me. I need an outside opinion from a royal who isn't related or married to me."

"What your father said. I know Aaron. He risked his life to

get me to help find you once before. I know he has faults, makes mistakes, is foolish at times, but where you are concerned … It's because he's young, and with you, his heart always wins."

Alex threw up her arms in frustration. "Then where is he, Harold? If he cared at all about me or our son, he'd have come to Warren. Without a sorcerer to bring him, it still only takes days to travel from Datten, not months."

Harold's face fell. "I don't know," he said, rubbing her shoulder. "I haven't spoken to him since Edward's meeting. After what he did to you, Edith was furious, and my wife's happiness matters more to me than anything in our world."

"Speaking of your wife, I'm sure she is desperate to catch up. We should find the others to join us for lunch."

Alex turned to leave, but Harold took her hand. "If you ask me to, I will write to Aaron. Perhaps he'll answer me."

Alex squeezed his hand in response.

Edith and the others were settling down for lunch when Harold and Alex joined them. They were dressed informally, and Alex appreciated that they kept it a quiet affair so they could enjoy lunch and catch up. Michael gave Edith an update on Jessica and little Jerome, while Stefan and Lynx talked to Macht about how things were going for them now that the sorcerers were free. Alex found herself moving her food around on her plate.

Your fork can't eat that for you, Gryphon thought at her.

Stefan followed Gryphon's attention.

I'm not hungry.

They are. Gryphon pointed across the table at the basket of rolls. Stefan nodded and passed them to Gryphon, giving Alex his best brotherly look.

Alex grabbed two rolls and stuffed the entire first one in her mouth.

"Love the manners," Edith teased. "I see Jessica has been working hard with you."

The entire table broke out in laughter, and Gryphon handed Alex his mug so she wouldn't choke on her bread. Alex rolled her eyes and stuffed the second in her mouth, making them all laugh harder. After Michael managed to shove three rolls in his mouth at once, Alex finally broke into a giggle and joined the conversation.

It didn't take long for the food to disappear. Edith had the servants fill the breadbasket three more times. Everyone was full and happy. Edith and Michael offered to stay with Alex so Harold could show Lynx and Stefan the animals they kept and those that roamed around the mountains. Lynx bounced with excitement and almost dragged Stefan down the hall.

Alex headed to her room with Edith and Michael in tow. Gryphon had vanished, but Alex knew he'd turn up eventually.

"I remember this," Michael said. "This is the room they gave Aaron when we first came to Betruger to ask for Harold's help."

"Harold requested you be put in here," Edith said.

Alex leaned against the balcony door, watching the waves on the sea. "How was that just over two years ago?"

"It really is hard to believe," Edith said. "It feels as though we've lived an entire lifetime in these few years."

"You had it easy," Michael teased Edith. "You had your family and didn't have to move towns or change your rank or anything."

"I had to help Alex get her footing."

"We all did."

"You still do," Alex turned to her friends and smiled.

"How are you doing?" Edith asked. "Keeping in mind that I can tell when you lie now."

"As good as you'd expect. I miss Aaron so much I can't

breathe at times. The guilt makes me nauseous, and I cry myself to sleep every night, knowing the man I love doesn't want me, and I'm married to his cousin. And on top of it, my father's been more distant than I've ever seen him before. And I *always* have to pee."

Edith wrapped her arms around Alex. "I still don't believe that Aaron doesn't want you."

"I wish I could just go to Datten and know he's all right." *Maybe I should.*

Michael frowned. "You forgot that the fury is stirring."

"Stirring how?" Edith asked. "I expected it to escape with violent force the moment you were betrayed."

"So did I," Alex whispered. "But Gryphon and I found a book written by Merlin. He had some spells to try, but Michael's right. She's getting louder and I'm losing my grip on her."

"You never told us that," Michael said.

"How?" Edith asked. "Is it like when you think, or like with Daniel?"

"I hear her in my head, like when Gryphon talks to me. But lately she keeps asking me to let her handle things." Alex paced, trying to burn off her nervous energy. Edith wrapped her arms around her chest and Michael narrowed his eyes at Alex.

Alex could feel her temper stirring. "Michael ... stop staring at me."

"I'm trying to get a read on the fury. Hold still."

Alex stopped and rubbed her forehead.

"What exactly is going on inside your head?" Edith asked.

"I think ..." Alex tugged her shirt, causing Edith to rush over.

"Whatever it is, we're here," Edith said, and embraced Alex.

"I think I have to release her," Alex whispered.

"Why would you?" Edith asked.

"She comes when I'm emotional—frustrated or hurt or …"

"Broken." Michael finished and Alex nodded. "Well, that explains why she hasn't emerged yet."

"Hopefully it stays that way," Edith said.

"I can't think of a reason I'd ever let her out, except the voice is getting louder and harder to ignore."

"Do you think it's because of everything you're going through with Aaron, or because of the pregnancy?" Edith asked.

"I can't say. For all we know it's because my father's mortal."

Michael pursed his lips. "What if …" He rubbed his chin as the girls both leaned toward him. "What if it's the babies that are keeping the fury back? You are carrying the most powerful sorcerer that will ever be born."

Alex bit her cheek and considered Michael for a long moment.

"It would make sense," Edith said.

"I'll see if I can find anything else in my grandfather's journals. Or ask Gryphon. He's been spending every free minute he has in the lab reading them."

"There's another thing," Edith said. "Julius is lying."

"About what?" Michael asked.

"He's avoiding me so I can't ask and find out, but I see it on him anytime he's around. He knows something. And Matthew taught all his boys, that lies of omission are still lies."

"So now we have to find out how to keep the babies away from the fury should she escape and figure out what a general's son could be keeping from us?" Alex asked.

"Sounds about right," Michael replied.

CHAPTER 58
AARON

Aaron paced the library as Jerome, Bernhard, and Randal read over his list of ideas. A month had passed since he'd been sent home in disgrace, and the fact that one of his best friends had been the one to do it made everything so much worse. Matthew had sent word to Jerome, so the Datten general had been waiting on the border of Warren and Datten to take Aaron home. Julius had barely said two sentences to Aaron and Cameron the entire time they travelled away from Warren. He'd said even less to Jerome, only reminding him that next time, Aaron would be thrown in the dungeon.

Aaron had done a great deal of research to come up with his plan. Randal and Bernhard could sneak him in better than any Datten knight could. Once inside, they'd hide at either the Nial or Strobel estate and take their time figuring out how to get him to Alex.

"What if she doesn't believe you?" Bernhard asked.

"Then Gryphon's mind reading magic will be helpful to me," Aaron replied. "He can see the truth with one touch."

"Doesn't that mean Alex can too?" Jerome asked.

"I don't think they have all of each other's powers now," Aaron said.

"Have you asked Harold to lend you the pearl?" Randal suggested.

"Add it to the list."

"Aaron, are you sure this is a good idea?" Bernhard asked. "If you're caught sneaking into Warren a second time—"

"I respect your opinion, Bernhard, but I'd give up my crown to get her back."

Jerome huffed, a sound Aaron knew all too well. His general seemed prepared to say something Aaron wouldn't like, and he braced himself.

"What if she doesn't want you back? You both signed the divorce papers, and your marriage is over."

"Our marriage is *not* over. Not until I hear that from her."

"Aaron—"

Aaron slammed his fist on the table and glared at Jerome. "I don't care what I signed. Alex is carrying my—*our* child—a fact I was never told until *after* Edward forced me to sign that document. You, Bernhard, my mother, were all there. You saw it. Alex needs to know the truth, and then she'll decide if she's willing to let me make it right. And I will, no matter how long it takes."

There was a knock at the door of the library. "Enter," Aaron ordered.

Caleb entered the room with a happy and surprised look on his face. "We have a visitor," he said.

"Who?" Jerome asked.

Caleb stepped back to reveal Jessica bouncing her and Michael's son, Jerome Jr., in her arms. Her father crossed the room, kissed the top of her head, and gleefully took the baby.

"What are you doing here?" Aaron jumped to his feet.

"Everyone thinks I'm here to visit my father while they're in Betruger, but I lied," Jessica said, making her father look back at Aaron. "I brought the baby as an excuse, because I'm really here to see you. Consider me your one chance."

"One chance?" Randal asked.

She glanced at the other men. "His one chance to convince someone in Alex's inner circle that he's telling the truth about Edward."

"You got my letters!"

"Stefan and Megesti have been burning every one they got their hands on. So was Michael, until a few days ago. He broke down and confessed. He hadn't burned the last letter you sent to the Veremund estate. I read it, and what you wrote sounds..."

"Mad?" Bernhard offered.

"Honestly, yes," Jessica replied.

"It's true," Aaron said. "Every word."

Jessica narrowed her eyes. "Really? It's all Edward's fault? You never accused her of being unfaithful and wouldn't even give her the opportunity to explain?"

Aaron ran his hand through his hair. Jessica slapped him across the face.

"Jessica!" Jerome shouted, making the baby cry.

Without a word, Aaron held his hand out to stop the men in the room from interfering and turned his other cheek to Jessica. She slapped him again.

"How dare you! You are supposed to be the King of Datten, the kingdom of Honor above all, and yet you accuse your wife of infidelity and now blame her father for protecting her!"

"That's all true, but see it from my perspective, Jessica. She was gone for months and then shows up pregnant, reeking of Gryphon. I reacted badly, but when I told Edward I was wrong, he forced me to sign the divorce papers by threatening war."

"Three months. She showed up pregnant after three months! You saw me at three months. Alex was much larger. Why in Torian did you assume she became pregnant there?"

"I wasn't thinking clearly, Jessica. I smelled Gryphon on her and just snapped. But even if I had thought about it, I don't know how fast sorcerer babies grow. For all I know, they have shorter pregnancies! Why would I have assumed she was pregnant when she left? After what happened the first time, she *promised* to tell me when it happened again. And she didn't!"

Jessica pushed her hair back and put her hands on her hips. *She's thinking. I'm making sense to her.* "We hadn't considered that," she said.

Chairs scraped. Bernhard and Randal came around the table. "We'll leave you two to talk in private," Randal said.

"I'm going to take the baby to see Her Majesty," Jerome said. "Please, dear, don't assault my king again while I'm away."

"I make no promises," Jessica replied. She waited until the door closed behind them. "You were doing so well with maturing and staying calm. Why did you lose your temper with her?"

His stomach sank. Aaron motioned for his childhood friend to join him on the couches behind the library table, and they took a seat. He noted that Jessica sat on the furthest seat. "I was so frustrated about not being able to get to the Forbidden Lands. I had just found out that yet another thing hadn't worked, and Lynx looked so awful, and I knew Alex would have hated that, and then the Rassgats showed up with this *ridiculous...* never mind. Anyway, then she just walks in! Pregnant! And all I could smell was *him.* No flowers, no sea salt, nothing Alex, just him, and he wasn't with her. My mind got away from me, and I went to the worst plausible scenario. And then he showed up, threatening me, telling me to stay away from Alex and *his* child. I saw red. I just wanted to make him bleed from his stupid, smug face."

"So that's when you fought him and threw her out?"

Aaron nodded and hung his head.

"You had another chance, though! We came to collect her things, and Edward tried to talk some sense into you. What then?"

Aaron laughed out loud. "Talk sense into me? Is that what he told her? Jessica, he didn't even try. As soon as you, Stefan, and Gryphon left, he threw the divorce papers at me and threatened me!"

"No!"

"Yes, and if you doubt me, ask your father. He was there." Aaron rubbed his palms on his pants. "So was my mother. They both ... they both told me to sign the papers."

Jessica's mouth dropped open. "But why?"

"Because Edward said if I didn't sign the papers, he'd take it as an act of war. We couldn't take on the Betruger and Warren."

"Why didn't my father tell us? Or Julius for that matter?" Jessica finally asked.

"Julius had no reason to take my word over his father's and Edward's. As for your father, he's my general. He wouldn't say anything unless I told him too."

Jessica moved down the couch, reached across the gap, and patted Aaron's knee. "Well, you're stuck with my help now."

"You believe me?"

Jessica nodded. Feeling his heart speed up, he watched Jessica's face closely when he asked, "Is it true *she* picked Cameron?"

"Yes, but don't make that face. He sleeps in Michael's old bed. Cameron agreed to help her raise her children and stand at her side as a husband in public, but behind closed doors, they're friends. Nothing more."

"I have no right to ask but—"

"As long as you breathe, you are and always will be her husband. Those are her exact words."

Aaron felt a weight lifted off him. *She still loves me. Even after everything I said.* Aaron told her of his plan to have Randal and Bernhard sneak him to the estates. "But once I'm there, I'll need more support. I don't think Alex will ever believe her father is lying to her just with my word."

"Cameron and Michael are getting suspicious of Edward's behavior. It's why I'm here. Someone needed to hear your side. Hopefully, by the time you arrive, I'll have Stefan and Megesti willing to listen too."

"What about Gryphon?" Aaron asked.

"I'll just tell him he gets to torture you."

Aaron's mouth dropped open. "You wicked Wafner!"

"That's Veremund now, Your Royal Highness."

Aaron smiled. "Not in Datten. Here, you'll always be a Wafner."

"So how soon do you think you can get to Warren?"

ONCE IN HIS ROOM, Aaron dropped his crown on the red velvet couch and took off his royal tunic, leaving him in his simple red shirt. For the first time since this whole mess had started, he felt hopeful. Jessica believed him. *And I didn't even need to use any magic to prove it to her. Maybe, just maybe, we can figure this all out.* He walked to a lonely, empty bookshelf and took a well-loved volume to his favorite couch. They'd forgotten to take *Plants of the Dark Forest*. Alex had given it to him when he'd come to Kirsh for his honor rite. Warmth spilled from the fireplace and illuminated the pages as Aaron flipped through it, looking for the flowers he knew Alex liked to grow in the garden.

He'd finally found the section on wildflowers when he heard a thud from above. He froze, listening intently, and heard another softer thud, followed by a whistle of wind.

The latch on the balcony doors must have come open. He put down the book and crept up the stairs. His journal and a letter from his mother had fallen from his bedside table, and the balcony door flapped in the wind.

He rushed outside to find a figure in a black robe walking across the empty courtyard. Turning on his heels, Aaron took the stairs two at a time to get his sword, then bolted down the hall toward the courtyard doors. He burst through them and raced for the figure, thinking back to the nightmare Alex had in their room, and knowing Lygari was fond of arriving where he wasn't wanted. Ready to fight, Aaron reached out, but in a second the figure vanished, and he was left holding his cape.

"Sorcerers," Aaron grumbled. Staring at the cape in his hand, he moved it to his nose and sniffed. Flowers.

His heart sped. "Alex?"

CHAPTER 59
GRYPHON

Gryphon got up from the table, shoved his chair aside, and shouted, "I am not cracking to Datten to kidnap Aaron in his sleep!"

"Well, I don't trust myself enough to do it." Megesti picked up his mug and took a sip of ale. They had all gathered around the dining table at Michael's estate, the only place they could speak in private.

"If he's not confident, he'll end up cracking him into a wall, and that would be bad for everyone," Lynx said.

"That depends," Stefan said, wrapping his arm around Lynx and pulling her closer. "If they arrived up a tree, that would at least entertain us."

"Until Aaron falls out and breaks his leg, or worse, his neck," Michael said.

Jessica giggled. "He's not you, dear."

"We need actual ideas, not foolishness," Gryphon snapped.

"Gryphon's right," Lynx said. "We're wasting time. Michael can only keep Alex busy for so long."

Stefan motioned to Jessica. "Tell us again, exactly what he said."

Jessica repeated everything Aaron had told her for the third time, trying her best to find his exact words.

Cameron rubbed his forehead. "Forcing his general to lie to all of us? Outright lying to his own daughter? That's cold."

"He's doing what he thinks is best," Megesti said.

"So did Arthur," Cameron said.

"I don't care," Gryphon said. "He can't just ignore what she wants. He took the choice from her, and that's unacceptable."

Megesti sighed. "She's been sneaking to Datten to check on Aaron."

"What? When?" Stefan and Gryphon demanded at the same time.

"She confessed when I caught her returning last night. She's traveled there a handful of times, trying to find some proof about how he feels about her. She's stopped now, because the last time, he almost caught her."

"Gryphon, what do you remember of the day we went to Datten with Edward?" Jessica asked. "Stefan and I were sent away before anything was said."

"I was sent away soon after you, but I asked Kharon to speak to some of the ghosts. Apparently Edward threw it in Aaron's face that Alex was expecting twins. It was obvious Aaron didn't know. After that, he demanded Aaron sign the divorce papers or else it would mean war."

"That sounds like coercion to me," Lynx said.

"Did Aaron say anything about wanting to make it right?" Megesti asked.

"He wanted to talk to her, but Edward said no," Gryphon said.

"So, her father threatened her husband. Lovely," Lynx groaned.

"Honestly, I think we need to bring Aaron here so he and Alex can hear each other out," Jessica said, and pointed her finger at Stefan. "And before you say anything nasty, brother—"

Stefan grabbed her hand and lowered it. "I believe you. You've known him as long as I've known Alex. If you think he's telling the truth, I believe you. But we need to be certain, for Alex's sake. She plays the part well, but inside, the guilt is eating her. Michael and I see it."

Lynx raised her hand. "I'll go. I'm not a threat in Datten, and Edward has no ill will against me. Although honestly, I wouldn't care even if he did. My loyalty will always be to Alex."

"And your husband," Gryphon teased.

Lynx elbowed Stefan. "He knows his place."

"And I'm very happy there."

"We also need to discuss what to do about the fury," Jessica said. "In Betruger, Alex confessed to Edith and Michael that she's hearing a voice in her head, and she's pretty confident the fury is stirring."

"No!" Cameron shook his head. "He can't have broken her that badly, could he? I mean she's still longing for him, so her hope isn't gone."

"What if the betrayal was not going to come from Aaron?" Lynx asked.

"Explain," Gryphon replied.

"The premonition. What if it was her father's betrayal that was predicted?" Lynx asked, taking Jessica's hand in hers.

"Alex doesn't know that yet. Maybe she has to know about it for the curse to take effect. Did you figure anything out when you were trapped in the Forbidden Lands, Gryphon?" Stefan asked.

"Nothing good. We found Merlin's lab and he wrote Alex so many journals. We tried some spells to help her gain control of her powers and others to help her overpower the fury. Apparently the only way to stop a fury is with the combined power of a Head and Heart. If we lose Alex to the fury, I will not be powerful enough to stop it."

"What about the baby?" Megesti asked.

"The baby?" Stefan asked.

"Gryphon and Alex's," Megesti said. "As the child of a Head and Heart, shouldn't he be a Head himself?"

"We'd need to wait for him to be old enough to take his power," Lynx said.

"Not if we age him up," Gryphon said, tapping the table with his fingers. "I've been thinking about this."

"That Tiere spell hasn't been used for centuries because of how dangerous it is," Lynx growled as Jessica's teacup clattered to the floor.

"That's why it's the last resort," Gryphon replied.

CHAPTER 60

ALEX

"That was a fantastic idea, Michael." Alex plopped down on the couch in her new sitting room and shook off her boots.

Michael chuckled and set their bows in the corner. "I'm glad you had fun. It's been forever since we went rabbit hunting, but maybe you shouldn't tell Jessica. Somehow, I think this would not be on her list of appropriate activities for a pregnant woman."

"She worries too much." Alex chuckled. "We've been going rabbit hunting since I could hold a bow. Though I should probably change, just to be safe."

Michael patted her. "Let me get your comfortable clothes, and then I'll get us a late lunch while you change."

"Yes please," Alex said. "Extra bread and—"

"Cheese? Of course."

Michael brought Alex her newly tailored training clothes. These fit her more loosely, and the shirts had ribbons running up the side to allow her to pull them over her bump without issue. She dressed in her clean clothes, and while she braided her hair, she had a wonderful idea. *I could surprise him and get Jessica. It would be nice to have some time with the two of them.*

Grinning, Alex cracked herself the Veremund estate.

CHAPTER 61

AARON

Ever since Aaron had been a boy, working with his horse had helped him clear his mind. So, it was no surprise that he found himself, now king, standing in the stables. He breathed in Thunder's scent as he considered his ever-growing list of issues. The guard training went well, and the new councils were making tremendous improvements to people's lives, but he was lonely. Caleb, Hunter, and Lucas were doing their best to keep him company, but they were no substitute for Alex and their group of friends. It didn't matter that Stefan glared at him, or that Gryphon taunted him, or that Jessica and Megesti scolded him. Without them, he felt alone. The brush grazed along Thunder's rippling muscle again and again, as if each stroke could brush away his own worries. *This waiting is killing me.*

He was hanging the lead line when two silhouettes appeared at the door.

"There you are," Stefan said. "We need to get you out of here without anyone noticing."

"What?"

"You might have spies." Lynx smiled, and Aaron felt a twinge of hope.

"Jessica told you?"

"She did," Stefan replied. "And while I suspect something bigger is going on, I'm not ready to put this behind us until Gryphon digs through your memories and confirms whether you're telling us the truth."

"Of course," Aaron said. "I'll use the pearl, drink a potion, let Gryphon poke through my head—anything you need."

Stefan's face softened in relief.

You believe me ... oh no.

"What did Edward do?" Aaron asked.

The younger Wafner pursed his lips. "He's not listening to Alex. He says he's trying to protect her, but he's suffocating her instead ... something I'm more familiar with than I'd care to admit."

Lynx held her hand out to Aaron. "Ready?"

AARON COULDN'T HELP but feel awe at Michael and Jessica's Warren home. He'd spent much of his youth with Jessica and could see every little touch of hers in the foyer—the embroidered pillow on the couch, the small touches of red and gold, and the perfect layout for entertaining. Stefan and Lynx were whispering to each other, until Lynx came over and gave him a hug. Aaron stiffened for a moment and then softened into her embrace.

"Good luck." Lynx released him and disappeared.

"Where is she going?"

"Fetching Megesti and Gryphon. They'll be here shortly." Stefan motioned toward the main hallway, and Aaron followed him. "Alex might get suspicious if we all vanished at once. Megesti and Gryphon made a point to bump into her earlier today. Lynx and Michael are going to keep her busy while we're here."

"I don't get to see her?"

"Not yet," Stefan said. "I won't set her up for more pain and disappointment, but if we believe you … we'll bring her here."

The walls were mostly bare, but the family portrait Alex had found in the treasure room hung proudly in the center. Aaron couldn't remember much of Mattias since he'd been with his father, but Catherine had spent time with his mother and Victoria. He remembered her as a kind and gentle woman. Michael took after her. A little farther toward the hall, Aaron found a painting that made him gasp.

"Uncanny, isn't it?" Stefan asked, pausing at the painting with Aaron. Smaller than the family one, but just as treasured by Michael, it depicted a four-year-old Alex and a likely five-year-old Michael, but that wasn't what made it special.

"I've never seen a painting of Alex as a child smiling," Aaron said. She wore a green dress instead of blue. Michael proudly wore the Veremund crested shirt, his chest puffed out, but the mischievous grin on his face gave him away. Her smile, her eyes, the way she beamed with delight—she might have grown since then, but these things remained. Aaron missed her so badly his heart hurt.

"Michael's grandmother had it in Datten. She sent it as a housewarming gift," Stefan explained.

"It's incredible," Aaron whispered.

"That's because they are," Jessica said, stepping out of the doorway at the end of the hall. "Are you two going to get in here or do I have to ask Gryphon to summon you?"

"Sorry." Aaron forced himself away from the painting and gave Jessica another hug. "Thank you for helping me."

She squeezed him back, then patted his cheek. "You deserved a chance to tell the truth."

"Who else is here?"

Cameron stepped into the hallway. "You aren't going to punch me, are you?"

Aaron marched up to Cameron, reached out, and gave him an even bigger hug than Jessica. "Thank you for protecting them."

Jessica peeked into the sitting room and announced that Gryphon and Megesti had arrived. The others followed her in. Aaron stood from his seat, desperate to have Megesti hear him out.

"You're a mess, kingling," Gryphon said.

"Megesti, please believe me. This wasn't what I wanted."

Before Megesti could reply, Gryphon cracked to Aaron's side and grabbed his head. Aaron screamed as a pain burst through his skull. He struggled to open his eyes and saw Gryphon's mouth twisted into a scowl as he squeezed Aaron's head harder. His eyes were glowing blue.

"Gryphon, let him go!" Stefan shouted, but Aaron thrust out his hand to silence him. *Gryphon is my one chance to be believed.*

When Gryphon finally released him, Aaron took a step forward, but dizziness overtook him, and he stumbled. Stefan steadied him. Closing his eyes, Aaron pressed his hand to his forehead to make the room stop spinning.

"He told the truth," Gryphon said. "Everything about Edward refusing to let him see or speak to Alex is true. He even threatened him with war if he tried to delay signing the papers."

"I never thought Edward would stoop so low," Jessica said. "We've been at peace for centuries."

"Edward would throw that away to protect Alex," Aaron said. He was starting to feel normal again. "He would have done anything to keep Alex and me apart."

Megesti stared at the door.

"Is everything okay?" Stefan asked Megesti.

"Yes." Megesti turned back to everyone. "I thought I heard something, but must have been imagining it.

"Why didn't you come to me?" Cameron asked Aaron.

"I tried," Aaron said, and explained what happened the day he and Caleb had seen them at the pier.

"Edith told Alex and me that Julius was lying about something," Michael said. "Clearly, he didn't agree with Edward and his father sending you away.

"That's why I started writing you each a letter every day. I hoped between all of you, someone would answer eventually and I'd have a chance to explain myself."

CHAPTER 62
ALEX

Alex covered her mouth with her hand to keep herself from making a sound.

He didn't want the divorce—came to Warren—wrote letters? Aaron was trying to get to me ... to make things right. He loves me and wants the baby? But how? My father said—

Thunder rumbled outside. Alex's emotions were getting away from her. Hearing footsteps inside the room, she cracked back to her suite at the castle, but her aim was off, and she tripped over the couch. She landed on her knees and cursed as she cut her palm on the floor.

Lynx opened the door and walked in carrying a jug. "I couldn't decide, so I brought every cheese."

Michael followed, carrying a platter of cheese, bread, and fruit. The moment he saw Alex on the ground, he dropped the platter, which shattered on the stone floor, and rushed for her. "Are you all right?"

Lightning flickered outside the window. Lynx squatted down and examined the cut on Alex's hand. Alex winced at the

293

pain, but never took her eyes off Michael. She searched his face for the truth.

"How long have you known?" she whispered.

"Long enough that I should have told you," he whispered back.

"You let me believe he hated me. You let my father lie to me."

"I didn't know how to convince you Edward was lying."

Lynx helped Alex up. "How did you find out?"

"I went to get Jessica to surprise Michael, and ... he's there. They're *all* there. I heard them. Everything."

"Alex, I'm sorry." Michael came to hug her, but Alex stepped back.

"No." She pointed at him. "Not you."

"Alex." Michael moved closer, and Alex stumbled backward to get away. His face went ashen. "You have to calm down."

Liars. The fury whispered. *All of them, but your father most of all.*

No. He was protecting me.

He betrayed you, just like Michael.

"How could you?" Alex spat at him. Michael closed the distance as Alex's control over the fury slipped and she slapped him.

Lynx gasped in shock.

"I expect this from Gryphon, Stefan, my father ... everyone. But not you. Never you." Her voice was gruff and guttural, and all trace of Alex was gone.

He's the same as the rest. Liar.

"Alex ... I'm sorry. I don't have an excuse." Michael held his hands out as if calming a wild animal. "But you need to breathe. Don't let the fury take control."

Alex wanted to scream at him, but stopped when the room turned ice cold, and a ghostly figure appeared.

"Emmerich?"

"Alexandria, you have to save them!" he begged.

"Who?" Alex asked.

"Our people. Datten's people are under attack! You must go before it's too late!"

Alex whipped her head toward Michael and Lynx. "We have to go to Datten now! They're under attack." She grabbed both of them without another word and cracked.

CHAPTER 63
AARON

"Her father lied to her. How do we tell her without breaking her heart?" Jessica asked.

"As gently as possible," Cameron said.

"Forget gentle," Megesti muttered. "How do we tell her without releasing the fury?"

"Perhaps the knowledge that her kingling never gave up on her will help her accept Edward's lies," Gryphon replied.

"We can't just walk Aaron into the castle against the king's orders," Stefan said.

"I *can*," Gryphon said.

"But you won't," Aaron replied.

"We could bring Alex here," Jessica suggested.

"Maybe," Stefan said. "But Edward and Matthew check on her constantly now."

"You'd think they don't trust you," said Aaron.

"What if Michael and Jessica invite Stefan, Lynx, Alex, and me for dinner?" Cameron asked. "It is completely reasonable for a new Duchess to want to entertain."

"That could work," Aaron said.

"How soon can you arrange this, Jessica?" Megesti asked.

"A small dinner? I'll have it set for tomorrow."

"We only need to keep Aaron here in secret for one day," Cameron said. "That won't be too hard."

The door flew open, and everyone jumped. Julius entered, sword in hand. "They're in here," he called.

Footsteps stomped down the hall, and the senior Bishop arrived. "It seems your sources were correct. Well done, son." He patted Julius on the back and stepped into the room. Jessica readied to defend her home, but Aaron held his hand out to stop her.

"You caught me," Aaron said. He surrendered himself, hands outstretched, and stepped in front of Megesti.

"You were warned about what would happen if you came to Warren again, Your Royal Highness." Matthew approached Aaron. "A night in the dungeon should be enough to smarten you up before we send you back." He affixed iron shackles to Aaron's hands.

"You can't do that," Jessica said. She jerked on Aaron's arm, but Julius held firm.

"Don't make this harder than it has to be, Duchess Veremund," Matthew said, glaring at her. "Your punishment will be decided once your husband is found. Luckily, Michael was smart enough not to get mixed up in this."

Julius turned toward Stefan. "Too bad the Wafners were not smart enough to follow him."

"I demand an audience with Edward," Cameron said, standing up and facing Matthew.

"Cameron, sit down," the general snapped back.

"That's Your Majesty to you, General Bishop. The King of Datten is visiting his family—me. As Prince of Warren, I order you to bring him before the king. I will not allow you to remove him from my protection without the king's express orders."

"The king is busy," Julius said.

"We'll see about that," Gryphon said, as he snapped his fingers, bringing the entire group to the throne room.

As soon as they arrived, Matthew's grip clamped down on Aaron's arm.

The throne room had been transformed since the fire. The paintings had been replaced by new ones, ones from which Datten royalty were conspicuously missing. Only one throne sat in the center of the dais, and Aaron wondered if Edward was becoming more controlling or if he simply refused to give Cameron any actual power. *Probably both.*

"Matthew, what is the meaning of this?" Edward shouted from across the room. Aaron recognized the master Betruger builder standing beside him. "You?!" Edward pointed at Aaron and charged across the room. "I warned you what would happen if you showed your face in Warren!"

Aaron stood his ground and wouldn't budge. His wrists throbbed from the shackles, but he refused to show any weakness.

She could be just behind that door. If I shout, she'll hear me.

"Why would I listen to you? You're trying to keep me from Alex. You lied to your daughter. Refused to let me speak to her. Told me to my face you were planning to manipulate her and tell her I wanted nothing to do with her. You threatened me with war to make me sign divorce papers!" Matthew's grip loosened on Aaron. He glanced at the general's face, but he was watching Edward closely.

Matthew looked at Edward in surprise. "You told us he wanted nothing to do with Her Highness, or their child."

"He called my daughter a whore," Edward snarled, stabbing a finger toward Aaron. "Would you let a man near your granddaughter if he called her that?"

"Perhaps not," Matthew said as his fingers released from

Aaron. His face contorted in a look Aaron recognized as pain from whenever Jerome disagreed with his father. "But I would respect her enough to do as she asked. Alex sobbed for days and begged you to fix things with Aaron, and you told her he refused. One of you is lying, and I owe it to my future queen to find the truth."

"Edward is." Aaron held out his hands and watched Matthew glance from his king to Aaron. "If you doubt me, Matthew, then go look at the divorce papers. I didn't sign it."

"That's preposterous," Edward shouted as Matthew unlocked Aaron's shackles. "Your own mother watched you sign it."

Aaron faced his godfather. "Last time I checked the laws of Torian, any proper document requires the person's full name."

"It does," Matthew said.

"Leaving out Edward or Arthur in your name won't make the divorce invalid," Edward said.

"You're right, but signing *princeling* instead of my name would."

A hint of a smile twitched at Gryphon's lips.

Edward's eyes widened as he glared at Aaron.

Matthew nodded. "That would mean your divorce is invalid, and Alex's marriage to Cam—"

Edward interrupted Matthew. "I told you in Datten that document was a formality. As far as my kingdom and council are concerned, you and Alex are through."

"Lucky for Aaron, we don't care what you, your council, or your kingdom think," Stefan said, joining Matthew at Aaron's side. "The only opinion I care about is Alex's."

Edward rubbed his face in frustration, and Aaron took his chance. He raced to the throne room door and ran for Alex's suite. "Alex!"

"Gryphon! Megesti! Get him out of here, now," Edward shouted, following Aaron.

Aaron threw open the door to Alex's room. He heard Gryphon and Megesti crack in after him. They found a shattered platter and a pile of bread and cheese all over the floor.

"What happened here?" Gryphon asked.

"Michael? Alex?" Megesti called as the others followed them into the room.

"Get him out of here, *now*," Edward shouted at Matthew, but his general stalled in the doorway, unsure of what to do.

"Give him a chance, Matthew," Stefan said, and the general nodded.

"Alex?" Aaron called, but the room remained eerily silent, until Kharon and Birch cracked into the room.

"Datten is under attack!" Birch announced.

"*What?*"

"Your brother came to find me," Kharon said. "The Titans and elders are ripping Datten apart, trying to find Alexandria."

"Why are they looking for her?" Edward asked.

"They want the baby," Gryphon snapped. "Ours, not Aaron's," he added quickly. "The baby we made to mask Aaron's. But now that he exists, they won't allow their next Head to be born in the mortal world."

"Tell them the rest," Birch said.

"They want Alex back in the Forbidden Lands when she gives birth," Kharon said. "If they get her, they'll kill her and the mortal baby as soon as Gryphon's is born."

"Our child will be the strongest sorcerer ever born," Gryphon snarled. "They want to corrupt him and raise him to be the monster I never was."

"Why attack Datten?" Megesti asked.

"We never protected Datten," Gryphon said. "Alex and I

intended to put protection spells on all the kingdoms, but with things how they are—"

"Did she go there?" Edward asked.

Gryphon closed his eyes and groaned as he burst into blue light. "I can't tell. She's blocking me."

"She would have gone to help," Stefan said. "Datten's people still matter to her."

"Then what are we waiting for?" Cameron asked.

Aaron turned to Gryphon. "Take us to Datten!"

CHAPTER 64
ALEX

The town square—the place Aaron had brought her years before on their secret trip to Datten together—lay in shambles. Fire consumed the roof of the Lion's Chest, where Datten knights often gathered to relax and share stories and where Alex first kissed Aaron. Pieces of smashed market stalls littered the ground along with chunks of stone torn from the walls of houses. Some were almost as large as Michael. All around them, people screamed, fleeing the chaos. Alex scanned the other side of the square, but she couldn't spot the sorcerers responsible for the carnage. Despite the mixture of terror and rage swirling inside her, the fury had gone silent —likely biding her time to cause the most damage.

Lynx stepped away from them, sniffed the air, then shook her head sadly.

Michael's hand dropped to his sword, which he must have forgotten to remove when they arrived at the castle. He took in the space, but left his sword sheathed. "Everyone here is a citizen," he said. "Where is the damage coming from?"

Alex closed her eyes and slowly let her breath out, opening

her well to summon her power. Opening her eyes, she focused on a group of mortals cowering on the street. Among them, little Ruby Reinhart's face shifted from fear to relief when she saw Alex. Alex returned her smile and cracked the first group of people into the castle. It took her several minutes to get all the panicking citizens of Datten away from the flames and crumbling ruins of their town square, but soon it was empty of people except for the three of them.

The flames were growing larger and spreading to the other houses that hadn't been damaged yet. Alex went over to the well in the central square and rested her hand on the stones. Effortlessly, she pulled the water from it, and soon, large rain clouds formed over the area. As it rained, Alex focused the water on the burning buildings.

With the fires extinguished, Alex could survey the full extent of the damage. The tavern would need to be rebuilt, along with at least a dozen of the houses. Some buildings were in near-perfect condition, but the theater leaned to the side, making Alex nervous it would collapse and hurt someone. Someone grabbed her, and Alex shrieked.

"It's just me," Michael said.

"She's silent. I don't know why," Alex said, shaking her head. "This can't be everything they planned."

"Of course it isn't," came a voice from behind them. Alex and Michael spun toward the castle. *Lygari.* The sorcerer wore a deep violet robe, his sleeves rolled up to reveal his betrayer mark. At the sight of it, Alex's own scar itched, but she resisted the urge to scratch it. Pain and rage rippled through her.

Not now. She growled at the fury inside her.

"What do you want, Lygari?" Lynx growled and leaped in front of Alex, one hand already outstretched and glowing green, the other hovering protectively over Alex's swollen belly.

"Besides revenge?" He adjusted his cloak as he strutted toward them.

Kill him, the fury purred. Her Ares powers began to seep out, unbidden, and she struggled to maintain control. It felt as if someone were stirring her well from within.

I can help, the fury whispered. *Let me deal with him once and for all.*

Stella appeared beside Lygari, glowing maroon, and Alex could smell the ash on her despite the rain. "Did you think we'd leave you unscathed after you murdered my mother?"

"I am your Head," Alex said, pushing Lynx to the side and moving in front of her friends. "I'm not frightened by either of you. Leave now, or you'll regret coming after my home."

With a yip, Lynx vanished. Phobos appeared where Lynx had been a moment before. "The Forbidden Lands is your home now, Head. It's time you stopped listening to these traitorous sorcerers who mingle with worthless mortals and return to your *proper* home."

"Datten *is* my proper home," Alex spat at him.

"Will it still be once we burn it to the ground?" Stella asked.

<h1 style="text-align:center">CHAPTER 65
AARON</h1>

Aaron had grown accustomed to being cracked, but this time he slammed into the stone floor of his throne room so hard it knocked out his breath. The clang of metal on metal echoed all around him. Jerome and Avery lead a group of knights against Gryphon's hexa and her lackies, Orion and Fenrir. Only Gryphon arrived on his feet, already growling at the other sorcerers.

Cameron scrambled up and reached Aaron. "We have to get out of here and find Alex."

"You're not going anywhere, mortals," Fenrir snarled. He transformed into his wolf form and stalked toward them. Aaron drew his red steel blade, brought it up to his shoulder, and put himself in front of Cameron.

Stefan leaped from the side and kicked Fenrir in the snout. "Matthew, we've got Cameron. You take Edward to find Alex!" he shouted across the room. Warren's general nodded and pulled Edward by the arm toward the door.

"Not so fast," Eris chimed as she burst into an orange glow. A breeze circled the room, as the stench of fear permeated the air. She moved toward Aaron, but Gryphon and Megesti cracked between the sorceress and him.

"Stay away from him," Megesti snapped.

Eris smirked, unfazed. "You're certainly braver than your worthless father. Did you inherit anything worthwhile from him, or is your only power from your mother?"

Gryphon burst into orange to match his hexa, but before he could do anything, Birch cracked in front of the withered sorceress and punched her in the face. Eris fell back on her rear, and Birch exploded in a light green color. Vines burst through the stone floor and ensnared Eris, Orion, and Fenrir, dragging them down to the ground.

"Don't you dare speak to my son."

Fenrir bit through his vines, leaped into the air, and deftly landed on his paws. He cocked his head toward Stefan and sniffed the air before growling.

"Touch him and I'll rip out your throat," Gryphon said.

Jerome and the Datten knights had made it to Aaron, and the sorcerers backed away from them in unison. *They're speaking through their thoughts.*

"Last chance, Gryphon," Eris said. "Come with us and help us find *your* sorceress, otherwise we'll consider you a traitor and whatever we do to her ... well, let's just say her blood will be on your hands."

Aaron swallowed hard.

Gryphon stared at his hexa. "You won't hurt her. You need her and the next Head she carries. Without her, I can't have another child, and your line will end."

"After the disastrous state you and your mother left our line in, maybe it should end."

"Ares disagrees with you," Gryphon snapped.

Eris' face went pale. "Ares visited you?"

"He summoned all three of us," Aaron said. "Gryphon,

Alexandria, and myself. He must value us, regardless of what you think."

Fenrir had reverted from his animal form, staring at Aaron wide-eyed.

"What did he say to you?" Orion asked.

"What my line founder wants from me is not your concern," Gryphon replied.

Aaron felt the air cooling. Kharon stood in the corner, glowing gray. He mouthed some words, and a flash of light flew through the room, and then some new ghosts were standing there, facing the intruders. Aaron recognized Victoria, Merlock, and an older sorcerer who resembled Megesti. Eris stumbled back and cracked away, leaving Orion and Fenrir behind.

"Orion and Fenrir!" the older ghost shouted. "If you do not leave my line alone, I will see to it that you learn what the Merlins are truly capable of. It is not merely the Usurper and Head powers that run in my descendants' blood, and unlike you, I fear neither founders nor gods."

"Is that ... Merlin?" Aaron asked Megesti, who shrugged.

Orion and Fenrir glared at the ghosts, then, with wicked smirks on their faces, they cracked away.

A shiver rushed through Aaron, and he heard voices and shouting coming from the throne room. Jerome rushed past him and, together with Stefan and Avery, opened the ancient doors that led to the spare hall.

"What in Torian?" Avery asked as Ruby ran through the doors and jumped into her father's arms.

"She saved us, Daddy! I knew she didn't abandon us. She still loves us."

"Who, dear?" Birch asked as Caleb's mother entered the room.

"Alexandria," Lady Reinhardt said. "She removed all of us

as some wicked sorcerers were destroying all our homes. They set the entire marketplace on fire. See for yourself."

Aaron raced from the throne room and charged down the stairs to the main castle entrance. Gryphon caught up, using magic to throw open the monstrous oak doors. From the top of the steps, Aaron had a clear view down the road he'd walked thousands of times, houses smoldering far into the distance. All of the roofs and wooden structures were gone. Further down the road, a colossal storm cloud spread, unleashing sheets of rain that drowned the flames.

Jerome stood beside him, surveying the charred remains of the houses of the knights. Their homes were located closest to the castle. "We'll rebuild."

Aaron turned and marched back into the throne room. Determination pulsed through him. *I'll get my people safely out of the castle and town grounds, then I'll find her.*

"Ruby, I need your help," Aaron called.

The youngest Reinhart hurried over. "Anything, King Aaron."

"Take your mother and the other families down to the lowest floor. Do you still know where the food storage is? I know it was years ago that you played down there with your brother and me."

"I do!"

"Perfect. Go down that hallway until you see the locked door with no handle. There, you'll need to tell the door, *show me the way, from Datten I won't stray.*"

"That's silly!"

"And that's why you won't forget. Now, go and make your father proud."

Ruby curtsied to Aaron and spun around to her waiting mother. She pulled her by the hand toward the stairs, and the rest followed. As they vanished down the hallway, Aaron turned to the others.

"We have to split up and make sure no other sorcerers are hiding in the castle. Gryphon and Stefan, you go to town and try to find Alex. Birch and Kharon, we'll need healing and sleeping potions. Megesti—"

"I'm not leaving you."

Aaron looked at his friend for a long moment. "Okay. You're with me. Avery, stay with Matthew and Edward."

"If you think I'm going to sit around while my daughter is out there, then you are sorely mistaken," Edward snapped.

"You'll stay here in case Alex comes back. Cameron, you can stay with Edward or join Megesti, Jerome, and me."

"I'm with you," Cameron said, joining Aaron.

"Then let's go. Those sorcerers gave up much too easily. I suspect there is more going on than we realize."

CHAPTER 66

ALEX

"We aren't going to ask you again," Lygari said. "You come with us willingly, or you'll live to regret this."

Memories of his and Moorloc's abuse filled her mind, and Alex let her Ares powers take over. Rage burned through her veins and an orange light emanated from within her. The rain stopped, and she took a step toward him. He scrambled to get away. She smiled. "As I expected. Without your father to protect you, you're the same coward you always were. I've died, faced Cassandra, and threatened Ares himself. I'm not afraid of silly half-mortal boy sorcerers, who spend their time torturing children. I am your Head, and you will obey me or suffer the consequences."

"Sounds like the fury is making herself known." Phobos' voice boomed around Alex, but she couldn't see him.

"We can take from you too, little Head," said Fenrir. He appeared, alongside Phobos, in the courtyard. Sniffing the air, he shook his head and shifted into his giant wolf. Alex switched her stance and threw her wind at him, but nothing happened. She reached for it again, but her Poseidon powers had depleted themselves by creating the storm and putting out the fires.

Alex screamed and leaped back as Fenrir stalked toward her.

Michael unsheathed his sword and shoved Alex behind him. Fenrir bared his teeth and snarled, but Michael gripped his red steel blade with both hands. "Alex, get out of here!" he shouted.

A cold force grabbed Alex, trying to pull her away from Michael. "I won't leave you," Alex replied.

"For once in your life, do as I ask." Michael swung the sword at the wolf and missed. The creature swung its head to the side and lunged for the blade. Lygari cracked between Alex and Michael and drew a short sword from his robe. Alex glimpsed the hideous skull on its hilt and recognized it from Moorloc's castle. Lygari lifted his arm and before she could scream, he slashed Michael's lower calf. Blood sprayed from his leg and he crumpled to his knees. Moving with lightning speed, Lygari kicked Michael with such force that he skidded across the ground into the wall with a sickening crack.

"Michael!" Alex shouted. She threw Lygari out of her way and charged toward her best friend, stopped only by a warmth running down her belly followed by a sharp pain.

My babies!

A solid steel spear had been rammed through her midsection, making her head swim.

"That's for my mother, you witch!" Stella twisted the spear and Alex could feel it ripping through the muscles in her back. Her entire body went stiff, and the surrounding voices became muddled. She saw a glow, and Emmerich's voice ripped through the garbled sounds. "Run!"

But Michael ... I have to help Michael.

"You can't help him if you're dead. Flee to fight another day." Emmerich vanished, and Alex desperately searched for Michael, finding only a pool of blood. Sorcerers closed in on her, and as a tear ran down her cheek she cracked.

CHAPTER 67
GRYPHON

"Alex! Lynx! Michael! Someone answer me!" Stefan shouted.

Gryphon would usually have groaned at Stefan's constant shouting, but right now all he cared about was finding Alex and Lynx. They were running down the main road checking down alleys and in the open doors. Both of them were drenched to the bone. *At least the rain means she's all right.* The darkening sky fed Gryphon's anxious energy, though.

"Can't you sense them?" Stefan asked.

"If I could, we wouldn't be running still."

They arrived at the marketplace, and Gryphon immediately recognized it as the epicenter of Alex's storm. Wherever she was now, the spell had originated from here.

"Gryphon?" Stefan's voice was shaking.

"Yes?"

Stefan squatted on the ground, his voice soft when he asked, "Can you tell whose blood this is?"

Gryphon crouched beside him and his heart stopped. Whoever had been injured here had lost a lot of blood, enough that they might not survive it. He dropped to his knees and slammed his hands into the blood. Even in this chilly rain, it was still warm. A sword slash followed by a spear being jammed forward came into his mind unbidden. "I can't tell for sure. It's more than one of them."

"Lynx!"

Stefan's bond mark glowed through his wet shirt. He reached out to Lynx without even realizing it. *Their connection is stronger than I'd surmised.*

Gryphon stood up, letting the rain wash the blood from his hands.

An icy wind surrounded him. "Victoria?"

"Save them! Go to the stables, where Daniel died. *Now!*"

"Gryphon, who are you talking to?" Stefan asked.

"Think of the stables Daniel died in," Gryphon shouted and grabbed Stefan's arm.

CHAPTER 68
ALEX

Alex cracked into the burned-out stable, struggling to stay upright with the heavy spear sticking out of her midsection and back. She closed her eyes and focused on sending her healing magic into her body. She could just pick up the heartbeat of her babies, but they were much weaker than normal.

"Please, no," Alex sobbed. "I can't lose you too." Her pants were soaked with her blood, and she felt dizzy as her hands grew cold and trembled.

Alecto ... please save my babies.

What will you give me?

Save them. I'll give you my oath. As long as you never hurt them, you can do with me whatever you want.

"Wake up." Daniel's voice sounded far away, but when she opened her eyes, he hovered over her.

"I'm so tired and cold. Why is it cold?" Alex whispered.

Daniel's face had a look of increasing terror. "Alex, you have to stay awake. We can't get help if you go to sleep."

"Go," Alex whispered, and Daniel vanished.

Alex went to take a step but her legs gave out on her and she dropped to her knees. As the back of the spear handle smacked the ground, she shrieked in pain making the ramshackle structure tremble. The pain jerked her fully awake.

Icy air surrounded her. "They're coming, my love. Stay awake," the ghost of her mother said. Heat burned through Alex's cheeks.

"Alex, stay with me. We're going to help you." Stefan's words sounded like an order but his pale complexion and wide eyes told Alex he was anything but calm. She had to tell him about Michael. She opened her mouth but only a hoarse croak came out. She moved her hand to touch his face.

"Grab her left arm," Stefan ordered.

Gryphon looked destroyed. His mouth hung open and his pupils were almost black.

"Gryphon!" Stefan shouted.

He finally snapped to attention and gripped her arm. Stefan reached around the other.

I'm going to crack us as gently as I can.

I understand.

We're going to save you, Alex.

I don't care what happens to me. I only care about the babies.

Without you, they don't stand a chance.

Alex nodded weakly, and Gryphon took them away.

Despite how carefully he moved her, the spear jostled as they landed in Datten's spare hall, and Alex shrieked in pain. The castle walls rattled around them as her scream left her and bounced off the walls of the room. The joining doors were thrown open and Aaron rushed in with Megesti and Jerome at his side. After only a few steps all three froze in shock at Alex.

"Birch!" Gryphon shouted, and the Celtic Titan appeared. Her surprised gasp echoed through the room.

Alex shook violently, her energy draining. Faintly, she heard Gryphon's terrified thoughts. *She can't stay like this forever.*

"Help," she croaked at Birch.

Birch burst into green light and rushed toward her. The moment she touched Alex's face, the icy cold was gone, replaced by a warm, comforting feeling—like a mother's hug. Her panicked breaths slowed.

A loud bang followed by Edward's voice echoed across the room. "Alexandria! What have they done to you?"

"Stay back," Megesti ordered. He took Alex's hand and burst into a violet glow. "Take what you need from me."

Alex could only nod.

"Gryphon, you're going to need to remove the spear." Birch's voice was nearly drowned out by Edward and Aaron's shouts, echoing from opposite sides of the hall.

"Enough!" Stefan boomed. Jerome joined his son, and Alex could tell from his stance that he was ready to step in if needed. *Even against my own father. Even against Aaron. How did this happen?* Stefan bent low and calmly addressed Gryphon. "You're the only one who can remove the spear and cauterize the wound at once. You have to."

Gryphon shook his head. She'd never seen him truly afraid, and it was almost worse than her physical pain. Alex reached out. *Please Gryphon. You have to ... for our baby.*

Gryphon took a breath and closed his eyes. He sent his Salem powers down his arms in a bright red, glowing light. He sucked in a breath as the magic intensified and soon his hands were glowing like a sword heated by a blacksmith. Exhaling sharply, he gripped the spear, and Alex shrieked as the metal turned orange from the heat of his flames.

"Pull it out *now*," Birch ordered.

Gryphon wrenched it out, and Megesti embraced Alex. They both erupted in a gold light so bright, the others had to cover their eyes. As their light dimmed, Alex's glow lingered on the wound the spear had left and on one side of her midsection.

"It's not enough!" she cried, grabbing Megesti for support. For a moment, her face went stoic, then cold and her eyes went black.

No, Alex. Stay with us, please!

Footsteps echoed from across the room, followed by a scuffle. "Alex, don't give up. We'll get you through this!"

Aaron? Alex's heart fluttered for a moment when she turned her head just enough to see Aaron rushing toward her. Edward fought him, but Jerome restrained the king despite his protests.

Birch put a hand on Megesti's back, while Stefan paced beside them.

"*Do* something, Gryphon!" Edward bellowed from across the hall but Jerome's grip only tightened on him.

Gryphon sent his power surging into her.

It's not enough. I can't feel my babies. I want Aaron.

Alex sobbed, as her gold light flickered and dimmed. As if he'd heard her plea Aaron nudged past Megesti and bent down to touch her cheek. "I'm here, Alex. I love you. Stay with us, *please*."

The moment Aaron's hand touched Alex's face, a wave of heat burst from him, warming everything around them before rushing into Alex and removing the chill that had taken her over again. Alex was finally calm enough to take a full breath. As her lungs filled with air tears streamed down her face and she managed to lock eyes with Aaron. *My Aaron.*

Then she realized Aaron glowed as brightly as she did.

CHAPTER 69
AARON

Aaron felt strange. His entire body tingled the way his fingers did when he came into the warm castle from the stables in the dead of winter. Megesti, Birch and Gryphon were staring at him, wide-eyed. *Am I glowing? Did I take Alex's power? What is happening right now?*

The others released Alex and slowly stepped back. They stared into each other's eyes and the gold light grew even brighter.

I wish you could read my mind like you can read Gryphon's, so I could tell you how much I fought to get back to you, and how much I love you. I want you. You, and both of these babies. Don't leave me again.

Alex's eyes widened for a moment almost as if she'd heard him. The golden glow faded and the color drained from her face. Aaron braced her midsection before she could collapse, and looped his arm under her legs to hoist her up. She was so limp, he struggled not to lose his grip on her. Stefan rushed over and despite his fears Aaron allowed Stefan to take her.

"Take her to our room, Stefan," he asked. "Birch, can you change her?"

"Of course—"

"She is not going anywhere with you," Edward snapped finally wrenching himself free of Jerome and striding forward. "Stefan, bring her here, and we'll return to Warren."

Aaron held his hand out to Stefan intending to stop him, but Stefan took several steps back, moving Alex further from Edward and behind Aaron.

"No. She came to save *our* people," Aaron said. "and she's not leaving until she wakes up and tells me what she wants to do."

"You have no say over my daughter." Edward pushed against Aaron to get to Alex, but Jerome yanked him away by his collar, as if he were a family pet and not royalty.

"She stays," Stefan said. "You lied to your daughter for months. She deserves to hear the truth and make her own decisions."

"Their marriage is over!" Edward shouted, shoving Jerome off him. The general raised his brow—a warning Aaron knew too well. "She isn't anything to Datten anymore!"

"You're wrong. She's my wife and our queen. The contract isn't valid." Aaron said, making Edward stop in his tracks. His head was still foggy, and his heart hammered in his chest, but he would not let Edward take her from him before he could talk to her. *This might be my only chance.*

Edward groaned. "I already told you; I don't care what name you signed. My counsel declared you divorced once Alex signed the papers."

"Alex never signed the paper either," Stefan piped in. "Michael forged her signature. He can replicate both Alex's and my signatures with alarming accuracy."

"What?" Edward shouted.

"She never wanted the divorce," Stefan replied. "You forced her into it. If anyone in this room betrayed her, it's you, not Aaron."

Edward spun, eyes wild as he searched for any ally. Finding none, he threw an accusing arm at Aaron and Stefan. "If you think I'm going to let you take my daughter hostage—"

"I won't allow them to keep her here if that's not what she wants," Birch interjected. She gently touched Edward's arm, lowering it. "But you have to let Alex make this choice for herself."

"She's a *child*," Edward snapped.

"She stopped being a proper child the day her mother died," Birch said. "That kind of trauma changes you forever. I'd know."

Edward opened his mouth, but a faint green light left Birch's hand and entered his chest, so he closed it. "Alexandria is a queen, and in a few short months, she'll be a mother. She'll always be your daughter, but she's a grown woman, and Victoria would insist she be allowed to make this decision herself."

Edward dropped his head in defeat and nodded. Birch turned to Aaron, as if waiting for instructions.

Aaron stood tall. "I promise to summon you the moment *Alex* asks to see you, Your Royal Highness. Until then, Birch will return you and your men to Warren."

For a moment, the kind godfather who'd protected him from his own strict father for so many years looked back at him. Aaron bowed slightly to show respect to the king he recognized, and then Birch cracked the Warren men away.

Moments later, Aaron was in Alex's suite with a smaller group.

"Lay her here," Birch said, pointing to the bed. "I'll get her changed, and you can all go help whoever needs it in town."

"I'm not leaving her," Aaron said.

"Lynx and Michael are still missing," Stefan said. The same worry line formed between his eyes that Jerome got.

"I'm staying here. Take your father, Gryphon—whoever you need and go find them."

"I don't want to leave her either," Gryphon said. Aaron shot him a warning glare, then softened.

"If she wakes up and Lynx and Michael are still missing, she'll be devastated. You'll be more help in finding them than I would."

Gryphon rubbed his eyes but nodded. "Let's go, Wafners." And the trio departed.

"As soon as she's changed, Megesti and I will join Kharon and begin work on as many potions as we can make to help everyone who might have been injured," Birch said.

AARON DRAGGED a chair up from the main floor of their suite while Birch changed Alex out of her ruined clothes. Nothing in her wardrobe would fit her anymore, so Birch improvised and put Alex in one of Aaron's larger sleeping shirts. It fit, but barely, snug around her baby bump. Birch fussed over the pillows and tucked Alex in for a few minutes before leaving.

Finally alone with her, Aaron changed out of his blood-soaked tunic and plopped down into the chair on Alex's side of the bed to watch over her. For a long while, she barely moved. Aaron watched her chest rise and fall with each breath, and anytime it slowed even slightly, he'd slide to the edge of his seat, only for her to breathe again. When it became clear she would not stop breathing, he took a moment to look her over. Despite the amount of healing magic that had filled the hall, many unhealed cuts and bruises still littered Alex's body. On instinct, he moved to push her hair out of her face, but stopped short.

"Stefan, Cameron, and Megesti all said you were fighting for me, for us. I tried to fight for you, but your father made it impossible. Until I know for sure…" Aaron pulled his hand away and sat back on the chair. "I'm so sorry, Alex. How is it you're three years younger than I am yet so much wiser than me?"

"That would be from the hardships she grew up in," came a voice from the stairs.

Aaron's mother entered the room, and he hurried to take her hand. "You should have evacuated with the other nobles."

"And leave without knowing my son, goddaughter, and grandchild are all right?" She examined her son, placing two fingers on his chin and tilting his head to the side. "If you intend on standing guard at her bedside, you should wash her blood off yourself. No one wants to wake up to that."

"I'm not leaving her."

"You will bathe. But I will stay with her while you do so. You and I both know when Alexandria drains herself, she's out for at least a day." When Aaron frowned, she thrust a finger in his face. "And don't think just because you're king that you can order me around."

"Yes, Mother," Aaron muttered to himself as he hurried down the stairs. He flung off his clothes as he went, so he was nearly naked by the time he got into the bathing suite. Despite the cold water, he cleaned himself in record time, leaving the tub water a dull pink. He found the clean tunic he'd been wearing, but he'd been so bloody that this one dripped with it. He tossed it in the bathing suite and listened to his mother's voice, as he quietly climbed the stairs.

"You've missed so much, dear. Ruby is growing into a fine young lady, and her mother is beside herself. She's becoming more Edith than Jessica, and her parents don't know what to do with her. The cook's youngest boy is thriving exactly as you said he would. He loves working in the stable and has a true knack for horses. He's almost as good as you are. I'm handling all your duties, so nothing is being missed."

Guinevere had forgone the chair, sitting instead on the edge of Alex's bed. She tucked the loose hair to the side and told the sleeping Alex all the things that had happened in Datten in the last six months. Aaron swallowed hard. He'd been so focused on his own feelings, he'd never considered how much Alex being gone would affect his mother, let alone everyone else.

Guinevere smiled sweetly. "That's much better. We can't have you scaring her half to death when she wakes."

"Thank you."

"Of course. You are a wonderful delegator and king, Aaron, but as a husband, you have much to learn."

"I know. I only hope she gives me the chance to work on it."

"She will."

"How do you know?" Aaron asked, moving to his mother's side next to Alex.

"Two reasons." She squeezed his hand. "I was told she never signed the divorce papers, so that means in her eyes, you are still her husband."

"You can't know that."

"I can because of the second reason." Guinevere picked up Alex's hand and held it up, pointing out a traditional Warren wedding ring with a huge blue sapphire on it.

Aaron ran his hand through his hair. "How does her wedding ring to Cameron prove she loves me?"

"It's on the wrong hand." His mother lifted Alex's left hand gently off the bed. His grandmother's ring was in the same spot he'd slipped it on her finger at their wedding.

CHAPTER 70
ALEX

Alex felt so stiff she struggled to move her arm over her head to block the light from her eyes. *Why does everything always hurt?* Alex grabbed her belly. *The babies!* As if her children sensed her terror, both kicked. Alex closed her eyes and covered her face with her hand, letting tears of relief fall. When she finally caught her breath, she could take in the room.

This bed isn't red, but ... the bed I shared with Aaron is. Alex reached for Aaron's side of the bed and found it empty. She was in Datten, but where? A snore drew her to Aaron passed out in a reading chair. His hair was a mess and his face sported several days of stubble. He'd balanced his elbow on the arm of the chair to hold up his head. He snorted in his sleep and Alex smiled.

Is it true? Have you been trying to get to me for months while it was my father who kept us apart? Do you still love me?

Alex leaned out of the bed and stroked his knee. He startled awake and his head slipped and he almost punched himself. He reached for her, and Alex felt a rush of peace and warmth, but he stopped his hand a slight distance from her face and withdrew. The happy warmth turned to stone. Alex took a deep breath and decided to take a chance.

She pressed Aaron's hand against her face. That broke whatever spell was on him, and Aaron leaped from the chair, sending it flying, and came to her bedside.

He cupped her face in his hands and pressed his forehead to hers. "I'm so sorry. I ... I lost my temper—"

Alex fisted Aaron's shirt and yanked his face down to her, giving him her reply with a kiss. A wind ripped through the room, sending the balcony doors crashing open. Outside it thundered and rained. Even the vase of flowers on her bedside table bore blooms much too large for winter.

"You seem to have a lot of feelings," Aaron whispered.

She pulled him into the bed. Aaron held her tightly in his arms. A long moment of silence passed between them while Alex considered how to express all the feelings swirling through her.

"Is it true?" Alex finally asked.

"Is what true?"

"That you changed your mind, and have been trying to reach me since that day ... and that ..."

"Your father lied to you and has been keeping us apart? Yes."

"Why?"

"He no longer thinks I'm worthy of you and he didn't want me anywhere near our son."

Their baby moved, so Alex put his hand on her belly over their son. She knew he'd react, since neither baby was fond of other people touching her stomach.

Aaron gasped the moment the baby moved, and Alex smiled. "He's saying hello."

"All I wanted for these last three months was to get back to you and the babies."

"Babies?"

"Yes. I know everything that happened in the Forbidden Lands. I wasn't planning on having to rear a child with Gryphon, but Gryphon's son will still be our son's brother, and he deserves to be with his mother as much as his father."

"You'd accept them both?"

"Yes. I made a stupid mistake sending you away. I love you."

Alex pushed Aaron away slightly. "Are you only accepting the other baby to get me back?"

"No. I'm messing this up," he muttered. He took a breath. "While you were in Warren, I read the queens' journals. Some of our best families started under less-than-ideal circumstances, but Datten kings stand by their wives. And I've always said I love all of you, and that baby is part of the sorceress in you, and so that baby will be our magic baby."

"Magic baby?"

Aaron nodded. "An unexpected blessing. The same way Cameron was a gift to his parents from your mother, and the way my mother helped raise Jessica, getting the girl she would have loved to have herself."

Alex's heart swelled so much it was hard for her to breathe with the babies pushing on her lungs, but she pulled Aaron close and kissed him again. "We obviously have a lot more to talk about, but knowing that you want *us* is all I need right now." Aaron held her, sending relief through every bit of her. While she craved the stillness, the empty room made her feel something was amiss. "Where is everyone?"

Aaron hesitated, and she knew it couldn't be good. "They're still searching for Michael."

Alex twisted in Aaron's lap. "You haven't found him? How

long was I asleep? What about Lynx?" Alex fought to free herself from the blankets around her legs.

"You've been asleep two days. Lynx arrived late last night. She was cracked into a forest she'd never seen before, and it took her ages to get out. She saw some ... disturbing beings there."

Alex's foot became tangled as she tried to climb out of the bed, and Aaron caught her.

"Two days? We have to go get him." She rushed to leave.

"Alex, you can't just barge out of the castle like this."

"Aaron, I've made a lot of mistakes recently. Losing Michael will not be one of them."

"Okay, fine! We'll go together, but you need pants!"

The cool air on her legs finally reached her awareness. "Oh."

Aaron dug through his wardrobe and returned with a pair of his older training pants. "These should fit. Shall I leave while you get dressed?"

"No," Alex said. "We can talk about this later, but know that Cameron and I were never anything but friends. He played the role for my father, but behind closed doors, he touched me even less than Stefan does. There was only ever you."

Aaron smiled. "He told me. May I help you?"

"Please." Alex held Aaron's shoulder for balance as she stepped into his pants and pulled the drawstring below her belly.

Aaron threw open the door to the hallway. "Caleb, fetch the Wafners—all of them."

"Is she—?"

Alex pushed Aaron aside and smiled at Caleb. "Awake? Alive? Staying in Datten? A yes to all."

Caleb beamed at Aaron and hugged Alex. "Thank you for saving my mother and sister."

Alex hugged him back tightly. "What kind of queen would I be if I didn't? You're all family to me."

Caleb left, running down the hallway to find the Wafners.

"You're planning to stay?" Aaron asked tentatively.

Alex turned back to Aaron. "I only left to give you space, but then I stayed away because of what my father told me. I know that truth now. I'm coming home. Have someone send word to my father that I'm alive, but that I have no desire to see him after the lies he spread for months."

"Alex, he won't believe it."

"You're right. I'll write the note and crack it. Then we'll find Michael."

CHAPTER 71
ALEX

Lynx cracked them back to the town square where they'd arrived a few days before. Despite knowing Stefan, Lynx, and their other friends were all uninjured, Alex struggled to rein in her tremulous feelings, and the storm raged around. Branches snapped off the remaining trees and littered the ground around them as they searched for their missing friend. It hadn't even taken a full minute for them all the be soaked by the downpour that followed her.

Lynx tried to sniff the air, but the scowl on her face made it clear the rain and constant gusts of wind made tracking him impossible. Alex inhaled deeply, hoping it would slow the wind, but instead the rubble heaps rumbled as if they were trying to implode. Alex closed her eyes to slow her breathing and keep a vortex from forming and turning the debris into weapons.

"Where did you see him last?" Stefan asked.

Alex walked over to where she'd faced the sorcerers when Lygari had cut down Michael. Despite all the rain, the blood was still visible on the pale gray cobblestone. She detailed the entire attack, and they searched for where he could have gone after being thrown by Lygari.

Splish splash.

The fury's taunt made Alex's stomach churn. "The well!" Puddles had already formed on the ground. Desperate, she ignored her spinning vision and staggered toward the broken well.

"If he's in there, he'd have drowned," Aaron said.

"No. Alex drained the well to make the rainstorm," Lynx said.

Alex had nearly reached the well when someone pulled her away. She whipped around, expecting to scold Stefan, but it was Gryphon.

"If he's down there, and it's bad, you don't need to see that."

Alex wrenched out of his grip. The surrounding storm rumbled, and the rain grew heavy, pelting them harder. Lightning struck a tree behind the row of damaged houses, making a crack vibrate through them all.

"Any chance you could be less annoying?" Stefan asked, shoving Gryphon away from Alex. "The storm soaking us is coming from her, and upsetting her is only going to make it worse."

Gryphon stepped up to the well, rubbed his hands together to produce a large enough fireball that Alex's rain wouldn't extinguish it, and dropped it into the well. It didn't even take a minute for him to gasp and lean into the well. "He's down there, and I think he's still alive."

Alex hurried to his side. "Michael!" she shouted, but there was no reply. "We have to get him out. Now!" The storm above rumbled again, and with a deafening crack, lightning struck the road a small distance from the market, sending stones flying through the air. Megesti threw his hands up, sending a wind strong enough to divert the stones that would have hit them.

"It's too dark to crack safely down there," Gryphon said. "Someone has to climb down to get him out."

"I'll go," Megesti said.

"I can do it," Gryphon argued.

"No," Megesti said. "You're all sorcerer. I was trained by several Wafner generals to manage these sorts of mortal situations."

"Several?" Stefan asked.

"I'm almost seventy, Stefan. You're my fourth generation of Wafner." Megesti removed his robe and handed it to Alex. Stefan untied the bucket from the well pulley. The wall had been damaged, but the pole that held the bucket and pulley was still functional. Megesti tied the rope around himself, and Aaron tightened it until Megesti made him stop.

"Stefan and Aaron will lower you down while Gryphon sends light down for you," Alex shouted above the storm. "Once you reach him, crack out."

"Understood."

As Alex stepped back to give room to the others, Lynx slid her arm around her. "They'll get him out."

"I know. I'm just worried about what I'll do if he doesn't survive."

Lynx squeezed Alex tighter as Aaron and Stefan lowered Megesti into what remained of the well.

CHAPTER 72
GRYPHON

"Get out of my way, Gryphon!" The desperation in her voice made Gryphon's heart hurt. Aaron shrugged at him, as pained by Alex's pleas as he was.

"Alex, you have to trust our friends and the doctor," Aaron said.

"I'm the Titan of Cassandra! I should be in there."

"Megesti has Cassandra powers too." Gryphon leaned on the closed door to the lab as another muffled scream came through.

Aaron tried to rub Alex's shoulders, but she growled at him, so he stepped back.

"I order you to move," Alex said.

Gryphon didn't move. "Alex, you cannot help him. You drained all of your magic to save yourself and the babies. If Megesti and I hadn't shared ours with you, all three of you would have died. It'll be at least a month before you have enough magic to heal anyone."

"I can help without magic!"

The door opened, revealing Lynx and Stefan. Stefan was drying his hands on a towel. "It's done."

"Is he—?"

"He'll make it," Lynx said.

A sob broke from Alex, and she finally let Aaron console her. "We're going to go update my family," Stefan said. "You should go see him before they arrive."

To Gryphon, Lynx whispered, "Be ready. She's going to need both of you after she sees him."

Stefan and Lynx were gone by the time Alex calmed herself enough to go in. Gryphon let her lead and shared Lynx's cryptic warning with Aaron. The two of them hurried after Alex and immediately froze.

Michael lay in a large bed, unconscious. Unlike all the other rooms Gryphon had seen in Datten, these sheets were black. *Easier to hide the blood.* Gryphon hoped Alex hadn't heard that particular thought.

Michael had been propped up by several pillows. His face was swollen, and his arms and bare chest were littered with deep cuts that had been stitched up by the doctor. Large bruises were already forming around his rib cage—but that wasn't what Lynx had warned them about. His left leg was propped up on three pillows, his entire knee wrapped in several layers of bandages soaked in dried blood. The bottom half of his leg was gone. Panic and nausea overwhelmed Gryphon, and he knew it was coming from Alex. She crept toward Michael's bed, unable to take her eyes off his missing leg as her entire body began to tremble. Gryphon's gaze settled on the tray of bloody saws that had been left on the table near the end of the bed. He flicked his fingers to crack them away before Alex noticed them.

"There was nothing you could have done, Alex," Megesti said.

"If I had my magic—"

"Your Royal Highness," the royal physician said. "I worked with your mother, and his injuries were severe enough that they would have been beyond even her abilities."

"It was his leg or his life," Megesti whispered.

Alex glanced back at Gryphon and Aaron. Gryphon nudged Aaron forward. Slowly, he took his place at Alex's side as she took Michael's hand.

After you're both healed, we'll figure out what we can do to help him.

Alex gave Gryphon a nod, and he took it as a sign he could leave, so he slipped silently out of the sickroom and cracked to the Verlassen Castle. After checking on Cerberus to make sure the beast was happy, he went to the lab to check the books.

He had two things to look up. He remembered reading a book by a Tiere or Salem Titan about crafting artificial limbs. That information was best found in the larger library in the Forbidden Lands. But the Cassandra books were here, and he needed to find something even more important.

Gryphon read until his eyes burned. Alex's sorrow and pain were to be expected, but the way it all flowed into him made it difficult to focus. After hours of reading, he'd barely made it through ten pages.

There was a soft knock at the door. Expecting Birch or Kharon, Gryphon waved his hand to open the door and turned to greet his guest, but was shocked to find Megesti.

The Titan of Merlin crossed the room to the shelves, which were now fully stocked, and lingered near an herb Gryphon suspected was peppermint, the tea he favored when given the option. When Megesti idly tugged at his own collar, Gryphon decided to help the poor sorcerer out.

"She'll survive this, Megesti, and so will Michael."

"That's not what I'm worried about."

"Then what?" Gryphon asked.

Megesti slunk across the room to sit at the table with him. "Did I do something wrong? What if I hurt him?"

"Ah. The kingling. You think you sent magic into Aaron, and that's why he glowed gold."

"I haven't found anything else that makes sense," Megesti groaned.

"That's the reason I'm here—to see if any of your books can give us a hint about what happened with Aaron. And I seem to recall a book that talked about magical limbs ..."

"Lynx has the limbs book, or a copy of it. She already gave it to my mother. Is it really possible to regrow a limb?"

Gryphon's weariness wore on him, and he rubbed his eyes. "No. But there have been times where a limb was lost and the titans could craft one from nature, by enchanting it. That's what Lynx, Birch, and I all thought of. He won't ever be the same again, but if we do it correctly, he'll be able to walk."

"That's amazing. Will we be able to use this to help other people, too?" Megesti asked.

"I can't see why not," Gryphon replied, and Megesti smiled. "What?"

"I think we may have found Michael another career to go with advisor," Megesti said. "And I'm sure Alex will insist on funding it."

Gryphon felt a twinge of hope ripple through him. "I hope so."

"Do you have any theories about Aaron?"

Gryphon tapped his fingers on the table. Megesti stared at him with the same nervous hope sparkling in his emerald eyes as Alex had. "I have a few. He could have magic left from the curse, and it took the form of the magic we were using. Or Alex —or you—may have unintentionally sent it to him to heal something in him during the struggle."

Megesti chuckled. "Or he's secretly a sorcerer and just never told us."

Gryphon laughed. "Or that."

"I wonder who he'd get it from, his mother or father?"

"That's actually my last theory ... that Victoria put a spell on him to protect him after I was sent to kill him. Did he heal easily as a child?"

"He'd have to get sick to heal quickly," Megesti replied. "Aaron has been healthier than anyone living in Datten, and yes, when he injured himself, he healed faster than the doctor or my father expected."

"So, my final theory holds merit."

Megesti stilled and groaned.

"What is it?"

"Her blood!"

In Gryphon's estimation, it took the Merlin Titan far too long to finish his thought. When Gryphon cleared his throat, he finally did.

"Alex gave Aaron some of her blood before she went to Moorloc's castle. She did it so Aaron would be able to see the castle when we came to get her back."

Gryphon nodded, figuring out where Megesti was going. "So, it's likely when she needed every last bit of her healing magic, she simply took it back from him."

AARON

Aaron struggled to convince Alex to leave Michael's side. Even with Jessica, Stefan, and Jerome watching over him, she didn't want to go. Stefan finally stepped in and insisted that she leave, claiming Jessica needed to sit with her husband. From the sorrow on Alex's face, Aaron could tell Stefan's request had broken her heart.

Stefan must have realized his mistake. "You should eat something and rest. I'll send for you as soon as we need a break."

Alex hung her head and slunk away, wordless. Aaron followed, but Jessica stopped him.

"We're not mad, Aaron. You need to know that," she said. "I just need to be here with him when he wakes up. I have to figure out what this will mean for our future. All our plans ..." Jessica swallowed. "I know he was doing his job, but Alex rushed here without her proper guards, and it was Michael who paid the price."

Stefan growled. "Alex got here in time to get innocent people out. If she hadn't, who knows what would have happened? Michael's oath to Alex means he would lay down his life for her—the same as me, and the same as our father. You knew that when you married him, so do not blame Alexandria for risking her own life, as well as Michael's and Lynx's, to save hundreds of Datten citizens."

"She should have brought more people," Jessica snapped.

"Had she asked for more help, she would have been delayed," Jerome piped up. "She's carrying the future king of two kingdoms. Matthew and Edward would never have allowed her to come, and would have done everything possible to keep her there. Many of the Datten families we care for would have been injured or killed. But as it stands, Michael's sacrifice allowed everyone to get out."

"Everyone?" Jessica asked.

"Everyone," Jerome repeated. "From what I've heard, there were no other casualties."

Stefan nodded. "Not to mention that my pregnant wife went with her too, and she's perfectly capable of making up her own mind. I don't blame Alex for Lynx's choices."

"Lynx is pregnant?" Aaron held his hand out to Stefan to congratulate him.

"Thank you. Apparently, I'm going to be the next Randal. Lynx insisted that if she can't keep me for more than my mortal lifetime, she wants only daughters so they can live with her after I'm gone." Stefan patted Aaron's back. "Go. Alex needs you. We both know she's going to blame herself for all of this."

Aaron rushed down the hallway to his suite. He flung open the door, but didn't see Alex. He searched the library, the kitchen, the nursery, and the lab, but he couldn't find her. He felt ready to give up when Kharon came around the corner. "Have you seen Alex by any chance?"

Kharon looked startled, but their eyes flashed gray for a

moment. "Your brother says she's taking out her anger on the old stables. Don't put the fire out. She needs this." Kharon patted Aaron's shoulder, and he found himself in the overgrown field looking at the stable where his brother had been killed. It was surrounded by three other stables, and all four structures were ablaze. Standing between him and the raging inferno was Alex.

Aaron trudged toward her. Her sobs rose over the crackle and pop of the fire. Every word he'd planned to say to her left him, and he approached in silence. He cupped her hand in his, and she trembled, wordless. For a moment, he saw the scared little girl he'd coaxed into being bad and playing in the Datten woods. She threw her arms around him, and he finally embraced her. Neither of them spoke. The stables crackled and burned around them; their flames reflected in Alex's eyes.

Once all that remained was smoldering ash, Aaron kissed the top of Alex's head, then went rigid when he realized what he'd done. *You've been away for six months—three of which you thought I hated you. Is this okay?*

Alex must have sensed his sudden nervousness. She wove her fingers into his and squeezed. "Shall we walk or crack?"

"It's nice out. I'm up for the walk if you are."

Alex nodded, and with her hand still locked in his, they headed toward the castle. "Have they started the repairs?" she asked.

"Yes. The throne room is half done."

"What happened in the throne room?" Alex asked.

"There was—a fire."

"I'm sorry, Aaron. Gryphon and I knew the sorcerers could break through our old spells once we became Head and Heart. We fixed all the protection spells in the other kingdoms, but I couldn't face you, because I thought ..."

"It isn't your fault, Alex."

"They were looking for me and the babies."

Aaron stopped and gently pulled her toward him. Trembling, he reached toward her cheek. Alex leaned in, and he cupped her face. "You and our baby are the most important thing I have in my life. I'd give up my kingdom, my crown ... I'd give up my life for you both."

Alex closed the distance between them and placed her hands on his chest, sending heat rushing through him. "I love you, Aaron. Despite everything we've been through, and the things we will go through ... I love you with every beat of my heart, and there is no one I will ever love the way I love you." She leaned in to kiss him, but her belly bumped him and she couldn't reach. Aaron chuckled and leaned down to kiss her instead.

The heat in his gut spread through his entire being, and the bond mark on his shoulder itched terribly. *Slow down, Aaron.*

"Alex—"

"Aaron—"

They both grinned at each other and Alex's cheeks turned red. "We have a lot to figure out."

"Yes, we do," Aaron replied. "But before we get into all that, I need you to know that I lost my temper with you because I was already furious with Wesley and Nathanial. It's not an excuse, but I just want you to know that you are not the cause of it. I never intended to go through with a divorce."

"I understand. Gryphon and I knew it was a possibility you'd be angry when I returned."

"Wait, you did?" He felt his cheeks reddening. *I thought I was doing better.*

"We did, but not because you did anything wrong. I was gone for months, and came back pregnant because I never told you before I left. I was so surprised by your anger because I saw a vision of you and Gryphon parenting your children together and didn't connect that the children were older, and that it would take us time to get to that point. And it wasn't me who snapped at you."

"The fury?"

Alex nodded. "I intended to stay in Warren just long enough to let you calm down."

"Neither of us expected Edward to try to break us up."

"Do we have to talk about my father?" Alex asked. "I'm not ready for that conversation yet. I'm furious with him, but my mother must be even more upset. He betrayed me and you, made me use poor Cameron, again, and hurt your mother and uncle because he decided he knew what *I* needed. Everything that happens now is his fault."

"What do you mean?"

"The last crime needed to free the fury was betrayal. It was never you who'd betray me, Aaron. It was my father."

Before her words could fully sink in, she stumbled.

CHAPTER 74

ALEX

Everything spun out around Alex and she teetered.

Aaron's voice sounded strange, oddly distant when he spoke. "Alex? Are you saying you think the fury is going to get free?"

Alex closed her eyes. The world still spun, but in darkness. She managed to nod at Aaron. "I don't think ... I know, because I made a deal with her."

"What kind of deal?"

"When I learned my father betrayed me, it snapped the last of what was holding her back. I'm still able to fight her, but only to a point. When the babies were killed, I made a deal with her. She helped me bring them back, and in exchange, I'll step back once they're—"

The field began to spin, and spots danced before Alex's eyes. Alex felt herself go down, Aaron's voice fading away. But instead of hitting the hard ground, she felt herself lifted into the air. Warmth filled her body, and when she opened her eyes, Aaron looked down at her. She wrapped her arms around his neck to help him hold her.

"Have you eaten since you woke up?" he asked.

"No."

"So you haven't eaten since you left Warren?" Aaron asked. When Alex nodded meekly, Aaron called out for Megesti.

A soft breeze hit them as both Megesti and Gryphon appeared.

"What happened?" Gryphon rushed to her and quickly scanned her with his eyes, groaning. "Why do you insist on skipping meals?"

"I didn't mean to. A lot has happened."

Gryphon narrowed his eyes, so she turned away and buried her face in Aaron's chest.

"Could one of you crack us to our suite so we can get her something to eat?" Aaron asked.

"Megesti will take you to the room. I'll go to the kitchen."

Alex felt Gryphon's eyes boring into her back, and he raised his eyebrows. "Really? You want venison?" he asked. "I thought you only wanted fish right now."

"I'm in Datten. I eat venison here."

Aaron chuckled and pulled her closer.

Megesti brought them to their suite, and still, Aaron refused to let her go. Alex surrendered and let him set her on their couch by the fireplace on the main floor. He brought her pillows and a blanket from their bed to make sure she was comfortable. When Gryphon arrived, he set down a giant tray covered with enough bread, cheese, dried meat, and fruit to feed a small army. Alex smiled and grabbed the sunflower roll and venison sausage. Aaron sat next to her, and both men relaxed when they saw her eating with so much gusto.

Aaron waited as long as he could before he finally asked the question Alex was trying to avoid. "What did you mean when you said you made a deal with the fury?"

Gryphon choked on his bread, coughing uncontrollably.

Aaron stood and smacked him on the back until the bread dislodged and flew from his throat. Gryphon turned orange, and Alex felt his rage flow through her. "You *what*?" he sputtered.

"I had to," Alex whispered, avoiding his eyes in favor of her own fingers on her lap. She explained the deal she'd made with her fury to the fathers of her babies. Their lives for eventual control of hers.

Aaron dropped to his knees, gently tugging on her hands until she met his eyes. "We'll figure this out. Let's give it a few days for things to settle down, and then we'll bring everyone in on it, and see what we come up with."

Gryphon growled and cracked away. Alex tried to block out his emotions. Still rage tickled at the back of her mind.

Aaron touched her cheek. "Let him get out his frustration. I'm confident he's feeling like he failed you, so give him some space."

"Since when are you such a Gryphon fan?" Alex teased.

"Since he took care of you and my son for months. And also, since he saved our baby's life?" He rose and settled down beside her and let her snuggle up against him. "Who else knows?"

"Edith and Michael likely felt something because of their gifts. That is if Michael survives what I let happen to him ..."

"Alex," Aaron said sternly. "We went over this. Michael did his job, and you saved the lives of every citizen of Datten. If Jessica, Stefan, or anyone makes you feel guilty for that, you tell me."

"Stefan agrees with you," Alex said. "Jessica's been a bit cold, but I understand. This is even worse than when Stefan was injured at the Verlassen Castle."

Aaron kissed her forehead. "If it continues, let me know. I won't tolerate anyone disrespecting you."

Alex turned to face Aaron. "Jessica expressing her opinion is not disrespectful."

"It could be misconstrued as that. A lot of rumors have been flying around since you left."

"Such as?"

"That you hated Datten."

"Who would say that? I love our people."

"I'll give you one guess," Aaron said, and Alex groaned.

"Wesley."

"And he hates what you do to me. All these changes you've inspired—giving the working class a say. How dare I!"

Alex couldn't help but giggle. For the first time since she'd been back, she really looked at him. He'd let stubble sprout across his face, and new worry lines stretched across his forehead.

"What?"

Alex traced his forehead line with her finger. "You've aged."

He grabbed her finger and kissed it. "That happens to mortals. We can't all look nineteen for decades."

"I like it. Makes you look more distinguished."

Aaron struck his best kingly pose a moment, but couldn't hold it before he cracked up. "Now, I know it's early, but I think you should get some rest, so we should—"

"Go to bed?"

Aaron laughed. "I've never seen you this excited to go to bed."

"I missed *our* bed and having you beside me."

Aaron stood and scooped her up in one motion.

"Aaron put me down. I'm huge."

"Nonsense." She wrapped her arms around his neck, and he steadied his grip on her. "You're perfectly sized for a queen expecting an heir and a spare."

Alex stuck out her tongue at him, and he growled at her.

The sound set something off inside Alex, and she felt her cheeks heat.

Once in their bedchamber, Alex went over to her wardrobe to change, but Aaron approached her with a pile of clothes in his hands.

"What's that?"

"My mother took the liberty of getting you some items from the seamstress to hold you over until you can be fitted for new clothing."

Aaron dropped the fabric, and a shimmering night gown unfurled. It was Aaron's favorite shade of red, and Alex's preferred style.

"She knows us both so well," Alex said.

"Let's get my old shirt off you."

Aaron helped her remove his shirt, and she slipped into the nightgown. On the balcony, Alex let the wind make her gown gleam in the moonlight. The city's streets were deserted, and the buildings were blackened with soot.

Before long, Aaron joined her and wrapped his arms around her, gently caressing her belly and kissing her neck. "What are you thinking?"

"How long will it take to rebuild? Their homes were destroyed. Where will they stay?"

"Many of the families are staying with relatives, or in the inns on the outskirts of town that weren't damaged. *We* paid for them to remain there until we finish rebuilding. In fact, I'm going to Betruger tomorrow. Care to join me? I wanted to let Harold and Edith know everything that's happened in person, and get their help for rebuilding the town."

Her husband had made good choices in her absence, and she felt proud. "And get back in their good graces?"

"Only if my wife thinks it appropriate."

Alex cupped his face. "She does. Very much so." She pulled his face down so she could kiss him.

"We should get you to bed," he said, "It's been a long day."

"Long day, week, year."

"Exactly. So no arguments." He kissed her.

"I would not argue about going to bed," Alex whispered, bringing Aaron closer. "What I have in mind works best in bed." She led him to the bedroom.

Aaron shook his head. "You need rest."

"I slept for three days! I'm not tired at all," Alex said as Aaron latched the balcony door shut. "I know what you're going to say. You think I need to rest, and you want to be sure this is what I want."

Aaron grinned and nodded.

Alex ran her fingers gently along his biceps until she felt him tremble. She narrowed her eyes at him. "You always want to be honorable, but let me make this clear." He swallowed in anticipation, and she continued, "I love you, and for the last six months I've been away from you. I don't know how much you know about pregnant women, let alone pregnant sorceresses, but it's been a very challenging six months. And now that I'm back with you, I don't want to suffer the way I have without you."

Aaron tilted her chin up. Alex slid her hands along Aaron's bare chest. "What did they do?" he asked.

"What did *who* do?"

"Gryphon. Cameron. The other sorcerers. Whoever made you suffer."

Alex smiled at Aaron. "They didn't make me suffer. Being away from you while being pregnant did. A sorceress needs to be near the father of the child she's carrying, or else it's uncomfortable. Gryphon helped as much as he could, but he's not you."

A smirk spread across Aaron's lips, and he leaned down and kissed her. His hands snaked around her chest and pulled her flush with him, letting the heat from his body overtake her. "I remember Michael being worn out when Jessica was with child," he said. "I assume these needs are stronger in sorceresses."

Alex nodded, refusing to move too far from Aaron's lips.

"Then worry not, because we are most definitely on the same page."

Aaron kissed her again, and Alex felt on fire. It made her think back to the night in her suite years ago when he'd kissed her for the first time. The same excitement coursed through her and nestled in her stomach before moving lower.

When Aaron gripped her harder and kissed her more deeply, a soft moan left her. "I thought I was going mad without you," he whispered.

"I was," Alex panted back.

Aaron firmly gripped her hips, holding her in place. "How do we? I mean, is it safe?"

"For the babies? It is."

"You're sure?"

"I asked my father's physician. I had to make my fake marriage convincing."

"I'm glad you picked Cameron. He's the only available person I'd trust with you." Aaron's fingers squeezed Alex, and she gasped when his lips found her neck. Her legs felt weak, and she used his body to steady herself. Aaron's kisses coated her neck, and the cool air from the balcony made her skin goosebump.

"No more talk of anyone, especially not my other husbands," she ordered.

Aaron chuckled and moved his kisses to her ear. Alex ran her hand up his chest and grabbed his neck. Gripping her hips,

Aaron jerked her toward him. Alex pushed him onto their bed, resting her hands on his shoulders. A sweet smile spread across Aaron's face. Alex felt her body tense with anticipation. She slowly drew a finger over her bosom and slipped off one strap of her nightdress. Aaron's breath hitched when they locked eyes.

"You still blush with me?" he whispered.

"Only when you look at me like that." Alex leaned down and lightly kissed him, drawing herself to standing to slip the other strap off her shoulder. Her nightdress pooled on the floor between them. Aaron gasped, loud and rough with hunger, but he gently caressed and kissed her belly, sending warmth into her.

"You're even more beautiful than when I married you," he said.

Alex lowered her lips to Aaron's and kissed him. He pushed himself back on the bed, struggling to pull his sleeping pants off while not breaking the kiss with Alex. Before Alex could shift to lie beside him, Aaron positioned her so she straddled him. She settled on top of him and gasped at how hard he was under her. He gripped her hips and lifted her enough to slip inside of her, making Alex moan loudly. He lifted himself, cupped her cheek with his hand, and kissed her. Alex's skin burned with need at every kiss from Aaron. His caresses started off gentle but soon grew more desperate. Alex's breaths grew faster and faster, as she ground against him, feeling him thrust up in her.

Aaron moved one hand lower and squeezed her buttocks. Alex wrapped her arms around his neck and pulled him roughly against her, riding him more roughly with each thrust. He shifted slightly and began to kiss and bite her neck, making Alex moan louder. She slammed herself against him harder and harder, feeling her entire core seize before she cried out.

Her entire body trembled as she came. Aaron shifted just enough that he could wrap his arms around her to hold her, even with her belly pushing him away.

The door flew open with a loud bang, and Caleb stood there. "Aaron, if you're hurting her, I swear I'll—"

Caleb froze in the doorway to their bedroom.

"Your Royal Highnesses ... I'm sorry."

"Caleb, get out," Aaron ordered.

"Enough of this, Caleb," Alex said. "He will not hurt me, and if he ever tries to again, I'll freeze him."

Caleb's eyes had dropped to the ground, but he nodded his head, turned tail, and ran from the room.

Alex turned back to Aaron, and he smiled. "What?"

"I love you."

Alex pressed her forehead to his. "I love you too."

CHAPTER 75

GRYPHON

Gryphon dropped another book on the floor and rolled his neck to crack it. Megesti yawned and stretched his arms over his head.

"How many spells have we found?" Megesti asked.

"Three." Gryphon groaned. "But that includes the one we need to show Birch to see if she understands what the old Celtic names for the plants are."

"So almost none. I wanted good news for Alex."

"Alex will be fine. We just need one spell to help Michael get back on his feet—or leg in this case, and she'll be thrilled. I'm more worried she expects him to be back to his old self, because that isn't likely."

Megesti drummed his fingers on the table. "I don't think she expects us to get him back to his *old* self, but the new man he's becoming. Since you took over being her guard, and they figured out Michael's history, he's been more advisor than guard. Most Veremunds took that role at an early age."

"That, I think, we can manage."

"Are you going with them to Betruger tomorrow?" Megesti

352

held up a letter from Alex. Since her return, she'd developed a habit of cracking notes to the sorcerers she needed. She claimed that as head, she could more easily sense where the sorcerers were to crack things to them, but Gryphon suspected it had more to do with the fact that they were all titans. He was just happy she was being cautious.

"Going to Betruger? Why would I?"

"Because Michael can't and Stefan likely will want to stay behind with him and Jessica."

"If Alex wants me to, I will." Gryphon went back to flipping through the book in front of him, but felt Megesti still looking at him.

"How are you handling everything?" Megesti asked.

"What do you mean by 'everything'?"

"Pick one. Alex carrying your child, her father lying to her, her being back with Aaron, or your discovery that she is our Head. You haven't said much since you figured out how to break free from the Forbidden Lands."

"I'm fine. It's just—it can be a strain. Alex is expecting our child, and because of that, every part of my being is driving me to protect her from everything, and that includes Aaron. It's hard, but I know he loves her and is taking care of her."

"Really?"

"Yes. I'm just glad she knows the truth. She may be upset with her father now, but she is happier and more at peace than she was when she thought Aaron hated her. Now we just have to keep her from hating herself for what happened to Michael and Lynx and—"

"Lynx didn't get hurt," Megesti said.

"Lynx spent two days lost in some terrifying woods with monsters she won't discuss. Whatever she saw there scared her half to death."

"Ah. That is something Alex would blame herself for." More

than most sorcerers, Megesti knew Alex's heart. They both worried for her. "When are you going to tell everyone how to protect her from the fury?"

Gryphon straightened in his chair. "Did you go through my things?"

"No. You left your notebook open in the lab. I glanced."

"Fair."

"What are we supposed to do if removing the fury requires the combined power of both a Head and a Heart to perform the spell?"

"We found the books we were told about—the ones that made no sense—and managed to put them together to figure out which powers are needed, and the spell to perform a removal."

"Perfect! Let her have the babies, and then you two cast the spell. If she's weak, I'll give her a boost."

"It's not that simple. It has to be only the Head and Heart, and it can only be used *after* the fury has been released."

Megesti's face went ashen. "But if we lose her to the fury, then we don't *have* a Head."

"That's why I considered aging up the twins. But that puts Aaron's baby at risk because who knows how long they will live, and I know Alex would never forgive me if I risked her children to bring her back. And that's the problem I'm trying to solve without having to endanger *our* child."

※

Gryphon knocked on the door and waited. He was about to leave when the door opened.

Aaron crossed his arms. "Long night?"

"Not particularly, why?"

"You look like Megesti when he spends all night in the library."

"Ah. Well, that's accurate. He told me you wanted to visit Harold yourself, so I'm here to offer my services, since your usual guards are busy."

Aaron stepped back and allowed Gryphon to enter the royal sitting area. "Did you and Megesti find any spells that could help Michael?"

Gryphon strolled along the bookshelves, scanning the titles. He frowned at the lack of magical books. "A few, but ultimately it'll be up to Birch which ones to try. I'll let my Titan of Celtics try to make a wooden leg that matches Michael's fleshy one in both size and weight. Birch has the magic to do it, but to achieve the needed precision, we'll need Alex or Megesti's help too."

"Why couldn't you do it?"

"That's not my area. I'm fire and chaos. Alex has plants and water powers. So, Betruger…"

"You should come," Aaron said. When he stepped through the door, rubbing his face, his pants hung loose on his hips.

"Did you lose weight?"

Aaron self-consciously adjusted his pants. "What?"

"Your pants don't fit. And you can certainly afford new ones."

"Afford them, yes, but make time to get measured for them? No. I was busy the last few months trying to get my wife back from my father-in-law, and that left little time for drinking with my friends."

Gryphon resisted rolling his eyes. "Don't let Alex see. She needs nothing else to feel guilty over."

"I won't."

"Good. As soon as Alex has the energy, we'll put the same

protection spell on Datten that the other kingdoms have. It should help keep the sorcerers out, at least for a while."

"We also have to have a serious discussion when we return. We still have to figure out what to do about my deal."

Alex descended the final steps with her arms wrapped around her chest, quiet as a ghost. Without thinking, Gryphon moved to help her, but she took Aaron's outstretched hand instead. Pulling her close, Aaron kissed the top of her head and wrapped his arm around her. Alex explained the circumstances of the day they almost lost her and the babies, refusing to make eye contact with Gryphon.

Aaron rubbed Alex's back during her quiet contemplation.

You did what you had to. I'll never be angry at you for protecting our child.

Gryphon moved closer to Alex, and Aaron nodded permission. Gryphon tilted her chin up and felt his heart swell when her eyes glistened in the soft torchlight. "You are not alone, Alex. We will figure this out."

Alex opened her mouth to reply but closed it.

"And I don't mean you and me. I mean, us. Your kingling, Megesti, Birch, Lynx, and everyone else who loves you. We will not lose you to that beast inside of you."

Alex moved so fast, Gryphon couldn't prepare, and she threw her arms around his chest and hugged him. *Thank you.*

And I promise, Megesti and I will keep looking for answers. For Michael's leg. The safest way to handle the fury. We suspect Aaron glowed gold because of the blood you gave him years ago, but we'll figure that out for certain too. No harm will come to any of them.

Alex looked confused.

How do you know the glow didn't hurt him?

"Okay, enough mind reading, you two."

Aaron's hands moved to Alex's shoulder, and Gryphon bit

back the Ares urge to go after him for it. Instead, he merely asked, "When should we leave?"

CHAPTER 76

AARON

Alex had insisted they eat before leaving, and Aaron was never one to stop her eating, especially in her current condition. Only the knights were awake this early. As they were leaving the dining hall after breakfast, Alex stopped and asked Hunter to bring food to Jessica, Stefan, and Jerome. Aaron couldn't help but laugh at Caleb standing behind Hunter, unable to make eye contact with Alex or Aaron.

After they'd dressed, they waited in their suite for Gryphon. When he finally arrived, Aaron snickered. Aaron and Alex had dressed simply, but he wore flamboyant robes of a rich and heavy fabric that appeared to be stitched with gold.

"I thought visiting another kingdom called for formal attire," Gryphon said.

"Usually when visiting another kingdom, convention would require it, but I'm visiting Edith as a friend, not as queen," Alex said.

"And I'm trying to be humble when I visit Harold," Aaron said. "I will be groveling for forgiveness and whatnot."

Gryphon rolled his eyes, but cracked them to Betruger,

regardless. The trio landed in the courtyard, and within seconds, Alex rushed away from them, and Aaron heard Edith's squeal.

"Oh, thank the kings you're all right!" Edith threw her arms around Alex and squeezed her as Harold strolled up to the queens. Aaron nodded to Gryphon, and they followed Alex.

"We're fine, all three of us."

Edith released Alex and stepped back to look her over. "I'm glad to hear that. How are Michael and Jessica? Lynx wrote to us to tell us what happened."

"He'll survive, thanks to Alex helping us find him," Gryphon said.

"How are you doing?" Harold asked.

"Honestly, I'm not sure," Alex said. She wrapped her arms around Aaron's waist. "I am thankful that everything I'd been told about Aaron was a lie, but I don't know how long it'll be before I can trust my father again."

"Or even speak to him," Gryphon added. Alex shot Gryphon an angry look, and he threw his hands in the air. "If you didn't want me to tell them, then don't yell your thoughts at me. Besides, she knows if you're lying."

"Well, I think it's time we leave the kings to talk about rebuilding the damage done in Datten, and about how our blacksmith can help the sorcerers with Michael's leg," Edith said. "Would you care for a stroll in town?"

"I'd love that," Alex said.

Aaron opened his mouth, but Edith beat him to it. "Soren, please summon Macht to escort us?" The young knight Aaron hadn't even noticed nodded, and left the grounds.

"You didn't think I'd let your pregnant wife wander around unprotected, did you, Aaron?"

Aaron chuckled, and Harold patted his back. "Have fun, ladies."

"Join us in the library when you're finished," Harold added.

Edith looped her arm through Alex's and led her away, whispering. Soon they vanished into the hall, leaving the three men alone. Harold turned to Aaron and crossed his arms.

"What are you intending to do about Edward?"

"Nothing. I can't retaliate for what he did. He's still my godfather and Alex's father. He hurt her much worse than he did me, and as angry as I am at him, helping Alex get through this is more important to me."

Harold turned to Gryphon. "And you?"

"I'm preoccupied with helping Michael and getting revenge for what the sorcerers did to Alex. They tried to murder her and my child. I'm going to kill them all."

"Are you even capable of that?" Harold asked, and Gryphon merely nodded. Harold turned to Aaron. "I can see why you made him a guard." Harold motioned for them to follow him, and they headed to the library.

Aaron loved the Betruger library. It reminded him of the library in the Verlassen castle. Every surface was covered in books, and even the doors themselves were camouflaged as shelves. Gryphon scanned the shelves, running his finger along the spines of the books. Aaron glanced around to see if anything had changed since Harold had married Edith, and found it easily. A bookcase that had been mostly knick-knacks now burst with books.

Harold smiled. "Spotted my new collection?"

"It's impressive. How did you get so many new books?"

"They're Edith's. I can smell Warren sea air coming off them." Gryphon continued to scan the books until he found something interesting and removed it from the shelf. "Do you own any books on magic?"

"A few," Harold said.

Aaron did a double-take. "You have magic books?"

"Moorloc was my father's advisor for many years. I still have some of his journals."

Gryphon loudly closed the book he was reading. "I suspect Moorloc is the reason for that hatred and suspicion you had of sorcerers, until Aaron showed up."

Harold nodded. "When my mother became sick, my father did everything he could to save her, including making a deal with that sorcerer. My father offered him anything, provided he saved my mother, but all his attempts were useless. He left Lygari here to help after she died, but then my brother died. My father always suspected Lygari was behind it."

"An educated assumption," Gryphon said.

"I'm glad you decided to help me despite your history with sorcerers," Aaron said.

Harold smiled. "As am I. It proved to be an impressive decision of my kingship, and one that will forever be remembered."

Aaron grinned. "The king who made peace with the vicious Dattenites." Gryphon lingered at the bookshelf, looking lost in thought.

"What's wrong?" Harold asked.

Gryphon replaced Moorloc's journal. "I just remembered a book that Alex and I discovered when we were trapped in the Forbidden Lands," Gryphon said. "It could help us with Michael's situation."

"How?" Aaron asked.

"It told of an extra-thin and strong metal that could be crafted. If I give the recipe to your blacksmiths, we should be able to strengthen this wooden leg."

"I know my personal blacksmith would be delighted to try," Harold said.

"I'll go hunt for the book. If you're ready to leave before I'm back, have Alex bring you back." Gryphon paused. "Is it safe for me to leave you?"

"In Betruger? Yes," Aaron said. "Macht is with Alex and Edith at the moment, and I'm here with Harold, so we should be fine. You managed to cast the protection spell here, didn't you?"

Gryphon nodded.

"Then go." Aaron blinked, and Gryphon disappeared. Harold handed Aaron a book. Aaron tapped its spine against the table twice. The Betruger king was quiet and focused. "Harold, I believe we need to clear the air."

"Do you mean because I sided with Edward?"

Aaron's chest tightened. "Yes."

"Of course. You know why I did it, don't you?"

"Because of Edith."

"That's part of it. I sided with Edward because Edith knew Alex would need us. You had Edith's father in Datten. If Edward believed I was on his side, then we thought you might have a way to get information through Randal."

Aaron's jaw dropped. "You were planning to play both sides?"

"No, we were always going to do what was right for Alex. If she decided she was done with you, we would not have pushed it. But as long as it was clear you both cared for each other and someone else was between you, we made sure we had a way to bring you two back together."

Everything clicked at once—the tense conversations with Edward and Harold's reactions, Edith's cold shoulder—and Aaron exhaled slowly. "Thank you."

◆◆◆

AARON SPENT hours working with Harold. Together, they found many resources that could help the Datten master builders rebuild structures that could withstand magical attacks. Alex wasn't even back by the time they'd finished. When she finally returned, smiling and giggling with Edith, both women refused to tell their husbands what they'd been up to or where they'd gone. Even Macht wouldn't utter a word, claiming he'd been sworn to secrecy by his queen.

Now back in Datten, watching Alex sleep peacefully, Aaron wrote in his king's journal, recording not only his successes in Betruger and the plans to improve the lives of his people, but also his fears about Alex. He worried that the fury would control her and ruin everything they had fought for. She hid it from many people, but Aaron could see through her façade to the pain she was enduring. Her nightmares were back, making it nearly impossible for her to get any proper sleep, and her features were starting to show her weariness. Her hair had lost its shine, and her emerald eyes no longer sparkled. Aaron once found her arguing with herself. She'd denied it, but after he'd reminded her of their promise to be honest, she'd confessed it all. She finally accepted Birch's help, and for the first time in weeks, Alex was sound asleep.

Setting his journal on his nightstand, Aaron leaned down to Alex. "I know you're scared, but you're stronger than anyone I know. You'll get through this, and we'll send that fury back where she belongs."

He moved her hair out of her face and kissed her.

CHAPTER 77

ALEX

The following two weeks passed quickly. Lynx, Megesti, and Birch worked without ceasing to figure out what to do for Michael, and when Alex, Gryphon, and Kharon weren't casting the protection spell across Datten, they were scouring Merlin's books for any insight into how to hold back the fury after the deal Alex had made.

A few days after they returned from Betruger, Alex called meetings with the councils Aaron had set up while she was in the Forbidden Lands. Aaron seemed thrilled that she was jumping back into her role and feeling up to meeting with their people. Alex insisted that even if the castle would pay to fix the houses, they should have a chance to say what they wanted in their homes. The same went for the builders and craftsmen, who were facing more changes to the city than had been done in hundreds of years. Guinevere, Avery, and Randal accompanied them to the meeting so that every citizen would have the opportunity to be heard by a highly ranking member of the court. Everyone in attendance enjoyed the meeting, especially with the food Alex insisted they serve. By the end of it, Aaron seemed to beam with a new energy, and the knowledge of exactly how every house and business should be rebuilt.

Alex felt intense relief being back with her people and seeing with her own eyes that no one—*other than Michael*, she winced at her omission—had been seriously hurt when the sorcerers attacked. Now with the protection spell on not only the castle, but the entire city, Alex felt at peace. *The only thing left to worry about is how we'll keep my babies safe from the fury. Hopefully Edith's plan works.*

"Alex?"

"Huh?" She jerked upright, realizing she was in the library reading with Kharon.

"Are you all right? Do you need some water?"

"I'm fine."

Kharon glanced behind her. "They disagree."

Alex chuckled at the ghosts over her shoulder. "Emmerich and Daniel, I'm fine. I'm just tired. We've been reading for hours." The Datten men crossed their arms. Alex scoffed and rolled her eyes.

"They love you," Kharon said.

"I know. But I have enough overprotective men in my life."

"That's not a bad problem to have."

Alex sighed. "Can I ask you something?"

"Of course."

Alex twisted her tunic in her fingers. "What do *you* know about the furies that isn't in our books?"

"I haven't thought of them since I was a young child studying with my father. What I remember is they originally worked with my line's founder, Hades. They were created to seek revenge against those who hurt their own family or those who can't protect themselves. They were seen by some as beautiful. Others saw them as monsters."

"The violence against my family would explain why they are in the Cassandras."

"I believe so. From what I've pieced together, Ares demanded Hades cast the spell to ensure no other Cassandra would be hurt the way his daughter was when her mother abandoned her."

Alex laughed and rubbed her face with her hands. "I was hurt as badly as she was, long before the final betrayal happened. If he was trying to keep us from being hurt, he failed, and honestly he should have known better."

Kharon reached their hand across the table, and Alex placed hers into it. "Indeed. We cannot run from our pain, but if we learn to harness it, and use it, we can overcome it."

"How are you always so calm?"

"What do you mean?"

"Aaron, Gryphon, and Megesti are losing their minds, worrying I might be taken over by a monster. Lynx and Birch are trying to help Michael, as if fixing him will ease my guilt and allow me to better fight the fury, but you ... you're here with your books and no panic or terror about what might be."

Kharon smiled at Alex. "Hades and Cassandras have a few things in common, my Head."

"You don't have to call me that."

"I know, but when I'm advising you I like to. For the first time in my life, I actually respect the living Head, and I intend to enjoy that."

Alex's cheeks heated, and she nodded at Kharon to continue.

"Many lines share qualities or personality traits. Ares and Salem are known for their tempers and violence. Tiere and Celtics, their love of nature. But Cassandras and Hades have a unique ability to accept things as they come. You can see the future, so you know what to accept and what to fight to fix. I know that ultimately we all end up in the same place, even if how we arrive there and what we do with the time given varies. We all have skills to use in our time."

"And what are your skills?"

Kharon grinned. "I've always been a fast reader, and exceptional at puzzles."

"So that's how you figured out the journals that didn't match so quickly."

"It is."

"You have that in common with Megesti," Alex said.

Kharon nodded. "That's why he's been spending so much time with me. I'm teaching him what I know about reading and analyzing the texts we now have. You may have lost Merlock's journals, but Megesti knows them by heart. He's working on rewriting them."

"I did not know that," Alex said.

Kharon pinched their lips. "If I ruined a surprise, you'll act shocked won't you?"

"Of course. Your secrets are safe with me."

AFTER HOURS of analyzing the new books, Kharon and Alex had found some useful spells for amplifying or hiding powers. Alex bid Kharon good night and left with a book she wanted to finish reading in bed. The Datten town bells rang. It was already almost nine.

Alex's stomach grumbled, and she patted it. "I know. I'll get something to eat. I wonder what was for dinner?"

Alex hoped to find Aaron in their suite so she could ask him to bring her dinner but their room had been empty so she went for the couch to keep reading.

"Hello."

Alex trembled and dropped her book. The thump it made echoed through the room. Stefan dashed over to brace her.

"I haven't seen you this speechless in years," Michael teased. He lifted his cane off the ground and leaned down to pull up his pant leg. Beneath it was the artificial leg. Harold and Gryphon had shown her sketches of what they were planning, but she hadn't expected them to finish so quickly. His new leg was shaped the same as his other leg, even fitting into his boot. The metal was one she didn't recognize and she suspected it was magical. At the top of the leg, a pair of leather straps wrapped around it, and rested above Michael's knee to keep the magical leg in place.

Alex covered her mouth and broke into tears. Michael dropped his pant leg and hobbled across the room. He walked like a newborn foal, trembling with each step. When he made it to her, he held his arms out, and Alex hugged him as tightly as she could. She worried she might knock him off balance, but he squeezed her so tightly she couldn't move.

"No escaping," Michael said. "I know you feel guilty for what happened, but I'm just glad you and the babies are safe. I did what I did to protect you, and knowing I almost lost you hurts far more than losing my leg."

Alex frowned.

"I mean it," he said. "Since Gryphon came and Jessica had the baby, I have done little guarding. Mostly, I've been advising and keeping your company."

"That's what Veremunds do," Alex whispered.

"I know," Michael said. "That's why I'm okay. Birch says I'll get used to the leg, and eventually walk almost normally. I'll still be able to use my bow and go for rides with you. I just can't chase sorcerers anymore."

"What about little Jerome?"

Michael chuckled. "I should be able to chase him by the time he can walk."

"You were always better with Alex's emotions than I was," Stefan said, wrapping his arms around the two of them.

"And you were always better at invading her personal space to protect her."

Alex snorted and laughed, while Stefan groaned and released them. "You should talk to my sister," Stefan said.

"Why?" Alex asked.

"She wants to apologize for yelling at you," Michael said.

"Oh," Alex said. "She doesn't need to. I know she was scared."

"She wants to," Stefan said. "She knows it wasn't your fault the sorcerers came here."

"But it was."

"No," Michael said. "You weren't even here when they attacked, and you came to protect the people."

"That's something a Wafner should appreciate," Stefan added.

"Jessica is a Veremund now. Not a Wafner."

At a knock, Stefan leaned back to open the door. Jessica stood there with her father behind her. "May we come in?"

"Of course," Alex replied, releasing Michael.

Jessica nervously adjusted her dress skirt, but Alex didn't give her a chance to say anything before pulling her into a tight embrace. "You have nothing to apologize for," Alex said. "If Aaron had been injured protecting you, I'd probably have set something on fire."

Jessica squeezed her back. "At least I don't have to worry about him running into danger anymore," she whispered, and Alex burst into laughter.

"What did she say?" Michael asked.

"Nothing," Alex and Jessica replied in unison, and fell into another round of giggles.

Lynx tightened the ribbons to tie up the back of Alex's dress for her.

"Are you sure?" Alex asked the royal physician.

"I can't be completely certain, as your mother is the only sorceress we have records of giving birth, and you were born in Warren. I believe you could go into labor anytime. Most mortal women who have twins give birth earlier than those who only have one."

Lynx leaned forward and sniffed Alex. "You smell different, and your belly is lower."

"While I can't speak to the smell, the stomach being lower is a sign I recognize."

Alex playfully swatted Lynx away.

The physician turned to Lynx. "Would you like me to check you as well, Lady Wafner?"

Lynx's nose scrunched at Alex, and she bit back a chuckle. "Sorcerers go by their title or first name," Alex explained to the physician. "So, you should address her as Lynx or Titan of Tiere. Sorceresses do not change their title or rank after marriage."

"Apologies ... Lynx."

"Thank you, but I'm all right. Birch is my midwife and has been monitoring my pregnancy."

"I didn't know she was a midwife," Alex said.

"She and I helped deliver Gryphon. In the absence of a Cassandra Titan, or daughter of Cassandra, the highest-ranking Tiere sorceress assists. Imelda hated my father, and I was still quite young, so Birch came as well."

"Would you like me to inform His Royal Highness?"

"No thank you," Alex said. "I'd like to tell Aaron."

"Of course. I'll be back in a day or two to check on you." The physician nodded a goodbye to the ladies and left the room.

"You look nervous," Lynx said.

"I thought I had more time." Alex settled onto the couch in her suite. "Mortals take nine to ten months to deliver. It's only been eight."

"You're actually on time for a sorceress," Lynx said. "Depending on the line, we take as little as five months, and as long as ten."

"Only five months? Which line is that?"

Lynx smiled. "Tiere. If we've been given our animal by nature, many of us take after them. My mother was only pregnant with me for five months."

Alex rubbed her belly. "I missed so much about sorcerers growing up around mortals."

"Then it's a good thing you have me to help you." Lynx plopped down beside Alex. Her eyes sparkled with wisdom and mischief as she brushed her hair out of her face, letting it fall down her back. "If you have something to ask me, then do so."

Alex tilted her head and opened her mouth to speak, but then shook her head. Grunting, she got up and waddled across the suite. She tugged on her gown, struggling to find the words, when a pair of warm hands snatched hers and gently tugged her. Lynx locked eyes with her. When Lynx finally dropped her hands, Alex felt calmer.

"How loyal are you to me?" Alex asked.

"Explain."

"If I need something of you, could you keep it from Gryphon? Or Stefan?"

Lynx sucked her breath sharply exposing her teeth. "I ... I ... I think it would depend on what you were asking."

"Why?"

"You took an oath to let us in, so if you're putting yourself in danger—"

"But asking *you* for help would mean I'm not alone or in danger."

"Alex—"

The door to the room opened and banged shut. Aaron beamed at them and strutted across the room. "How did the appointment go?"

Alex embraced him. "All is well, and it could be any day now."

"We'll catch up later." Lynx nodded and fled through the closing door before Alex could say anything.

"Did I interrupt something?" Aaron asked, rubbing Alex's arms.

"No. I wanted to ask her to help with our plan."

"You really think she can keep that from Stefan and Gryphon?"

"That's what I was trying to find out."

Aaron pressed his forehead to hers and held her. Alex sighed contentedly, letting her lungs fill to the brim and enjoying the scent of pine that always came off Aaron.

"Are you sure you want to go through with this?" he asked.

Alex opened her eyes to find Aaron staring at her. "We have to. It's the only way to keep them safe from her."

"I understand, but ... it feels wrong."

"Hard choices, Aaron. Your mother warned you that being a king and a father would require hard choices and—"

"Sacrifice. I know. I just never realized keeping plans to yourself was so much work." Aaron stepped back from Alex and ran his hand through his hair, but this time, he shook his hand to tousle his hair.

"What are you doing?" Alex couldn't help but laugh as Aaron's naturally unruly hair became as wild as the Dark Forest that surrounded Datten.

"I have a surprise for you."

"What is it?"

Aaron held his hands out, waiting for Alex to take them. "If I told you, it wouldn't be a surprise. Come on."

Interlocking their fingers, Aaron took Alex over to the bookcase door that led into the queen's suite, which his mother had converted into a nursery. Aaron's fingers skimmed the shelves until they stopped on a copy of *Torian Tales*. He pulled out the book, opening the door. Alex let Aaron lead her into the room, and her jaw dropped at the second, new crib beside the one Aaron had used as an infant. Alex slowly crossed the room and reached her hand out to touch the crib, making sure it was real.

"I figured out which carpenter made my crib. Well, my father's crib. So they match."

Alex turned back to Aaron. "Emmerich slept in it too?"

"The crib was made for him, and my mother insisted on using it for Daniel and then me."

Alex walked around the second crib, noting all the same tiny details in it as Aaron's. It had the same wood stain and identical carvings. The only difference was the older one had some scratches and dings in it. Inside both were gold blankets. Alex ran her fingers along the fabric and sighed. Aaron wrapped his arm around her, and warmth spread around her middle.

"I picked gold rather than red, since both babies will have a Cassandra mother."

Alex turned and wrapped her arms around Aaron's chest, letting him pull her closer.

"I meant what I said. I want the twins raised together. I won't deprive my son of his brother just because he's Gryphon's and not mine. But I have one request."

Alex waited, knowing what came next would be important.

"We have to tell everyone our son was born first. Datten law gives the throne to the oldest, and I just want to make sure there is no question about that."

"I can do that," Alex said. "And thank you for doing this."

"Of course." Aaron kissed the top of her head.

"You went to all this trouble, and for all we know, these cribs will never be used."

"They will."

Alex turned to face him. "You don't know that. Once the fury gets out, how can we stop it without my powers as Head?"

Alex ran her hand along her bump. Aaron's hand slid on top of hers, stilling her movement. "We'll find a way."

As long as my babies are all right, I don't care what happens to me.

"You need to make sure they are protected. No matter what."

"We will."

"Do you promise that?"

"On my life."

CHAPTER 78

GRYPHON

Gryphon finished lining up the books on the shelf and stood back to admire his handiwork. Months after the fire, the new, bigger-than-ever Datten lab needed no further work. Megesti had been kind enough to involve Alex in the planning of the lab, even though he would oversee it. Alex had surprised them both by insisting Gryphon have a say, too. After all, she'd said, Gryphon had seen more labs in his time than they had, and could come up with a layout that would allow them to get the most use out of theirs. Aaron had ordered the two guest rooms along the back wall to be removed, which doubled their size. Now they had an ingredient pantry as large as a knight's suite, and Gryphon couldn't be happier.

Not only was it large enough to serve as a meeting place for all of the sorcerers, but it was also strong enough to contain Gryphon should he lose control and unleash his beast inside the castle. He'd agreed to that after Lynx reminded him that they didn't know what Alex's child would be capable of, so having the ability to keep a magical beast contained would make Datten safer for all.

With a wave of his hand, Gryphon summoned all of the flames in the torch-less room into himself, sending the room into darkness. He left, closing the door behind him, but then paused, unsure of where to go. For weeks, he had been diving into books to help Michael, but now the mortal focused on building up his strength with his new wooden leg. Gryphon was free, but after the endless stress that had been his last few months, he wasn't sure what to do with himself. He closed his eyes and searched for Alex, but he couldn't sense her.

She's probably napping. The last few days have been exhausting for her.

Gryphon set off down the stairs. Maybe Lynx or Megesti would be free to get into some fun. As he rounded the corner on the second floor, he heard shouting. He dashed down the steps two at a time until he landed on the main floor. Stefan and Jessica were arguing with Michael.

"Why do you think I know where she is?" Michael asked.

"Because you're her best friend," Jessica said. "And her Veremund."

"And I can tell when you're lying," Stefan said.

"What's Michael lying about?" Gryphon asked.

"Where Alex is," Stefan replied.

Gryphon felt nauseous. "She's not just sleeping? Where is she?"

"I don't know," Michael said.

Lies. Rage erupted through Gryphon. He launched himself at Michael, but before he could reach the mortal, Lynx appeared between them.

"Leave him alone. If Alex wanted you to know, then you would."

"Wanted *us* to know?" Jessica said.

"Do *you* know, Lynx?" Stefan asked.

"Yes, but I'm not telling. I gave my word to my Head and queen. I will not break her trust."

Jessica crossed her arms. "How could she tell you and not us?"

"Simple. She told those of us she knew would respect her wishes." To Gryphon's surprise, Stefan wasn't fazed.

"Where is she?" Gryphon asked.

"Somewhere safe," Michael said.

"Safe, according to whom?" Stefan demanded.

A door closed, and Aaron appeared in the hallway with Jerome behind him. When he saw the gathering, he sighed. "You've realized she's gone."

"You know, too?" Gryphon asked.

Aaron nodded. "I helped her leave."

"You allowed our queen to leave without our knowledge?" Jerome asked.

Aaron held his hand up to his general. "It isn't simply about her leaving. This needed to be done not only for her safety, but for the babies, and ours. We don't know how to stop the fury before it gets out. Now we have to focus on getting Alex back after it takes control. So rather than standing around bickering, maybe you could put your energy to better use."

Stefan opened his mouth to say something, but Jerome gave his son a look, and Stefan grunted and left. "Excuse me," Lynx said and chased after him.

Jessica glared at Michael, but when he rubbed his leg and grimaced, her expression softened, and she looped her arm through his. "Come on. You should rest your leg. Keep your energy up in case Alex needs you."

Gryphon was still seething. Now that he was alone with Aaron and Jerome, he could feel himself scowling.

"I told her she shouldn't leave you out of the loop," Aaron said.

"Then why did she?"

"Because she didn't think you would let her leave and have the babies without you."

"She's right!" Gryphon shouted. "The only sorcerer in this world who has a chance of protecting our children from what Alex will become is me."

Aaron grabbed his arm. "And that's why she didn't want you there. Our children are being taken into hiding. I don't know where, but I know only two people will know where each child is. They will be safe until we figure out what to do."

Gryphon pulled away from Aaron and rubbed his face with his hands.

"If you need to blow off some steam, then go. I'm sorry I didn't get to tell you immediately. I told Alex I would, but then I got distracted by some noble issues."

"But they're safe?"

"She's safe and cared for right now. Lynx will go to her when she goes into labor, and return here once the babies are safe. Hopefully, the fury doesn't take her right away, and then we'll still have some time. But if it does ..."

"What are you planning?" Jerome asked.

Aaron looked grim. "Then, Gryphon, you may be our only hope."

CHAPTER 79
ALEX

I waited too long.

Alex paced in front of the oversized fireplace, despite the fact that doing anything while in labor was excruciating. The small hunting cabin, tucked away where the Ogre and Crimson Mountains met, had been furnished with all wood furniture and more animal mounts than Alex had seen in a single location in all her life.

During her last visit, Alex and Edith had searched Betruger for a safe place for her to give birth, and Macht had offered the cabin that had been in his family for generations without hesitation. Edith assured her Macht could be trusted, and he gave the queens his oath that he'd never say a word to the kings. Though both Aaron and Harold knew the ladies were up to something, neither pried further.

For the last week, Alex had remained in the small cabin, preparing for the birth. Edith arrived daily with Macht to bring her food and check on her, but outside of that, Alex had been alone. She'd spent the time talking to her babies about their families, the kingdoms they'd get to live in, singing to them, and even embroidering a small blanket for each of them. For eight days, nothing happened, and Alex had begun to wonder if the physician was wrong. But she'd awakened that night in a puddle with severe pain, and now she dragged herself across the room in her nightdress, moaning. She'd sent the secret sign for Lynx to come—a pair of gryphon feathers in a red bag—but now she feared she'd waited too long.

"I can't do this myself!" Alex cried out as the next contraction hit her, sending pain throughout her body. The slightest breeze hit her. She wanted to see who had arrived, but stopped when the pain became too much.

"Good thing you won't have to."

Alex cried out in relief and pain at the sound of Michael's voice.

"We're here too," Lynx added. Edith didn't speak, but Alex knew she had come.

Tentatively, Michael made his way across the room, taking each step with care, until he arrived at her side. "Take my hand. I'll lead you to the fireplace. You have to stay warm."

By the time they'd made it there, Edith and Lynx had set up a slew of blankets on the stone floor to cushion Alex and to keep her warm. Edith gathered the towels while Lynx put the water over the fire to heat it.

"Lie down," Lynx said. "I'll have a look."

Alex did as told, and Lynx checked on her progress. "You're doing wonderfully, and it won't be long now."

Outside, it began to rain and thunder loudly, sending hail beating down on the cabin. The cabin was well-built, but could the roof handle everything her emotions threw at it?

"Macht assured me this cabin has survived *dozens* of sea storms over the centuries," Edith said. "A sorcerer storm, even one from a Head, won't bring it down. You just focus on those babies."

Alex nodded and forced a slight smile. Michael and Edith took turns holding her hand and encouraging her.

I wish they were here. It isn't fair that they're missing this. I wasn't supposed to do this without Aaron or Gryphon. Alex sobbed. Edith and Michael squeezed her hands, and Lynx ordered her to push.

Alex held her breath, clenched her jaw, and pushed until she no longer felt resistance.

The silence that filled the cabin felt like an eternity, and Alex agonized over the quiet until Lynx held up a bundle in a towel. Lynx wiped the baby, and then they all heard a small cry, barely loud enough to compete with the rain outside.

Surprise crossed Lynx's face, and Alex shook her head in reply. *Keep my secret. Please!*

"This one is Gryphon's," Lynx said.

"How do you know?" Michael asked.

Lynx handed Alex the baby whose entire head was covered in black hair, except for a streak of brown that ran from above the left eye.

"That most certainly is Gryphon's," Edith said.

Holding the tiny sorcerer in her arms, Alex felt her heart break in a way she'd never known in her life. She'd never known it was possible to love something this much in a second. Struggling to control her emotions, Alex kissed the baby's head and took in the tiny fingers and toes.

"Ten of each. Like I said, perfect," Lynx said, and Alex marveled at her baby.

Another contraction hit, and Alex winced. "I think the other is impatient." Alex handed Michael the baby, and he stepped back from Alex, allowing the ladies to tend to her. This one came out even faster, and when Lynx lifted him, his golden blond hair revealed his parentage. He cried loud enough to drown out the hail outside.

The instant her second baby was in her arms, Alex broke down crying. She clutched her and Aaron's baby to her and let out all her fears and sorrow at not being able to stay with her babies.

"We don't have to take them right away," Edith whispered.

"Yes, you do," Alex sobbed back. "I can't risk it."

"You don't seem like you're losing yourself," Lynx said.

"She is," Michael said. "Cassandra gave me the gift to see the fury. You may not see her, but I do. Alex is already slipping away."

"Clever Veremund," a voice sultrier and huskier than Alex's left her mouth. She turned back to Lynx. "You should listen to him, kitten."

Lynx swallowed and dropped the bloody towel she'd been holding. "But we aren't done with ..."

"We'll be fine," the voice insisted. Lynx cracked Edith, Michael, and the twins away.

No, don't go!

Alex felt her body rise and cross the room to the mirror. The body, hair, and face were hers, but the eyes and smile were another's. The fury examined herself, and everything around Alex faded until it went dark.

PART FOUR

THE FURY

CHAPTER 80

GRYPHON

She was in on it and lied.

Gryphon paced the grounds, feeling more rage and betrayal than he had in decades.

I'm not surprised Alex wouldn't tell me. She's trying to protect us from the fury. But Lynx is my best friend, and she lied. She knew where Alex went, and it didn't matter that I was making myself sick with worry ... she stayed silent until last night when she vanished.

He summoned a fireball and threw it across the field. It set the ground on fire. Watching the plants burn brought little relief.

"I swore I'd never be like my father. I swore I'd be better, and I wasn't there. I didn't even have the choice to be there. My best friend and the mother of my child took it from me."

Gryphon threw another fireball. It struck a bush and burned to ash. It wasn't nearly as satisfying as he'd hoped.

"I know it would have been dangerous, and I probably wouldn't have wanted to leave our son once he arrived, but I should have been asked. I should have been given the choice."

He summoned another fireball when a branch snapped

behind him. "Birch, I'm not in the mood for sage advice right now."

"How about violence?"

Gryphon turned to face Stefan, a pair of staves in hand.

"If you'd rather be alone, I can go, but I know Alex feels better when she works out her frustrations with sparring, and I wouldn't mind the chance to work out mine too."

"You're frustrated?"

Stefan banged the bases of the staves on the group. "I wasn't entrusted with their location either. I won't presume to know how you feel at not being there for the birth, but I'm worried about Alex and the babies, and also Lynx. She's pregnant and now she's run off to trap herself in a room with the fury. We don't know how fast it'll come out or what it'll do if she refuses to talk."

"I hadn't considered that."

"So if you could take a break from burning things, maybe we could help each other out."

Stefan tossed a staff to Gryphon, and he spun it in his hand before assuming his stance. "I'm going to use my magic."

"I didn't expect anything else."

CHAPTER 81

AARON

Aaron shifted on his throne.

I wish I knew she was all right. I wish Lynx or Michael or someone would just let us know how things are going. Being a king is challenging enough without your wife giving birth in secret somewhere else. I hate feeling helpless.

"Are you all right, Your Royal Highness?"

"I'm fine, Caleb." He'd been paying just enough attention to the knights and addressed the concerns they'd brought. "Hunter, you're excused from duties until your father's arm heals and he can resume his duties."

"Thank you."

The door behind Aaron's throne banged shut, and Aaron stood and straightened his shirt. "You're all excused if there's nothing else." His three friends stayed there, looking at him in concern. "What?" he growled.

"We couldn't help but notice that Her Royal Highness isn't here. Is everything all right?" Caleb asked.

Aaron clenched his jaw to calm himself.

Megesti must have seen him and responded for him. "Dif-

387

ferent sorcerer lines choose to give birth differently. Offspring who are special, or very powerful, can be seen as a threat, so the mothers go into hiding to deliver them. Alexandria is fine. Lynx is with her."

Aaron's friends sighed with relief, bowed to Aaron, and set off down the aisle to the exit.

"Should I give you a moment?" Jerome asked.

"Yes please," Megesti replied. Jerome remained in place until Aaron nodded. Then he followed the knights out of the hall.

"How angry are you, really?" Megesti asked.

"I'm not angry." Aaron left his throne and walked toward his friend. "She asked me before she decided to leave to give birth. I'm scared."

"Lynx and Michael will be back as soon as they can."

"Are you sure about that?" Aaron raised his eyebrow at Megesti. "I wouldn't put it past Alex to send Michael and Lynx into hiding with the babies."

Megesti's mouth dropped open. "I never even considered that."

"And you call yourself her cousin."

"I'm blood, but I don't know her as intimately as you do." Megesti shivered.

"What's wrong?"

"I ... I sense kin."

A commotion outside the throne room caused them both to hesitate. Then they turned in unison and ran for the door. Jessica's shouts reached him through the door. He took a few steps before the person responded to her. *Michael!*

Aaron burst into the hallway, startling Jessica, who shrieked. Michael held a bundle in his arms. Aaron couldn't believe what he was seeing. "Is that—?"

"Your baby," Megesti replied. "I can sense Alex's magic coming off of it from here."

"Aaron, you can't be here," Michael said. "You can't know where I'm bringing him."

"Then why are you here?" Jessica asked.

"Because it happened faster than expected."

Aaron took a step toward Michael and his child. Instinctively, Michael clutched the baby closer, and Aaron heard crying. The sound made his knees weak. "Ferflucs," Michael muttered and bounced the bundle. Aaron could only watch, speechless.

"What happened?" Megesti asked.

"The fury," Michael muttered. "She came out so fast. Lynx tried to crack us away, but the fury followed. We ended up in three different locations before we lost her. Megesti, I need you to send me where I'm supposed to go. And give me your oath that you won't tell anyone."

"I give you my oath—"

"Megesti!" Aaron snapped.

Megesti thrust his hand at Aaron, never taking his eyes off Michael. "On my life, I shall never reveal the location of Alex and Aaron's child."

Michael relaxed slightly and turned to Aaron. "You can look, but I can't let you hold him. If it were me, I know I could never give my son back."

Aaron held his hands up beside him, away from the baby, and crept toward Michael. Michael leaned closer and pushed back the bundle, exposing a small, wrinkled little face. Aaron's heart shattered. Little wisps of blond hair stuck out of the blanket. His baby yawned and opened his sleepy eyes.

"He has Edward's eyes."

"He does," Michael said.

"He's all right?"

"Healthy as a horse, according to Lynx. And good lungs. His cry could wake the dead."

"And Alex?" Aaron whispered.

Michael shook his head. "The fury has her. If she's even still …"

Aaron held up a hand to stop him. "Megesti, take Michael wherever he needs to go. Then get Harold for me. I don't care if Edward is still angry. If we have any hope of getting Alex back, we need to work together."

"What can I do?" Jessica asked.

"Find your brother. We're going to Warren."

FURY

"Come out, kitten. I know you're here somewhere." The fury remained still as a statue and listened for any sound. She'd followed Lynx to almost a dozen random locations now, and the pregnant Titan of Tiere was running out of energy. Along the way, she'd lost track of where Lynx had left the raven-haired beauty and the monopod. Now her only chance at finding the Head's spawn was to stalk the sorceress and force the answer out of her.

If I can't get the answer out of her, I'm sure I can find another use for her.

The wind moved the leaves in the thick forest canopy above her head. The wind that wove through the Dark Forest rarely blew harder than a breeze, meaning the fury could hear every sound around her, a fact any clever Tiere sorcerer would well know.

"I will not hurt you, Lynx. I only hurt those who have betrayed the Cassandra, and you are not on that list. Your *husband,* on the other hand ... let's just say, ignoring Alexandria's wishes to justify 'keeping her safe' for over a decade was not the best choice on his part."

A branch snapped, and the fury cracked toward it. She could hear Lynx yip and leap back. "Hear me out before you run again, kitten."

Lynx gulped. She strode out from the brush and held her hands up to show she meant no ill will.

"You must be tired of running from me, so hear this. I have seen what your husband is truly capable of. You have been nothing but loyal to Alexandria, and I shall repay that kindness, as I would punish those who hurt her."

"What do you mean, repay?" Lynx asked.

The fury examined Lynx carefully. She was in good health —strong, and fit, but behind her eyes was a pain she recognized, a pain that could only be caused by the betrayal of a man. Lynx trembled, as if she knew what the fury had sensed. "You have suffered at the hands of a man."

"It wasn't Stefan," Lynx spat out. "He would never do that. He isn't like that. It happened before he was even born."

"As I said. I've seen what he is truly capable of. Should you ever find yourself in need of refuge, you are welcome to join me. I will protect you and ensure no harm comes to you."

"If you truly mean that, then let me leave."

There are other ways to learn the truth.

The fury nodded. "Go."

Lynx stared at her, confused, for a long second. Then she vanished.

The fury wiped her hands on Alex's bloody gown. "First, I need to find something to wear. Then we'll actually start the hunt."

CHAPTER 83
GRYPHON

Gryphon walked the castle perimeter, breathing in night air. Lynx had returned utterly exhausted from fleeing the fury, putting everyone on high alert. As a precaution, Megesti and Gryphon had suggested a sorcerer remain in each of the castles to sound the alarm, should she arrive to cause problems. Gryphon had volunteered to guard the Verlassen Castle.

Before they'd split up, Gryphon had asked Kharon what the chances were that the fury would head to the Forbidden Lands instead. Kharon suspected that until she completed the revenge, the fury would remain on this side of the Oreean Sea. While that gave Gryphon a bit of peace, he still feared for Alex. No one knew if she was merely trapped inside herself the way Aaron had been when he was cursed, or if the fury had already hollowed her out entirely.

Gryphon finished his final patrol by checking on Cerberus. While not thrilled to see Gryphon, the now thankfully normal-sized dog did enjoy the dinner Gryphon provided him. Satisfied he would not be causing any issues, Gryphon left to get some sleep. Only a few knights remained in the castle when Aaron and Alex were absent. While that made sense, tonight Gryphon wished it were empty.

If the fury shows up, I have to not only protect everything in here Alex holds dear from her mother, but also all the mortals. Too bad the Vinirs and Rassgats aren't the only ones here. Then I wouldn't have to care.

Gryphon reached the door to his room on the second floor. He grasped the handle and felt for any extra magic in the space, but found nothing. He flung open the door and waved his hand, igniting the fireplace to take the chill out of the air. Breathing deeply, he threw his clothes on the floor between the bed and the wardrobe and searched under his pillows until he found his sleeping pants. Once he'd pulled them on, he climbed into the bed.

All the bedrooms in the Verlassen Castle had four-poster beds elaborately carved with different sorcerer line symbols on them. When they'd allowed him to stay, Alex had insisted he choose his room, so he'd hunted for the bed with the moon and clouds of his Mystics line. The idea of sleeping in an Ares bed made him nauseous, and on nights like tonight, when he struggled to sleep, he appreciated looking at the carved moon and clouds on the ceiling of his bed rather than a battle ax. Soon enough, his exhausted body won the battle and he slipped into slumber.

"Gryphon," a sultry voice whispered.

He groaned and rolled over slightly.

"Sunset, wake up," Alex's voice whispered, and the mattress shifted beneath him. Gryphon's eyes popped open, and he sat up sharply, coming face to face with Alex. She strad-dled his thighs and used her knuckles to keep her full weight off him, so he hadn't awakened until she spoke.

"There's my favorite sorcerer." She smiled seductively at

him, and he couldn't stop the excited pace of his heart. But then she blinked and the emerald green of her eyes vanished, replaced by black. She was slimmer, having given birth to the twins, but despite how recent it was, she moved smoothly, almost feline. She wore a black silk nightgown, and her hair cascaded over her shoulders. Gryphon tentatively moved her hair off her left shoulder to inspect her bond mark.

The body is hers. But are you still inside there, Princess?

The fury leaned closer, forcing Gryphon to lean back awkwardly. "I can still hear you, Sunset," she whispered. "That bond you have is tied to this body."

"That's a shame," Gryphon replied. "I would have preferred the link to my Head remain with her."

"But where would be the fun in that?" In a flash, she kissed him. The familiar feel of Alex's lips on his sent lust surging through his veins. His bond mark burned, and his Ares powers rushed to the surface, demanding he give in. They clearly didn't get the message that this sorceress wasn't actually Alex. Gryphon pushed her away.

The fury frowned. "That wasn't very nice, Gryphon."

"Sorry, witch. You may look like my sorceress, but you aren't her."

The fury shoved him back on the bed and leaned over him, draping her hair around his head. It felt cool against his skin. "You expect me to believe you have no interest in this body?"

Gryphon laughed. "Does Alex's body arouse me? You know the answer to that."

A smirk spread across the fury's face as she leaned down to kiss him, but Gryphon turned away. She growled in annoyance. "You just admitted to wanting me."

"No, I admitted that I find Alex's body arousing, but it's her mind and heart that I want. I'm not interested in some lowly substitute."

The fury sat up and slapped him across the face. "I don't care what you want. You're going to do what I say, or else."

"No, I'm not." Gryphon sat up and rubbed his cheek. "I'm not stupid."

The fury moved off him and glared at him with growing rage.

"You can't find her twins. You were either hoping to use me to find my baby or trick me into getting you pregnant again so you could have a powerful sorcerer to do whatever it is you want. But it takes both of us to make a bonded child, and I will never give you that."

The fury screamed and clawed at Gryphon's face. He shoved her off the bed, then jumped to the floor. She scrambled to her feet, hissed, and cracked away.

Gryphon wiped the blood off his face. "That's going to scar." Sighing, he decided against getting dressed and cracked.

CHAPTER 84

ALEX

Alex shivered so hard her teeth chattered. Tears streamed down her cheeks and she closed her eyes, desperate to block out the horror.

"Please go away, Alecto."

"Regretting your choice, little one?" Alecto's voice was eerily similar to Alex's uncle Moorloc's. The memory of his blade slicing her flashed in front of her, making her open her eyes. But then she saw the bodies and screamed.

"Tsk tsk," the fury said, sending Alex shuffling backward across the dirty dungeon floor to get away. "You shouldn't have left them with your friends. They clearly didn't care about you or your babies."

"No. They wouldn't do this," Alex said between sobs. "It can't be real." Lying on the floor were the bodies of her dead infants.

Alecto squatted beside Alex and rubbed her back. "I'm so sorry. After everything you went through to save them. To lose them because you did what Cassandra told you and let them *help* you. If only you'd listened to me and done it yourself … they'd still be alive."

Alex sobbed so hard she hyperventilated. Her brain screamed, and she saw spots.

"Nothing we can do now." The fury stood and moved across the icy stones to the door. "Though, if you wish, I could help you end your pain."

Alex shook even harder. She nodded, and her mother's red steel dagger landed in front of her. She picked it up and felt its cold weight. She remembered finding it in her mother's lab. The memory moved to Aaron's proposal, and then losing their first child, and now her twins. Their tiny bodies were too much, and Alex turned her back on them. She stuck out her arm and jabbed the knife down, carving along her entire fore-arm. Blood poured from the wound and collected at her feet, but before she could move the dagger to the wounded arm to cut the other side, the cut lit up in a golden light.

"No!" Alex cried.

The wound stitched itself back together.

"Oh dear," Alecto said. "It seems you'll have to live out your punishment, you selfish little wretch who gets everyone killed. You will watch them all die at your own hands."

Alex pulled her knees to her chest and buried her face in them as the fury's footsteps faded.

CHAPTER 85
AARON

Harold sat at the table, watching Aaron pace. "If you keep doing that, Edward's going to need to replace his floor."

"Is that your way of volunteering to tell Edward that we lost his grandchildren and his daughter has turned into a vicious monster?"

"I'd rather not."

"Then let me pace."

A knock at the door had Aaron rushing toward it. Megesti thanked Julius and entered the room. "I found Matthew. He said both Edward and Cameron are in a council meeting. He's going to interrupt them so they can wrap it up and come here."

"Well done," Harold said.

Megesti never took his eyes off Aaron. "Do you know what you're going to say?"

Aaron grimaced. "No. At least I can tell him his grandson is alive and safe, but I can't say the same for Alex."

"Has Michael returned yet?" Harold asked.

"I don't know," Aaron said, looking at Megesti.

Megesti ignored him and focused on Harold. "How about Edith?"

Aaron raised his eyebrow at Harold. "Edith?"

Megesti nodded. "I assumed if Michael took the first child, Edith had the second. Who else would a Warren trust?"

Aaron marched up to Harold. "Did you and Edith hide Gryphon's child?"

"I don't know," Harold said, shaking his head. "Edith never told me anything."

The three of them jumped when the door flew open, slamming into the wall. "Matthew had better be mistaken," Edward roared.

"About what?" Aaron asked.

"That we lost Alex, and she's turned into the fury," Cameron said.

Aaron's body stiffened. Megesti went ashen, and Harold looked toward a bookshelf. He'd have to face his godfather and cousin on his own. "I don't know how it went down exactly, but from what we've pieced together, she gave birth, and immediately the fury took over. The body is hers, but she's not in it."

Edward's anger slipped away, and the expression left was one Aaron had hoped never to see again. The anguish on his face was the same as the day he buried Victoria. "What about the babies?"

Megesti spoke up. "They were born healthy but were taken into hiding to keep the fury from finding them."

"Do we know where?" Cameron asked.

"No," Aaron said. "Alex wanted it that way. The fewer people who know, the less chance the fury has of getting them."

Edward dropped to the ground. "Your Royal Highness!" Matthew rushed to his side, but Edward pushed him away.

"This is all my fault. I did this."

"Edward, you couldn't know…" Aaron began, but didn't know what else to say.

"I should have," he whispered. "You're young, and so like your mother … but you always had your father's honor."

Aaron kneeled before Alex's father and rested his hand on his shoulder, as his own father had when they'd said goodbye to Victoria. "You made mistakes, as any father would. But you never had a role model of what a good father is, and you didn't get to father a girl or a young princess. You were expected to father a grown woman, and a very stubborn one at that."

"She's never going to forgive me."

"Alex loves you. You're her father."

"I mean Victoria," Edward whispered. "I was supposed to protect our daughter and I failed her."

Aaron looked at Matthew, unsure of what to say.

"I know my aunt," Megesti said. "And the only way she wouldn't forgive you is if you give up on Alex now."

Edward whipped his head toward Megesti. "I'll never give up on my daughter."

"Good," Megesti said. "Then get up. You have the Kings of Datten and Betruger here, and while both are very capable, they are young and will need your guidance in this."

Harold had crossed his arms and looked less than impressed with Megesti, but Aaron kicked him under the table. He grudgingly uncrossed his arms.

"What do we know?" Edward asked. He patted Aaron's shoulder and took a seat at the library table.

I guess that means he no longer hates me. Alex couldn't convince him, but Megesti did it in two sentences.

"We have a sorcerer at each of the places she's likely to go, so we'll know as soon as she turns up," Harold said.

"And where are the generals?" Matthew asked.

"Macht is in Betruger with Edith," Harold said.

"Randal went with Kharon to Moorloc's, and Jerome is in Datten with Stefan and Lynx," Megesti said.

Cameron took a seat beside Aaron. "Your mother is back with my parents in case you were worried."

"Thank you," Aaron said. "Do we know where Alex gave birth? That might help us figure out where she goes."

Julius' startled cry came from the doorway. They all spun to see Gryphon standing there.

"Where are your clothes?" Cameron asked.

"Probably being hexed by that wicked witch," Gryphon grumbled and sent the fireplace blazing.

"Julius, get Gryphon some clothes," Edward ordered.

Megesti went over to Gryphon, looking at him with concern. "What happened to your face?"

Gryphon smacked his hand away. "The fury, that's what. She hasn't found the babies, so she decided it would be easier to make another one."

"She *what?*" Aaron shouted.

"Don't worry, kingling. I turned her down," Gryphon said. "That's what got me clawed in the face."

Julius returned and threw one of his guard uniforms at Gryphon. He pulled the shirt over his torso and stepped into the pants.

"So she got into the Verlassen Castle?" Megesti asked.

"With no trouble," Gryphon said. "I was sound asleep and woke up to her in my bed."

"She just gave birth. Shouldn't she be resting?" Cameron asked.

"She doesn't look or act as if she just birthed twins. Unfortunately, I think we underestimated how powerful Alex truly is. This fury clearly knows how to wield Alex's abilities better than she did."

"Where will she go next?" Harold asked.

"Datten," Edward said. "If she went after Gryphon, there is only one other person in all of Torian who can give her what she wants."

Everyone turned toward Aaron. "Obviously I won't."

"*We* know that," Cameron said. "But she doesn't."

"We need to warn—" Harold was cut off by the entire castle shaking so violently Edward's décor flew off the shelves. Matthew opened the door just in time for the sound of screams to reach them.

CHAPTER 86
GRYPHON

Screams echoed through Edward's room, and the men leaped to their feet. Gryphon threw open his well, letting his Ares powers not only overtake him, but also spread through the room, sending rushing orange light into every one of the men around him. The silence that penetrated the room terrified him more than the screams, until Jessica appeared in the doorway.

Closest, Cameron moved to her, but Gryphon stopped him, sensing something was wrong. Alex's lady gently shook her head, a warning. Her clenched fists trembled.

"What do we have here?" A husky voice filled the room, and Jessica was shoved forward. The arm holding the back of her head gave her away before the rest of her body even appeared. There were three Xs carved into the skin. "If you're going to hold a meeting of the most powerful royals in Torian, shouldn't you include your Head queen?"

Gryphon's orange glow grew brighter as the fury walked into the room. Alecto still wore the simple black nightdress she'd had on when she tried to seduce Gryphon. She hadn't even bothered to put on shoes. *She must have followed me here.*

"Alex, what are you doing?" Cameron asked.

The fury said nothing, smirking at Cameron and then looking them each up and down slowly. Jessica pulled away, but immediately Alecto's eyes went completely black, and she wrenched her head back. "I told you not to struggle if you valued your life, girl. The only reason I kept you alive is because someone who loves you might know where my child is."

Julius reached for his sword, but the fury was too cunning. Before his hand could even grip the hilt, she thrust her hand back toward him, and he vanished without a sound. Her head whipped toward Matthew and Cameron next, and they also disappeared. "I suppose I don't need to keep all of you." A dagger appeared in her hand, and she slashed at Jessica, sending her crashing to the ground before she too cracked away.

"Tell me you didn't hurt her!" Aaron shouted, and Gryphon realized sending Ares rage into Aaron may not have been the best idea.

"What I do with my friends is none of your concern." The fury tossed the dagger in the air and sent it away. In her other hand, she held a mass of Jessica's fire red hair. "I didn't need the girl for what I intend to do. Her hair will suffice."

Alecto took a step toward them, and at once, the men readied themselves. Megesti burst into violet light, and the three kings drew their swords.

"Tempers, gentlemen. You might want to pull back on your chaos, Gryphon, before the mortals hurt themselves."

Gryphon withdrew his Ares powers. The mortals shook their heads, as if clearing themselves of the violent influence he knew his Ares magic would bring out in them.

"That's much better, isn't it?" The fury smiled, but there was none of Alex in it.

"What have you done with my daughter?" Edward demanded, moving beside Gryphon at the front of the table.

"She's still here," the fury said softly, placing the hand holding Jessica's hair upon her chest. "At least for now, and as long as you all behave." Her tone shifted to threatening as she clenched the red locks and narrowed her gaze on the men.

"Now, who's going to tell me where my children are?"

"We can't," Harold replied. "Because we don't know."

"You expect me to believe that none of you, including the babies' fathers and grandfather, know where they're being hidden?"

"Alex knew you'd expect us to, so she made sure none of us did. Even she didn't know," Megesti replied.

"That is unfortunate, for you," the fury replied and snapped her fingers. A gust of wind exploded from her and threw them all against the walls of the room. The wind was not only strong enough to hold them in place, but also kept them from being able to even move their hands from their sides. Slowly, she walked toward Gryphon first. Once she reached him, she burst into Mystics blue and pressed her free palm to his forehead. She dug through his memories, not caring how loud she made Gryphon scream. By the time she finished, Gryphon was in so much pain that had he been on the ground, he'd have simply retched and passed out. One by one, the fury checked them all, trying to find the truth, until she hit Aaron.

"Interesting," she whispered, pulling away. "So, the redhead's husband knows."

The fury snapped her fingers, the wind vanished, and they all fell onto the ground in an instant.

"Lucky for you all, you've been helpful to me, so I will leave you this time. But the next time I see you two," she pointed at Aaron and Edward, "you will pay for what you did to Alexandria." She cocked her head at Harold and Megesti. "You two, however, have nothing to fear from me. So long as you don't interfere, no harm will come to you."

"And if we try to stop you?" Harold asked.

"Then you'll die, as slowly and painfully as those you love."

Gryphon heard Harold gulp. He understood. Having Edith, Harold finally had someone worth losing, and he wouldn't risk her, any more than Gryphon would risk Alex.

"Goodbye boys." The fury cackled and cracked away, leaving them all on the ground, still recovering from the pain of her ripping through their minds.

"How is she that strong?" Megesti asked when he'd caught his breath.

"Alex is the Head. She has more magic in her than any other living sorcerer," Gryphon replied.

"But she's never been able to use it like that," Edward said.

"That's because Alex is young and still learning," Gryphon replied. "Alecto is centuries old and knows how to wield the magic running through Alex's body. We'd hoped she'd be limited to Alex's knowledge, but she clearly is not."

"So, what do we do?" Edward asked.

"We regroup," Aaron said. "Summon our friends and see what we come up with."

Gryphon frowned. *The best idea I've found* will *work. But you'll have to choose between your son and Alex.*

CHAPTER 87
FURY

Alecto strolled across the courtyard engulfed in fire. Cerberus scampered around her. The giant dog had been delighted upon her arrival, and she had decided he would be a useful companion. Alarm bells rang out, but they didn't bother her in the least. *It isn't as if these mortals could actually hurt me. I am, after all, in the body of their beloved queen, and they certainly won't risk losing her permanently. It's a pity, really, that they don't know they already have.*

A group of knights raced at her, but she merely flicked her wrist, and a hurricane gust sent them flying across the field until they struck the inner wall of the courtyard. They fell to the ground with a satisfying clank of armor on armor. Cerberus growled at them, and Alecto cackled and cracked them away.

Perhaps the mortal lover will be more reasonable. After millennia trapped in the underworld and then these compassionate Cassandras, I can wait a few more decades. I'll soon have what I need, and my sisters will be free to join me in my pursuit of vengeance.

Alecto reached the castle entrance and barely flicked a finger to send the enormous wooden door flying open. "Cerberus, make sure no one is hiding." She motioned for the dog to go, and he trotted down the deserted side hallway. Alecto crossed the main hallway to the royal suite.

"There better be something in here to wear." She stripped the black nightgown off her body and tossed it into the fireplace. Immediately, the fire burst into life and reduced the gown to ash before she even hit the stairs leading to Alex and Aaron's bedroom.

She paused at the stairwell, disgust curling her lip. "This is a royal suite? I will have to change everything to make it acceptable." She stroked the soft blankets. "Perhaps these may stay."

She sauntered over to the mirror on the wardrobe and crooned. Once again, she examined her new body and smiled. *Even after having twins, the young head has a lovely figure. I'm going to enjoy my time in this body.* She opened the wardrobe and flipped through Alex's dresses until one caught her eye, a black dress with gold detailing. Alecto ran her fingers along it, then took it off the hanger. She stepped into the dress and lifted the cups to her breasts. A quick glance in the mirror made her smile.

"Mortal," she shouted, and the door opened, and Jerome stepped inside the room.

"You summoned, my Queen?"

Alecto smiled. "Yes, tie my dress." Jerome crossed the room and did as ordered. When he finished, she straightened his collar. His uniform had blood in a few spots, from where he'd fought bravely to protect his family from her, and yet he'd failed to protect himself, the only one she intended to take. "And mortal, never remove the talisman I gave you."

"Of course not, my Queen," he replied in a deep voice, moving his hand to the magic amulet that hung around his neck. "I would never dream of removing your gift."

"Wonderful. Now take me to the sorcerer lab. I need to make more gifts."

"As you wish."

CHAPTER 88

GRYPHON

"Birch! Kharon! We need you now!" Gryphon shouted, applying pressure on Lynx's arm to stop the bleeding. The throne room had quickly been turned into a medical camp, with uninjured guards trying to help those hurt.

"Stop helping me and fix Stefan!" Lynx shouted.

"Don't you dare stop helping her!" Stefan said between his screams of pain.

Megesti shoved Gryphon aside and took over Lynx's care, making her yell in agony while he tried to stop the bleeding. Cameron held Jessica back, trying to calm her. Everyone else struggled to help Stefan.

"Ferflucs," Aaron grunted. Gryphon joined him and put pressure on Stefan's side. "Harold, how's Lucas?" Aaron shouted.

"He's unconscious, but alive."

Edward and Mathew attempted to put Avery's shoulder back into its socket. "What happened?" Edward demanded.

"We were attacked," Avery said.

"By who?" Cameron asked.

"Please tell me Alex didn't stab you, Stefan," Aaron said. Megesti finished with Lynx and came to examine Stefan's wound, replacing Gryphon and Aaron.

"If she did, we'll never hear the end of it."

Birch and Kharon appeared and audibly gasped.

"The fury is out," Stefan said.

"But Alex didn't stab Stefan," Lynx said. "Jerome did."

"What?" Edward exclaimed.

"She's done something to him," Lynx said.

Stefan screamed when Megesti pressed on his wound. "Your father has excellent aim," Megesti said. "He knows how to make it hurt."

"What did she do?" Kharon asked them.

Lynx explained how the fury had arrived and despite their best attempts to keep her away, she managed to put some chain on Jerome. The moment she did, he turned on them all.

Birch looked at Kharon. "Do you think she made a talisman?"

Kharon nodded. "It seems so."

"You'd need an immense amount of magic to create one," Lynx said. "How could Alex's body have that after everything she's been through?"

"The fury is better at using Alex's magic than she was," Gryphon said. "When I held her powers for those few months, I could barely handle them myself."

"And you only had *half*," Megesti reminded everyone.

Once patched up, Stefan explained how Jerome had attacked everyone. He'd gone for Stefan and Avery first, and then went after other knights. The fury sat on Aaron's throne, giggling as the guards were injured, knocked unconscious, or tied up. Lynx had worked to get the innocent people out of there, and when she'd tried to protect Stefan ended up being thrown aside by Jerome.

Gryphon hugged Lynx, while Megesti finished checking over Stefan. The throne room door opened, and Bernhard entered with Michael and three dozen others who Gryphon could sense were every Warren healer and midwife.

Cameron looked stricken at the sight of his mother, Elfriede. "What are you doing here, mother?"

"Helping." She tossed a pile of rags to one of the young knights.

Cameron opened his mouth to reply, but his mother pointed at him fiercely. "And don't you dare try to tell me to go home! I'm a Bishop by birth and Strobel by marriage. I shall do my part." Julius snorted and went over to help Elfriede with the rest of her supplies.

"Michael!" Jessica hurried across the room and threw her arms around him. "I was so worried."

"Your hair," Michael said, touching her face. A large chunk of her red hair had been cut out, leaving it uneven.

"It'll grow back. Is Stefan all right?"

"I'll survive," Stefan replied. He winced, but still pulled Jessica into a tight hug. "I'm just thankful you're okay. When we saw your hair, we feared the worst!"

"You're going to hurt for a few days, Stefan. I'm sorry I couldn't do more," Megesti said.

The moment Stefan released Jessica, Lynx grabbed his face and kissed him. "Don't you ever scare me like that again."

"Enough smooches," Gryphon said.

"Gryphon's right," Aaron said. "The fury has already arrived at the Verlassen Castle, Warren, and now Datten. She's clearly more powerful than we expected."

"And now she has my father under her control," Stefan said.

"But she doesn't have the babies," Lynx said. "So at least there's that."

. . .

IT TOOK MOST of the day to get everyone tended to and situated safely in Warren. Both Cameron and Michael offered to let Aaron stay with them, but Edward refused to hear of it. It seemed that despite their recent disagreement, the king had come to his senses and saw Aaron as Alex's husband again. Aaron had agreed to remain in the castle, though Gryphon could sense his unease. Aaron stayed in his and Alex's suite, while Stefan and Lynx took their places in the adjoining guard room. Gryphon went to his usual room, in the wing near Megesti, Birch, and Kharon. Megesti had told him the room had once been Daniel's, and Aaron's for a short time before he'd married Alex. Standing in the middle of the room, Gryphon could feel the history of it weighing on him.

After he opened the balcony doors to let some fresh fall air into the room, he changed from his soiled clothes back to his simple, sorcerer garb of black pants and an orange tunic. He leaned on the balcony door, breathing deeply and reaching out for Alex. When nothing came back, it sent a shiver down his spine. *Could our bond actually be broken? I didn't think they could break.*

A loud knock, followed by the door swinging inward, revealed Stefan.

"We need to talk."

"About what?" Gryphon replied.

"Not here, and not us. Lynx sent me to get you, and have you crack us to the Verlassen Castle."

"That seems dangerous, considering how attached Alex is to her mother's home."

"We suspect the only reason the fury went there was for you, and since you made it clear you will not help, she has no reason to return."

"You seem to forget all the valuable sorcerer books sitting in that lab."

"And you seem to have forgotten the first King of Warren's scepter that Alex hid in her mother's bedroom," Stefan replied.

"That was only helpful before the fury got out," Gryphon said. "With Alecto released, it's just a pretty rock."

CHAPTER 89

FURY

Alecto took her time selecting the materials for her talismans. Jerome's had been made out of a small stone she'd found in the cabin where Alex had given birth. She'd crafted it using what little she had on hand. Bewitching a mortal to perform her bidding was simple for someone with the level of magical knowledge Alecto had amassed over millennia, but to control a sorcerer as powerful as the Heart, or one of the older titans in the Forbidden Lands, would require a more specific item. Drumming her fingers on the table, she examined what she'd chosen for the sorcerers: the root of an old oak tree, a small jar of graveyard dirt, some gryphon feathers, a lava rock, an emerald, a bone fragment, and a small pile of rocks for the mortals locked in the dungeon for the time being.

"Nothing here speaks to the Merlin sorcerer. I'll need to learn more about him before I craft his talisman. What I have now should do in the meantime. I'll prepare a few for Gryphon's meddlesome hexa and her friends in case the old witch gets any ideas."

Alecto spent the next few hours combining ingredients and mixing a potion in the largest cauldron available. Soon, it bubbled and turned a deep navy with flecks of red and white. Once it reached a rolling boil, she wrapped each talisman in a leather strap and submerged them all in the liquid. Each glistened for a minute, absorbing the portion. When she finished, she hung them along the wall.

Satisfied with her talismans, she turned her attention to the books that covered the entire small room at the end of the lab. *I wonder what delightful spells we have?* She picked up a book and opened it to find it empty.

"What trickery is this?"

"No trickery. Old magic."

Alecto turned around to find the ghost glowering at her. "Victoria. What brings you to my new home?"

"Release my daughter."

"Now why would I do that? I waited forever to be allowed to return to this world, and I will not give that up."

"I'll do anything," Victoria pleaded, her anger instantly gone.

"That's a lovely sentiment, but you're dead, and as such, you have nothing I want."

"There must be something."

"No. There's nothing. Now leave, before I banish you. We both know I'm better at it then your daughter, so if I do, you'll never come back."

Victoria clenched her fists, but then slowly faded away.

"For being dead, she has good sense." Alecto turned back to the stacks of Merlin books that she couldn't use. "I'll have to find another way to set an alarm around my new home, before I decide how to dispose of any mortal stragglers."

CHAPTER 90

AARON

Aaron waited in the rooftop garden with Harold. The sun vanished into the trees of the dark forest surrounding the Verlassen castle. A *thunk* from behind broke the silence, and they turned to see Michael standing at the top of the stairs.

He'd brought out his cane, and Aaron felt a twinge of guilt. "You should have sent one of the younger knights to retrieve us, Michael," Aaron said. "There is no reason you had to climb those stairs."

Michael grimaced for a moment. "My injury does not relieve me of my duties."

Aaron realized his error. There was no reason to injure his pride in addition to all he'd been through.

"Any reason you left Edward out of this?" Harold asked.

"We brought you and Matthew instead. We don't need a hundred people," Aaron said.

"It just seems like so few. You and Stefan aren't representative of all of Datten."

"No. But we understand Alex and Jerome better than anyone."

"Edith and Macht are joining me from Betruger," Harold said. "I thought having your Nial would help."

At the mention of Edith, Michael smiled. "I suspect it will."

The three found their friends waiting in the library. They had rearranged to allow for a large table to be placed in the center. Kharon and Edith set out the food and drink on a side table while Matthew and Macht reviewed a large parchment.

"Your Royal Highnesses." Matthew nodded to the kings as they filled their cups. Edith gave Aaron a quick hug.

"We'll get her back. I promise," she said.

"I've assigned seats," Macht said. "We'll put each of the three kingdoms on one bench and the sorcerers on the final side."

The group took their places, and Macht revealed a floor plan of the Datten castle.

Aaron examined the old parchment. Every room was there in great detail, although the secret passageways and the changes made after the fire were absent. "Where did you get this? I'm shocked by its accuracy."

"Datten gave it to Warren as a show of good faith during their second peace treaty," Matthew said.

Aaron turned the map to him and pointed out the changes that had been made in the last few decades—Megesti destroying the third tower, the repairs from the recent battles, and his father's own secret additions.

"Why are we looking at this?" Lynx asked.

"To figure out how to break in," Macht said. "If this sorceress has control of Alexandria, then we need to find a way in that she is unaware of."

"We can split up and try to catch her unawares," Matthew said. "There are enough of us."

"That'll only work if we figure out how to remove the fury," Edith said.

Gryphon shook his head. "So far, everything we've thought of requires both a Head and a Heart. Without Alex, I'm not powerful enough—even if I combine my powers with Megesti."

"Could we put her to sleep until we figure this out?" Stefan asked. "That way, she can't hurt anyone or do anything Alex couldn't live with."

"You mean like having your own father stab you?" Aaron asked.

"What if we got a spy?" Edith said. "If one of us could convince her they are leaving our side to join hers—"

"But who?" Harold asked, narrowing his eyes at Edith.

"I would be an obvious choice—" Edith replied.

"I'll do it."

Everyone turned to Lynx.

"Why would she believe you?" Michael asked.

"Because she already offered me sanctuary."

"Absolutely not," Gryphon said. "You are not risking your life or the life of your pup for this. We'll think of something else."

Lynx opened her mouth, but Stefan cut her off. "You do not decide for my wife."

"You're right, but I do decide for *my* Titan of Tiere."

"Enough," Aaron said. "The last thing Alex would want is everyone fighting. Lynx, do you think the fury would believe you?" He didn't want to put any of Alex's friends at risk, but there was no way around it. They were already all at risk.

"I think I could be convincing enough." Lynx's face shifted from uncertainty to determination, and Aaron knew she would do whatever it took.

"Then we have one plan. We need to come up with more."

"Michael and I have a connection to the fury and Alex," Edith said. "We could try talking to her. Maybe we can get through to Alex."

"Too risky," Harold said.

"You don't get to shoot down my idea just because I'm your wife."

"I shoot it down because two people cannot take on this fury," Harold said. "I do not doubt your ability."

Edith huffed, but let Harold pull her closer.

"Do we know what she wants?" Aaron asked. "I know the fury is supposed to avenge all of Alex's betrayals, but what exactly does that mean?"

"Kharon suspects the fury will turn the tables," Gryphon said. "Whatever someone did to Alex, the fury will do it to them, but worse. Who she decides to start with is the real question."

"She could have gone after Edward or Aaron but didn't," Harold said.

"But she has taken control of Jerome along with several Datten knights," Matthew said. "Whatever she's planning must be large."

"Turning our men against themselves was evil," Aaron said, remembering how it felt to be used the same way.

"Is there any magic we could use to defeat her?" Macht asked. "We only have a bit of red steel, and we know it doesn't hurt Alex. But could it hurt this fury?"

"I doubt it," Gryphon said. "She is in Alex's body. I believe she has Alex's healing abilities."

"And therefore her weaknesses?" Stefan asked, and Gryphon nodded.

"I don't see how bad needlework will help us," Edith said.

"What if we aged them up?" Lynx asked. Confused faces peered back at her.

"Aged Alex up?" Megesti asked.

"Not her," Lynx said. "Birch has a spell to make plants grow. What if we could apply that to the twins somehow? If Gryphon's child were aged up, that would give you a Head!"

"It's too risky," Gryphon said.

"How do you know?" Aaron asked.

"I already thought of this. I found the spell, and ruled it out."

"You don't get to make choices like that on your own," Matthew said.

Gryphon groaned and gave Aaron a sorrowful glance. "It would take Birch, Megesti, and myself to create the potion, and there would be no way to test it. Because they're twins, we'd have to age both. If I aged them too much, it could kill Aaron's child. He'd die of old age, even if mine didn't have all of his powers yet."

"Oh," Aaron and Lynx replied together.

"That's why I never brought it up," Gryphon said before turning to Aaron. "And I don't think Alex would forgive us if we ended up killing your son to save her. If we went with this plan, it would have to be because we are out of options, and need to save everyone in Torian from her."

The meeting went all night. Any idea, no matter how outlandish or terrible, was considered. When everyone headed off to bed, the list of accepted ideas was far shorter than anyone had hoped. Aaron did not sleep very long or very well.

CHAPTER 91

FURY

"I want to keep him, him, and him." Alecto pointed at the unconscious men in the Datten dungeons.

"What of the rest, my Head?" Jerome asked.

Alecto snapped her fingers, and they all vanished.

"Did you kill them?" Jerome's lips turned up into a wicked smile.

Alecto chuckled. "That wouldn't be sporting. I sent them to the middle of the woods. Let them find their way home, or anywhere else."

"As you wish." Jerome bowed extra low.

Alecto patted his head. "Take me to the treasure room next. I require something sparkly."

Datten's treasure room was buried deep beneath the castle. Alecto descended the stairs, lifting her skirt. The cold stone floor sent a shiver through her bare feet. After so long being stuck inside the boring, always trying to do what's best for others Cassandras, Alecto relished the sharp, icy sting this body could feel. Jerome silently led the way, illuminating the

423

darkness with a torch that emitted a glow so bright the stairs appeared lit by the midday sun.

The door that guarded the entrance was formidable enough it could have easily been found on the outside of the perimeter walls. Alecto placed her hand on it. It took longer than she would have liked, but it soon began to smoke and catch on fire. Soon, the door disappeared in a raging inferno. Alecto summoned her ice power, poised to quell the fire if need be, and waited until it was reduced to ash. Fire could be so satisfying.

Alecto waited for Jerome to draw his blade and enter, then she stepped over the smoldering ruins. She'd seen vast fortunes in her life, but they wouldn't hold a candle to Datten's wealth. There was gold, not in coins, but smelted into bricks. There were stacked many deep and all the way to the ceiling. The other side was a wall of treasure chests. Judging from the few open on the floor, they were filled to the brim with diamonds. Along the far wall sparkled shelf after shelf of jewels. Alecto strutted the length of the room until she reached the crowns, tiaras, necklaces, and other trinkets crafted from every imaginable stone. Alecto wiggled her fingers in the air, trying to read the pieces.

An intricately carved box brought her to a halt. She lifted its lid and removed an ornate gold crown with black gemstones protruding from its top like the points of a spear. Etchings circled the entire crown. Smiling to herself, she ran her finger along the gold, using her fire power to mark the crown with wispy lines that resembled cobwebs before she placed the crown onto her head.

She turned to the chests, selected matching jewelry, and whistled for Jerome. "Carry these."

The general trotted over like a loyal dog, nodded, and accepted the jewels, carrying them back upstairs.

The guards she'd enchanted earlier were all still standing in place when they reached the main floor. "Such good boys," she chortled, petting a few of them on the head as she walked by them. Behind her, she heard claws skittering on stone, and she turned to face Cerberus. "Who's a wonderful dog?" The beast raced to her and lifted his front paws to beg.

"I see you remember my training." She scratched the middle head behind the ear and turned to the closest guard. "Take Cerberus to the kitchen and feed him your finest hock of venison."

"Yes, my Queen." The guard walked away, and Alecto sent Cerberus after him.

Alecto turned to the others. "I want lookouts on the top of the castle and all the grounds. We have control of this castle, but the mortals will no doubt try to get it back." She paused and pointed at Jerome. "Or at least try to rescue you. We wouldn't want that, would we?"

Alecto tilted her head, letting Alex's chestnut curls fall onto her chest. The sight of her wholesome, warm locks made her sick. "I must do something about this." She rubbed the hair between her fingers before throwing it over her shoulder. "See that I'm not disturbed."

Once in the lab, she waved her hand, removing all the homely touches Alex and her friends had put up. Without them, the room became dark with gray, black, and bloodred accents representing her and her two sisters. Over millennia, the trio had found ways to distinguish themselves. Tisiphone avenged murder, making bloodred her favorite shade. Megaera preferred black, for her black heart and the grudges she held. Being the most relentless sister, Alecto preferred silver and gray. Like the morning fog and the moon in the sky, she was unceasing in her pursuits.

She swung the enormous cauldron on its hook over the

fireplace and brought the fire to life. The potion came together quickly, and the moment it cooled enough, Alecto took a swig of the foul mixture. When she turned to the only reflective surface in the room, she could already see the magic taking effect, her brown hair slowly replaced by silver.

"Much better. Now to find some allies before the boy returns."

ALECTO SURVEYED the men before her. Several of the highest-ranking Datten families had refused to see reason and were being removed from her sight. She'd expected more of a fight, but they held their heads high as they were dragged away to whatever fate her new pet deemed appropriate. That left five families, and while there were fewer than she'd hoped, they were better than nothing. She passed out the pendants she'd created, and the instant they touched the chests of the mortals, their eyes flashed black, and they went stiff.

The final family made Alecto pause. *The same blond hair as all of the images of the king.*

"Who are you?"

"Wesley Rassgat and my father, Nathaniel."

"You're related to the king?"

The men nodded. She sniffed, and a stench filled her nostrils. Decay—the sign that he was rotten inside, and had done something to Alexandria that would now earn her wrath. Slowly she looked him up and down until he spoke again.

"Like what you see? The princess did too, until my cousin influenced her."

Alecto crossed her arms. "Influenced her?"

Wesley leaned forward. "I was trying to be polite. My

cousin helped himself to her, knowing their fathers would turn a blind eye."

"Really."

Wesley and Nathaniel nodded, but Alecto shook her head and closed the distance between her and Wesley. "Don't lie to me. I have her memories. I know you are the one who put your hands on her."

The color drained from Wesley's face.

Alecto's voice came out as a growl when she spoke. "In fact, you should be on your knees thanking me that I don't gut you where you stand for your crimes."

Wesley looked to his father and Alecto took his chin and made him face her. "I said on your knees." He dropped like a stone throne in the ocean. She held her boot out. "Now kiss it."

"What?" Nathaniel asked.

Alecto snapped her fingers, and he fell over unconscious, and her attention went back to Wesley. "I said kiss it and I might spare your lives."

Shaking, Wesley bent down and kissed Alecto's boot. She slipped a talisman around his neck and leaned down to whisper intimidatingly, "Good boy. Now make yourself useful, and drag your worthless father back to your estate. Then return here for more orders."

"Yes, my Queen." Wesley struggled to drag his father away by his ankles.

"What fun." Alecto rubbed her hands together and spun to look around the room. "Next, I think some redecorating is in order ... and a new wardrobe."

ALECTO REJECTED another dress from the royal seamstress Valaria, throwing it on the floor like discarded refuse. The older woman trembled like a leaf, and Alecto relished her fear. "I want the neckline lowered and the entire back removed. And since we're making it more fitted, add some slits so I can climb these incessant stairs more easily."

The seamstress hesitated. "Are you sure you want to show so much, Your Royal Highness? That isn't what a queen would wear."

Heat flooded the fury's veins, and she clenched her fist. She slowly turned toward the mortal. "I don't care what you think. I will be queen of this entire world, and shall wear what I see fit. Is that understood?"

Valaria's eyes dropped, and she nodded her head, vigorously gathering the dresses strewn around her.

"Good. And stop cowering. I would hate to have to hurt you."

Valaria fumbled and nearly dropped her scissors, and Alecto burst into a cackle. "I was only teasing. You are far too valuable to me to kill. Besides, you've done nothing worthy of my wrath, so as long as you continue to do as I say, you will not be harmed."

The fury narrowed her eyes at a knock at the door, trying to decipher who could be disturbing her so late. "Come in."

Alecto smiled at Jerome, but stopped when she sensed something. He'd brought a visitor. "Leave us," she barked at the seamstress, who took the gowns and hurried down the stairs. When she'd gone, Jerome went back into the hall and ushered in a cloaked figure. The general then left Alecto along with the stranger. She sniffed the air. *That smell ... Lynx?*

"Well, Lynx, do tell me. Are you here as a spy, or have you come to your senses about your husband?" Alecto chuckled until Lynx pulled her hood back. Alecto couldn't stop the gasp that escaped her. Some part deep inside her cared for Lynx, and the sight of the Titan of Tiere was enough to hurt her heart. Head hung down, Lynx stepped forward and twisted the bottom of her shirt. A sharp coppery scent overwhelmed Alecto —blood, sweat, and fear.

"What happened?" Reaching Lynx, Alecto used her first two fingers to force Lynx's chin up, and her breath stopped in her throat. The blood smell had come from the cut on her cheek and her split lip, but it was the large black eye that sent uncontrollable rage coursing through Alecto.

"I'm sorry to disturb you ... I just ... I had nowhere else to go."

"Who did this to you?"

Lynx continued tugging on her shirt. "Stefan. He was furious at me."

"What for?" Alecto's heart broke for the sorceress. She could still picture the self-serving face of her own abusive partner from millennia ago. *But this might be a trick.*

"Because I don't know where the babies are and I didn't tell him Alex—"

"Aghhh." Alecto roared at Alex's name, and Lynx threw her arms up and stepped back, trembling like a newborn cub. The sight of a terrified titan calmed Alecto. "I'm sorry." She held her arms out, and Lynx gingerly crept into Alecto's embrace. "You're safe now, and if he shows his face here, I'll take care of him."

And then, my kitten, I'll take care of you.

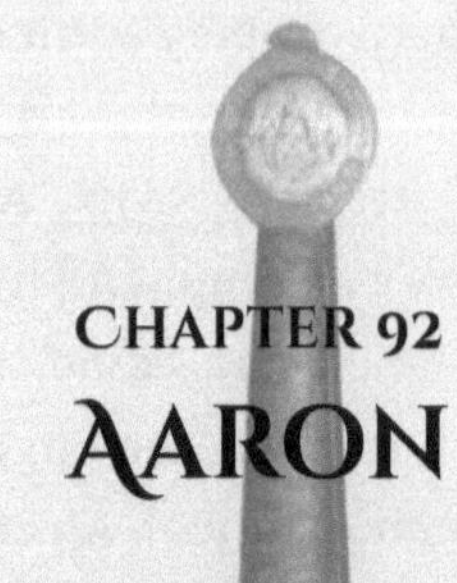

CHAPTER 92
AARON

"*We have to save her, or all will be lost!*"

Aaron woke up in a cold sweat, panting. The nightmare he'd had a few months before had returned. He quietly got up and left Randal asleep in their tent to get a breath of fresh air. The dew on the ground glistened as he wandered between the various colored tents of his friends and their men until he'd made it all the way to the edge of the camp, where he heard voices. Something in him urged him on. Soon, he found himself in the woods, using the dim moonlight to avoid the branches of the trees trying to ensnare him.

"Is that really the best we can come up with?" Michael's voice found him first. Aaron turned to follow it.

"We don't have any more red steel," Harold said.

"Even if we did, Alexandria doesn't react to it the way other sorcerers do," Macht said.

"Well, locking her in the sorcerer dungeon isn't any better," Stefan said.

"At least she'll be safe there," Gryphon said.

Aaron reached a small clearing and found his friends in the midst of a heated discussion.

"You cannot make this decision without involving Aaron," Megesti snapped.

"He's not thinking rationally," Gryphon said.

"Of course, I'm not," Aaron announced, stepping out of the trees. "I'm terrified this monster will kill the Alex we love, if she hasn't already." He ran his hand through his hair. "But that doesn't mean I won't listen to reason. Something is coming, and I think it's on our side."

"What are you talking about?" Michael asked. "Why aren't you angry at us for sneaking around?"

"He should be," Stefan said, glaring at Aaron as only a Wafner could. "He must be keeping something from us."

Aaron sighed. Stefan knew him too well. "I'm hearing things in my dreams."

"We all hear things in our dreams," Macht said.

"No," Aaron said. "This is different."

"How do you know?" Michael asked.

"Because Alex said it was."

"*Alex* said—?" Gryphon crossed his arms. "Are you saying you have been hearing a voice in your dreams for some time, and never told us?" Gryphon's hands lit up in orange, and he stuffed them in his armpits, which only made them glow instead.

"That's right. Alex figured it was my father or brother communicating with me. She had a conversation with Kharon about whether it was possible, and when she learned it was, we stopped worrying."

"Then why tell us now?" Stefan asked.

"Because I think the voice is warning us about going to Datten."

"What has it been saying?" Harold asked.

"That if I don't go with them at once, everything we fought for will be lost."

"I suggest we wake the generals," Stefan said.

AARON'S FINGERS were white from the pressure of gripping Thunder's reins. They'd decided to send ahead a smaller party, exactly as Aaron had done when he'd gone to the Betruger a few short years ago. Publicly, their mission was to reason with the fury so that she'd allow the remaining Datten citizens to go free. But their true goal was to see if there was anything left of Alex to save. Following behind Randal, Gryphon, and Macht, Aaron heard the strange voice from his dream echoing its warnings. Harold rode beside him but hadn't said a word. A quick glance told Aaron Harold was deep in thought.

"You can speak to me, Aaron," Harold whispered.

"I didn't want to interrupt whatever you were thinking about."

"I can think about Edith later."

"We're going to confront the ferocious and vengeful goddess that has taken over my wife's body, and you're daydreaming about your wife?" Aaron suppressed his urge to groan or roll his eyes at his friend.

"Of course. When in times of danger or turmoil, Edith's love grounds me. Our future is what I fight for. Are you not thinking of Alex?"

"I am, but she's the one we're going to see in order to get my people back."

"Do you see her as this monster who holds your kingdom hostage, or as a woman you love and wish to save?"

"Both. I worry I'll lose her to the monster, or I may already have."

"We're getting closer," Randal whispered. "I suggest we remain quiet to avoid detection."

"Don't bother," Gryphon said.

Ahead, Jerome and several of Aaron's favorite knights blocked the path, swords and spears drawn.

"Dismount your horses, hand over your weapons, and we'll escort you to see the queen," Caleb ordered, his voice a growl.

Aaron bit back the snarky retort that jumped to mind, deciding in favor of remaining peaceful. Randal and Macht shifted uneasily, but Gryphon lowered his head, and his hand slipped behind him, glowing red.

"As you wish," Aaron said loudly, making everyone turn toward him. He slipped off Thunder and drew his sword. Caleb held out his hand. Had it been someone he despised, Aaron could have killed them in that instant, but his childhood friend's face stared at him, and so he handed over his red steel sword, and his comrades did the same.

"Very good. I told her you'd be reasonable under the circumstances," Jerome said. "Have your sorcerer take you to the throne room."

"Have your sorcerer?" Gryphon muttered to himself. He tensed up the moment Aaron patted his shoulder. Annoyed, he reluctantly nodded and snapped his fingers, sending them into the throne room.

A group of guards was on them before Aaron could even blink, forcing his arms behind his back. The guards ushered them toward the center of the room, where the throne had been relocated, allowing more guards than he'd ever seen in the throne room to stand around it. They were shoved down to their knees in front of the fury sitting upon his family throne on the hulking stone dais.

He searched her face, desperate to find any sign of the woman he loved. Her hair was now silver, and everything from her dress to her shoes was black. The dress was not only tight but also very revealing. Alex wouldn't even have worn that to bed, unless she intended for him to rip it off her in a matter of minutes. Even the crown on her head was wrong. He had expected her to wear his, since he was the ruling royal, but he'd never seen this one before. It looked ominous.

Her eyes were as black as night, and a wicked little smirk spread to the corners of her mouth. "Welcome, gentleman," she crooned, and pressed her hands against the throne arms to push herself up. "How kind of you to visit me."

She strutted down the stairs, and Aaron couldn't help but stare at how her body swayed. Although the gown hugged her figure, the slits on either side of her dress allowed her legs to move about freely. She paused near the bottom and interlaced her fingers, pressing her index fingers to her chin. "There are fewer of you than we saw at a distance. You must have sent out a scout party, like you did with the Betruger. Hopefully, it wasn't a mistake."

She stopped in front of him. The scent of flowers and sea salt surrounded him, mocking him, and he swallowed hard. The creature—equal parts still Alex but not *his* Alex—leaned down and gripped his chin so tightly she could have cut his skin with her nails. She wrenched his face toward hers.

"I think you and I should have a conversation, Princeling."

Aaron blinked, and the throne room vanished. She brought them to the kitchen. Memories of sneaking cookies with Alex and Daniel hit him out of nowhere. Scanning the space, nothing had been altered. He found Alecto standing at a tall table with a sharp knife in her left hand. In the other, she held a shiny green apple. Aaron stayed silent as she sliced off a piece of the fruit and popped it into her mouth. She chewed, staring at him as if trying to read his thoughts.

"Why did you bring me here?"

The fury shrugged. "I was hungry." She pointed her knife at a bowl behind Aaron. "Help yourself."

"Thank you, but I've lost my appetite." Alecto shrugged and plopped another apple chunk into her mouth.

Eating Alex's favorite fruit must be a sign.

"You've come all this way. Tell me what it is you want."

"My people. I want you to release everyone."

"No."

"You can't possibly want to take care of an entire kingdom," Aaron protested.

She narrowed her eyes. "For your safety, I would suggest you not presume to know what I want."

Aaron ran his hand through his hair, trying to figure out what to say. The fury kept munching on her apple. His eyes roamed from her face to her hands, hair, legs, and back to her face. *Be in there somewhere, Alex. I refuse to believe that you're gone. We fought too hard for too long to lose us like this.* "Understood ... I just meant that you must have plans of what you intend to do, and the needs of the people would only interfere with your plans."

"For all you know, my plans are to destroy all of Datten."

"If that were the case, you'd have done it already."

"True." Alecto tossed the core into the air, and it vanished.

"So tell me what you want for my people. You wouldn't bring me here to talk alone if you didn't have a price in mind."

"Such a clever mortal. I can see what the girl saw in you."

"Do you mean Al—"

"Do not say her name."

Why? Will it strengthen her? Summon her? Please tell me she's still in there.

"None of those. I simply despise hearing it after all the years trapped inside her."

Aaron stilled, trying to quiet his mind. He leaned against the table and waited for the fury to make her demands.

"I require the sorcerous."

"Kharon?"

"Yes."

"I don't have the authority to give you a sorcerer. They have free will and a mind of their own. I cannot simply give them to you."

"Such a dull king you are. You have persuasion over them, and I need their skills."

"For what?"

"Why should I tell you?"

"Because," Aaron said, shifting his palms to the table and leaning toward the fury, "if you don't tell me, I won't help."

Alecto cackled. "You foolish boy. You think you have power here, but you have none. If you don't help me, I'll simply find another way. But first, I'll murder every innocent mortal in this kingdom and send you their heads."

Aaron's heart stopped. *No. You can't.*

"Tsk. Poor boy, you worry what your wife would do if she learned *we* committed mass murder." She crossed the room and now she stood right in front of him, looking down and smirking. "You don't have to worry about that, because she's never getting out."

Aaron forced himself to breathe slowly so the fury wouldn't sense his excitement. *Getting out? That means she's still there.*

CHAPTER 93

GRYPHON

Gryphon threw open the doors to the Warren lab. *Ferflucs! Where is that titan?* The fury had given them only a few hours to hand over Kharon. It was Gryphon's job to convince them to go, and now they were missing.

An icy wind surrounded him, and Gryphon pinched his brow. "Daniel, I swear if you are here to annoy me, I'm going to do something you will not like."

"Victoria was right. You are a petulant child."

"Merlock?" Gryphon turned to face Megesti's father. Unlike Victoria and Daniel, who could hold their form and appear almost human, Merlock struggled. His apparition was an opaque, vaguely body-shaped cloud.

"I don't have long, so be silent and listen."

Gryphon nodded once, and Merlock went on. "Kharon can go to the fury, but they must not, under any circumstances, do what she asks."

"What does she want?"

"To raise the dead."

"That's not possible, even for a Titan of Hades."

"The Hades line has more power than people realize. But it is imperative that Kharon not help her."

"Why?"

"Because if they do, there will be no hope for Alexandria."

"So you believe there's a chance we can get her back?"

"You know as well as I do what is possible with magic. Regardless of what the others say, make your potion."

"Which potion?"

"The aging one. It's the only way—" Merlock groaned, and the cloud dispersed for a moment before reforming. "If you want to save her, you must find the twins and age them. If you do, they'll come to you."

"What about Aaron's son? If I age them too much, I could kill him."

"You know what is at stake! Risk it."

"Alex would never forgive me if I brought her back at the expense of her son."

Merlock's image faded. "Gryphon—if you don't ... everyone will die at her hand."

Gryphon panted out foggy breaths, heart hammering in his chest.

There was a soft click, and Kharon entered with their nose in a book. "Hades, it's cold in here." Looking up, they dropped their book. "What's wrong?"

"I need you to come with me. The fury is holding all the Datten people hostage, and the only one who can help them is you."

Kharon pursed his lips. "I wondered what she would do to get her claws into me."

Gryphon shivered until the death cold finally abated. "You were expecting this."

"It was inevitable, Gryphon. Do you remember nothing of our studies?"

Gryphon nodded. "The legend of the furies—the goddesses of vengeance, created by Hades himself."

"And only he could control them. Well, now I am the closest thing in this world to their creator, and I suspect Alecto wants to use me to reunite her with her sisters."

"Aaron mentioned something about bringing back the dead."

"Gods don't die. They merely take on a new existence."

"But you can't mean—"

"The fury wants me to bring her sisters into this world, and the only way to do that is to put them into someone's body and wait to see who wins."

Gryphon's stomach dropped. "I let Lynx go to her! Why didn't you say anything?"

"It's Lynx. Even if she knew, she'd have gone."

"But she could have prepared—you could have prepared her!"

"I understand your fears, Gryphon, truly I do. But nothing would have changed, except Stefan and the others would worry even more for Lynx than they do now."

"I guess I know why she wants my child so badly."

Kharon nodded. "Three sisters. Three bodies." Kharon handed him the book they'd been reading. "I will go to Datten to ensure their people are freed. This book contains a spell to protect the mortals from her influence."

"Will it work on us too?"

"No, and it isn't foolproof. The closer the mortals were to Alex, the more the fury's influence blooms inside them."

"The more they love her, the easier it is for her to corrupt them."

"Precisely. So be sure to give Stefan, Aaron, and Michael

extra protection." Kharon straightened their robes and gave Gryphon a small smile. "Don't be frightened. She won't dare hurt me, at least not until her sisters are in sorcerer bodies."

Gryphon nodded and drummed his fingers on the book's spine. Kharon tilted their head, and Gryphon rushed to them, throwing his arms around them.

Kharon embraced him, squeezing him back even harder. "No matter what your parents told you, your love is not a weakness." Kharon released Gryphon and patted his cheek. "Your love is your strength, and you *can* do this. Believe in yourself, in the bond you share with Alexandria, and in the child you made."

"I will."

"Good. Where are the others?"

"In the woods outside of Datten. Megesti is there."

"All right. I'll crack to Megesti, and you make that potion. I gathered the ingredients already. They're in the crate under the table."

Gryphon set the book down and turned back to Kharon. The titan straightened their gray robes, seemingly unconcerned about the dangers that would face them. "I have a favor—"

"No worries. I will."

"I didn't even ask."

"You didn't have to. I'll ensure no harm comes to Lynx or Alexandria's body." And then Kharon disappeared.

Gryphon opened the book, letting the cover slap against the table. A ripped piece of parchment protruded from the pages, and Gryphon flipped open the book to the potion Kharon had told him to prepare. He swung one of the cauldrons over the fire pit and waved his hand to ignite it. He left a crate of supplies on the table and cracked to the Forbidden Lands.

He couldn't help but shiver standing in his and Alex's library. All the other libraries in the various castles were just hers, but this one belonged to both of them. Silently, he crossed the room toward the shelves he'd set up.

He needed to find the book that contained the aging potion. Luckily, he'd grouped the books with more dangerous spells together. His fingers danced along the wooden shelf, hunting for the one he needed. There it was—a small violet book they'd retrieved from Merlin's cabin. He remembered the joy on Alex's face when she'd come running out of the cottage. She'd found something so precious and meaningful to her, and he was honored to help her bring it to their home.

What if that Alex never comes back? What if we're already too late?

Clutching the book in his hand, he closed his eyes and reached deep inside himself for his Ares side. *If we're too late, and that witch has taken Alex from me, I'll become that monster my father always wanted me to be.*

CHAPTER 94
AARON

"Where is he?" Aaron demanded. Megesti shrugged, and the generals didn't even look up from their maps and castle layouts. The fury had sent them away, and they had only until sunset to provide their answer. At the edge of a clearing in the Dark Forest, the light dimmed with each passing moment. "If we don't send Kharon in, the fury will kill my people."

"Kharon won't let that happen, Aaron," Birch said. Her tone was soft and reassuring like his mother's, but Aaron caught her looking away.

An owl cried nearby. Aaron turned toward the west. Darkness swept across the Dark Forest. Orbs of glowing fire appeared to light up their camp. He reached toward one and poked it, making the fire inside flicker.

"We failed," Aaron whispered. Someone cracked nearby.

"Aaron, hurry!" Harold shouted.

Fire orbs chased Aaron through the trees, helpfully lighting his way. He reached an opening in the trees where he could see the protective wall that surrounded Datten. Below, throngs of people were streaming out. They were carrying bundles in their arms and pulling carts behind them, while his former soldiers stood at the wall entrances barking at them. They were evacuating. *Why is she letting them out?*

Gryphon and Harold came up beside him. "I found Kharon," Gryphon said. "They accepted our request and turned themself over to the fury to help your people."

In the distance, the silhouette of interlopers on the keep—*his* keep—mocked Aaron. This was the same keep where he'd watched his father leave and return from battle a hundred times, the one his parents had stood upon when he left to get Alex, reassured by their watchful gaze. Now, the fury watched his citizens leave the city, and he could make out Jerome, Lynx, and Kharon standing beside her.

"But don't worry," Gryphon went on. "Kharon won't give her what she wants."

Below him, Aaron's people abandoned their homes, and all he could do was watch. *I'm a failure. I put my love of Alex above my people, and now they're paying for it.*

"Gryphon, can you crack them all to Warren?" Aaron asked. "Or do you need help?"

"I can do it, but—isn't Datten twice as large as Warren?"

"Some can stay in Betruger," Harold said. "I already spoke with Edward. But we need to decide who will go where."

Gryphon nodded. He held his hands out over his head, and the people streaming through the gates began to vanish.

✦

IT TOOK HOURS, but the trio remained at the edge of the clearing until every Datten citizen had been sent to safety. By the time it was done, Gryphon was so exhausted, he summoned Megesti to bring their group back to Warren so he could rest.

As soon as the women saw them, Edith hurried to Harold, and Jessica to Michael. Aaron looked to Stefan for solidarity from the only other man whose wife was at risk of not coming home. Stefan motioned toward the side hall and ducked out. Aaron hurried around the corner after him, but ran into Edward.

"Aaron. I hoped to find you. Do you have a minute?"

Aaron tried to follow Stefan down the hall with his eyes, but he was already gone. "Of course, Edward."

The King of Warren led Aaron down a small side hallway into his personal suite. He motioned for Aaron to sit and removed his crown. The spot at the table he preferred was directly behind Edward, so instead, Aaron sat in what had been his father's spot for decades.

Edward sat across from Aaron, a worn leather journal in his hands. He opened it and slid it to Aaron. "I owe you an apology, Aaron."

Aaron picked up the book and read.

LIFE HAS BECOME ALMOST UNBEARABLE. My father is livid that I married Victoria, and his hatred of my chosen wife makes living with him difficult on all of us. My people need me to balance my father's overbearing ruling style, but with Victoria expecting, it's much better for her in Datten with Guinevere and Gwendolyn. Trying to be there for my people while protecting my wife from my father's wrath is more challenging than any military campaign Emmerich dragged me on. Truthfully, if it wasn't for my dear friend, I don't know how I would cope. I'll be forever indebted to him for his support. When the time comes, I'll repay his kindness by helping Daniel learn to juggle all that comes with being a crown prince with a young family.

. . .

"I PROMISED myself I would help your brother when he took the throne. And I'm so ashamed that I didn't help you more. You married my daughter, but I became so blinded by what she was going through that I never cared enough to look at your struggles."

"Edward—"

His godfather held his hand up to silence Aaron. "Becoming king is not a straightforward task, Aaron, whether you're young or old. I should have looked past your youthful mistakes and helped you, as Harold has. I'm truly sorry."

Aaron closed the journal and slid it back to Edward. "Thank you. You were right when you said you wouldn't have had to protect Alex from me had my father been alive. He would have known what to do. I'd have fought him the entire time, but ultimately, I would have done what he said. He had an innate ability to see things other people didn't."

Edward tossed him an old brass key.

"What's this?"

"It's for your father's office."

"An office? In Warren?"

"Only the generals are privy to the knowledge that Datten kings have always had an office in Warren's castle. When there were battles to be planned, your father and grandfather needed a quiet place to work. If you're ready, I'll take you."

Aaron nodded.

Daily life in Warren's castle happened mostly on the two main floors, but the building had a few floors below the main one for storage and crypts. Edward led Aaron past the library to an alcove with an old statue of Daniel, the second-born son of Warren's founder, Arthur Warren, and Aaron's own brother's namesake. Aaron couldn't help but shiver. This was the exact spot he'd found Arthur ranting before he'd attacked him. Edward leaned in front of Aaron and pushed down the first

Daniel's sword handle. With a click, the wall beside him swung open. Stairs led up into the darkness.

"Why am I not surprised that the Datten king's study is hidden beside the prince who would marry our last princess?"

Edward smiled and patted Aaron's shoulder. "Because you're a great king, Aaron. I know you don't believe that right now, but getting your people out was the right thing to do. We'll get her back, somehow. If she'd learned you let your people—*her* people—suffer for her, she'd be furious."

Aaron stepped into the doorway and paused. "Edward?"

"Who do you need?"

"Stefan. Then Harold and Michael."

"I'll have Matthew bring Stefan. He can get the others when you're ready."

Aaron stepped into the dark. He'd expected a damp, musty odor, but was met with the slightly astringent smell of pine and bright, almost floral fresh-cut wood. He took the steps two at a time and reached an enormous door. Oddly, it had neither a keyhole nor a handle. He ran his fingers over it and found a seam. It was actually two doors. He caught his index finger on a sliver and jerked his hand away. It was bleeding. A keyhole appeared, and he heard a voice in his head.

Welcome, King Aaron of Datten. Son of Emmerich, son of Aleric, son of Daniel.

The door swung inward, and the voice continued to rattle off the names of all Datten's former kings. *I hope it doesn't do that every time.*

Aaron crossed the threshold. The dust all over the room made it clear it hadn't been used in over a decade. An enormous black-pine desk called to him, and when he reached it, he found an unfinished letter upon it.

"June 1538. A month after Victoria and Daniel died. Shortly before my father lost his desire to battle the Betruger."

Aaron meandered, examining every book and figure on the shelves: maps, compasses, battle plans, weapon sketches. He had the confidential military thoughts and history of all Datten's kings at his fingertips. Aaron brushed the dust off the chair and sat down at the desk. Only when he stopped moving did he hear the footsteps.

"This is quite the setup," Stefan said from the top of the stairs.

"It is," Aaron replied, still looking around the space. They sat in silence for a few minutes, taking the room in when Stefan finally cleared his throat.

"I had a thought."

"Speak freely, Stefan."

"What if the voice you're hearing isn't Daniel or Emmerich? What if it's a future voice?"

"Like from Alex's premonition dreams? But how?"

"I've been thinking about it for a while. Aaron—I saw you glow gold. What if conceiving a child with Alex transferred some of her magic into you?"

"Could that even be possible? Megesti assumed it was from when she gave me her blood."

"Whatever the reason, Lynx has some ideas," Stefan said. "She thought we could use it as a distraction against the fury. We could fake that you have magic and use it to get back into the castle. Then have Gryphon crack us to you and take her unaware."

"That's a very interesting idea. Once Gryphon recovers, we'll discuss it with him and Birch. We're getting rather low on sorcerers with Lynx and Kharon in Datten, but hopefully there's enough magic to pull it off."

"If not, we'll come up with something. The three of us are more alike than any of us care to admit."

Aaron smirked. "What's wrong with being handsome and

heirs to powerful families?”

"I was referring to our stubbornness and unwavering need to keep Alex safe."

"Fair."

"Aaron, when you were cursed—"

Aaron sat up sharply. "The man who stabbed you isn't really your father. We'll get him back too."

CHAPTER 95
FURY

"Why is this taking so long?" Alecto screeched. "It's been over two months!"

Kharon continued writing in their journal, then calmly dropped their quill. "Since the night I surrendered myself to free the Datten people, I have been working nonstop to find a way to release your sisters from the underworld. If you would leave me alone and stop screaming at me, I would be better able to concentrate."

Alecto slammed her hands on the table. "You are the Titan of Hades. How hard is opening the underworld? That idiot boy Lygari managed it when he sent the mortal king after my body."

"Opening the underworld is not the problem. You are asking me to bring up the souls of goddesses—"

"That makes no difference."

"Goddesses that Hades himself trapped down there. That's the struggle. I need to outwit a god to free your sisters before the next Cassandra is born."

"Ah," Alecto groaned. "You're useless."

Kharon stood up and walked toward the door.

"Where do you think you're going?"

"If I'm so useless, then I'm taking a break to get something to eat. It's been two days."

Kharon opened the door to leave, and Lynx appeared in the doorway. They passed her and nodded. Alecto crossed her arms at the Tiere sorceress who lingered a little too long watching Kharon. When she turned back to Alecto, a mischievous smile bloomed across her face.

"I'm bored. Can we do something?"

Alecto pushed down her anger and forced a smile. She needed to keep Lynx happy so that when the time came, she could put one of her sisters into that body. "What do you feel like doing? I could have the mortals duel again."

"No, that's dull."

"Well, aren't you a cranky sorceress?"

"I'm not cranky." Lynx crossed her arms, resting them on her now enormous stomach.

"I know. You're just uncomfortable." The fury patted Lynx's shoulder. "Perhaps a stroll in the woods would help."

Lynx dropped her shoulders. "Maybe. I do like to see all the strange animals the mortals have here. So many more of them are fuzzy than in the Forbidden Lands."

"Then go, dear. I won't ask you to bring a guard, since you're clearly capable of taking care of yourself, but if anything feels off, come back at once."

Lynx cocked her head. "What do you mean 'feels off'?"

"I woke up with a strange feeling yesterday. I think the mortals are planning something."

Lynx chuckled. "Nothing for you to worry about. If they tried to enter the castle, your alarms would let us know."

Alecto smirked. "I know. But that doesn't change the fact

that they're going to come for my body one day. They persist in their foolish belief that they can still save their sorceress."

"Do you have a plan?"

"Fear not, Lynx. I have more than one plan, so when they arrive, I'll be ready."

"That's reassuring."

"Now, go enjoy your walk, and I'll continue my work preparing for our unwelcome guests."

Lynx nodded and cracked herself away.

Alecto went straight to the sorcerer lab. *She was much too eager to go tonight. They must be getting close.* When she got there, she extinguished the fire. Summoning ice against the heat, she reached up into the opening of the chimney and removed a chain-mail satchel. She brought it to the table and scattered its contents. Six talismans remained. These were specifically designated for Aaron, Megesti, Stefan, Michael, Gryphon, and Edward. The others could be controlled by a simple talisman. Alecto reignited the fire and began the arduous task of making another batch.

When the potion was done, she strung bits of stone across it to soak, then slipped out of the lab and crept down the hallway. The back of the castle was deserted. All the mortal guards were on the roof watching for the kings Alecto knew would come.

At the end of the hallway, she pulled a small pin out of her hair and pricked her finger, then used the blood to unlock the door to the queen's suite. Since banishing everyone, she'd taken the king's suite as her bedroom, and the queen's as her office. She went over to her desk, picked up the ledger, and updated the number of talismans she had. Then she grabbed the notes she'd compiled of the men she expected would be on their way.

Aaron's weakness was his mother, his dead brother, and his endless love for Alex.

Edward would give anything to save his daughter.

Stefan would fight to the death for Alex, but would struggle to raise a sword against his own father.

She added a note about Stefan. Lynx could be used against him as well as Gryphon. The fury paused with her quill over Megesti's name. His section remained stubbornly incomplete. As a sorcerer and relative of Alex, he should want to protect her. On the other hand, his mother and best friend were with him, so he was as likely to sacrifice Alex for their safety. Dropping the notes back on the desk, she opened the top drawer and removed the two charcoal sketches she'd been working on.

I wonder if my sisters would even recognize me?

She traced Megaera's face. She'd been the fury assigned to Victoria. The sisters hadn't all been together in over two thousand years, when Hades and Ares uttered the curse that bound them to the Cassandra line. In all that time, not one daughter of Cassandra had even come close to releasing her fury, until Alex. *Such a clever line. Ensuring their daughters held all the power while the sons received a pittance. It would take generations of sons to build up enough power to heal anything.* Alecto crept over to the small mirror she'd hung on the wall. She leaned in, and her black eyes shifted to green. They grew large with fear.

"That's right, little one. You're dreaming again, and that's where you'll remain until our lives' end."

Closing her eyes, Alecto shook her head, willing Alex to leave. When she opened them, they were black once again. She smirked and, twirling her silver strands in her fingers, gathered a pile of parchment from her desk.

"The kitten's right. I may have nothing to worry about when those useless mortals come calling, but it certainly wouldn't hurt to have a little backup."

She dipped her quill into the ink and began the first letter.

Eris, *I believe it's time we settled things, sorceress to sorceress.*

PART FIVE

THE BATTLE BEGINS

CHAPTER 96
THE NEXT HEAD

On the other side of the ocean lay a wooden cabin. It was small, simply decorated, but delightfully homey, not wholly dissimilar from the one where the future head had been born. In the corner sat a small wardrobe filled with a collection of simple green and yellow sparring clothes in various sizes and styles.

Good choice, Mother. Hiding me in Betruger was brilliant indeed. Just like in the labyrinth, the strange stones would block my father—and his psychotic family—from finding me.

A black pair of pants and a green tunic would work nicely.

"Ready or not, little brother. Here I come."

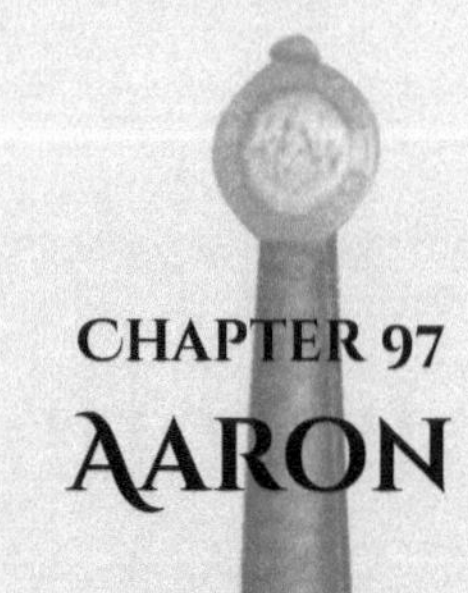

CHAPTER 97
AARON

"You have lost your mind!" Aaron shouted.

Gryphon crossed his arms and shrugged. "No, I was following orders from a higher power."

"Since when do you listen to anyone but yourself?"

"You can shout until you're blue in the face," Gryphon finally yelled back at Aaron. "I did what I needed to in order to save Alex. I'm not sorry."

"You had two months to talk to me—warn me!"

"I didn't say anything because nothing would have changed my mind. This was our last resort, and it was all we had. Saving Alex is too important."

"You don't get to make decisions on your own that affect other people's lives."

"Why not? You do!"

"Because I'm a king."

"And I'm the sorcerer Heart. It's the same thing."

"That's enough, you two," Harold said, grabbing Aaron's arm. Megesti took hold of Gryphon.

"We need to prepare to sneak inside, and your shouting will not help," Randal added.

Aaron's temper flared, but the general merely held his hands up in a mild surrender. "Aaron, I understand why you're afraid, but I trust Gryphon in this."

Aaron opened his mouth to bite back, but Megesti spoke first. "Aaron, Gryphon was told to do it by Merlock. My father would not have risked your son if he weren't confident this would work. He clearly knows something we don't."

"It would have been nice if he'd told us," Aaron muttered, running his hands through his tousled hair.

"That doesn't seem to be how any of your families work," Harold said.

"Is everyone in position?" Gryphon asked. He continued to adjust his tunic, not used to the form-fitting cut of a knight's shirt.

"I think so," Megesti said. "I couldn't find Michael, but he's likely off sulking somewhere."

"He'd better be," Gryphon grumbled. "Now, where is the little Wafner with my potions? He should have given them to the others and been here by now. Forget it. I'll get him."

Gryphon vanished, leaving Aaron alone with his friends.

Randal glanced nervously at Harold. "I just hope Edith listens."

"We should all keep our eyes out for them," said Aaron. "I wouldn't put it past this generation's Nial and Veremund to ignore our orders and head right into the thick of things."

Gryphon reappeared with Stefan at his side. "Found him."

"Excuse me for taking a leak before we head into battle."

"Not the time, Wafner." Gryphon handed the bottled potions to everyone. "Drink up."

"Is this batch as bad as before?" Harold asked, eyeing the sludge in the jar.

"No, it's worse. I strengthened it," Gryphon said. "But it's the only thing we have that might help. Without it, we'd fall under the fury's control in minutes."

"Thank goodness for Lynx." Randal unscrewed the jar and chugged the drink.

When the putrid smell wafted over to them, the other men gagged. Aaron followed Randal's lead. It tasted even worse than it smelled, like goat's milk left in the sun. It needed to be chewed to be swallowed, but somehow Aaron got it down without retching. Megesti, however, did not, and Gryphon handed him a spare jar to try again.

"How many traps and alarms do you think she—" Randal stilled at the sound of leaves crunching behind them.

"Over a dozen," Lynx announced, stepping out of the bush. "And she's expecting you to strike. I'm not sure if you should go through with it tonight."

Stefan dashed across the group and pulled her into a passionate kiss. When he finally let her go, his voice was almost a whisper. "Are you well?"

"I am. Living with the fury and doing nothing to save your father or Alex is frustrating, but the fury is a very attentive captor. I'm well cared for, and couldn't ask for more."

"I'm glad," Aaron said. "Alex would be happy to know you were being taken care of."

"Do you have any news?" Gryphon asked.

Lynx nodded and told the group about Kharon's success at stalling and how the fury had been influencing the higher-ranking lords and guards.

"So she has everyone under her thumb?" Randal asked, and Lynx nodded.

"Which magic is she using?" Gryphon asked.

"Talismans. She has one for each of you, so you all need to

stay far away from her. I don't think she knows yet, but if she realizes I've swapped them, she can make new ones."

"Isn't that dangerous?" Harold asked.

"I'll take the risk to help us get Alex back. Besides, I told Kharon, and they intend to take the fall if it is revealed. They spend more time in her lab than I do." She sounded resolute, even though her voice wavered slightly at the end. Regaining her confidence, a moment later, she spoke to Aaron, "What's your plan?"

"We have a few options," Aaron said.

"Aaron, Megesti, Harold, my men and I will arrive intending to speak to the sorceress," Stefan said. "We'll ask for you and the other important members of Harold and Aaron's kingdoms to be returned."

"The fury made it clear she wouldn't tolerate another visit," Gryphon added. "So, while they're meeting, I'll be sneaking in with Macht, Matthew, Randal, and Birch. We hope that since we'll also send guards with the first group, she won't notice the missing generals. Our goal will be to get you and Kharon out and undo the talisman magic."

"I'll be with Aaron," Megesti said. "That way, if anything goes wrong, I'll get him and the others out."

Lynx nodded, thinking. "I know we all hate to think about it," Lynx said. "But what if we can't get Alex back? How do we decide when she's gone?"

Aaron's stomach dropped. He'd tried hard not to think about that possibility, but he knew if it came down to it, the call would be his and Edward's to make. He crossed his arms. "We'll cross that bridge *if* we get to it."

Lynx shifted awkwardly. "I should get back before I'm missed."

"You should stop by the stables and hug a few smelly horses," Gryphon said.

"I will," Lynx rolled her eyes, kissed Stefan's cheek and cracked away.

"Horses?" Megesti asked.

"To hide my scent," Stefan said.

"Does everyone know their role?" Randal asked. Megesti scratched his neck but nodded. Stefan and Harold were much more confident in their agreement.

"Then I suggest we split up into our groups and get some rest," Aaron said.

AARON HAD SPENT years of his life exploring the dark forest around his home, but tonight felt different. Gone was the familial warmth and safety, and in its place was a menacing aura of dread that burrowed into his gut. Most of the others were sleeping, but like Aaron, Stefan had too much to lose in their battle.

"Lynx will be all right," Aaron said, trying to put his friend at ease.

"I'm not worried about her. Pregnant or not, she can take care of herself. It's my father and Alex I'm worried about."

"Jerome was one of the people who helped me the most when I came out of my curse. Hopefully he'll be able to heed his own counsel. But he's going to need help. He'll be furious when he finds out what she made him do."

"Honestly, this whole situation has made me more sympathetic to what you went through."

"I wouldn't wish it on anyone," Aaron said.

Stefan squeezed Aaron's shoulder. "We don't always see eye to eye, Aaron, but as far as Alex and my father are concerned—we'll always be on the same page."

CHAPTER 98
FURY

Alecto woke to an icy chill.

She sat up and raised her arms, sending light orbs floating around the room. "Whichever ghost is harassing me tonight better leave." A blur rushed past her, making her shiver violently. *I need to get Kharon to remove these pesky mortal ghosts. They're worse than the rodents in the cellar.*

Slipping out of bed, Alecto thrust her arms into her robe to take the edge off the chill lingering in the air. With a wave of her hands, she threw open the doors to the balcony and stepped outside. A faint light tinged the dark forest.

"A violet dawn ... a premonition of change on the horizon." Smirking, Alecto rubbed her hands together and strutted back into her room to prepare for the day.

Dressed in her new favorite black gown, she set about ensuring that everyone was doing their job. The sunrise had made her suspicious of everyone, and she felt the need to confirm the mortals were at their posts, watching for anyone who didn't belong there. *But first things first.* She cracked into Lynx's room.

Minimal walnut wood furniture—a bed, reading chair, and wardrobe—and various shades of green found in nature adorned the room, giving it the feeling of a more functional animal den. Unlike the other bedrooms, there was no rug in here—Lynx had not been able to conceal her disgust at using animal hide for flooring. Slipping through the shadows, Alecto found the Tiere sorceress curled up in her moss green blanket, purring in her sleep.

Alecto crept toward the side of the bed and inhaled deeply. The unexpected stench hit her so hard, she stumbled backward, covering her nose. *I suspected she'd smell like a wet cat, not a stable. Ugh.* Pinching her nose, Alecto cracked away.

Kharon was more difficult to track down. The sorcerous wasn't in their room, the library, or lab. Alecto was readying a summoning spell when she heard footsteps from a narrow stairwell on a far wall. She waited for them to appear at the top. "What were you doing down there?" she demanded.

"Visiting an old friend," Kharon replied and brushed past her.

Alecto scoffed and thrust her hand out at them, causing them to freeze in place. She spun her fingers, and the Titan of Hades rotated to face her. "Manners, Kharon. I'd hate to dispose of you." Kharon's eyes narrowed at her, and she snapped her fingers, releasing them from her hold.

"You're free to do with me as you see fit, my Head. But know that there isn't another Hades alive who would stand a chance at helping you." Kharon's lips pulled up ever so slightly, and they turned to head down the hallway, leaving Alecto alone.

Kharon vanished into another stairwell, and a scowl spread across her brow. "I'm well aware. If you weren't, I'd have killed you the first time you talked back to me."

With a sharp exhale, she thundered up a small side stairwell leading to the roof of the castle. The narrow column echoed with her every step until she reached the keep and guard walkways. The mortals were in their appropriate locations, except for the general. She snapped her fingers, and the closest guard came over. "Boy, where's the general?"

"Inspecting the secret tunnels."

"Secret tunnels?"

"Yes, my Head. There are evacuation tunnels under the basement, for escape in the event of a siege."

"Thank you…"

"Hunter."

"You've been most helpful."

Taking two steps at a time, Alecto hurried down the stairs toward the basement, calling Jerome's name. She needed to find the general and make sure he wasn't up to anything. After exploring a few dark hallways, she heard a door slam and followed the sound to see him rattling a door.

"What are you doing?"

"My Head, I am ensuring the magic doors cannot open from the other side."

Alecto crossed her arms. "And?"

"They have no handle on the other side, so they should remain sealed."

"Good. If they don't, you'll be paying with your head."

He didn't flinch, simply replying, "Understood." He calmly waited for her next order.

Good. Her talismans were holding strong. "Go and tell the chefs to prepare a feast. We'll be having visitors tonight."

Jerome bowed and left.

Alecto examined the wooden door Jerome had tried. She could feel a strange magic emanating from it. She reached out to determine which line it was, but as soon as she touched it, she screamed and wrenched her hand back. Blisters burned across her palm, making her hand burst into gold light to tend to the injury.

She had her answer. This was old magic. Victoria and Merlock hadn't been the first sorcerers in Datten! Alecto dashed back up the stairs to the lab, where she interrupted Kharon sitting at the table, reading. Without moving anything other than their eyes, the aged sorcerous returned to their journal.

"Who?" Alecto demanded.

A brief pause followed by Kharon rubbing their temples with their fingertips. "Could you try speaking in complete sentences for a change?"

"Who protected this castle?"

"Victoria and Merlock."

"No! I mean before them."

Kharon's eyes softened, and his mouth opened slightly. "You think someone else did first?"

"I *know* someone did. A door burned me."

Kharon looked even more confused. "That isn't possible. Unless it was during the great sorcerer war, there wouldn't have been another sorcerer here before them."

"*Someone* was here."

"I don't know who it could be," Kharon said.

Alecto narrowed her eyes at them and waited for any sign of deception, but it appeared they genuinely didn't know. *I suppose if the ghost isn't here, no one would tell Kharon.*

Kharon impatiently drummed their fingertips on the table. "I can stop working on this to sort it out, if you prefer."

"No," Alecto snapped. "You will continue working on a way to free my sisters. I will sort this issue out myself. Hopefully, before our guests arrive."

CHAPTER 99
AARON

Aaron pushed Thunder harder along the trail through the Dark Forest, familiar scents of pine and dew filling him. Nostalgia and grief twined around his heart. He was *heading home*, but it wasn't really *his* home now. Not anymore. Everything was familiar, but wrong. His personal guard—his friends—guarded someone else, and now he marched into his home to ask for an audience with a strange sorceress, who was actually his queen. Who was wearing his queen, his *wife*'s, body. Around them, the only plants that bloomed were noxious thorns and thistles. The closer to Datten they rode, the barer the trees became, with vines hanging down from the branches, as if waiting to ensnare anyone travelling along the road. The forest that had been so full of life, even in the harsh winter, looked dead around them.

He glanced at Megesti, Stefan, Harold, and the handful of soldiers behind them, and doubt slithered into his heart. *Did we bring enough people? What if we're killed? What if we cannot save Alex because I listened to Randal and Gryphon? What if—*

"Don't doubt yourself, Aaron," Megesti whispered. "We

sent Gryphon with the generals. With their combined skills, they're sure to find a way."

"Am I an open book to you?"

"No, but your panic is all over your face," Harold said.

"Of all the times to lock up that annoying cocky version of yourself," Stefan muttered, moving his horse ahead of them.

"Point taken. I'm a fierce Datten king. I'm going to get this audience, and we'll achieve everything we set out to. Better?"

"Much," Megesti said.

Aaron pushed his shoulders back and stuck out his chest to appear confident to his friends, but as soon as they continued on, he sagged. All the havoc that the fury could have done in the castle these last few months weighed heavily on Aaron, and sweat gathered on the nape of his neck. They carried on in silence until the Dark Forest thinned out and the protective walls surrounding Datten became visible.

"Won't be long now," Stefan said.

They picked up their pace, and the horses' hooves kicked up the dirt on the path, leaving a dust cloud behind them. Aaron strained to hear the familiar sounds of castle life, but none could be heard. In their place, beating drums and the clanking of metal on metal rang, as though an entire army marched behind the wall. Then he heard the sounds of horses galloping toward them at a great speed.

Here they come.

They rounded the next corner, and Jerome appeared with a large group of guards behind him. Every one of them, besides the general, was dressed in full Datten battle armor. They were outnumbered four to one, more than Aaron had expected, but he kept his composure as they closed the distance between Jerome and his men. The stench of burning wood overwhelmed him, ominous in its warning.

"Hello, General."

"Aaron."

"That's Your Royal Highness," Stefan corrected, pulling his horse beside Aaron's.

"Gryphon said it best," Jerome said, scowling at his son. "Are you really a king when you don't have a kingdom?"

Biting his tongue, Aaron tightened his grip on Thunder's reins. "I'm here to see her."

"What business could you possibly have with my Queen?"

"That is for me to discuss with her," Aaron replied.

"So do your job and take us to her," Harold snapped.

Jerome considered Harold. Time stopped for Aaron. Led by Jerome, his former men stared unblinkingly at his friend, the tension growing. The sweat on Aaron's neck beaded and trailed slowly and uncomfortably down his back as he waited for the general to say something.

"As you wish," Jerome finally broke the tension. He pointed two fingers at the men and the guards moved to separate Aaron and his friends. With two guards flanking him and one behind, Jerome led them through the wooden gate and into the Datten city proper.

Aaron took in the changes to his beloved home, biting his tongue to keep from making a sound. Every step Thunder took into the city filled Aaron with a growing sense of despair. The streets that should have been filled with his people going about their daily lives, were deserted with barely any Datten-ites left. The central market area that should be filled with life and noise was now an empty wasteland. Broken stalls littered the ground—others had been burned to ash, their goods and produce strewn around as if they'd been upturned and simply left there. The cobblestones were stained dark. He turned away quickly, unable to bring himself to look too closely for fear of what he'd learn. They arrived in the royal courtyard, where guards marched to and fro in a trance. A guard hesitated at the sight of Aaron, a glimmer of recognition rippling across his stony visage. *Caleb? You saw me—really saw me. You're still in there ... and if you're still in there, then Alex must be too.*

"What's taking you so long?" Jerome asked. Some squires came dashing out of the stable across the courtyard to get their horses. Aaron picked up his pace to avoid angering the general. The area where Jerome had trained him in combat for years was gone, and in its place, a fire as tall as a catapult burned. Knights threw wood, chairs, and even rugs into it. Furnishings he recognized from various rooms in his home. Unable to take his eyes off the flames, he handed Thunder over to a squire, and immediately they were led through the front doors. Aaron entered his family castle with his head held high, but when he caught sight of his home, he winced.

Inside, the palace was unrecognizable. The few family treasures that had decorated the halls were gone. All the ancient tapestries portraying the history of Datten were removed, and in their place were terrifying images—people sword fighting in a dark fog, monstrous beasts ripping soldiers limb from limb, and bloody battlefields brimming with bodies. The blood and gore of the artwork made the Betruger throne room art look like a children's story book.

"Whatever you say about her, she has unique taste. These put even my own dining hall paintings to shame," Harold whispered to Aaron, as if hearing his thoughts.

"What are these?" Megesti asked.

"Art," Jerome snapped. "The new queen's tastes lean toward the more violent parts of Datten's past."

It wasn't the only thing amiss. The suits of armor that belonged to his father and brother were gone. They'd stood guard on either side of the doors leading into the throne room, but now statues of horrible, deformed dogs with huge teeth and glowing red eyes took their place.

"What are those?" Megesti whispered.

"I don't know," Aaron said.

"Hellhounds," Stefan said. "Those are the things that chased Alex through the fog at Moorloc's castle after she escaped her grandfather."

From behind, someone struck his shoulder, and Aaron nearly stumbled.

"Move." Hunter glared at him. Stefan moved toward the knight, but Aaron shook his head. Growling, Stefan turned around and gripped the door to the throne room. Jerome pushed the men through and shoved Stefan away from the door. He nodded to Hunter and slipped into the throne room, making sure none of them could see inside.

"We'll see if the queen is ready for you or if you are to wait in the dungeon," Hunter said.

"How could she be ready for us? We sent no word ahead," Harold said.

"We were told to expect visitors today."

Aaron gave Harold and Stefan a look, then turned to Megesti, questioning him.

"The fury will have some of Alex's abilities, but we can't know which ones and to what extent," Megesti replied.

"Not all of them?" Stefan asked.

"No. Some are attached to Alex's body, and others..."

"What?" Aaron asked.

"Those she was born with are part of her physical self and her spirit. But her gifts from being a Returned One tie her to the afterlife and are not something the fury would have access to since they belong to Alex's spirit."

"What powers, exactly?" Aaron asked.

"I'm not sure," Megesti admitted. "I never knew her without powers. She also gained more powers when she became Head, and I can't tell them apart from her Returned One powers."

Aaron scratched his head, and a powerful hand squeezed his shoulder. "We have to know for sure," Stefan whispered.

"We will," Aaron replied. *How are we going to figure out if Alex is really in there? What would she know that this fury wouldn't?* Aaron wished he could read what Stefan was thinking.

"Would she have Alex's memories before?" Harold asked.

"Before what?" Stefan asked.

"Before her magic arrived."

Understanding what Harold implied, Megesti came to life. "No. When Alex was a child, she had no magic. If the fury is only taking control of her sorceress side, she wouldn't know anything from Alex's past until the moment she fell through the ice."

A loud knock shook the stones beneath their feet. "You may enter."

Jerome shoved himself between the young men and threw his weight against the throne room doors. The enormous solid oak doors pushed open, and Aaron inhaled deeply before following the general into the throne room. Their footsteps echoed through the nearly empty hall. All the paintings he'd grown up with were hidden away under a curtain of rich velvet, the one of his parents replaced with a golden-haired prince holding a princess with deep blue eyes like his own. The couple emanated love in an oddly familiar manner. Outside the room, the walls portrayed only death and violence.

"Does my choice in art confuse you, Aaron?" Alex's voice using the fury's intonation sent a chill down his spine.

The fury rose from her throne and strutted down the dais,

the same black crown upon her head. She wore a dress in the same black shade as last time, but even more revealing, a feat Aaron wouldn't have thought possible. While the slits up the sides were the same, the bodice of the dress was made from lace that reminded him of spider webs, and barely covered Alex's breasts. Her entire stomach was visible, and the fabric wrapped around her back from her breasts. From his distance, Aaron had no idea how the bodice stayed up.

"For my throne room, I selected art that *I* enjoy." She threw her hands up, and with a snap of her fingers, the velvet fabric lifted. Gone were the faces of royalty and nobility of Datten, all replaced with sorcerers. Some, Aaron recognized, like Victoria, but he didn't know most of them.

Alecto sauntered toward the one that hung where Daniel's portrait had been. "You can tell their line by the background color." A stern older man with gold eyes and wild, windswept salt and pepper hair stood against a gray background. "This one is my favorite. Hades, the god who founded the line, and the one who created my sisters and me."

"Does that mean the others are ...?"

"Very intuitive Megesti." Alecto clapped her hands together and turned toward him. "The others are indeed the remaining line founders, and a few sorcerers that I particularly admire."

"Such as Alex's mother?" Stefan asked. He emanated such rage that Aaron could feel it coming off him.

"Calm down," he whispered through clenched teeth.

Alecto smiled. "Of course, I have Victoria. How could I not include the sorceress who birthed the one to free me?"

Stefan moved for her so quickly neither Jerome nor Aaron could stop him. Alecto shot her hand out, and Stefan froze mid-step. Jerome slapped Aaron down on his knees, stopping him from intervening. The other Datten guards followed their general's example, and soon all of them were on their knees aside from Stefan.

"Leave him be," Aaron said. "We just came to ask for the rest of my people."

"No, you didn't." She shoved Stefan down to the ground. "Such a shame you can't be trusted. But after what you did to my little kitten, better safe than sorry."

"Ryan and Olivia say hello," Stefan grunted.

Your dead siblings? How do they— Alecto's eyes flashed green so fast Aaron barely caught it, but by the change in his expression, Stefan clearly did.

"Stupid mortal," Alecto growled and leaned down. "That will be the last time you betray me."

In the blink of an eye, Alecto dropped a chain around Stefan's neck.

CHAPTER 100
GRYPHON

"It reeks down here," Gryphon grumbled as he followed Randal, Matthew, and Macht down the tunnel. He'd made enough fire orbs that each of them had one floating nearby to see by.

"We're buried beneath the moat," Matthew said.

"How do you know their door won't be locked?" Macht asked.

"It will be," Randal said. "But that's why we have Gryphon."

"Three generals and a crazed sorcerer. We'll be fine," Gryphon said.

"I'm just thankful Edith and Michael finally saw reason and stayed behind," Randal said. "The last thing I needed was my daughter being in the middle of all this."

Gryphon rolled his eyes but kept his mouth shut. *If you think those two aren't going to find another way in, then you don't understand their devotion to Alex.*

"What's the plan after we get through this magical door?"

Macht asked. "Datten doesn't have hidden paths like Warren, right?"

The others stopped abruptly and turned to Macht, wondering how a foreign general would know about Warren's hidden tunnels. "Edith," he said.

"It will depend on where the fury has taken them," Matthew said. "But it's likely they'll be in the throne room, and there aren't very many good hiding spots there, but maybe we can get in from the dining room."

Gryphon squeezed past them in the narrow passage and examined the ancient wooden door—spells were carved into its surface. He moved his hands apart, growing a light orb. Some of the marks were fresh.

"These marks here." He pointed them out to the generals. "They're less than an hour old."

Randal moved to get a closer look and bumped Gryphon, who caught himself on the door. When his mystic powers connected with it, he cried out and ripped away his hand.

"Are you all right?" Randal asked.

"The magic in this door is old. And it was opened already, by a descendant."

"Like the blood spell on Victoria's lab door?" Matthew asked.

"Exactly," Gryphon said. "Someone more powerful than I am is here. We'll need to be extra careful."

Gryphon avoided touching the door as they filed through, letting Macht close it behind them. Still, no matter how far they ambled through the tunnel, he could feel the door and how it had burned him.

The tunnel opened into the basement of the castle. The group crept along the hallway, frequently pausing to listen. It was as silent as a crypt.

"It seems they didn't expect anyone to get past the enchanted doors," Randal whispered.

"A reasonable assumption," Gryphon said. "We should take the servants' stairs."

The men ascended the stairs two at a time, to minimize their footfalls, but before they reached the first floor, they heard footsteps. Halting, the generals drew their swords, and Gryphon summoned his fire. A figure appeared above them.

"There you are."

"You were supposed to meet us in the basement," Gryphon said.

"Apologies," Kharon said. "Lynx told me your plan, but I lost track of time in the library. This way."

They ascended the remaining steps to the doorway. "Where are they being kept?" Randal asked. Kharon stepped into the hallway and paused. Their eyes flitted around, and they cocked their head as if listening to a whisper.

"The halls are clear," they finally said. "Jerome took them into the throne room."

"Better there than the dungeons," Matthew said. "Let's go."

Datten's hallways felt eerie without the usual hustle of knights and busy castle life. As frustrating as it was to constantly be dodging mortals on a normal day, the silence of their absence was far worse. Gryphon avoided the painted images of the underworld. Instead, he sent his Mystics powers to locate Megesti and Lynx. He couldn't sense the fury with any detail. She had ripped him from her mind shortly after she'd taken control of Alex, but Gryphon could sense Megesti's unease. His cousin's fear sent a shiver up his own spine.

"We need to see what's going on in there," Macht said.

"The fury ripped the rooms apart, so there isn't anywhere

to hide," Kharon said. "I have come up with a way for you to blend in." They led them to a narrow door.

Gryphon raised his brows. "Blend in?"

Kharon opened the door, and their plan became obvious. They'd entered the guard uniform room. Matthew slowly shook his head as he took in the space. "Kharon, you're brilliant," he said.

The sorcerous smiled. "Get dressed, and then come to the throne room. I'm late and need to go there now. The general summoned the senior guards to the room, so I left you all the darker red tunics." With that, Kharon cracked away.

Randal held a shirt out to Gryphon. "This one should fit you. Just ask us if you're unsure of anything. In Datten, a senior guard who's not dressed properly will stick out as much as a blue uniform would."

Gryphon nodded, took the shirt from the general, and disrobed. The others all turned their backs to each other, so Gryphon did the same. In a matter of minutes, they were wearing full Datten knight garb. Gryphon couldn't help but slouch under the weight of the steel uniform. *Warren uniforms aren't this heavy. Datten needs to take fashion advice from its allies.* No one else seemed bothered by the armor, so Gryphon took the spot at the back as they marched toward the throne room.

Luckily, several other knights were running late as well, and when they arrived at the entrance to the throne room, they were pushed into the room by the crowd unnoticed. Gryphon lost his footing, swept up by the actual guards, but managed to regain it as Aaron and his group were shoved to their knees. Alecto was saying something about Victoria, and Stefan foolishly went for her. Alecto was fast and stopped the younger Wafter in his tracks. He could see the chain glisten in her closed hand. *Don't let her put that on you, Stefan. I don't know if my potion is enough to keep her from controlling you!* But it was too late. Alecto dropped the talisman onto Stefan, and he stiffened immediately. *Ferflucs!*

Another door banged open. All eyes turned toward Lynx. She strode across the room toward Alecto and Stefan. "What is he doing here?" she demanded.

The fury smiled wickedly. "I told you I'd take care of him." Holding the chain around Stefan's neck with her fingers, she chuckled. "Now he'll do whatever I want."

"What *you* want?" Lynx stopped, her gaze flitting between the fury and her husband.

"Of course. You didn't expect me to fall for your little story, did you? I'm over three thousand years old, girl. You can't fool me."

"If you knew—why keep me?"

The fury's lips twisted into a terrifying grin. "I need your body for my sisters. It may be a little older than I would have preferred, but you are lovely." Alecto thrust her palm out, sending a stream of gold light at Lynx's midsection, and she screamed in pain. "Don't worry, dear. I have no intention of hurting your pup. But making you suffer will make our Heart show himself. It's only a matter of time."

The light grew brighter, and Lynx's screams became louder, drowning out the fury's terrible laughter. Lynx met Gryphon's eyes, and nausea roared through him.

CHAPTER 101
FURY

That's right, little witch. Find the Heart for me. Alecto followed Lynx's eyes, but there were only her Datten guards. The Tiere sorceress doubled over in pain, whining like a cat. Approaching her, Alecto spoke gently, "Tell me where he is and I'll release you."

"Never," Lynx hissed. "I'll die before I let you find him."

Alecto scoffed. "Gryphon is a grown sorcerer. He can take care of himself." Lynx's face went blank. *You didn't know I was talking about Gryphon. That means ...* Alecto's heart sped. "You know where the babies are!"

Alecto closed her hand to release Lynx from the spell. The Tiere sorceress dropped to the ground, panting for breath. "Tell me or I'll kill him." Alecto raised her hand, sending magic flying across the room at Stefan. Lynx shook her head violently and sobbed.

Alecto squeezed her hand, making Lynx sob harder. Stefan struggled to breathe, his breath growing ragged. "Tell me where my body's babies are, or your bonded mate won't live to meet your daughter."

A door behind them banged shut, and Alecto growled in frustration. "Now what?"

Wesley dragged Kharon toward her. "I caught this one hiding guard uniforms in a spare room. I think he's helping them."

Kharon slapped Wesley's hand, freeing his robe from the Rassgat's grip. "I was doing no such thing. I simply wanted to test a spell."

The fury didn't have time to question Kharon, because Wesley laughed loudly and hurried over to the mortals who still knelt. "Well, well, well, what do we have here?" Wesley squatted down in front of Aaron. "Looks like my father was right. You were never worthy to be king."

Megesti struggled to free himself. Aaron leaned over to Wesley and whispered something. A second later, the Rassgat stumbled backward and got to his feet. Fixing his tunic, he returned to Alecto's side but never turned his back on Aaron.

"What did he say to you?" Alecto asked.

"Nothing of consequence. I know you'll take care of him soon, and I won't have to worry about him any longer."

"Go be useful, Wesley. Tell the maids to prepare the dining hall for our guests."

"You're serving them dinner?"

"No. I mean my proper guests, not these invaders." Alecto turned back to Lynx and Kharon. "I'll give you two minutes to make Gryphon reveal himself, or else I'll start killing people." Her eyes fixed on Lynx. "Starting with your—what do the mortals call it? Ah yes, husband."

From the middle of the guards came a loud crash of armor, and in a flash, Gryphon was standing between Stefan and Alecto. "Don't touch him."

"I'm surprised at you, Gryphon." Alecto approached him and reached her fingers toward his face, but he recoiled. "I never thought you'd risk yourself for a mortal—least of all him."

"Just because you don't understand caring for another doesn't mean the rest of us are so heartless."

Alecto giggled and brushed some dirt off his red tunic. "I was heartless, but now you're here."

The throne room doors opened, and Wesley returned with a group of servants. They followed him into the dining hall attached to the throne room.

Throwing his head toward Wesley, Gryphon said, "I thought your entire purpose was to dispose of those who did Alex harm, or wronged her."

"It is."

"Then why is *he* still here?"

"He'll have his day, as will all of you. Well, except that one." She pointed at Megesti.

"Me?" The sorcerer sounded confused.

"Everyone here has wronged Alexandria, except you. You may have deceived her when she first arrived home, but your blood oath to her mother means she never held you responsible for it. You are the only one who hasn't wronged her."

"What did Harold do?" Kharon asked.

"Nothing, but I find him annoying," Alecto replied. "Jerome?"

The general stepped out from the group of guards where Gryphon had been hiding. "Yes, my Queen?"

"Gryphon would not have come alone. You have spies among your men. Find the others and bring them to me."

Gryphon grabbed her arm. "You don't have to do this. You want me? Fine, I'll stay and do your bidding. Just let the others go—all of them."

Alecto savored the strength and power emanating off him. Inhaling deeply, she could smell the campfire. She smiled coquettishly, leaned close to his body, and whispered, "You'll do my bidding? Does that mean you'd wear my talisman? Give me complete control over you?"

"You won't have to. I'll give you an oath."

Alecto pouted and reached for Gryphon's cheek, but he jerked away. "I want a puppet, and you are not capable." She flicked her fingers at him, and vines sprang up from the ground. They slithered up Gryphon's leg so fast he couldn't even light a fire before they gripped his body up to his neck.

"Gryphon!" Lynx cried out, running to him. Alecto cracked to her and struck her in the face, sending her to the ground.

"I'll deal with you later, you treacherous little mutt. If I didn't need you—"

The entire room rattled, and a group of cloaked sorcerers appeared in the entrance to the dining hall.

"Looks like my guests have arrived," Alecto chirped.

CHAPTER 102

AARON

Still on his knees, Aaron glanced at the entrance to see the worst possible group of sorcerers he could imagine. Eris, Fenrir, Orion, Phobos, Lygari, and Stella were all dressed in the more formal sorcerer robes in the colors of their lines. Phobos stood at the front beside Eris, and the pair crossed the room, where the fury waited to greet them with open arms.

We're outmatched, outnumbered, and despite that brief second, there doesn't seem to be anything else left of Alex in that body. Aaron turned toward Harold. The Betruger king nodded as if he were reading Aaron's mind. *If we're going down, we'll go down fighting.*

"I brought you the gift you requested," Eris said, scanning the room until her eyes landed on Gryphon. "Would you like me to do the honors?" Her eyes glowed a threatening orange.

"Please," Alecto replied. Eris walked toward Gryphon, reached into her robe, and removed a large gold ring. She whispered to it, and it popped open.

"No," Aaron whispered, watching Gryphon's face turn white with fear.

"Is that—" Harold's question was answered when Eris snapped the collar onto Gryphon's neck. It lit up in an orange glow, and he cried out.

"You now have complete control over the Heart, my Head."

"Much better than killing him." Alecto smirked and rubbed her hands together. "I'm sure after a few decades he'll learn to behave."

The look on Gryphon's face was one that Aaron suspected only Alex got to see. He was vulnerable and terrified, like a little boy. Eris slapped him across the face hard enough that Aaron heard it across the hall. Harold sucked a breath beside him. On his other side, Megesti vibrated with a rage that Aaron never thought possible in his friend. "Calm down. We'll get to him."

"Are we going to eat now?" Lygari asked.

"Not just yet," Alecto said, turning back toward the sorcerers. "These mortals think they're smarter than us, and we need to put them in their place."

"Delightful," Stella said, looping her arm around Lygari's.

"All right, mortals. I know you're here. I can smell you." Alecto snapped her fingers, and Cameron, Edward, Jessica, and his mother appeared, sending Aaron's stomach into his throat. Cameron pushed Jessica behind him. She caught Aaron's eye and mouthed, *sorry*. Alecto rubbed her chin, turning toward Lygari. "Are there more?"

"Yes. The other generals." Lygari closed his eyes. When he opened them, they were violet, and he snapped, making Matthew, Randal, and Macht appear on the ground beside Aaron.

"Leaving Warren unguarded? Delightful. I shall have to visit when we're done here." The fury's giggle was nearly enough to make Aaron retch. She waved her hand, sending Cameron and the others to a side wall. Cameron struggled to step away, but his legs were locked in place. "Eris, you're welcome to join me if you'd—"

An arrow whizzed past her face.

Still frozen in place, Aaron could only watch the fury pick up and examine the arrow, her face flushed with rage.

"This is red steel. Who shot this?" The entire throne room went as silent as a crypt. She fisted the arrow shaft and shouted, "Who ... shot ... this?" With a twang, another arrow from a different direction landed at her feet. This one had a note on it. Alecto unfastened it. After reading it, she screamed and burned the letter to ash. "General, search your men," she said.

Jerome turned and ordered the knights to remove their helmets. They were all under Alecto's control. She clenched her jaw, her chest heaved, and she searched the room for her attacker. A young-looking kitchen maid with black hair tucked into a head wrap timidly approached her and asked whether they should return the food to the kitchen. The fury screamed at her. The poor girl was on the verge of tears, and dropped to her knees begging forgiveness, when another maid hurried over. Aaron narrowed his eyes at the raven-haired maid. Edith winked back as she led the young girl away.

The first arrow flew when Jessica was discovered. It had to be either Edith or Michael.

Orion and Phobos moved to flank Eris. Alecto returned to the mortals, straightening her dress. "So, who shot the arrow? Who thought they were so clever shooting a red steel arrow at me? Well, not only did you miss, but red steel doesn't kill Cassandra sorcerers!"

"But an arrow still hurts," Aaron muttered, hoping to distract her from his mother and friends.

It worked. Alecto stormed over and struck him. "No one asked for your opinion."

Another arrow flew across the room, this one on fire. It struck one of the new oil paintings and burst into flames. The kitchen maids screamed and tried to flee, but Wesley shoved them aside to get to the door. Many of the enchanted guards simply stood still. Alecto screeched and summoned her water magic to douse the flames.

Something in the room seemed to shift. Aaron felt a heaviness fill the air, and it wasn't the smoke. Alecto's chest heaved, and a loud bang echoed through the room. It came from behind the throne.

"Got you now," the fury whispered. She threw out her hands, and the heavy wood doors slammed shut, and the metallic clink of the lock echoed through the room. With a snap of her fingers, the massive obsidian throne and dais vanished, revealing a pair of men wearing cloaks. Each held a bow at their side.

One man leaned slightly. *Michael!* The other man was unfamiliar. He was taller than Michael and had the broad chest and shoulders of a Wafner or Betruger knight.

Alecto scoffed and strutted toward them. She threw up her hand, and a wind flew across the room, blowing their hoods off to reveal their faces.

Aaron had been correct about Michael, but the other face made him swallow hard. The features were unmistakable: his father's nose, a darker complexion, and Edward's eyes. *My son. Daniel.* Once Gryphon had decided to age up the twins, Aaron knew he would leapfrog his son's childhood, but he hadn't anticipated how much he would immediately love him.

What came next happened fast. A few steps away from Alecto, the men both dropped their robes, revealing more weapons than Aaron would have thought a guard could carry.

Two familiar broadsword handles were visible over Daniel's shoulders, telling Aaron his father and brother's swords crossed his son's back, and an ax head balanced between the handles with the blade visible around his hair. A leather holster strapped across his chest held at least eight different daggers, and a huge hunting quiver hung from his hip, stuffed full of arrows. Alex's favorite bow was in his hand.

Michael selected two arrows from the quiver strapped to his back, took aim, and sent them flying. A bundle dropped from behind one of the curtains and slammed to the ground where the servants were still cowering. Edith scooped it up and tossed it to her father, who was still locked to the ground.

Daniel deftly switched his bow for a dagger and sword. Even from across the room, Aaron recognized Victoria's red steel dagger and his father's blade. Daniel stood in perfect form, daring Alecto to come nearer.

Alecto paused and snapped her fingers again. Jerome and Stefan appeared beside her. "Deal with them," she ordered, and retreated back to where Eris stood.

Aaron strained every muscle, trying to get up and help his son. He was at the point of retching when Daniel locked eyes with him and winked. With a powerful thrust, Daniel spun, slamming Emmerich's blade against Jerome's and kicking Stefan in the knee.

Randal had passed the bag down the line, so all of them were now armed, but still unable to rise. The stones around them glowed orange, sending heat up into Aaron's legs. Aaron looked to Gryphon, but he seemed just as confused about the source of this magic. When the glow faded, Harold elbowed him and lifted his knee off the ground slightly.

We're not trapped anymore. But who did this?

A psychotic laugh rang through the room.

CHAPTER 103

THE NEXT HEAD

Victoria rose from the group of servants, among whom she'd gone unnoticed. With deliberate steps, she marched toward the sorcerers, lighting up the stones beneath her feet with each step. The room fell silent, and she locked eyes with her father. *Let them see.* She removed her scarf, and a midnight black braid dropped to her hip. All eyes were on the streak of chestnut brown hair that started above her left eye.

I'll make you proud, Father. Victoria lifted her hands over her head, her tunic sleeves gathering around her shoulders. Out of the corner of her eye, she saw Daniel miss a step and almost drop his sword while battling against Jerome and Stefan.

No one hurts my baby brother. Victoria thrust her dominant hand toward the fury and burst into violet light. A gale force threw Alecto across the room. In the same breath, Victoria's other hand shot out toward the mortals stalking toward Daniel. The stones beneath their feet trembled so violently that the men and guards around them dropped to the ground.

Daniel gave her a quick nod, switched his sword for his bow, and took aim. The arrow sailed toward their mother's body.

Alecto, having regained her footing after Victoria's wind, summoned a gust barely strong enough to divert the arrow's path. Terror wormed its way into Victoria's gut as the fury advanced on her brother. *I can't live without him.* She cracked herself between Daniel and the fury, and her glow brightened until her hands burst into massive flames, ready to scorch the earth to protect him.

"What do I have here?" Alecto asked, strutting toward Victoria. Eris, Phobos, and Lygari followed closely behind.

Victoria extinguished the flames on her hand and crossed her arms at the witch who had taken control of her mother.

"You're ... but you can't be!" Lygari said.

"How?" Phobos demanded.

Victoria shrugged as if she had no idea. Eris reached for her, but Victoria growled.

The elderly sorceress yanked her hand back. "You're a girl."

"And?" Victoria snipped. The fury examined her carefully, holding her gaze on her patch of brown hair, exactly like Gryphon's own gold streak.

"You were supposed to be a *boy*," Eris said.

"Why? Because a Head is supposed to be male? My mother proved that false."

"Who says you're the next Head?" Alecto said.

Victoria scoffed and burst into flames, forcing all the sorcerers except Alecto to step back. Letting the fire burn hotter, she stared at the fury until the flames extinguished and Victoria's line marks became visible, seared onto her neck—an ax, an infinity symbol, and a crown. "So, you can all surrender now."

"Why would I do that?"

"Because it takes a Head and a Heart to send you back to Hades, and with me here, we have that."

Alecto chuckled. "You seem to have missed the part where Gryphon was put under my control."

"I'm not talking about my father."

The ground beneath them exploded. Vines burst through the stone slabs as if they were made of soil. They slithered like snakes, encircled the legs of the bewitched knights, and dragged them to the ground.

"Birch!" Eris screeched.

She cracked between Daniel and Michael and was already taking control of the treacherous knights around them. Daniel nodded at her, dropped his sword, and ran from Michael's side.

Victoria turned away from the fury and ran for Gryphon as hard as she could. Fireballs flew at her, but in a flash, Daniel was beside her, sending his arrows flying at the attacking sorcerers. When she reached Gryphon, she ran her hands along his collar, searching for the opening.

"What do I say?" she asked her father, her voice jumping an octave. "This wasn't covered in our lessons."

Gryphon took her hands, stopping her progress. He stared at her for longer than Victoria expected. He reached up and brushed her cheek, but she batted his hand away. "Yes, I'm your daughter. Not a son. Alex is my mother. Daniel is my twin. There'll be time for all this later. Right now, you need to tell me what I say to get this *ferflucsing* collar off you."

Gryphon's eyes widened, and in an instant, Victoria lay on the ground with Gryphon on top of her. She felt searing heat and even her father winced. "Daniel!" Fear burned her chest far worse than the flames that surrounded them. She shoved her father off and leaped back to her feet. A breath later, Gryphon was at her side, and the room had gone eerily quiet. A glacial ice wall had split the room in two, trapping the fury and her bewitched guards and guests on one side. A chill filled their side of the room, where their friends and the mortals had been safely gathered beside them. Taking in his daughter, Gryphon let his mouth fall open.

"Now can you tell me how to get it off?"

CHAPTER 104

THE NEXT HEART

Daniel groaned and stepped away from the wall that stood between the sorcerers and most of the mortals. *Please be okay, Michael and Edith.* His palms smoked and crackled from the freezing cold of the wall he'd erected to protect them from Stella and Lygari's fire. Without thinking, he placed a hand to his neck. There, he felt the sizzle of his line marks, and the heart he knew was there.

"You're a Merlin *and* a Cassandra?" Megesti said in disbelief. The cold in Daniel's fingers switched to heat, and he burst into a gold light for an instant before it vanished.

Lynx came over and sniffed him. "You're full sorcerer. But you're obviously Aaron's son. What is going on?"

"Our mother is the most powerful of our line ever born," Victoria said, arriving at Daniel's side with Gryphon a few steps behind her. He tugged on the collar, trying to get it off.

"It's quite simple," Victoria said. "Mortal Cassandra sons passed on their powers for over thirty generations without knowing it. Then Victoria made herself a daughter—our mother—who inherited the Warren descendants' collected magic."

"And I got Datten's," Daniel said. He took his sister into a tight hug.

"I don't understand," Harold said.

"The first queen of Warren was the original Cassandra," Aaron whispered.

Daniel nodded, and Aaron's hand went to scratch his bushy hair. "Their firstborn, Teon, passed her powers through Warren until Edward gave it to Mother, and their second son, Daniel, passed it through Datten until you gave it to me," Daniel said.

Something slammed into the ice wall, and it rattled. Kharon appeared beside them. "Alecto is raging. She's getting Phobos, Eris, and Orion to destroy your wall. We only have minutes, but I made sure the servants were sent to safety."

Daniel nodded and reached to his back for Emmerich's sword and two others. He passed one to each of the generals, then turned to Megesti and Lynx. "I'm about to do something very dangerous and I need you to protect our bodies."

"Your ... bodies?"

"Daniel—" Victoria started, but he held his hand up.

"Don't argue with me again. You don't have Mystics or Hades."

She scowled at him. "There are other ways."

None that are fast enough. "Now do what we agreed. Your father fights with you and mine with me." He turned back to Kharon. "Is everything prepared?"

Kharon nodded.

"Prepared for *what*?" Gryphon demanded. Lynx grabbed his collar and spun it, making him wince in obvious pain. When she found what she sought, she snarled.

"What?" Megesti asked.

"They used the bracelets?" Gryphon asked weakly, and Lynx's angry growl gave him his answer.

"That doesn't explain it," Harold said.

Daniel stepped to Gryphon and put his hand on the sorcerer's shoulder. Feeling peace overtake him, he released his healing magic into Gryphon. Gryphon glowed gold, and Daniel felt his sister's fear turn to relief.

"You have healing?" Lynx whispered.

Daniel nodded and removed his hand from Gryphon. "What it means, Harold, is that Gryphon's family reused the two bracelets they'd locked onto him when he was in the dungeon after my mother was rescued from Moorloc."

"How do you know that?" Aaron asked.

"Apparently strong Cassandra males can see the past *and* the future," Daniel said.

The ice wall shook again.

"We're running out of time," Victoria said.

Lynx squeezed back to Gryphon's side and yipped at the collar, releasing it from Gryphon's neck. Instantly, he dropped to his knees, groaning in pain, but Daniel pulled him to his feet. "Sorry Gryphon. I know that hurt. But Victoria needs you."

Daniel looked over the group of knights and royals around him, and a warmth washed over him. "They're almost through. Cameron, you, Randal, and Megesti need to guard our bodies."

"But—" Randal protested.

"Harold and Macht will get Edith," Aaron said, and Randal nodded, flanking Aaron.

"Lynx and Jessica, try to remove the talismans Stefan and Jerome are wearing. If you get them off, they'll be free of her control. Kharon, can you open the underworld?"

"Yes. I don't know for how long, or what else will come out, but I can do it."

"Victoria—"

"Don't talk to me like you're the oldest. My father and I will keep that witch busy while you get our mother back."

"Exactly."

CHAPTER 105

AARON

Aaron barely understood half of what Daniel was saying, preoccupied instead with the same soft eyes as the baby Michael had held out to him what felt like days earlier. But instead of a chubby, squishy baby, a hardened warrior handed out swords that he'd brought, giving orders with the confidence Emmerich had possessed. If he was being honest with himself, he hadn't heard much after the part where he'd given Cassandra sorcerer powers to his son.

Over thirty generations of Datten kings, passing Cassandra magic to their sons. Never knowing or realizing our military planning, our foresight, our good health ... it's all because our last princess wanted to marry a sorcerer prince without knowing. Now my son is Crown Prince of Datten, Warren, and the Heart. And Alex thought *she* had a lot of titles.

You forgot Returned One.

How can you—

You're my Father, Aaron. Your blood runs through my veins.

The sorcerer winked at him. *Oh, and I'm also a mystic.*

In that instant, Aaron felt as if he were looking in a mirror.

497

Daniel braced himself against the ice wall. When the orange glow of the flames broke through, Daniel, Macht, and Matthew slammed into the ice with all the strength they possessed. It shattered, sending chunks flying at the sorcerers. Screams and curses echoed through the hall, and Daniel yanked on him. But instead of feeling the force of his body moving, he felt a breeze, and at that moment, Daniel's words made sense. Aaron's own body lay on the hard ground. Panic flooded his senses until Daniel's grip tightened, drawing his attention back.

You're fine. It's a Mystic power. Gryphon and mother can dream walk, but only alone. I can bring someone. We're going to get my mother back.

So, we're asleep?

Not quite. We're in between the living and dead. I'm the only one who can find her wherever the fury may have locked her, but I'll need you to bring her back.

A loud boom sounded, and Aaron instinctively covered his face with his arms to protect himself from the pieces of stone flying at them, but none struck him. When he removed his arm, they were engulfed in a dark gray fog, with a single glowing light in the middle. He squinted, and Kharon came into focus as the source of the light, holding open a door that hadn't been there a minute ago. Inside was completely black until two shrieking women ran out.

Ignore the furies. We have to go.

But we have to help.

No, we don't. Because they *will.*

The ghosts of Emmerich and Daniel stepped through the open doorway, followed by a few other men with the same golden hair.

Let our ancestors catch them. We have to get to my mother.

Aaron nodded and let Daniel pull him into the fog. They

wove through the space between living and dead, passing Michael exchanging blows with Stefan while Jessica. Lynx crept up on him from behind. Birch struggled to keep growing the vines holding back the knights. Aaron couldn't help but grin at Edith pummeling Wesley.

An orange glow wafted through the fog. Gryphon and Victoria combined their chaos magic with fire to throw at Eris, Alecto, and the other sorcerers.

Daniel slipped back into the fog, and Aaron sprinted after him. Magic rippled through him, letting him know Alex was near long before he could see the fury.

That's Alex ... not the fury.

I know. Take my hand so you don't get left behind.

Despite having no body, heat filled Aaron when Daniel's ghostly hand took his. They passed through the fog as if it weren't there, and in the blink of an eye, Alecto appeared. Busy using Alex's ice powers against Gryphon, she didn't sense them until it was too late. Before she could react, Daniel leaped into her body, bringing Aaron with him.

CHAPTER 106
AARON

Overcome with the feeling of falling, Aaron braced for impact, but it never came. Instead, he opened his eyes to find himself in a cavernous room that reminded him of the royal crypts, with a ceiling at least three stories high. Equally confused, Daniel inhaled, then shivered, and plugged his nose. Aaron sniffed and recognized the smell of wet earth soaked in blood. After the battle outside of Moorloc's castle, he'd never forget it. Tentatively, he took a step forward, hoping to learn the cause of the stench, hoping the blood he smelled wasn't coming from Alex. Soon, the eerie crypt was replaced by trees. Daniel hurried to catch up.

"This is not what I expected," Daniel said.

"Alex spent much of her life in the woods."

Aaron walked into the forest, and the smell of fire hit him. Screams sounded around them. Spinning to find the source, they saw a Datten house with flames engulfing it. A young girl and an older boy were shoving each other, and Aaron recognized Alex and Stefan. "We're in her memories. This is the day the Wafner house burned down."

"Her worst memories, it seems. But why would the fury torture her like this?"

Aaron sucked in a breath. "Because Alex fought her. She did everything to keep her from taking control, and now the fury's trying to break her."

"Guilt is a mother's weakness," Daniel whispered.

"One we'll save her from."

They left the children behind and moved further into the forest. As they jogged through, they came across the most terrible memories Alex had lived through. Each one seemed to get worse than the last, but Aaron couldn't help noticing the most traumatic ones were missing. After they'd run through her murdering Kruft's guards, childhood mistakes at the camp, and stupid disagreements she'd had with Aaron, her ladies, and her father, they heard crying. Slowing down to track the direction, they soon faced a well larger than the city square.

Aaron had never seen a well so large in his life. Daniel walked around it and stopped at the other side, calling Aaron over. At first it had appeared like a normal well with nothing special about it, but from the back, the wall opened to stairs. Slowly, Aaron took the lead. The instant his foot touched a stair, an animalistic scream Aaron recognized echoed up the well.

Alex!

Slamming his foot on the stairs, Aaron ran into the dark without thinking of his well-being. As they made their first turn around the spiral stair, a torch appeared at a sort of landing. Once both men were on it, a memory appeared in the open air beside them. Aaron recognized Victoria's body, and the pool of blood around her left him cold. Daniel looked a little ashen despite all he'd already seen today.

"It's not real," Aaron whispered.

"I know," he replied. "I just—I never realized how bad that was for her."

Swallowing the grief he could hardly contain, Aaron reached for Daniel's shoulder, expecting his hand to pass through, but when it didn't, he squeezed it, and they turned to continue on. Every turn around the well meant a new landing, a faint light, and a new horrendous memory. The pain on Alex's face at Reinhilde's death, and when she lost their first child, was enough to make him sick, but it was the kiss with Gryphon that had nearly destroyed them that hurt him the most. That was one he could have prevented if only he'd been strong enough to push her away ... to resist her.

Soon their footsteps began to echo, a sign they had nearly reached the bottom. Aaron and Daniel stepped off the steps and were plunged into complete darkness. Aaron remembered another time he'd ended up in the dark of an enchanted place, the day he'd proposed and Alex had found her mother's lab in the Verlassen castle, before everything had gone wrong. A sob filled the silence, and the two Datten men followed the sound through twists and turns until they faced a small alcove.

Alex wore the simple red version of her favorite dress, but the entire lower half was brown and heavy with drying blood. Daniel reached for her, and Aaron covered his hand, shaking his head. Alex rocked slightly as her sobs slowed.

"All my fault. It's all my fault. I killed them. Killed them all."

She leaned to the side, and the metallic smell intensified. *Blood! We can't be too late. I'd never forgive myself.* Aaron rushed into the alcove in time to see a gold light erupt in her arm and wrist, stitching the wound together. A horrendous scream left Alex and she threw the glass in her hand against the wall. Shards rained down around her.

"Alex?" Aaron whispered. The instant her eyes found his, she screamed and recoiled into the alcove.

CHAPTER 107
ALEX

The scent of pine surrounded her, overwhelming her senses. *Not again. It's not real. They aren't here. Just close your eyes and they'll go away.*

"Get out! You're not real! He's dead. They're all dead." Grabbing the broken bits of rock and glass around her, she chucked them at the men. Aaron didn't move to protect himself, simply watching as the debris struck his body. The ground squelched when he knelt, and the smell of blood overwhelmed her. Despite being trapped for what felt like an eternity, Alex hadn't realized the floor or her dress were soaked until that moment. They'd been saturated in the blood that had collected from all the times she'd tried to kill herself but couldn't.

Aaron gently reached for Alex, and her chest heaved. An icy shudder raced through her, forcing her to look away from Aaron, and when her eyes found Daniel, she rattled out another sob.

"No. You're dead. I let you die."

"You didn't."

"Fine, Lygari killed you. But you're still dead."

"I'm a Returned One, like you."

"No." Alex covered her face with her hands, shaking her head violently and slamming it against the stone wall behind her. It should have hurt, but it didn't. Nothing she did to herself in this cursed place made her feel anything besides despair.

"Alex," Aaron whispered. She couldn't stop herself from looking at him. Even knowing he was dead, and this couldn't be him, she still wanted to see him.

"We're here to bring you back. The fury is ruining everything we worked for. We need your help to stop her."

"I can't. Just go."

"We aren't going anywhere," Daniel said, his eyes boring into Alex. "I won't let you do to me what your mother did to you."

The metallic stench of blood hit her nose and Alex sucked in. The image of her mother's corpse surrounded in red flashed through her mind, haunting her even here.

"I'm not dead," Daniel whispered, squatting on her other side. "Neither is my twin sister. Something happened, and we're both... older now. Aaron is here too. I brought him to find you. But Victoria can't hold Alecto off forever. Please come back to us."

Alex paused for a long moment. There were too many details present that had been missing before.

In all the visions of you ... not one of them had your complexion right, as if she forgot what my father looked like. And you have Emmerich's build, my father's eyes, and Aaron's hair and chin. She never got you right.

"Daniel. Is it really you? Both of you?"

Aaron nodded and pressed Alex's freezing hand to his cheek. "The same prince you picked in a flower garden when you were four, and who then dragged Megesti through the woods, and then Harold across the Ogre Mountains to find you. We've been doing everything possible to get you back for months."

"Months?" Alex whispered.

Daniel nodded. The blood-soaked earth and dress stank of death and fear, so mismatched with the face of her son. "But you're a baby. I hid you."

"Gryphon did something. Only a Head and a Heart can free our line from the fury, but you were trapped, so he needed my sister."

"He needed you both," Alex whispered. She placed her hand on his cheek, and tears streamed down her smudged face. "My Heart."

"You knew?" Aaron asked, and Alex nodded back at him, feeling hope and relief awaken in her.

"I suspected it for some time. I'm sorry I didn't have a chance to tell you before."

Aaron moved toward her and pressed his forehead to hers. The scent of pine and forest morning pushed aside the pungent stench surrounding her. Alex moved her head and kissed him softly. "It is you."

"Always," Aaron whispered. "Now let us take you from here. Your daughter needs your help too."

Daniel moved back so Aaron could help her up from the floor. She expected him to release her hands once she was on her feet, but he didn't. Instead, Aaron turned her hands over, glancing at her scarred forearms. Alex opened her mouth to explain, but without a word, Aaron moved his face down and softly kissed each of the scars.

What do I do? She hadn't meant to project her thought, but her son heard her.

Trust me, Mother.

Alex relented, and Daniel ran his thumbs along her scars, filling her with heat. But it wasn't painful the way fire was. It was full of loving warmth—like a hug. When she finished examining him, both scars and her betrayer mark had vanished.

Thank you.

Always.

Alex shifted and wrapped her arms around Daniel's chest, and he returned her hug with more gusto than any other man in her life. When she was ready to let him go, the walls flickered around them.

"What's going on?" Aaron asked.

"Alecto knows I'm coherent again," Alex said. "It's time to face her."

Aaron intertwined his fingers with hers, sending warmth throughout her body.

"Whatever happens today, know you aren't alone," Aaron said as the walls shook.

"I'm the only one who can remove her, aren't I?" she asked Daniel, and he nodded.

Alex decided to trust the most important men in her life. "Then let's go."

They ascended slowly, taking each stair carefully, but the higher they rose, the more the walls shook. By the time they could see the wall around the top, it shook so hard that stones were being dislodged, nearly falling on them multiple times. Alex slipped once, and soon after, Aaron jumped to the edge of the stairs, making sure a stone didn't hit Alex. If Daniel hadn't been there to catch him, he'd have fallen into what appeared to have become a bottomless pit where the wind roared like a beast.

The test in the labyrinth. Edith overcame it. Was it to show me I could? Or do Michael and she have a larger role to play in all this?

At the top, Daniel hoisted himself through the opening and reached back for Alex. Aaron pushed her up toward their son until a loud crack sounded. Lost in her memories of the labyrinth, Alex reacted too late. The stairs behind them shifted and collapsed. Alex hit the ground hard, and when she turned back, Aaron disappeared back into the pit.

"Aaron!"

CHAPTER 108

GRYPHON

The fog grew thicker, and despite their orange glow, he and Victoria kept losing each other. It was as though the entire hall was shrouded in a hurricane. Thunder cracked and lightning continued to strike all around them, revealing terrifying glimpses of death and sorcerers long gone, along with the living monsters they were hunting.

"Victoria?"

A hand grabbed his, and heat rushed up his spine, but when he turned, it was Birch. "I've lost everyone," she said.

"I've lost Alecto and—"

Out of the fog, a scream erupted. *Victoria. No one touches my daughter.*

"No!" Without thinking, he raced toward the sound, but the hall went on forever, as if the size had increased ten or twentyfold. Finally, he neared a small orange light and smelled blood. His Ares powers burst from him with the same rage and power he'd felt when Alex had been threatened by Kruft and Moorloc. Another scream echoed around him, followed by a loud crash, and Gryphon burst into a clearing in the fog, finding the end of what was clearly a vicious battle.

Jerome lay unconscious on the ground next to a large chair, or possibly a table leg of some kind. Jessica kneeled beside him, her bicep bloody and her hair in shambles. She reached into her father's tunic and ripped the talisman from his neck.

"She saved me," Victoria muttered from the floor a distance from him. Jessica stepped over her father to get to Victoria. She extended her hands and helped up the young sorceress. "She fought him," Victoria said, pointing to Jerome. "The general had a sword, and she only had a chair leg, and she won."

"I don't care who your father is," Jessica said. "If you're Alex's daughter, you're mine to protect."

Gryphon gripped his daughter. Victoria did not have even a scratch on her, and without a word, he hugged Jessica as tightly as he could. "Thank you."

"Don't worry," she whispered, hugging him back. "I won't tell my brother you're a big softie. He might reconsider letting you be Alex's guard."

Releasing Jessica, Gryphon clutched Victoria. He'd never been more scared or more relieved in his life. In that moment, he knew he loved Victoria in a way he had never been loved by his own parents.

"Should we send my father away?" Jessica asked.

"We can't leave the room," Victoria said. Jessica nodded and retrieved her father's sword from beside his body.

"He'll be all right until he comes to. He taught me how to knock a man unconscious and keep him that way."

"I can't wait to get lessons from *you*," Victoria said.

"Remind me never to make you angry," Gryphon added.

"Go," Jessica insisted. "But if you see Michael or Stefan, tell them we're okay."

Gryphon nodded and followed Victoria back into the fog.

"Can you hear Alecto at all?"

"No. I'm trying, but they must be separated from us somehow."

"It's okay," Gryphon said. Ice filled the air, and Emmerich stepped out of the fog, Aaron's brother Daniel at his side.

"She's over there," Daniel pointed and stepped into the fog, but Emmerich remained.

"Gryphon, I have a request," the late King of Datten said, in his most gruff and serious tone. Victoria slipped her hand into Gryphon's and squeezed it. Looking at her, Gryphon suspected what Aaron's father would ask.

"Your Royal Highness," Gryphon said, "his children will be my daughter's family, and that means they're my family too. I will always love and protect them."

Emmerich smiled. "Thank you."

The ghost vanished as quickly as he appeared, and Victoria dragged Gryphon toward where Daniel had pointed. This time, they heard Alecto before they saw her. A shriek ripped past them that made Gryphon's stomach drop.

That sounded painful.

It did. Whatever my brother and Aaron are doing, it must be working.

Victoria stopped walking and took a few deep breaths, and to Gryphon's amazement, her orange glow faded, then disappeared.

How old did I make you? I still struggle with calming down my Ares.

I know. That's why you made me learn how to do it.

The pair crept into the fog, stepping as lightly as possible in the hopes of preventing Alecto from hearing or sensing them. Terrified about what they could be walking into, Gryphon moved to take the lead from Victoria, but the sorceress had inherited her mother's stubbornness and wouldn't let him get even a step ahead of her. Soon they could see silhouettes, and Gryphon knew from the smell alone that Eris and Fenrir were with Alecto. Afraid to even think near so many sorcerers, he hoped she'd figure out his plan on her own. Gryphon burst into flames, revealing their location, and immediately attacked Eris and Fenrir. By the time he'd gotten a few shots in and his hexa had reciprocated his volleys with the same violent force, he could feel the fury's pain and frustration burning through his bond.

It had been months since he sensed anything from the bond, and he couldn't help but look over at Victoria and the fury that inhabited her mother's body. Victoria's stance was weak in the same place Alex's was, but the fury did not share that weakness. Grounded and solid, she used her Poseidon magic to combat Victoria's Salem. The sweat running down Victoria's cheek and her loud breaths made him terrified for her. Eris noticed and sent an explosive force at him, sending him flying back into the fog, where he landed on a pile of debris. Once back on his feet, Gryphon winced. His hand came back bloody when he touched his left hip. Bringing flames to his hand he burned the wound, without even bothering to remove his shirt, and charged back at Alecto and Victoria.

But he was too late.

Alecto held Victoria by the neck, a satisfied grin on her face.

"Your mother should have taught you better, little witch. Oh right … I took your mother from you. Too late now."

Gryphon's heart left him in a way he didn't know was possible. He'd thought he loved Alex, but this sorceress—the sorceress they'd made, who was half Alex and half him—his love for her was infinite.

Victoria squirmed to get away, and Alecto laughed. "I am, however, feeling quite generous, so I'll let you choose. Would you rather be possessed by Megaera or Tisiphone?"

Gryphon dashed toward her, but Phobos leaped between. Finally, Alecto loosened her hand on Victoria's neck. Bruises were already forming from the force of her grip.

"Well? Answer me."

Victoria merely smiled, and Gryphon's heart raced. "Neither, because my mother taught my brother and me *very* well."

Alecto's smile vanished, replaced with a scowl. "Your mother is gone. She taught you nothing."

"Even while carrying us, she taught us. Spoke to us every day. And she taught us the importance of oaths, and what happens if you break one."

Alecto went ashen.

"When you made a deal with my mother to take control of her body, she only agreed to it *if* you never hurt us."

Alecto gasped, and her eyes landed on the mark she'd left on Victoria's neck.

"I may not be a Cassandra, but I know that strangling me breaks that oath."

The room shook, and the enraged fury reached for Victoria, but she was too quick. Gryphon took his daughter's outreached hand and pulled her out of Alecto's reach. The room shook again, this time causing the fog to dissipate and swirl low to the ground, finally revealing everyone in the room. Camcron, Randal, and Megesti held out their swords, guarding Aaron and Daniel's bodies, while Harold, Macht, and the ladies flanked Jerome, who had finally come to his senses. They used shields to stop Lygari and Stella's magic while moving closer to use their own blades. Birch and Lynx were busy sending their Celtic magic to ensnare Phobos, Eris, and Fenrir, while Michael struggled to get Stefan into a headlock likely to get at his talisman.

The next rattle shook the entire castle, bringing down stones from the ceiling. Gryphon sent his magic to slow them, while Victoria sent hers flying at the sorcerers. Picking a stone off the ground, Gryphon shouted. "Little Wafner, over here!"

He sent the stone whizzing at Stefan, giving Michael the distraction he needed to lunge at Stefan and tear the talisman from his neck. The charm flew and landed on the stones just as they shook again, but this time, the fury grabbed her head. Two ghostly women appeared beside her, comforting her as she dropped to her knees, screaming.

CHAPTER 109

AARON

Aaron closed his eyes and let the feeling of falling overtake him. *If I saved her, our son will have his mother, and everything will be right. It was worth it.*

His arm was jerked upward, sending pain shooting through his shoulder. Daniel had caught him, leaning over the pit. He gripped Aaron's hands, and beyond him, Alex's face and shoulders followed, reaching for him. He swung his free hand up and clutched her outstretched fingers, and together they hoisted him up. Alex kissed him, struggling to hold back her tears.

"You'll have time for that later," Daniel said. "Right now, we need to get out of here."

Back on their feet, they rushed through the trees. Aaron's heart raced and he sucked in ragged breaths. Ahead, a glowing light called to them.

"That's the way out," Daniel shouted. "It's going to hurt. And Father—you'll have to find your body once you're free. Mother, I don't know what will happen to you."

"I'll be fine," Alex said, and the three of them dove into the glowing orb.

Aaron felt his body slam into a wall. It hurt worse than when he'd been thrown from Thunder, worse than being shot by Alex's arrows, and worse than when he was gutted by her vortex at Verlassen. He needed longer than he'd ever admit to come back to his senses, but he'd landed near their bodies. Daniel already stood above his and motioned to Aaron to follow. He turned his back to his body and fell backward. A second later, his eyes opened, and with one deep breath, Daniel was back on his feet, sword up, ready to fight. Aaron did the same.

Cameron slapped him on the back, and the sound of metal on metal echoed around them. The knights they'd brought with them battled the ones wearing Alecto's talismans. "Don't hurt them," Aaron shouted. "Just remove their chains. They're bewitched!"

Stefan hurried toward him, helping Michael along. Cameron slipped his arm under Michael's other shoulder.

"I'm fine. I just slipped and twisted my knee," Michael said. "Leave me here and get back out there."

Aaron opened his mouth to protest, but stopped when a blinding light filled the room for several moments. When Aaron could finally look, Alex's body lay in the middle of the hall. Standing above it were the three furies—Alecto, Megaera, and Tisiphone. Far behind them, Kharon stood, still holding open the dark door. It was clear even from here that they were running out of magic, and if the furies weren't handled soon, they'd be stuck here. Before Aaron could move, a bright golden figure appeared.

Alex.

CHAPTER 110
ALEX

Alex let her Cassandra powers flow into her body.

"You don't belong here. You gave *me* control, little witch," Alecto snarled.

"But you broke our oath, and that set me free from your torture," Alex said. "So, I'm taking control and sending all three of you back to Hades."

The furies giggled, but Alex raised her hands and slapped them together. Vines and ice burst from the stones, binding and freezing the furies in place. More frosty vines burst from the rubble and entangled all the remaining sorcerers.

"Daughter of Cassandra, first of my line, I call on you to rid us of the curse your father placed upon us. Use your Ares and Cassandra gifts to help me banish the unwanted," Alex's voice boomed.

The room became frigid, and Alecto and her sisters turned pale. With a small pop, a sorceress identical to Alex appeared beside her, draped in a simple white toga. A gold wreath rested atop her chestnut curls. "Where is the other like me?"

"Victoria!" Alex called, and the young sorceress appeared.

The daughter of Cassandra smiled at Victoria and embraced her. "Like you, I am the child of a Cassandra and an Ares. Just as I was, you are the most powerful sorcerer to walk this world. Do not misuse your gifts."

"I have no intention of doing so, but I do intend to free my descendants from the burden of a fury."

Nodding, the sorceress held one hand to Victoria and the other to Alex. "Only another minute, Kharon. We're almost ready. Hearts and Usurper. We need you too."

Gryphon, Megesti, and Daniel cracked to them. Victoria grabbed Daniel's hand, and Gryphon took Megesti's and Alex's. The furies were desperately struggling to escape, but the ghosts of Emmerich, Daniel, Merlock, and Victoria loomed behind them, and they stopped all attempts to escape.

The daughter of Cassandra was the first to emit her soft gold glow, followed by Alex and Daniel, while Megesti took on their power and increased it. Gryphon and Victoria burst into orange, and the daughter of Cassandra blended their orange with her gold, creating a sunrise of colors around them. Their completed line moved toward the furies, heat swirling in the air between them.

"Stop. We can work something out," Alecto said.

"You touched my child," Alex snapped back. "You can choose death or the underworld."

Alecto opened her mouth, but before she could speak, Alex stepped out of the line and thrust her hands out at the furies. A blinding gold light assaulted them, and they howled. The others stood by Alex and mimicked her gesture, and the furies screamed and yelled threats until they were swept into the golden river that led to the maw of the underworld. Once they'd vanished inside, Kharon shifted their feet and cleared their throat. The Datten Kings of old who'd come out to help turned toward Alex, Aaron, and Daniel. Bowing slowly, they retreated into the door until only the ghosts of Emmerich and his son Daniel remained.

"I've never been prouder of you, Aaron," Emmerich said. "You'll make an amazing father, much better than I was."

"You were a brilliant father. Exactly the one I needed," Aaron replied.

The apparitions stepped into the underworld. Kharon lowered his hands, and the door shrank into itself, sucking in the dense gray fog that had engulfed the room until it vanished with a loud crack.

No one is moving. Has time stopped? Nausea overwhelmed Alex, and she swayed. Her son caught her.

"We need to get you back into your body." Daniel scooped her up and brought her over to her still, lifeless form on the ground. Alex knelt and reached out to touch it, unable to believe it was her. But the moment her fingers grazed her skin, a chill ran up her spine.

What if I'm dying? Terror drummed through her, and Alex lay down above herself.

CHAPTER III

GRYPHON

Gryphon held his trembling daughter, who couldn't stop staring at her mother's ghost.

Alex examined her body from the outside. So much had changed in it while she was the fury. Her flowy chestnut hair replaced by silver locks, her eyes black rather than emerald, her body slender and less muscular, as the fury surely wasn't spending her time sparring, running, or training the way Alex did.

Alex's ghost slipped inside her body, and then they waited. With Alecto gone, the bewitched knights had returned to normal, quelling much of the fighting, but Birch, Lynx, and the Wafners continued battling Eris and her lackies. Vines flew through the air, trying to strangle and distract the sorcerers so the Wafners could use their blades. Kharon and Megesti hovered over Alex, watching for any sign of her return. The minutes ticked by, each longer than the last.

A loud gasp for breath made them all jump back. Alex sat up and pushed her palm to her forehead, groaning. Gryphon couldn't tell if it was confusion or pain, but she was awake, and that was all he needed.

Victoria's warmth was dispelled when she and Daniel leaped for their mother. Gryphon sought out Aaron and found he too stayed back, letting the twins have her first. Tears streamed down Alex's face, and she took in her children, throwing her arms around them, sobbing and laughing. Daniel rose, bringing his mother and twin with him as if they weighed nothing. When Alex finally loosened her grip on them, she turned toward Aaron and Gryphon, but froze after only two steps, as if she'd noticed someone was missing. She spun to face the rest of the room, where her friends struggled to defeat their enemies by any means necessary.

Vines once again burst from the ground, but this time Victoria joined her mother. The vines slithered up the legs of the knights Alecto had controlled, and they all stopped and held their arms up to show they were no longer bewitched. Daniel joined his mother and sister, flicking his fingers out and sharply pulling them back. All the chains holding Alecto's talismans snapped at once, and restraints no longer needed, the vines followed.

Seeing movement out of the corner of his eye, Gryphon stomped his foot, sending orange light through the stones and helping him locate the sorcerers scattered throughout the room. Lynx snarled at her father and held the side of her face. Gryphon knew the smell of her blood, and he sensed the rage coming off Stefan as he tried desperately to get to her through the mass of knights. But Daniel didn't even blink. He cracked between Lynx and her father, and a second later, Fenrir stumbled backward with a red steel sword sticking out of his chest.

"No one touches my family," Daniel roared and used his foot to shove Fenrir backward, ripping his blade from the sorcerer's ribs. They snapped loud enough for Gryphon to hear the echo across the hall. Birch reached Lynx the moment Stefan did, and the two fussed over her, but she slipped past them and gave Daniel a big hug. He laughed and said something to Lynx that made her cover her mouth in awe as Stefan joined them.

Shouts of joy rang out as people were reunited. Randal found Edith and Harold. Michael and Jessica shoved their way through guards to reach Stefan, making metal bang on metal. A loud, wet crunch followed by a terrible scream echoed through the room. It took Gryphon a full minute to realize it was his hexa's beloved Orion. Cerberus had found him and ripped the sorcerer to pieces on the other side of the hall.

But Stella and Lygari weren't with them.

"Megesti!" Alex shouted in warning. Their cousin threw ice, vines, and everything he could muster all at once. Lygari couldn't keep up and backed into a corner of the throne room. The sorcerer had been trying to escape, and Megesti declined to let him. Aaron reached them and tossed Megesti his blade. The air seemed to leave the room, and Megesti drove his blade into Lygari's gut.

"That's for what you did to Alex, to Daniel," Megesti said and twisted the blade. Lygari gurgled and spat blood from his mouth. "And for taking my father from me and my mother."

Megesti removed his sword, letting it drop to the ground. Lygari stumbled backward, chest heaving, holding his blood-covered hands up to his face. Dropping to his knees, he spat up even more blood and finally fell to the ground, dead. The room went silent for a long moment, Megesti and Aaron looking down at the dead sorcerer. Aaron had moved and pushed the body with his foot, when a sinking feeling hit Gryphon's gut.

Where's my hexa?

The sorceress appeared behind Aaron and stabbed him in

the back. Alex screamed and ran toward him. Before Gryphon could even think to crack, gold light exploded through the hall. When it dimmed enough for everyone to see, Alex was still several feet away from Aaron, but Daniel and Megesti had their hands on him, and his wound glowed gold as if healing itself.

Eris screamed and stumbled back with her hand on her bleeding neck. Victoria held up the red steel arrow Harold had given Alex, which Daniel had shot at Alecto, her eyes glowing orange. It was slick with Eris' blood.

"You always wanted a ruthless heir, Eris. Well now, you have one. I hope your remaining days are as horrible as you are."

Holding up her other hand, Victoria closed her fingers into a fist, and the sound of shattering glass echoed around them. In a breath, Eris, Phobos, and Stella vanished.

Alex reached Aaron and inspected his wound. Only when the gold light vanished did her face regain its color, and Gryphon cracked himself to them.

"Vicious little thing aren't you?" he asked Victoria, making her smile.

"I'm a combination of my parents," she replied, hugging him. She accidentally squeezed one of his wounds, and Gryphon bit back a wince.

"The best combination, if you ask me," Daniel said, bumping his sister's shoulder. She released Gryphon to shove her brother back.

The hall was in shambles, and the groans of many injuries rose around them. But no mortals had died despite the heated battle. Daniel and Alex excused themselves to go heal those who needed it. Birch and Megesti followed them.

"Aaron, I'm so sorry," Jerome said, coming over to them.

"It's not your fault, Jerome," Aaron said, patting his general on the back. "If anyone understands not acting yourself because of a sorceress, it's me."

"I'd prefer you check."

Aaron turned to Gryphon. "Is the general back to himself? No lasting effects?"

Gryphon slipped into Jerome's mind, and after a minute nodded to Aaron.

CHAPTER 112
AARON

Aaron poked the fireplace while Alex groaned at the mirror. She'd been examining herself for almost ten minutes now, shifting her red nightgown to take in all the changes the fury had made to her while in charge. What seemed to most upset her was her hair. Aaron had never realized how much Alex liked her brown curls until she stressed over her straight silver strands.

"What if I'm stuck with this forever?"

"I'll love you just as much," Aaron replied. "And you know your father will too. He made that clear to you."

"She was not very good with my healing magic," Alex ran her finger along the fresh scar on her shoulder, sending healing magic into it. Aaron caught her face drop for a second at the sight of her forearms. There may not be any physical scars there anymore, but Aaron knew those hidden ones would linger longer than the others.

"What do you want me to do with the dress?" Aaron teased, lifting his eyebrows playfully. A flush crept up Alex's neck and cheeks. She marched across the room, grabbed the revealing black dress the fury had worn, and tossed it into the fire.

"Don't get any ideas, Princeling." She squealed playfully when Aaron took her around the waist, pulling her down onto his lap. Both stilled, prepared for an interruption, but there wasn't even a knock.

Alex wrapped her arms around his neck, settling into his lap. "It would seem our guards have finally decided to trust you again."

Aaron opened his mouth to tease her about them likely being afraid of her, but thought better of it. Instead, he leaned down and kissed her. The day had been exhausting. Alex had spent hours with Daniel healing all the knights, servants, and anyone in the kingdom the fury had hurt, even Wesley. They'd found him knocked unconscious on the floor behind the thrones, and eventually they learned it had been Cameron who put him there after Edith beat him silly. The other sorcerers had spent their time cracking to other kingdoms and bringing back any Datten citizens who wanted to return home. Aaron didn't have to ask to know guilt gnawed at her, and he intended to ask his mother and Jessica how they could start making things right with their people as soon as everyone was settled.

Alex had wasted no time ripping everything off the wall and replacing it, and while some of their things were still missing and likely gone forever, at least the room felt more like theirs again. He'd be forever grateful that his mother had saved the cribs before they had been destroyed. When they'd finally sat down to eat, it had already been evening, and despite Aaron and Gryphon's best attempts, the twins had revealed nothing of their lives, wanting to make sure their childhoods would be as natural as possible.

"Do you think they'll already be back to being babies?" Alex asked.

"Gryphon said likely closer to sunrise. It was supposed to be at least a full day."

"I missed so much with them already."

"They seemed to love you as adults, so you clearly do a wonderful job. And so do I." Aaron pulled her closer, engulfing them in the smells of sea salt and fresh blooms. "How are you feeling?"

Alex stayed quiet for a long while before answering.

"I feel as if I'm being pulled in a hundred directions. I'm scared of what our people are thinking, but so thankful no one is seriously hurt. I want to hide in our castle with my babies, but also make things right with everyone. I want to check on Gryphon, Megesti, and the others, but can't stand the thought of leaving your side for even a moment."

Aaron grinned and kissed the top of her head again.

"I wish my father had stayed here tonight."

"He said he'll return tomorrow. He just needs to make sure things are in order in Warren. A lot happened while we were all hiding out there."

"And I need to make things up to Harold and Edith, and of course, Michael and Jessica. But what if Stefan never forgives me? Or Lynx!" Alex grabbed his shirt and pulled it hard, making Aaron bite back a wince.

"Shhhh." Aaron squeezed her and traced small circles on her back. "All will be well. Our friends adore you and know the fury wasn't you. They fought to get you back, and we all just want you to be happy."

"How can I be happy with what I put everyone through?"

"Hear me Queen, Head, whatever title you pick. You did nothing. The fury did. An entirely different being that took control of your body and was sent back to Hades, where she belongs. We all saw it."

"I know."

"You stood up for me when I was cursed, and the fury was far worse than what I went through, so no guilt. I won't have it."

Alex's eyebrows knitted, and then the worry left her face. She snuggled closer to Aaron, and he let her scent overwhelm him. Nothing else had made him love the sea more.

"Now what can I do?"

"I don't know," Alex whispered.

"Do you want to go for a ride to clear your mind?"

Alex shook her head.

"Bang on Stefan or Michael's doors to make sure they're still in one piece and not mad at you?"

Alex pinched Aaron, making him playfully feign injury.

"Use your magic to rearrange the library?"

Alex snickered. "Maybe later."

It was well into the night, and everyone else was likely sound asleep, but Aaron knew Alex, and she wasn't going to sleep without some sort of assistance. Leaning closer, he whispered. "Then what will take your mind off everything that's happened so you can actually rest?"

Please, please, please, please ... be what I hope. What I desperately want to give you.

Alex turned her focus to Aaron, grinned, and pulled him down to kiss her.

CHAPTER 113
ALEX

Aaron's lips pressed against hers, waking Alex's entire body as if it had been asleep for months. Aaron's hand wound its way into her hair and pulled her mouth closer to his, instantly lighting up nerves she'd forgotten. The heat from his body invaded hers so quickly, the warmth of the fire behind them was barely noticeable. And though she couldn't read Aaron's mind, she knew exactly what he was thinking.

Finally pulling her lips from his, she refused to release his shirt. Aaron's forehead touched hers, and he brushed his nose against hers. "You're going to have to release me if you want me to move you somewhere more comfortable."

Alex reciprocated, brushing her nose against his and whispered, "And if I don't?"

"If you don't, I'm likely to take you on the stone floor of our suite, and I'd much rather you be comfortable after being without you for months, because I will struggle to be gentle."

"Good." Alex released his tunic and gently nipped his chin. "Because I have no desire to be gentle with you."

Aaron gripped her hips tightly, pressed her to him, and stood in one fluid motion, lifting her with him. Before, his strength would have surprised her, but now it was something she loved about him. Regardless of the circumstances around him, Aaron had been trained by Jerome and disciplined when it came to training and maintaining his strength. Alex now knew that his Cassandra gift was quick healing, and that would only aid him in maintaining his build. In a few short strides, he carried her to their bed, but Alex shook her head.

A little confused, Aaron waited for instruction. Alex motioned for him to lower her. He'd barely put her feet on the rug beside their bed when she ripped his shirt off him, letting the fabric drop behind them. Slowly, Alex moved her hands to Aaron's chest and ran her fingers across his muscled torso. He flexed his chest for her and stood patiently, recognizing her need to make sure he wasn't hiding any injuries. Only twice did he twitch. First, when she tickled his hip where the old scar from the vortex wound was almost healed, and when she bit his back at the end, letting out a wicked giggle. Aaron spun around and pulled her to him, kissing her and then pressing her back into the poster of their bed.

Aaron's mouth moved down her neck, making Alex moan softly. She couldn't even remember the last time she'd been with Aaron after all that had happened. Desperate to stop thinking of all that had happened, she closed her eyes and gave herself over to him. His hands slid up her thighs, pushing her nightgown up as he went. Alex tried to move her hands down Aaron's front, but he dropped her gown and grabbed her hands, holding them above her head.

"I let you check me," he whispered into her ear, sending a shiver through her where his breath tickled her neck. "Now be good and let me check you over."

Slowly, Alex turned to face Aaron and pretended to bite

him, making him chuckle. He released her hands and, in one motion, grabbed her hips and tossed her onto their bed. Alex screamed sharply in shock and then burst into laughter. Aaron climbed onto the bed, trapping Alex beneath him before she could scramble away. Looking at him, she brought her hand up and gently brushed the bushy part of his hair off his eyes, and smiled up at him.

"I thought I lost you," he whispered, taking her hand and kissing the palm.

"You'll never lose me. Not until the end of time. Promise."

Aaron moved his mouth to her, and Alex kissed him, feeling their bond mark burn on her neck, knowing their connection was strengthening after their time apart. Sliding her hands around his neck, Alex kissed Aaron with everything in her heart. She pulled him roughly against her, moving her legs so he lay between hers, making him groan. Ripping his mouth from hers, a mischievous glint flashed across Aaron's face, and he flipped them so Alex sat on top of his hips with her hands on his bare chest. Without a word, Aaron slowly pulled her night gown over her head.

Alex flicked her fingers, causing the fire across the room to grow and send enough heat into the room to take the chill out of the air. Aaron moved her silver hair off her shoulders and kissed her skin, sending a little shiver through her when he removed his lips, leaving the spot wet. Alex tugged on the drawstring of Aaron's sleeping pants and lifted herself off him so he could slip his pants off without needing her to tell him. Aaron didn't even have a chance to throw his pants aside before Alex lowered herself onto him and took his face in her hand, kissing him.

Groaning loudly, Aaron grabbed her back and pressed her against him. She kissed him, and his hands roamed across her body, his touch setting off memories of their most intimate and treasured moments together. It was as if the fury had somehow buried them, and Aaron gave them back to her with each touch. Alex whimpered and rocked against Aaron, feeling the pressure build inside her, ready to explode. The instant she switched her pace and sped up, Aaron kissed her and held her to him as her entire body was set afire, followed by the release of all the pressure and desire that had built up inside her. Waves of pleasure ripped through her, and Aaron flipped her beneath him to let her finish while pressing his forehead to hers.

CHAPTER 114

AARON

A faint gold light shone from Alex as Aaron ran his fingers through her hair while she breathed softly on his chest. He was so grateful she'd relaxed enough to get to sleep. Saving Alex from the fury had taken more out of him than he'd expected, and it felt as if he'd aged twenty years in one day, but their son Daniel was incredible. All Aaron had wanted to do was talk to him until he turned back into an infant, but Daniel had insisted Aaron be with Alex. He wanted all their memories to come naturally, and so he'd given in. Now, tucking her silver strand behind her ear, Aaron thought of all they'd done and learned today.

So many strange things from my childhood and life make so much more sense now. How Daniel and I never got sick, or how my father won almost every battle since he was thirteen. All Datten's military and battle planning came from unknown gifts of foresight. All because our last princess fell in love with a son of Cassandra from Warren. I wonder if Arthur figured it out, and that's why he hated Victoria so much. It doesn't really change anything for me, but if it

533

means I can give you sorcerer children—children who will outlive me, I'm forever thankful. You'll only have to bury me, and you will have them for the rest of your life.

Alex began to jerk and shake in her sleep. Aaron moved to check her, when Alex sat up wide-eyed and gasping for breath.

"Are you all right?"

Alex babbled incoherently and scrambled to the edge of the bed. In her hurry, she fell off the edge with a sickening thump. Aaron hurried after her. She leaped to her feet, collecting the clothes they'd thrown haphazardly when they'd been too focused on each other to care where they landed.

"Ferflucs, where is my shirt?"

Aaron grabbed his off the floor and handed it to her. Without a word, Alex threw it on herself and ran to the door.

"Where are you going?" Aaron called, pulling his pants up awkwardly as he hurried after her.

Alex opened a door, peered in, and moved on to the next. Soon, Michael, Stefan, Jessica, and Lynx followed, when Alex finally found the room she sought. Throwing the door open, her mouth dropped open, and her rosy complexion turned ashen.

"How could you?" Alex shouted. Stefan stopped the screaming queen, and Aaron raced in after them. He froze in his tracks when he found a shirtless Gryphon.

"What is that?" Aaron asked, pointing at the large, angry wound on Gryphon's side. The cut wasn't like any he'd ever seen in his life. It almost looked as if it was burning—no melting—his skin.

"Tabitha help us!" Lynx whimpered, entering last.

"What is it?" Michael asked.

"A red steel wound," Lynx answered.

Looking at the man who had once been his rival, the father

of his wife's daughter and his son's sister, Aaron knew he'd do whatever it took to make sure Alex didn't end up spending centuries alone.

To Be Continued ...

NEED MORE OF TORIAN?

If you enjoyed the book be sure to leave a review since they are a huge help to indie authors like me! They can even just be a few words that you enjoyed the book!

Join the Facebook Fan group to engage with other fans and get fun updates from Alice!
  https://www.facebook.com/groups/theheadheartandheir/

Sign up for the monthly newsletter via my website!
  alicehanov.com

Support Alice on Patreon and get early or exclusive access to things.
  patreon.com/AliceHanov

TORIAN TIMELINE

Sorcerers Arrive	No one Knows
Founding of Datten	year 0
Founding of Warren	50
Founding of six Southern Kingdoms	50-100
Merlock & Victoria arrive in Datten	1469
Megesti is born	1483
Arthur of Warren is born	1484
Gryphon is born	1488
Emmerich of Datten is born	1503
Edward of Warren is born	1510
King Emmerich is crowned King of Datten	1516
Prince Daniel of Datten is born	1522
Prince Aaron of Datten is born	1530
Princess Elizabeth of Warren (Alex) is born	1533
Princess Elizabeth vanishes	
Princess Victoria is murdered	
Prince Daniel is killed	1538
Princess Alex returns to Warren	1552
Princess Alex is taken by Moorloc	1552
Datten brings Princess Alex home	1552
Present day story	1553

KINGDOMS
DATTEN

Motto: Honor above All

Royal Family
King Emmerich (1503–)
Queen Guinevere (1504–)
Dead Prince Daniel (1521–1538)
Prince Aaron (1530–)

House of Wafner
Jerome (General of Datten) and dead Lady Gwendalin
Seven children: Patrick (Stefan), Jessica, dead Ryan, Arthur, Samuel, Olivia, and David

House of Merlock
Merlock: royal sorcerer and king's advisor
Megesti: sorcerer apprentice and Merlock's son

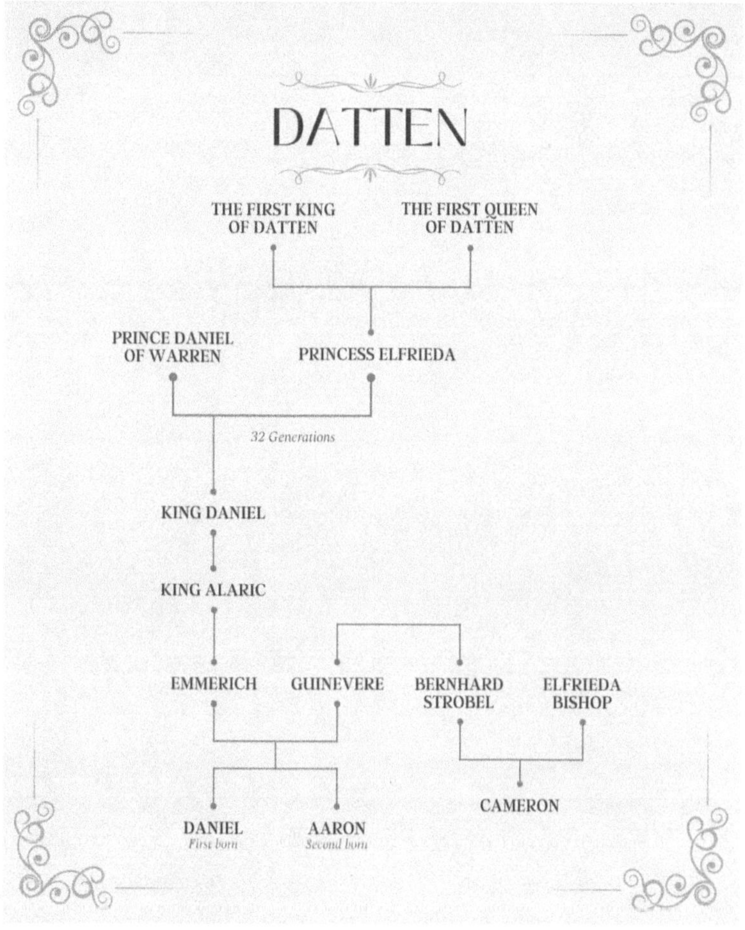

DATTEN
THE FIRST KING OF DATTEN
THE FIRST QUEEN OF DATTEN
PRINCE DANIEL OF WARREN
PRINCESS ELFRIEDA
32 Generations
KING DANIEL
KING ALARIC
EMMERICH
GUINEVERE
BERNHARD STROBEL
ELFRIEDA BISHOP
CAMERON
DANIEL
First born
AARON
Second born

KINGDOMS

WARREN

Motto: Prosperity through Courage

Royal Family
King Edward (1509–)
Dead Princess Victoria (1451–1538)
Princess Elizabeth aka Alex (1533–)

House of Nial
Randal (General of Warren) and Lady Judith
Three daughters: Abigail, Diana, and Edith

House of Bishop
Matthew (retired general) and Lady Lillian
Three sons: Marco, Aiden, and Julius

Motto: Prosperity through Courage

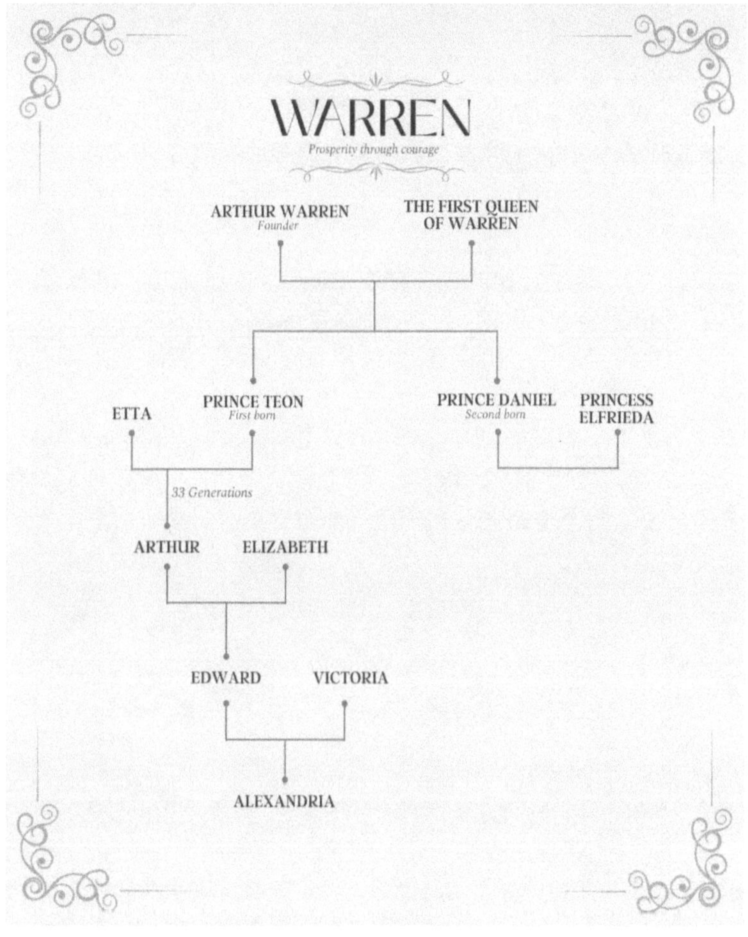

WARREN
Prosperity through courage
ARTHUR WARREN
Founder
THE FIRST QUEEN
OF WARREN
ETTA
PRINCE TEON
First born
PRINCE DANIEL
Second born
PRINCESS
ELFRIEDA
33 Generations
ARTHUR
ELIZABETH
EDWARD
VICTORIA
ALEXANDRIA

KINGDOMS

BETRUGER

Motto: Legacy Never Dies

Royal Family
King Harold (1525–)

House of Macht
Bruno (Head Guard of Betruger)

SORCERERS OF TORIAN

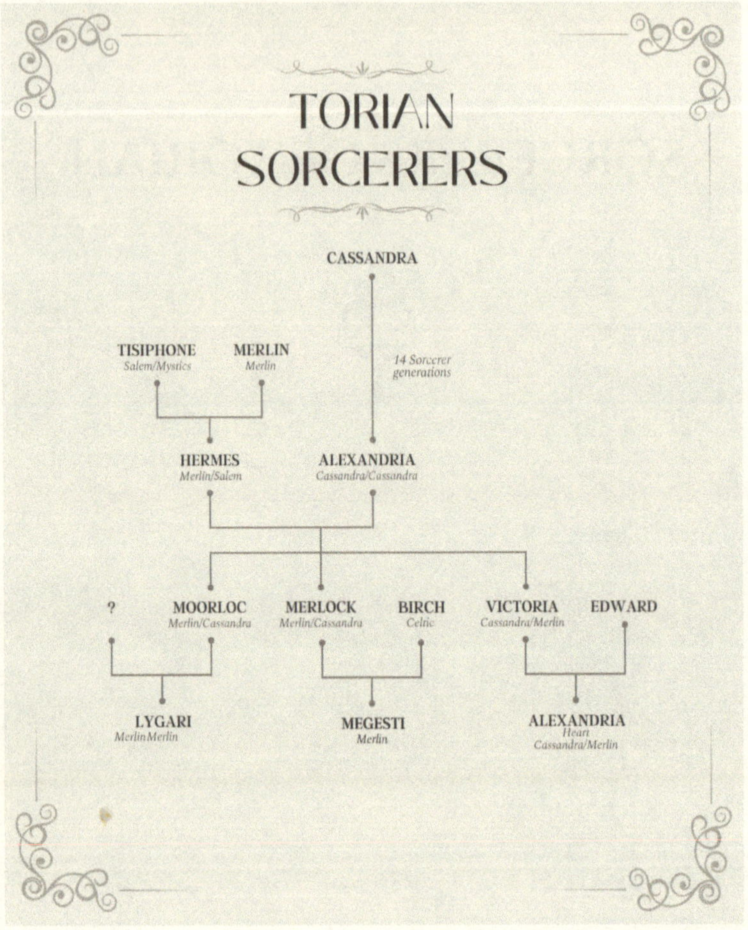

TORIAN
SORCERERS
CASSANDRA
TISIPHONE
Salem/Mystics
MERLIN
Merlin
14 Sorcerer
generations
HERMES
Merlin/Salem
ALEXANDRIA
Cassandra/Cassandra
?
MOORLOC
Merlin/Cassandra
MERLOCK
Merlin/Cassandra
BIRCH
Celtic
VICTORIA
Cassandra/Merlin
EDWARD
LYGARI
Merlin Merlin
MEGESTI
Merlin
ALEXANDRIA
Heart
Cassandra/Merlin

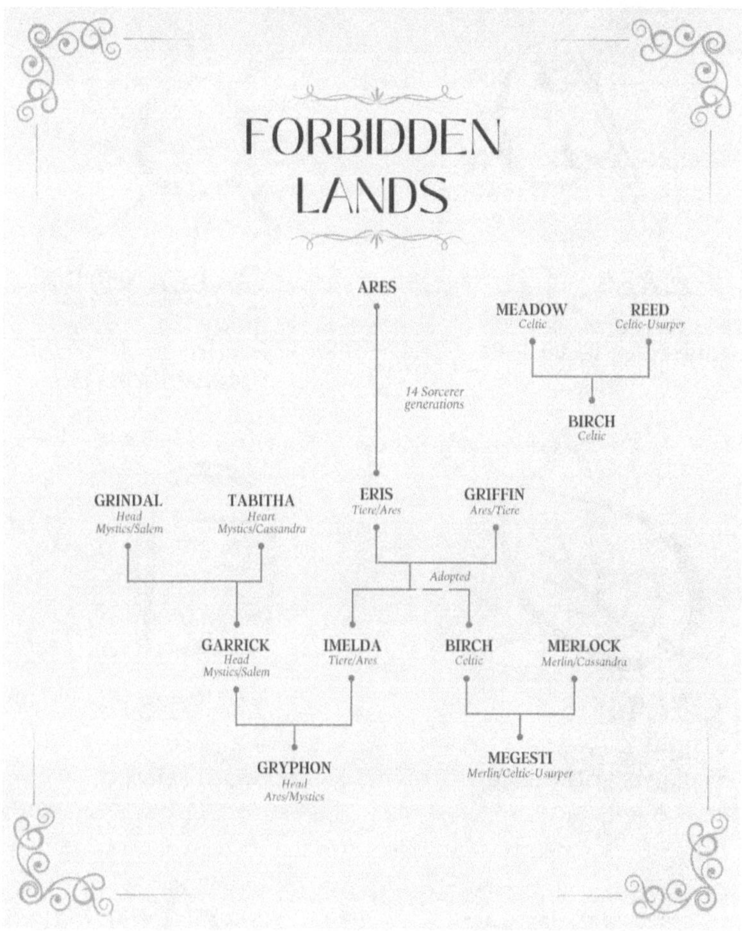

FORBIDDEN LANDS

ARES

MEADOW
Celtic

REED
Celtic-Usurper

14 Sorcerer generations

BIRCH
Celtic

GRINDAL
Head
Mystics/Salem

TABITHA
Heart
Mystics/Cassandra

ERIS
Tiere/Ares

GRIFFIN
Ares/Tiere

Adopted

GARRICK
Head
Mystics/Salem

IMELDA
Tiere/Ares

BIRCH
Celtic

MERLOCK
Merlin/Cassandra

GRYPHON
Head
Ares/Mystics

MEGESTI
Merlin/Celtic-Usurper

ARES

- orange
- chaos and violence

CASSANDRA

- gold
- healing and premonitions

CELTICS

- light green
- plants and peace

HADES

- grey
- death related

MERLIN

- violet
- varies

MIRE

- brown
- earth powers

MYSTICS

- royal blue
- mind control

POSEIDON

- dark blue
- water and weather

SALEM

- maroon
- fire and explosions

TIERE

- dark green
- animal powers

HEAD

- one of two strongest born in a generation
- logic ruled

HEART

- other strongest born in a generation
- emotional ruled

PRONUNCIATION GUIDE

Ares: Air-ease

Bernhard: Burn-hart

Betruger: Beh-True-Grrrr

Cassandra: Cas-an-draw

Celtic: Kel-tick

Datten: Day-ten

Ferflucs: Fair-f-looks

Hades: Hay-dees

Lygari: Le-garh-ee

Kirsh: K-ear-sh

Kruft: K-ruff-t

Merlin: Mer-lin

Merlock: Mer-lock

Mire: Mirr-ah

Moorloc: More-lock

Mystics: Myst-ics

Nial: N-aisle

Ogre: O-grah

Oreean: Or-ian

Poseidon: Poe-sigh-done

Rassgat: Ras-gat

Salem: Say-lem

Tiere: Teer-rah

Torian: Tore-Ian

Warren: War-en

GLOSSARY

Betrayer: term used for a sorcerer who tries to kill or severely wound their own family. Appears as three *x*'s stacked on top of each other on the left inner forearm.

Bond marks: a mark that a mated pair of sorcerers share. Each is unique, made up of their line marks, and can appear on the back of either shoulder or neck.

Hexa: sorcerer grandmother.

Hexen: sorcerer grandfather.

Line marks: images used to show the ten sorcerer lines.

Magician: insult that implies a person has no power as all human "magicians" were frauds.

Pearls: magical spheres that show the past (clear), present (white), and future (black).

Returned one: a sorcerer who dies but is brought back.

Sorcerer line: also known as a line, this is the legacy of sorcerers born from a founding sorcerer. For example, the line of Merlin includes all Merlin sorcerers born from him with Merlin powers.

Sorcerer awakening: a time in a sorcerer's life when they go through puberty and subsequently receive their powers and learn which line they are.

Sorcerer: sorcerer who identifies as male.

Sorceress: sorcerer who identifies as female.

Sorcerous: sorcerer who identifies as neither male nor female, nonbinary.

Titan: strongest sorcerer of a particular line.

Usurper: a special sorcerer born every two or three generations who can borrow or siphon the power of sorcerers around them. Only one can ever be alive at a time.

Witch: insult that implies a person has no power as all human "witches" were frauds.

ACKNOWLEDGMENTS

ALWAYS first. Thank you to my husband, Steve, and my children, Lillian, Katrina, and Zack. They believe in me, love my characters, and give up time with me to write my books.

To my mom, Elke, and stepdad, Al, thank you for supporting all my crazy dreams.

My amazing friend **Andrea** who is always there for me and gives me the best ideas and lets me ramble at her until I figure things out. I love you more than you know! And her cat is a lovely purrball.

To my amazeball friend **Brittany** you are AMAZING and I can't thank you enough for taking on my crazy.

To my amazing online BookTok and Bookstagram friends, thank you for bringing a smile to my face and giving me a safe place to vent and talk books and cry when I needed. To my fantastic author friends I found online—you are shining lights in my dark days. Killian, Nikki, Sonja, Rosalyn, Laura, Bekah, and countless more—you all make writing so much more enjoyable!

To my ferflucsing photographer, and FRIEND **Brittany Nosal**—I hate the way I look in photos, but you made the entire process painless and, more importantly, made me feel beautiful and gave me photos I love and can use knowing they captured the real me in all my happy, loving craziness! You are the best.

My editors are the bomb! **Sam,** my amazing developmental

editor! You love my characters a much as I do and I know they are always safe in your hands! **S. E.**, I can't thank you enough for keeping me on track and keeping things rolling. You are so easy to talk to you and I value you so much. **Kate** my amazing copy editor! Thank you for helping me keep things consistent and making sure people can read my words.

To my cover designers, **Alan and Ian**—I cannot thank you enough for making magic again! I love my covers.

ABOUT THE AUTHOR

Photo by Brittany Jean Photography

Alice Hanov was born in Germany and then raised on Pelee Island in the middle of one of the Great Lakes, spending her days imagining grand adventures in the woods around the island. She has never stopped writing and has a degree in rhetoric and professional writing from the University of Waterloo. Alice lives in Ontario with her hubby and three kids, various pets, and many, many books.

You can visit her online at alicehanov.com.